A NOVEL

IAN KARRAKER

Gray River Publishing

ISBN: 979-8-9878479-0-9 (Paperback)

ISBN: 979-8-9878479-1-6 (Hardcover)

ISBN: 979-8-9878479-2-3 (eBook)

Cover design by Ian Karraker.

First edition, 2023.

iankarraker.com

grayriverpublishing.com

CONTENTS

1

THE CLEARING

JULY, 1999

My God, the trees, David thought. His '97 Ford Taurus burst out of the woods and wound along a twisting driveway that crossed back and forth, back and forth up the hill to the asylum. Castle-like walls, curling iron bars, and a lawn riddled with arthritic trees gave Green Elm Home the appearance of an ancient estate, a gothic manor, time warped into the future. It was squat and archaic, stone ramparts lined from top to bottom in a thick maze of leafy vines, turrets rising severely into the clear blue, gardens rich and fertile—perhaps too fertile, monstrously fertile. Perched atop the roof were several large antennae and a conspicuously modern helicopter pad. There was also the unmistakably recent addition of the asphalt parking lot into which David now pulled. Heat rose in visible waves off the hood of the car and the craggy surface of the blacktop as the Taurus cruised to a stop, droplets of condensation dribbling from beneath as the A/C worked to keep the heat out. David pushed the door ajar and the July air rushed inside in seconds.

God, yes, the trees. He supposed they had been beautiful once. And in whole the grounds had all the signs of intended beauty. Green grass stretched from the arch of the door along a gentle slope, dotted with flower gardens planted in meandering circles, neat lines of lighter and darker shades fluttering in the breeze, proof of some recent mowing. Yes, all the signs were there—and squinting in the sun David saw people out even now, working the field in faded gray jumpsuits. The tiny blots of monochrome speckled the lawn, clipping, raking, pruning, but all their efforts could not overcome the much greater signs of neglect. The grass bubbled forth in messy blooms that gave the appearance of some titanic boiling pot. The flowers in the gardens were bright and vibrant, almost unbelievably so, but they clustered together with such fierceness that they bore a kind of feral look, a harsh look. And the *trees*... The wide, reaching arms of the elms stretched in agonized tendrils toward the forbidding building at the top of the hill. At first David thought for some reason they had been trimmed this way, but as he climbed out of the car and made his way briskly up the walk he saw that they had indeed grown into these strange shapes. All of them. Every trunk bent, every branch reached with clawing fingers, supplicants to the quiet fortress and its dark, leering windows.

David quickened his pace. The sun bore down on his suit; he felt the sweat wetting his back, his armpits, his buttocks, soaking into his under-shirt, into everything, making him hot and wet and uncomfortable. The top of his head burned—he felt a familiar pang of loss for the hair that had receded so aggressively in his mid-twenties—and beaded with sweat as well, running down into his face and making his glasses feel slippery on his nose. He pushed them back absently. In his opposite hand, the handle of his briefcase was warm and slick. He adjusted his grip. The walkway seemed impossibly long, the building impossibly far away. He remembered the way a mountain looked in the desert, close but never getting any closer. There was a small handkerchief in his suit pocket; he pulled this almost without realizing it and dabbed uselessly at his forehead, acknowledging for the thousandth time that he was miserably out of shape. The once powerful form he had gained during years in the Army was now a flabby wreck. He reflected on this glumly as he hitched up his pants and felt the tingle of sweat dripping down the small of his back. *Flabby wreck. Christ Almighty.* He flapped the lapel of his jacket and continued up the hill.

Slowly he grew level with the men in the jumpsuits. They were patients—inmates, really, with Patient ID Numbers stenciled in can't-miss-'em white blocks across their backs. Green Elm Home was a home for the insane, an asylum, a place for lunatics. Confined to these walls, reduced to gray shadows, they were, in a word, prisoners—as much as any inmate. Many stopped to watch his progress; others stared off into space; still others continued their work, dutifully oblivious. One man who met David's eye grabbed his own crotch in wild ecstasy and shouted with joy as he unzipped his jumpsuit and plunged an eager hand inside. A handful of orderlies in their white suits stood among the crowd, mostly silent, mostly watchful, and two of them peeled off to haul the man away. He shouted and yelped and fondled himself until his face—now jubilant, now furious—and his cries disappeared around the corner. A number of the grayscale souls around him grew restless too. One silver-haired patient dropped his rake and flailed, screamed:

"They're coming! Oh *God*, they're coming! Have you seen them? They hide in the *trees!*" More orderlies descended on him but he pushed them away, floundering, foaming at the mouth. A crowd gathered, murmuring, waving their tools. The orderlies quickly pulled the others to a safe distance but the man himself was wild. Two large guards came over the hill and seized him from behind, and in a flash one of the orderlies pulled a syringe and sank it into the man's arm with practiced speed. Still he shouted, clawed at his captors, shrieked until the moment his head lolled against his chest. "They're coming! Let me *go!* God, *let me go!* They're in the trees! You understand? The *trees!* Have you seen..."

David watched all this with curiosity but moved along. He gave those strangely shaped elms another meaningful glance. *Hell, I'd be scared too.* A few of the orderlies had their eyes on him; he nodded at them as he passed. They watched with interest as he gained the top of the hill.

At last—huffing, puffing, and clutching the stitch in his side—David reached the door, dripping with sweat and convinced his suit would be ruined. He ducked gratefully into the shade and gave his armpits a quick check, thanking the gods of antiperspirant that he at least did not smell as bad as he felt. He wiped his palms absently on his pants and rang the buzzer, gazing up at the door. It was a massive wooden door under a stone archway whose damp, cool shadow smelled of old earth. The building was quite old—how old David was not sure—but old enough that the camera staring out at him from the corner was an oddly anachronistic sight. They were everywhere in fact, set into nooks, mounted to walls, their unblinking eyes keeping silent watch over every square foot of the place. As he peered around at the cameras he made another unsettling discovery: also lining the walls was a grim assortment of birds. Vultures. Crows. They too glared, unblinking, out of sideways faces. And looking back down: dead bugs littered the porch, spiders and centipedes in fantastic numbers—and here came a patient with a look of total concentration, sweeping them away. Sweeping them off into the grass. The enormous door swung open, hinges groaning their displeasure, and a man in a doctor's white coat beckoned to him.

"Please, please come in, it's so hot outside."

David quickly obliged and the door swung shut behind him.

After the grandeur of the hill and the walls and the immense wooden door, David half expected to find an interior filled with suits of armor, vast hanging tapestries, ornate candelabras. Instead he found all the trappings of a modern medical clinic, decorated from floor to ceiling in a hideous pink-tan-blue paisley. Sterile fluorescent lights glowed down from the paneled ceiling onto a Welcome Desk manned by a squat, middle-aged woman in a floral print gown who sat typing away—*click clack click clack*—into a large computer console. Graying hair lined her head in a slightly frazzled bob that quivered and bounced in the rhythm of her typing, this way and that way, the ends of her bangs caressing the tops of her oversized glasses with every fussy little flop. Stern reminders to *Wash Your Hands!* and *Cover Your Mouth!* hung from the walls, next to diagrams of the human brain and an appeal to *Keep Our Facility Safe.* A bottle of hand sanitizer sat on a table in the corner, a ball of transparent gelatinous goop clinging to the end of the dispenser with clinical fortitude. All of this provided a bizarre form of relief, as if David had stepped out of some strange past and back into the present. Out of place within this comfortable and familiar world were two armed guards, solemn and serious and standing by the door.

"Doctor Alvarez," the man in the white coat said, extending his hand. "I hope our Mr. Smithfield didn't cause you too much trouble."

"Special Agent David Nolan," David replied, hands on his knees, the pomposity undermined by his wheezing breaths. It took a few seconds for him to notice Doctor Alvarez's outstretched hand, or to realize that he was referring to the screaming man with the rake. David twitched uncomfortably and pushed himself upright. "No, no, not at all. Uh—I believe we spoke on the phone?" He took the hand and shook it wetly. Doctor Alvarez looked at first as though he quite regretted this, but returned David's firm grip and quickly assumed an expression that was cordial but unsmiling.

"Yes. Yes, I understand you're here to visit a patient of mine. Mr. Wilford." Doctor Alvarez tilted his head forward and slightly to one side, the wrinkles in his brow punctuating the sentence with an unspoken question mark. Beneath his coat Doctor Alvarez was a meticulously well dressed man, a man of impeccable taste, with a shiny, bald head and a perfectly sculpted goatee complemented by a thin, similarly perfect mustache. His form was trim, even youthful, but the lines in his forehead and at the corners of his eyes betrayed his middle age and perhaps more than a little stress. He gave the immediate impression of THE PROPER GENTLEMAN, the nervous but well-put-together man who is fastidious and exacting, perhaps most in his element at dinner parties but generally neither seen nor heard when in attendance.

"I am." David nodded.

"And you said he's not in trouble."

"Oh God, no. Same story that sent him here in the first place, but you know how it is with these cold cases. Go back over the same old files, go talk to the same old witnesses. It's nothing. Between you and me, Doc, it's the kind of nothing job that comes up when someone wants a promotion. Just a goddamn formality."

Doctor Alvarez nodded, his eyebrows arched in an oddly paternal expression of long-suffering skepticism. "Well, no actually, I can't say that I know how it is. But I am relieved to hear it." He smirked joylessly and, apparently satisfied, led David further into the lobby. "He loves telling stories, I'm sure he'll be happy to tell you what he knows."

Doctor Alvarez spoke in a tone that was short and precise and conveyed that he was not at all interested in small talk, an idea reinforced by the hurried way he walked. David supposed that he probably had many places to be, many patients to treat or meetings to attend, or perhaps—and David's ego purred at the suggestion—he was simply nervous in the presence of THE LAW. In any case, David was not much interested in small talk himself, and was not especially good at it. He followed Doctor Alvarez at a trot. They passed under a vent which he suspected was receiving air from somewhere in the arctic and approached the woman who sat in bureaucratic dignity behind the desk. Doctor Alvarez cleared his throat politely.

"Uh—Marie?"

The woman, slightly surprised, looked up at them over her large plastic spectacles.

"This is Special Agent David Nolan, Marie. He's here to see our Mr. Wilford—patient 243. There should be an appointment on the calendar. Could you drum up the paperwork, and uh—we'll need an escort, please."

Marie raised her eyebrows in an expression that suggested this was a great inconvenience, and resumed her click-clacking.

"He's harmless, but...well you know, sometimes he gets excited," Doctor Alvarez explained. "Nothing to worry about, you'll have complete privacy. They'll just be waiting outside the door." His eyes flicked to the guards and back. "In case you need anything."

David graced him with a confident smile. "Sure, Doc," he said. "This ain't my first rodeo." And it wasn't. David had specialized in the criminally insane, had interviewed countless killers and small-time gangsters, many of them in institutions just like this. This man—this Patient 243—was small potatoes. Nothing, a nobody.

"You're all set, Agent Nolan," Marie said, with all the warmth of a dead penguin. She pushed a clipboard and a small plastic bowl toward the two of them. "If you could just fill out this paperwork and leave your gun, badge, and anything metal here at the desk."

David accepted the bowl with the best fake smile he could muster. "Of course. Where do I sign?"

Thirty minutes and several pages of disclaimers later, David was led into a small room with a window in one corner and a table with two chairs in the center. A bar ran up from the floor on one side of the table, made a loop, and connected to the flat metal top. David thanked the guard who had brought him in and settled into the chair on the other side, feeling the cold metal press his damp shirt against his back. He opened his briefcase and set a small tape recorder, a microphone, and a yellow legal pad out on the table, eyeing the camera that poked out of the corner of the ceiling, glassy eye staring, cold and unreadable. Doctor Alvarez stepped in as well.

"Now remember, Agent Nolan. He's harmless, really, but please don't do anything to get him excited. He'll probably want to cooperate. Sometimes he just gets a little—well—a little worked up. He can be a bit emotional."

David's smile was lopsided. "Relax Doc. I've done this a million times."

Doctor Alvarez stood for a moment in the door, looking uncertain, like he wanted to say something more, but he only twiddled his fingers and rubbed his hands together vacantly. "Yes, of course. I'll be right outside, if you need anything." And he left.

A moment later, a man in handcuffs and the now familiar gray jumpsuit was led into the room by two large orderlies, one tall and fit, the other short and round. The man himself was somewhat on the tubby side, early thirties, with hair that sprouted every which way in unkempt tufts. Across his back was the number *243* in huge stenciled blocks. They sat him down in the chair opposite David and carefully undid the handcuffs, pulling the chain through the bar in the table and then reattaching it to the man's wrists. Through it all, the man stared directly ahead as if catatonic, only moving when moved by the two larger men. A pair of enormous glasses sat perched on his nose, magnifying his eyes into large, comical discs. When he was settled, the orderlies nodded at David and left the room, shutting the metal door behind them with a heavy *thunk*.

"Good morning, Mr. Wilford," David said with a warm smile. The other man only stared. David waited a moment, but when it seemed a response was not forthcoming, he continued: "My name is Special Agent David Nolan. I work for the FBI. You're not in trouble, I was just hoping we could talk a little about your childhood."

Still the man sat silently.

"I understand you witnessed a murder. Possibly several. I'm sure it must be very painful to remember," David said, aware that he was talking loudly, slowly, as if the man was hard of hearing. He scooted his chair a little closer. "Could you tell me anything about it?"

The man said nothing, but turned his head slowly and fixed his eyes on David, who felt a sudden chill. Those eyes—there was nothing on the other side, they looked dead, cold. *He can be a bit emotional*. The words replayed in David's head. *Right. Sure.*

"If it's alright with you, I'll just record our conversation," David continued in that same loud voice, turning on the tape recorder. A quiet *whir* sprang into life and filled the silence. It seemed to awaken something in the man, who cocked his head slightly to one side but still said nothing.

"Anything at all will be helpful," David said. "I don't expect that you remember all the details, but, you know, even just broad strokes will be fine." Silence. "Anything. Anything at all."

The man cocked his head again, this time to the other side, still staring, and it was as if a light finally turned on behind his eyes. David waited for him to speak, waited for what seemed like minutes. And finally, slowly, the man did speak, in a voice that was strangely young, strangely childlike. His head was completely still; only his mouth moved.

"Have you ever heard of the Highwayman?" he asked, evenly, not breaking eye contact. His eyes were burning with passion, but with what passion David could not tell. They had lit up with that peculiar intensity, and now, as he spoke, they seemed to shine with muted excitement. It was not the twinkle of happy enthusiasm...not the glimmer of malice... It was something else. Something else entirely. A shiver ran up David's spine. He couldn't place it, but there was something about those eyes—they seemed to be searching him from the inside, probing for weakness, watching closely for hints of fear. They were the eyes of a predator. Yes, that was it: a predator stalking its prey. Playing with it. Possessed with the casual knowledge of its death. The man's voice gave away nothing, no hint; he might have been discussing the weather.

"I have," David said. He shifted a little uncomfortably in his seat, adjusted his tape recorder. "He was credited with multiple murders back in the seventies, but he was never caught. The murders were only linked because—"

"Funny that you should use the word 'credited,'" Mr. Wilford interjected, still looking at David with those wide, watchful eyes. His voice was flat, humorless. Then he smiled. "Like it was a good thing."

"I'm sorry, I didn't mean... There were multiple murders attributed to him..."

"Hey, that's fine, take it easy. You can say 'credited' if you want." He blinked. David realized suddenly it was the first time Mr. Wilford had blinked since entering the room. "Please go on."

"Right," David said uneasily, regaining his stride. "Well like I said, he was credited with multiple murders. The bodies were...unrecognizable, to say the least. That was what linked them, that and the timing. Otherwise there was no clear thing that could tie everything back to one person."

The man whispered something under his breath.

"Come again? Can you speak into the tape?"

"I said, there wouldn't be, would there?"

David's heart skipped a beat. Perhaps he really would make a breakthrough. God, wouldn't that be nice. He eyed the man carefully.

"Are you saying you know something?"

Mr. Wilford smiled, a coy sort of expression, like a kid caught in a lie.

"Why yes, I'd say I know a lot of things. But nothing that will help—not to catch the killer anyway—or killers."

"So there is more than one."

"You can't even begin to imagine," he said, his face falling, and then he smiled again. "The doctors and nurses may not understand why they keep me here—" he gestured vaguely at his surroundings, the first real movement since the blink "—but I do. They don't really get it, not really. But I understand. And I've learned a lot about people—"

"Like you," David finished, not really meaning to, the words seeming to bypass his conscious brain and coming straight out of his mouth.

"Yes, like me," Mr. Wilford said. There was silence for a moment, the noise of the tape loud in the still air. He looked almost introspective, except that his eyes were still glued to David's face. They had lost some of that strange light, but not all of it. For a few seconds David worried that he might have stuck his foot in his mouth, a phenomenon with which he was regrettably familiar. He watched to see how the man would respond. The soul on the other side of those eyes was somewhere far, far away. Tick. Tock. Still the tape whirred.

"But you aren't in here for murder," David finally said. "Not convicted, anyway."

"Tisk tisk, Detective. You wouldn't be talking about that sleazy trucker, would you?"

"No, I w—it's Special Agent," David said, flustered.

"Or maybe the girl."

"Like I said, not convicted," David said airily, but his mind supplied the phrase, *Not Guilty by reason of insanity...*

"I know why I'm here, and it ain't for my looks," the man said, and chuckled, as if it were a clever joke. Some of the light returned. All the while he kept staring straight ahead into David's eyes, and once again David had the odd sensation of being mentally dissected. There was another pause in which he felt powerless, naked before those gleaming orbs with their deep, dark pupils; then—

"Let's talk more about the Highwayman," David said, trying to keep things focused. These psych ward nutjobs could be tough to handle, but that was why they sent a professional. And a professional wasn't interested in jokes, especially not from the kind of man now sitting across from him. He forged ahead. "That's actually why I'm here."

"Oh, funny," Mr. Wilford said in a voice that suggested nothing was funny at all. "What would you like to know?"

"Everything you can tell me. Names, dates, locations, anything. Try to be as specific as possible."

Mr. Wilford smiled more widely this time. "You're hoping to catch him," he said through his big, disconcerting grin. For the first time David noticed that he was missing half a tooth. In another time and place it might have looked goofy, but set into Mr. Wilford's round, bespectacled face it was oddly unsettling. The remaining half descended in a sharp, curved line and formed a point. "After all this time you think you can catch him."

"Well, that is what we do at the FBI," David said. The man shook his head.

"Not this one. This one you'll never understand."

"Why is that?" David asked. He tried to make it sound like casual interest, but he couldn't help leaning forward and pushing the microphone a little closer to his subject—who had still not broken eye contact. And still had yet to blink again.

The smile faded into a sort of grimace. "I don't think anyone understands it. Not even me."

Once again, David spoke before he could stop himself: "To be fair, your perspective might be considered a little skewed."

Mr. Wilford's stare deepened, pulled David in, deep, deep into the black depths of those cold eyes, the pupils a pair of bottomless pits ringed by pale, dead oceans. David suddenly became terrifyingly, acutely aware of the man's enormous hands, how they were handcuffed to the table, how he had barely moved them once since the interview started but now restlessly ran them up and down along the bar to which he was chained. The man was unreadable, silent for a long time except for the metallic *scrape scritch scratching* as he fidgeted, and David, his heart fluttering, wondered if he had screwed the whole thing up.

"Yes, you could say that," Mr. Wilford finally said. David sighed unconsciously, but before he could say anything the man was speaking again: "But everything about that summer was skewed. Not *right*. Wouldn't you agree, Detective?"

"It's Special Agent," David said again.

The man shook his head, his eyes fixed straight at David even as his head wobbled from side to side. *"Wouldn't* you, though?"

David nodded slowly. "I suppose I would."

"Not right. Not right not right."

David nodded again. "Yeah. Not right. You've got it."

Mr. Wilford paused as if considering his next line. When he spoke, it was slow, deliberate—and quiet. "Do you want to know what happened?"

Silence greeted this. David tried to look up, but he couldn't quite meet Mr. Wilford's penetrating gaze. Sure, of course he wanted to know. Hell, that was why he was here. But now...confronted with the question...he suddenly wasn't sure. A current of doubt began to bubble up in the pit of his stomach, making him queasy and uncomfortable. He straightened the notepad, clicked his pen, flattened his tie. It was a simple question, yet it seemed to carry a terrible weight. He watched those hands, still running up and down the bar, up and down, up and down, all the while those eyes never looked away. The man's expression had hardened into an ugly, expectant leer, his pale eyes burrowing into David's face, watching, waiting. David opened his mouth, shut it again, then opened it and said: "Yes. I do."

"Well," Mr. Wilford said, his expression softening, his pale eyes relaxing but still focused squarely on David's brown ones, "really it begins several years before. At least I reckon it does. As best as I can place it."

"That's alright," David said, easing up a bit himself. "Any information is good. The tape is running, so whenever you're ready—"

"Several years before," Mr. Wilford said again, not listening. His eyes were far off now, no longer staring *at* David but *through* him. "In Vietnam."

David grabbed the notepad and started scribbling. "Vietnam?"

"Yes. Does that surprise you?"

"A little, I'll admit," David said, looking up.

"Well a lot of messed up stuff happened there. It's no wonder some of it followed people home."

David nodded, feeling strangely like a child who agrees with an adult simply because the adult says it is so. "PTSD," he mumbled, painfully aware of his own.

"No—well, maybe. But no, something else. Something much worse."

MARCH, 1968

It was 0716 and the morning sun shone brilliantly across the tops of the trees and rice paddies and painted the world in magnificent shades of green and orange, as Harry Ross sat cramped in the seat of his Army helicopter, a tired old Huey held together with chewing gum and hope, clutching his M16 and trying to shut his eyes for just a few more minutes. Down below the world was a cacophony of sound and light, the wash of the rotor creating a terrific disturbance in the morning air that could not be seen but was inescapably present. He shifted uncomfortably, deaf to the noise, and cradled his head in one hand. It had been a rough few months. Only two days ago, a member of his company, Charlie Company, had been killed by a land mine, the fifth since they had arrived in this God-forsaken jungle of a country. That was the way it had been from the start. No enemies, nothing to fire at, no outlet for the anger and frustration they felt at losing their friends. One day here, gone the next, obliterated in a fury of shrapnel and flame, blood, guts, limbs, everything flying in all directions. Harry squeezed his eyes shut harder.

He was the old man of the outfit, although no one would have guessed as much from his rank. Most of these kids were eighteen, nineteen; Harry was twenty-five, with a wife and a one-year-old son at home. He couldn't believe it himself most of the time, but he had *volunteered* to come to this shithole, to leave them behind, to leave everything behind, for what could only be described as sheer insanity. Back home he was nothing special, a dockworker going to night school on the side, but he would have traded his left nut—hell, he'd trade a lot more than that—to be back in his home town of Elmwood, with Jane and Willie, and his parents in the next town over. Willie was getting pretty close to his second birthday; Harry could just see his little face with a party hat on, his eyes wide with excitement, looking out from his highchair upon presents which had only begun to carry meaning but still brought sheer delight. A month or two ago, Harry would have had to fight back tears at the thought, but now (and he hated himself for this), although he missed them all more than ever, he felt mostly numb. There were days—weeks even—where he would not even dare to hope that he was coming home. It wasn't the brutal fighting—there hadn't been any of that. It was the random way they were all getting picked off by mines and booby traps. Twenty-eight casualties in all, and it had only been three months. He did the math, had done it many times.

Out the door, the horizon suddenly exploded in chaos. He looked up, feeling his pulse quicken. It was the artillery, the barrage meant to clear their landing zone. All around his squad-mates craned their necks for a look, wondering if it would work, if there would be any of the bastards left alive. Somewhere deep down, somewhere Harry would never admit existed, he hoped there were none left. They all talked a big game, sure, everyone did, but secretly he was terrified. He wanted revenge for his friends, but more than that, he wanted to get *away*, to survive. In the darkest, most private, most shameful part of his soul, he had no desire to fight them at all, these merciless, faceless Commies. But when the shelling started, the guys started cheering, and so did Harry. He forgot his fear for a moment, and that felt good, so he cheered louder. The shelling continued without pause, adding to the already incredible noise; the cheering subsided as the men went back to their solitary anticipation, each in his own way, all of them silent before the terrible power of the artillery.

Harry drifted back into memory. What was it his father had said? *Don't go lookin for trouble, ya hear?* He listened to the *kabooms* ricocheting off the treetops and thought with a sort of crazed amusement that trouble had found him anyway. His lip curled into something that was part smile, part scowl. His father had fought in World War II and was tough as nails, but that didn't stop him from the occasional bout of fatherly tenderness. When Harry enlisted the man had nearly lost his dinner; he stood up from the table (where Mom and Jane and little Willie also sat in stunned quiet) and proclaimed:

"No son of mine is going to fight in that *damned* jungle war! You hear me, boy? No goddamn son of mine!"

Harry was not so young that he wished to pick a fight with his father, so he sat in silence. His father, seizing the moment, launched into a description of all the grisly ways a man could die in combat, the spittle flying from his mouth and wet tracks forming on his face as he recounted tales from the Pacific that were far beyond anything he had ever dared to share before. Across the table Mom recoiled in horror at this sudden candor, her gleaming eyes huge and scared, and from his highchair Willie bawled and waved his chubby fists in the air. Somewhere in the back of Harry's mind a tiny voice whispered, *And that's how I could die too—like that!* But a much larger voice, the voice of plain stupid youth, retorted that he was not going to do any such thing, that he could feel deep down in his bones that he would survive the war, that he was actually invincible—

The bottom dropped out of his stomach as the helicopter swooped lower, pulling him forcefully from his reverie. They were approaching the site of the assault, and all at once the shelling ceased, and they slowly lost altitude. Glancing down, the earth was a wasteland of charred craters growing ever closer, the smoke rising in enormous plumes obscuring the sun, casting a pall on the bright morning, creating a scene like Harry had only seen in movies. The unmistakeable scent of gunpowder wafted up—Harry always thought it smelled like rotten eggs—and the smell of grass, trees, flesh burning, everything burning, rose with it, filled their nostrils, suffocated them. Harry choked. To his left, a guy smoking a cigarette flicked it out the open door in annoyance.

And then they were on the ground and someone shouted to *"GO, GO, GO, GET THE HELL OUT!"* and he unbuckled his harness and they piled out into a rice paddy, the air thick with the noise of their helicopter and untold others on all sides as the men splashed around in the shallow water. Harry gripped his rifle tightly, acutely aware that it was the only thing between him and death-by-lead-poisoning, and looked down the sight in anticipation of the attack. The attack that he knew would be coming at any second. It was not a question—it would come...*must* come. That was why they were here. This unseen force had harassed them for months, had harangued and picked at and booby trapped them for the last twelve weeks, and now they were here. Holed up in the quaint little hamlets dotting these fields. Out there. Somewhere. He scanned the horizon, nervously looking for any sign of movement. He saw no one at first, but then off to one side someone started shooting and he wheeled around to see...nothing. More of the same, the same tricks they had encountered time and again. His heart pounded in his chest, screaming that he wasn't ready to die, that he was in fact very much alive. The men set off toward the little huts bordering the field, and Harry followed, looking for anything that wasn't already dead.

Then from somewhere—oh, but who knows where?—a man! Off in the distance! A few of them rattled off rounds, but he was already gone. Vanished. In the back of his mind, Harry replayed the brief from the day before. *They're all VC—fuckin VC or VC sympathizers. So destroy every-thing. Everything that is walking, everything that is crawling, everything that is growling. If it moves, you shoot it.* There was little left to wonder about. Well—Harry thought, reloading—you didn't have to tell him twice. He had no intention of leaving this village today in a body bag, like so many men before.

They reached the village unmolested and entered in a line, rifles up, ready to fire, ready to unload 5.56 millimeters of American-made lead at—hell, anything. But there was nothing. Not a sound. Not a whisper. With every step he half expected to feel that sharp, blinding flash of heat and pain rip him apart—step after step after step. Adrenaline raced through his body. Where were they? Moments passed, minute after fucking minute of unbearable silence, with nothing but their own dusty footprints to keep them company, the nerves rising in Harry's chest and constricting his lungs, suffocating him. For one stupid second he considered if it really was possible to die of fright. All at once a terrific noise, a deep, sharp, bellow from off to one side, shattered the silence—and Harry jumped, his finger grabbing at the trigger, his heart in his mouth—but it was just a dog barking. A soldier to his right unloaded half a clip at the unfortunate mongrel, the bullets flying in a panicky spray, the man himself crumpling into a squat. The dog squealed and dropped dead. One or two men guffawed—someone patted the shivering Private on the helmet—and walked on. The Private let out a shaky chuckle, his face scarlet, watching the line move past him from his place in the dirt. At the back of the line were a handful of men with flame throwers. They torched the huts, sending rivers of black smoke hurrying into the sky.

"I'VE GOT SOME IN HERE!"

Harry heard his own pulse, felt his heart beating in his ears. He looked over: a couple of the guys had their rifles pointing into a hut, shouting, screaming, eyes wide, and after a few seconds a handful of skinny, malnourished Vietnamese made their way out. Harry saw them with their arms in the air, some dropping weapons, shuffling at gunpoint onto the dirt road. GIs crowded around them, shouting, straining for a look, for a glimpse of the enemy they had been so desperate to meet, until the villagers huddled

beside a grimy well and the soldiers formed a ring around them. The Vietnamese—*fucking VC gook faggots,* Harry thought—chattered anxiously in
their native tongue and some broken English, but the words were lost on
Harry. Meaningless. Nonsense. He felt a pang of hatred. These were the
shit-stains that had killed his friends. *Fucking murderers.* He had to fight
the urge to join the throng, to pick up rocks, sticks, anything he could use
on them. After an instant he remembered that he was carrying a rifle and
felt a strange rush of power as it dawned on him—dawned as if for the first
time—that he held in his hands the ability to kill them, to end them. It
was like a drug, a high. Euphoria. But no, that was...that was not right...
He swallowed his feelings and looked on from a distance. The soldiers
barked orders and the dweeby little bastards did their best to comply. Harry
tried to regain focus. These fuckers were under control. There were several
more huts to search. As he made his way further into the village he heard
crackling as everything behind him went up in smoke.

"NO VC! NO VC!"

It was sudden, shrill. Harry looked sharply over his shoulder. A Staff
Sergeant named Matthews held a man by his hair, dragging him into the
road as the man held up his hands and pleaded in the only English he
apparently knew. The GI's standing around them laughed nervously but
did not intervene as Matthews threw the man to the ground and shoved
the barrel of his rifle in the man's face.

"We already know you're VC!" he snarled. "Where the fuck are the rest
of you?"

"NO VC! NO VC!" the man bawled and broke into unintelligible Vietnamese.

"Speak—fucking—*English!*" He prodded the man in the chest with
each word, the bayonet drawing slivers of blood. "I can't understand a
fucking word you're saying!"

But the man was incapable of replying. He cried and pleaded, and then he reached up and feebly attempted to push the barrel of the rifle to one side. Matthews pushed it right back. The man shook his head, his lips drawn back in an anguished moan, his fingers patting the bayonet and his voice an anxious mumble. The exasperated Sergeant kicked him in the shoulder, and then—hesitation flashed across his face—rammed the bayonet into the man's gut. There was a second of silence, silence except for the wheeze of air escaping the man's sad little body, and then a hideous wail rose from the crowd and floated up to infinity. Matthews spun around, grabbed the wailing man by the collar of his shirt and dragged him to the well, beat him with the butt of his gun and heaved him over the side. Everyone in the square froze as they watched with a strange mixture of horror, clinical interest, and something akin to awe, oblivious to the mission at hand, only listening to the sounds of the two men, one gasping and gurgling as he bled out in the dirt, the other screaming from below the earth.

"What the—*fuck*—did you just do?" someone bellowed.

"What we came here to do," Matthews said, his cheeks flushed, his voice as thin as glass. He pulled a grenade off his belt and tossed it in after the villager, whose screams suddenly heightened in pitch until with an awful *bang* he was silenced. Smoke billowed up out of the hole, hanging on the air with terrible stillness.

All was quiet for a moment, an eternity trapped inside a few seconds. Finally someone said, "Nice one, Matthews." A handful of the soldiers laughed nervously. The remaining villagers wept. After a moment's consideration the group dispersed to continue their ordered destruction. Matthews fired a clip into the remaining Vietnamese before moving on.

Harry sniffled as the smell of burning wood and flesh mingled in his nose, bringing him back from some strange trance. He felt sick, a deepening horror settling into his stomach. This wasn't the way he had imagined it. Not at all. This wasn't combat, no this was—this was *execution*. He turned to continue his sweep, his mind racing, his heart pounding, and soon an uneasy rationale rose up to comfort him. They deserved to die. That was it. They deserved it because of what they had done. And he was here to do it. To make the town a crater, uninhabitable even for the Vietcong. Violence, sometimes brutal violence, was a part of war. Yes, it was all part of war. He closed his eyes and breathed deeply for a moment. These were not men, not even close. They were barely even human. No, these were...these were *animals*... Only animals were capable of the cruelty he had witnessed firsthand these last three months, and when an animal was dangerous it must be put down. Enough said. And with time more of them, more of the damned VC would show up, and he couldn't be lost down some rabbit hole of questioning and self-doubt. Eventually more soldiers, soldiers with guns, would show themselves, he was sure—in fact, he felt a stab of fear in his gut just imagining it. In war, the ends really did justify the means...

He rounded a corner and came across a strange sight, one which shook his conviction from only seconds before: what could only be described as some sort of small temple, with a throng of people, women and children mostly, crying and praying around it, some fifteen or twenty of them. Childhood images of going to church with his mother flickered across his mind: kneeling in the pew, flipping through the hymnal helplessly when he didn't know the words or the music, his feet dancing inches from the ground as he listened to the sermon. Then the wheels of memory screamed to life and he saw everything—Christmases, Easters, his son's baptism—all flew through his subconscious like some sped-up film of life's Greatest Moments of Church, until the reel rattled to an end and he was back in Vietnam, staring at this gathering of the faithful—faithful to what, he wasn't sure, but faithful—rifle hanging loosely from his fingertips, rooted to the spot. A few turned and saw him, but they didn't move. Where would they go? The sounds of destruction now came from all sides. Harry stood completely still, watching the sobbing parishioners, knowing he should alert the platoon, suddenly fearing what would happen if he did.

"Waiting for something?"

He looked around, startled. It was an officer, Fletcher, standing in his Second Lieutenant's uniform with all the commanding presence of a man perhaps twenty-two years of age. Even to Harry at twenty-five, the man looked so young, his face creaseless, but behind his eyes there burned the cruel flame of retribution. It was a look Harry had come to know well. He was hungry for blood, Harry knew it, they all were. Harry had seen the same look in the mirror, seen it in his own eyes. In his hand Fletcher wielded a pistol. Harry balked.

"Sir?"

"I believe you have your orders, Private. Don't stand there looking like a fool."

Harry blinked stupidly, not quite comprehending. He wasn't sure what he was hearing, couldn't believe it...wouldn't believe it. "Yes sir—um...these are just civilians," he said. He wished his voice didn't sound so high pitched...

The officer snorted with frustration, a great phlegmy inhalation, and spat on the ground. *Phht.* "D'you forget that we're here to shoot everything that moves?" He sounded like a man addressing a child, his voice laced with irritation. He cocked an eyebrow. "Huh?"

Harry looked down at the rifle in his hands, felt the grain of the wood, smooth under his fingers. He smelled the burning homes—it seemed the whole village was now in flames. In the distance he could hear screaming, screaming and laughing, all mixed up together, and machine gun fire. When did that start? He couldn't remember. It all felt so surreal, he sensed everything he stood for and thought the Army—hell, the *country*—stood for, crumbling, withering away in minutes, going up in smoke. The speed of it left him breathless. The kids around the temple... Some of them were the same age as Willie. He pictured his son kicking his own tiny legs under the pew at church, pictured him in his party hat, pictured the Vietnamese children laughing and smiling and enjoying their own birthdays. His heart broke. He gripped his rifle and looked back up at the officer, his eyes suddenly hot, his face burning. The sun shining hazily through the smog cast an unearthly light across the space between them.

"Sir... Yes sir—I mean no sir, I didn't forget," he said, willing himself to have misunderstood. His voice had cracked on the first *Sir* and he winced at his own inadequacy. "I just don't think they meant women and children, sir, it doesn't..." He trailed off under the withering gaze of the Lieutenant, who stared at him, disbelief twisting his face.

"Are you refusing to follow orders?" His voice shook slightly.

"I just—" Harry floundered, looking to the sky for inspiration (and finding none) and then back at the baby-faced man standing in front of him. "I can't. It ain't right, sir, you know it ain't right."

"Not *right?* I'll tell you what's fucking not right: five men, *my* men, blown to bits, itty bitty pieces, the kind you can't even send home to Mom, that's what's fucking not *right*. And you know who did it? It's no great mystery, Ross, it's these motherfucking gooks right here, the ones who look so innocent, but you know what?" He gestured wildly, the intensity of his emotions overtaking him. "We know better, Ross, we fucking know better. The VC look just like civilians. We see it again and again. They sure as shit do, you fucking know they do, I know they do, goddamn Ho Chi Minh sure fucking knows it, and he's using it against us. He's up in our fucking *heads,* Ross!" He tapped his temple madly. "He's up in our goddamn fucking *minds.* Now are you gonna fucking do something about that? You just gonna stand there like some chicken shit coward?"

Harry had no retort; he glanced back and forth between the officer and the crowd, willing them to go, to move, while there was still time, but of course there was no time. *Why don't they just move?* Harry thought desperately, but he already knew there was no chance for them. The smoke and the heat of the fire were closing in...closing in...

"GODDAMMIT!" Fletcher shouted suddenly, on the verge of tears, looking like an overgrown toddler. "It's a free fire zone—you understand that, you lazy sack of shit, a fucking *free fire* zone! YOU FUCKING SHOOT WHAT I TELL YOU TO SHOOT!"

"Sir—"

"THAT'S AN ORDER!"

Harry hesitated for a moment and swallowed hard.

"No, sir. I can't, I—I can't do it. I won't."

For a moment Fletcher looked like he might just turn and run. Then something clicked behind his eyes, a switch flipping into place, and with an eerie calm he raised his pistol at Harry.

"Do it, or I'll shoot you myself."

"What? Please, sir, put the gun down, please, don't—"

"We follow orders. You hear me? We follow orders, and if you won't do it, I'll make you do it."

"Sir, please—"

"DO IT! DO IT, YOU PIECE OF SHIT! I SWEAR TO GOD I'LL SHOOT YOU MYSELF, NOW *DO IT!*"

Harry looked into Fletcher's trembling face—Fletcher, whom he had laughed with and cried with; *not Fletcher, that's not possible, no way, no fucking way*—but the look in his eye was cold, stone cold, and fear ballooned in Harry's stomach. He would do it. Yes, he would do it. Harry felt afraid, more afraid than he had ever felt before, more afraid than on his first patrol when the guy in front of him stepped on a mine and exploded into bits. He felt afraid of the man pointing the pistol at his chest, and he felt afraid, in some unconscious way, for his own immortal soul, for the irreparable damage that would be done to it by this act of callous violence. He knew, in his core, without thinking about it or giving voice to it, that this was not something that could ever be forgiven. He wanted to say no, to tell Fletcher to stop, please...

But the gun aimed squarely at his chest scared him more. He turned carefully back to the crowd of villagers, still praying and crying, some of them chancing nervous glances at the two of them. Why hadn't they just *run?* He raised his rifle slowly, agonizingly slowly. Before him it seemed that his wife and son, multiplied by the dozen, stood gazing at him in judgement. In their eyes he saw them begging, pleading with him not to do it, their frantic prayers rising feverishly into the ash-gray beyond, but over his shoulder he still sensed the pistol at his back, and he felt so very afraid. He closed his eyes and put his family out of his mind, put his finger firmly on the trigger, his hand shaking, it seemed impossible he could actually do it, impossible...but he breathed and suddenly it seemed so easy...and he squeezed off a round.

Someone screamed—he didn't dare open his eyes—and he fired again and again and again until he couldn't bear it any longer—and finally he opened his eyes and his knees buckled. Seven people lay dead, women and children both, their bodies a ruin of blood and shattered bone, and three more were sprawled in the dirt spluttering blood. Sobbing, scream-ing...their cries drifted across the dark courtyard, dark even as the sun rose high above the horizon. But they did not dare to move as Fletcher brandished his Colt in a bitter expression of victory.

"About fucking time," Fletcher said, and took his pistol to the wounded villagers and shot them each in the head. The rest finally scattered and he emptied his magazine into their backs. One by one they crumpled in the street and moved no more. Then he turned back to Harry, stone-faced.

"War is hell. We can't let those Commie bastards live, they'll kill us in our sleep." Then without another word he left the square like a ghost.

Harry was in shock. He stared at the bloody, broken bodies, at the shards of pearly white bone, at the crimson puddles soaking into the dusty road. Limbs and guts, flies landing in a dizzying swarm, blind eyes staring through it all, gazing blank and cold, gazing into eternity. He had done it... It wasn't possible... It didn't feel *real*... *No, God no, please, please*... He couldn't believe it...couldn't accept it... He heard a rushing noise filling his ears, a great droning sound. Dimly it came to him that it must be the fire but...it was too loud to be the fire. It swelled up around him, surrounding him, enveloping him, this all-consuming noise. He couldn't think straight. He looked down at his hands, holding the rifle. Somehow he could feel every nuance, every imperfection in the stock, could feel the weapon heavy in his hands, the weight of death. His hands weren't even bloody. It was so easy. All around was a terrible commotion. He sensed that things were now completely out of control, heard through that awful drone the sounds of more people screaming, people in pain, people dying...but they sounded so very, very far away. He was floating...falling... No—he was standing in the smoggy light of day. And there in front of him was the bloody evil he had wrought; he, Harry, and in that moment he knew his soul was lost, would be forever lost. He fell to his knees, and then slumped onto his side in the dirt. And he cried.

JULY, 1999

"So the guy—Harry, right?—he shoots up a bunch of villagers. Maybe gives him a taste for blood?"

Even without moving it was obvious Mr. Wilford was seeing David again for the first time since he had begun the story. "You think Harry Ross was the Highwayman? That's laughable."

"I see you're not laughing though," David said, and immediately regretted it. Mr. Wilford leaned back in his chair—at least as far as the chain attached to his wrists would allow.

"Well I personally don't find the story particularly funny," he said, his voice rising to a sniff. "Do you?"

David looked quickly at his feet. "No. It's not funny."

"No, it's not."

Great, just fucking fantastic. David pushed his lips together in a wry smile, felt a retort struggling to push its way out between them. He did not like being lectured by anyone, especially not someone like Mr. Wilford, someone who was obviously a few cards shy of a whole deck. *The inmates are running the asylum*—he had heard that saying somewhere. He swallowed. "You know, it's fu—er—interesting you should bring this up. Mr. Ross was one of the original suspects in this case—back in the day. Thanks to this incident and his—uh, well of course his home life, and his murder conviction at about the same time. Back then there wasn't enough evidence to bring charges—for the other cases, I mean. But if you have some testimony that might help—"

"You're talking about the trucker again."

David paused. "Huh?"

"You're talking about the trucker, the one you suggested I helped murder."

David felt slightly off his footing. "Well—yes, Mr. Wilford, you have to admit it was an odd coincidence—"

"I already told you, Harry Ross was not the Highwayman. I told you."

"Yes, but—"

"You're not listening to me," Mr. Wilford said, his eyes taking David apart a piece at a time. "You keep interrupting."

"I'm sorry, I just want—"

"Promise you won't interrupt."

"What?"

"Promise you won't interrupt!"

David stared long and hard at the man across from him, willing him to buckle, to cave first, willing him to change his story. But the eyes behind those glasses were unwavering—unblinking. He glanced down at his notes, shuffled some papers, clicked his pen a few times.

"Okay. I promise. Please continue," he said, his stomach twisting into an angry knot. He looked back up. "You said he brought something back with him. Something terrible."

The man subjected him to another long, penetrating silence, his eyes as motionless as ever and yet they seemed to be searching his soul, unlocking doors and opening passageways, searching, crawling...

"Have you ever been in a war, Special Agent?"

"Yes. I was in Desert Storm."

"So you know that not everything you bring back with you is tangible. Not even as tangible as PTSD. Some things are so deep that they never get found. Some things are so deep you have no name for them."

Now David really puffed up; he had read this man's file, the guy had never even set foot outside New England. He had encountered these sorts of people before, the ones who thought they knew all about war because they had watched *Full Metal Jacket* or *Platoon* a half dozen times. The reality was very different, was a sore spot for David. But it wouldn't help to get worked up. He took a deep breath. "I suppose," he said, with effort. "You see that in a movie?"

"We all have our wars to fight," Mr. Wilford said vaguely. "What Harry Ross brought back with him was that kind of thing. Deep. Nameless. Nameless even to you." His eyes glossed over and he seemed to be drifting off again, but David was not done with him.

"So the guy has some disorder he gets in the war. PTSD, whatever, doesn't matter. Maybe a guilt complex. Wouldn't be the first time. But if he's not the Highwayman, then what are you—"

Suddenly they were interrupted by a loud noise as the door to the visitation room slammed open with a muffled clang and the same two large men in white suits and with white orderly hats perched on their heads stepped in, pushing a cart which looked as though its best days had been about fifty years prior. Of its four rusty wheels, one spun idly a millimeter off the ground and another squeaked shrilly with each pained revolution. *Eeek! Eeek! Eeek!* They stopped by the table—a safe distance, David noticed, from the man in the handcuffs.

"For you, Agent Nolan," the taller orderly said with a friendly smile, and yet it was slightly off-putting. His face was shiny with sweat and prematurely wrinkled. "Coffee and doughnuts. We thought you might be hungry."

David smiled back appreciatively. "Thank you, Mister..."

"Cameron. It's not every day we have visitors from the FBI."

"It's not every day I get to visit with such distinguished guests," David replied, tasting the lie on his tongue and nodding at Mr. Wilford. Mr. Cameron appeared mildly amused.

"Yes, well... The patients here certainly do attract a lot of attention—"

"The staff here are nothing if not considerate," Mr. Wilford said coldly, and for the first time he averted his gaze to stare at the orderly. Then he too smiled. "Thank you, Jason. I'm sure we're all just tickled. Are you ready to continue or aren't you, *Agent Nolan?*"

"Thank you for the coffee, Mr. Cameron," David said, pleasantly enough, but wanting the orderlies to leave. He turned to Mr. Wilford. "Yes, I'm ready." He paused for a moment, gauging whether to ask, feeling a stroke of inspiration. "Would you, uh—would you like some coffee as well?"

The man looked back at him suspiciously. So did the two orderlies.

"Sir, I don't think that's such a good—"

"Oh what the hell, can't a guy have a cup of coffee once in a while?" David asked. Internally he congratulated himself for his brilliance. Show the man some kindness. Just a bit. A cup of coffee for Christ's sake. And watch the wheels turn. Maybe then he would be willing to play ball. He saw the exasperated looks on the two sweaty faces and waved dismissively. "I'll take the heat. Tell the Doc I gave it to him."

Mr. Cameron and his companion looked at each other grimly, then back at David.

"Okay..." Mr. Cameron said slowly, and poured a little paper cup and placed it on the table by the metal loop. Mr. Wilford looked at it for a long moment, then up at the microphone, regarding both with an expression of extreme distrust.

"I like my coffee with cream and sugar," he said.

"You're lucky to get coffee at all," the shorter orderly snorted, a hairy man who made up in girth what he lacked in height.

"Please, please," David said. He acknowledged Mr. Wilford with a theatrical nod, and took the sugar and the small pitcher of cream and poured them both. All the while he sensed eyes on him from both sides. When he was done the orderlies left without another word and only a parting head shake, pulling the cart along on another agonized trek. The man across the table sat quietly and sipped his coffee, peering over the edge of the cup at David as if daring him to admit the coffee was poisoned.

"There are others, you know."

David looked up from his own cup, surprised. "I'm sorry?"

"There are other people who come to talk to me. They want to know how I did it."

David considered his response. He spoke slowly. "And what do you tell them?"

Mr. Wilford stared at him, but there was no light in his eyes now. They were hard, bitter. "I don't tell them nothin," he said with disgust. He sipped his coffee again, and David knew immediately that he would say no more on the subject.

"So where—"

But they were interrupted once more as the door swung open with that same thunderous *clank* and Doctor Alvarez swept in, eyes ablaze, the corners of his mustache drooping in apparent displeasure.

"Agent Nolan," he said curtly as he cleared the threshold.

"Doc," David nodded, perplexed.

Doctor Alvarez came to a stop by the table, his trim form bouncing up and down on the balls of his feet, his hands making their nervous way first to his hips and then sliding unconsciously into his pockets. "Agent Nolan. Forgive me. But after our conversation this morning, can you explain to me precisely *why* you are giving this man a *stimulant?*"

Agent Nolan fumbled with his pen, surprised. "Stimulant... The coffee? It seemed relatively harmle—"

"Well it's not. I told you not to get him excited, and I'm sure I don't need to explain to you the effects of caffeine. This man is seriously—" He paused as if suddenly remembering that Mr. Wilford was in the room with him and coughed uncomfortably. "—seriously, uh, ill. He cannot have caffeine. It will get him excited. Do you understand?" Doctor Alvarez gave David a meaningful look when he said "excited" and tilted his head forward and to the side in the same gesture with which he had first greeted David at the door.

"Yes, I understand," David said, nonplussed. "I guess I didn't think—"

"Apparently not. Please hand me the cup."

David glanced across the table and saw that Mr. Wilford had set the little paper cup down next to the bar. He began reaching for it and then remembered the man's large hands, handcuffed to the bar and sitting in his lap. He paused.

"Something wrong, *Special Agent?*" Mr. Wilford asked. Was it a taunt? Genuine concern? In his flat voice it could have been anything.

"No, nothing wrong," David said breezily, and with a rush of adrenaline he leaned forward until his hand was directly under the expressionless face across from him. He wrapped his fingers around the cup and, without meaning to, without wanting to, looked up and into those cold, pale eyes, so close, too close, close enough that he smelled the man's rancid breath, and immediately a deep, nameless fear gripped him. It twisted his stomach and turned his entrails to ice. That fear. It was powerful, inhuman. He was lost in it, drowning in it; he felt suddenly as though he could shout and no one would hear him; he fell into those dark, yawning depths and would never get out, and worse—something was down here in the dark, some unspeakable evil, the kind that has no face, no motive—

Agent Nolan, are you quite alright?

It was distant, far away.

"Agent Nolan?"

He blinked. He was still in the visitation room, still leaning across the table, the small paper cup in one hand, Mr. Wilford still staring at him and Doctor Alvarez looking at him with concerned curiosity.

"Yes, I..." he blinked again and his head cleared. "I'm fine." He sat back and handed the cup to Doctor Alvarez. "Just fine. Sorry for the trouble, Doc."

"I'm sure," Doctor Alvarez said stiffly.

"It won't happen again."

"No. Well, like I said, I'll be right outside."

Doctor Alvarez surveyed the two of them for a moment, distrust etched into the lines of his face, and then he walked briskly from the room. The sound of his fingers tapping nervously on the side of the coffee cup followed him out.

"Good work bud," Mr. Wilford said, once the door had slammed shut. There was even the faintest bit of humor in his voice.

"Yes, I—I'm sorry about the trouble," David said, still shaken.

"That's Green Elm Home," Mr. Wilford replied, the edge creeping back in. "Can't catch a freaking break."

"So, uh—where were we?"

"You were just starting to get upset," Mr. Wilford said.

"Was I?"

"Yes. You were upset because you think Harry Ross was the Highwayman. And I said he's not."

"I'm definitely confused," David said, and he was. He tried to muster his bravado from only moments ago and failed. "I'm not upset. Just—I just want to understand how it fits together." It was almost the truth; the frustration he had felt before was buried under a mountain of unease.

"Well you're not gonna see it if you keep interrupting. It'll all make sense. But you have to wait. Good things come to those who wait."

"I can wait," David said, noting the childish turn of phrase. The man across from him squinted a little and lifted a finger as if to say, *Just a moment.* The chain at his wrist made a dry clinking sound as he set his arms back in his lap. He resumed his piercing stare.

"The thing he brought back. It has no name," he said.

FEBRUARY, 1978

T om was eight years old when they moved to the lake house in the summer of 1977. Old enough to know better and young enough not to care, as his mother liked to tease. His father, Rob, was in a similar position of a more grown-up variety. He was a mid-level operator at the local power plant; experienced enough to be trusted, new enough to have no worthwhile opinions. Tom liked to think of them as being similar, perhaps not in this way—he lacked the age and maturity to put it in quite those terms—but in some way. Tom was an observant youngster, more observant than most, and even if he didn't have the words, he knew the meaning, could feel it deep down inside. His father knew it too, and commented on it a few times to his wife, in the small hours of the morning when they were finished making love and waiting to fall asleep, in those precious moments when the truths that normally go unsaid find a voice. Rob wasn't embarrassed by it—well, maybe he was. But he valued his son's experience all the same, and he cherished the idea that they were cut from the same cloth, that maybe they would keep this common bond forever.

They moved to the lake house when Rob took the job at the power plant, Elmwood River Atomic Energy. It was a promotion from his last job, with slightly better hours and a competitive pension. Deep down in his heart of hearts, Rob had no intention of retiring from Elmwood, but he had grown up close enough to the Depression to place a lot of value in pensions, and he was still young enough to want to impress *his* father—especially considering that a bad back had kept him out of the war. Besides, the pay was marginally better, and they fantasized often of living near the water, a small boat in the garage, fishing poles at the ready, swim trunks never hanging up for more than a day before being pulled on again, wet and cold, uninviting and chafing in all the wrong places. This dream they also shared in the dead of night, Rob and Kristin, alone in their tiny bedroom. So when the job offer came, it was with only slight hesitation that Rob took it, and sold the old townhouse, and took his family out to the lake.

Tom, for his part, loved the lake. He didn't have much concept of power plants or pensions or missed wars, not really, and he was mostly his mother's son, but he loved the mornings when his father would wake him early and take him out on the boat, the nighttime mist still clinging mournfully to the water's surface, the little bugs that skitter along the shiny mirror's edge dancing in the pre-dawn gloom. There Rob would show him how to bait the hook (he secretly hated that part) and cast the line out, far, as far as his eight-year-old arms could manage, and watch the little bobber wiggle up and down in the ripples from their boat. There was a special kind of joy when the bobber would disappear, rush beneath the water with an incongruous urgency, and his father would cry out, "You got one! You got one!" Tom thought there was nothing better in the whole world, even if he would never say so, not even years later. Rob thought there was nothing better too, and he never said so either.

The summer of '77 ultimately gave way to fall, and then winter, and the boat went back in the garage, and the mornings out on the lake came to an end. The swim trunks finally, mercifully, dried, and were folded and put away. The fishing poles were propped in a corner, the hooks threatening rust with every passing day. Rob was pulling extra shifts at the power plant, a small price to pay for the overtime he was making, but between that and the early evening darkness it seemed to Tom that he was never home. Sometimes Rob would come slouching in the door at eleven o'clock, well past Tom's bedtime, drop off his coat in the living room and shuffle slowly upstairs, and watch his son sleep. Dreaming of the days on the lake, perhaps. Rob certainly did. By February it seemed that winter would never end.

February, miserable gray February; it was a cold February morning of the worst kind. Buckets of rain—cold, biting, February rain—washed across the lake in sheets, melted the snow still clinging to winter's chill, soaked into the soil, dug little trenches and filled them with rivulets. It rushed, meandered, splashed, careened across the lawn until it dribbled into the icy surf. Kristin watched it fall from the safety of the window, musing that her husband's drive to work would be worse than usual. It was a part of his life that he hated, no question about it. He said so all the time. She kept her feelings private, kept the hateful things inside, but there could be no mistake that she carried her fair share. The part of her that worried, the small voice that whispered fearfully to her and conjured the specters of all her worst imaginings, echoed a lifetime of quiet misgivings, of anxious waiting. Waiting for the other shoe to drop. Waiting for the bombshell. She had no idea what it might be—actually, that was a lie, she knew perfectly well what—but she could not shake the feeling. It was a constant, ever-present companion, this fear, this *dread*; she buried it easily beneath a facade of wifely affection, contrived cheeriness, makeup, but it always remained. The incessant worry—all-consuming, steadfast, and secret—was a churning subterranean ocean, a world of its own that sometimes threatened to drown her—and which she was determined to maintain out of sight.

For one thing, Rob's vision was just not good. That was half the struggle of the drive, that and the traffic on the country roads. Despite his wife's fussing and the recommendations of countless doctors, he hated wearing glasses. He would for work—usually—but off the clock was another matter. Often was the time he could be found standing in one place, blinking hard and squinting determinedly, trying to clear up a blurry sight that no amount of blinking or squinting could remedy. Tom's vision was worse still, but he wore his glasses dutifully. His mother would turn her anxious gaze on him as he got ready for school, his eyes enormous behind the thick prisms perched on his nose, and worry about what the other children would say. What they actually said was a complete mystery, as Tom (or Tommy, as his mother called him), remained stoically silent about his time away from the house, a fact that worried her even more. By all accounts he was a happy child—the summer by the lake was quite possibly the happiest of his young life—but he was quiet and sensitive, and spent most of his time thoughtfully watching the goings on around him through those great Brobdingnagian spectacles, and saying nothing.

And Kristin worried. She worried about Rob's commute, and his glasses, and Tommy's glasses, and her father's failing health, and their finances, and the grocery list, and of course that thing, the thing she was waiting for, but most of all she worried about the incident with the cat.

Her hand rose to her mouth. Tommy had been three—no, four. Certainly too young to know what he had done. She could picture him even now with his bowl cut and his little suit, a miniature gentleman dressed to the nines. They were having a family portrait taken; an affair which had cost a substantial sum of money and a great deal of planning, but Kristin had insisted. They could use it for their Christmas cards, she said, and it could go on the bookshelf next to the pictures of Rob's parents. Tommy had been playing with the cat—he loved that cat, loved to chase it and pet it and watch its tail flick back and forth—but today it had scratched him, badly. He had an angry red line along his forearm and he had cried for a while, especially when his father dabbed alcohol on it, but he would be fine, just fine. And the photographer had come to their little townhouse with a van full of gear, a straight-laced professional who fixed Kristin's hair and covered Rob's acne scars and said things to make Tommy sit still and smile, and finally the pictures were done... Tommy had gone out back to let off steam...and she had stepped outside for a moment...she couldn't even remember why anymore...but there was Tommy sitting in the grass, his neat child's suit speckled with little red flecks, and playing with something...

Tommy, what are you doing, kiddo?

Just playing.

What have you got on your suit?

And the dawning horror, the realization that it was blood and the thing in his hand was a tail, a cat's tail—*their* cat's tail—white bone protruding in harsh contrast against the dark clotted red, and lying there just beyond him, a gory wreck smeared into the lawn, almost unrecognizable and covered with flies, the rest of the poor creature. And there was Tommy, himself in a cloud of flies and mosquitos, his glasses dotted with blood, his eyes bright and shining and unknowing... She had dropped something then, she didn't remember what, but it shattered...and she screamed, and Tommy started crying, great fat tears oozing from his eyes and down his chubby cheeks. He tried to wipe them with his sleeve but only managed to spread awful red streaks across his glasses...

With a familiar shudder she shook herself from the memory. How often had she wondered what that meant? What could be going on behind those big eyes, those eyes which looked so innocent, so pure? It made her feel incredibly guilty to ask, even just to ask herself, because this was her child, her sweet little boy, the baby she had nursed and cradled and loved more deeply than anything in her life. And anyway, that was years ago. On this particular morning those glasses were heavy with fog, and the dirty-blonde hair adorning Tommy's head in haphazard tufts was slowly turning a damp, cold brown as he stood on the other side of the glass from his mother, watching from under the too-small hood of his neon blue jacket as the school bus rolled up to the end of their driveway. She had kissed him goodbye when the bus rounded the corner, and he had trotted off, his little backpack bobbing happily to the edge of the porch until with a *plop*, he paused to watch it make the final stretch in his usual silent manner. Kristin, smiling in spite of herself, held a nervous hand to her lips until with a final cheery bounce his backpack followed him up the steps and the bus rolled away.

She turned from the window. There were other things to worry about, smaller things. To start, the house was a wreck. After a weekend at home with both of the men in her life there was no shortage of cleaning to do, and God knew Rob would never do it. She fell into the routine of tidying up and within an hour or two the swirling stormy ocean within receded and she felt a quiet calm return. She cleaned Tommy's room and folded his clothes and moved on to vacuuming the living room and (Heaven help her) Rob's study. There she found—predictably—another awful mess, the bane of her domestic experience. She simply hated messes and sometimes found it hard not to hate those who made them. With Rob it was always a struggle; the man was simply not built for maintaining a clean house. She winced as the vacuum sucked up bits of popcorn and potato chip, but it was a satisfied sort of wince, the kind that felt oh-so-good and yet fueled the ever-burning fire of frustration that smoldered just beneath the surface along with that treacherous sea.

She thought back to when she had met Rob. They had been undergrads at Vermont State, Rob a senior studying engineering technology and her a junior elementary education major. *Well, look where that got me,* she thought with a familiar undercurrent of resentment. Rob was six years older, and he had been so handsome then, so charming. And he was on the up-and-up, the sky was the limit, it seemed he could do anything but knew exactly what he wanted. She on the other hand felt directionless—elementary education was not so much a passion as a compromise with her father, and not a happy one. They met at a Halloween party and immediately hit it off. Rob was so sympathetic to the problems with her father, the ones she didn't talk about with anyone—although for some reason she opened right up to him—and even though the physical attraction was immediate, they spent that first encounter talking long into the night. Kristin fell asleep in the crook of Rob's arm and awoke to find him still there, still ready to listen.

Oh, she had fallen for him fast. Within six months she had dropped out of college and they had gotten married and only a few months later she was pregnant. An insidious thought came wriggling from the recesses of her memory then, puny and paper-white and reeking of indiscretion, but she pushed it away. Yes, pregnant. Talk about the best of times and the worst of times—she was sick almost every day but she loved carrying that little ball of life around in her *own body*, this thing that was a piece of her and yet brand new. And of course eventually she had to let it leave her and become its own life...but she promised herself that they would always be together, always be a family, and anyway there was no reason to worry because everything was just so beautiful and perfect and warm.

The vacuum caught on a paperclip under Rob's desk and the little motor inside cried with effort as it *smack-smack-smack-smack*-ed its way around the brush. She stopped to fish it out.

Yes, they had had a beautiful life there in the townhouse near the city, Rob just beginning to climb the corporate ladder, Kristin tending to their beautiful baby boy. From the first Tommy had loved her dearly, and she him. It was a special connection that she sensed right down in her gut and she knew—somehow she knew—that he did not quite have the same relationship with his father. Even though Rob loved the boy more than anything in the world—it was not the same. Tommy went everywhere with her, listened to her with wide eyes when she spoke and even gave her the strangest feeling that he understood every word she said. Rob was not afraid to change a diaper or two but it was Kristin who did the heavy lifting, and whether it was instinct or observation it paid dividends in the way that he looked at her when she woke him from his nap or set him in his highchair for dinner.

It took a few years for the cracks to show. Rob became increasingly dissatisfied at work *(The management,* he would say under his breath after a quick kiss to welcome him home, *The management have no goddamn idea what they're doing)* and she tried to make him feel better but the things that used to work just didn't seem to any more. He grew more and more tired, looked more and more—well—*old*, and as the veneer slowly chipped off their picturesque life so too did the rose colored glasses through which Kristin had viewed it. And of course there was the cat... She shuddered again, forced it from her mind. The move to the lake house might have been their shared dream, but whether Rob knew it or not—and Tommy *definitely* could not know—it was in Kristin's mind a kind of mental reset, a Take Two that she hoped could revive the old happiness they had lost along the way.

So she suppressed the frustration and she vacuumed, oh yes, vacuumed until she was numb from the soft vibration in her hand and the whirring in her ears. She mopped and dusted and washed and did everything she could think of to spruce up the house in the face of the unrelentingly gray, wet weather outside. By mid-morning it even seemed to have worked. The torrential rain finally turned over to a soft, sad drizzle, giving the outdoors a weepy, somber look, almost more depressing than the heavy rain had been, but inside things slowly returned to careful order. Still...Kristin caught herself staring outside, lost as if in a dream, contemplating the past, and pondering something...something shameful, something...something she didn't like to acknowledge. She shook off the unsettling feeling and continued her cleaning, but yes it...somehow it came back, creeping across her subconscious like some some sort of weed, or ivy, yes, just like ivy, and she drifted off again, staring out the window into empty space...and returned again, and started the cycle anew. The thought...the dreadful thought... What if it was *her* fault...because of the thing she had done... *No,* she thought, and pushed it away again. But it kept returning, monstrous, overwhelming, threatening to suffocate her; she felt that awful worry gnawing at her belly and the carefully ordered progress of the morning slipping away, slipping, slipping...

Ring... Ring... Ring...

The phone. *The phone!* It startled her, interrupted her morning like a shrill, unwelcome visitor. She looked over at it uncertainly. The anxiety was in full control, and somehow she knew, could sense deep in her solar-plexus that this was a call she did not want to answer. It was something terrible. Worse...it was her fault, it was all her fault because of that thing, she knew the one, the unspeakable thing... *No, that's not possible,* and she surfaced for a moment from the tumultuous waves crashing through her mind and gulped for air. Her thoughts, the thoughts she had, those awful *thoughts,* the ones she would not admit even to herself—they swirled and whined and pounded in her head for attention, but no, she could not give it to them, she would not—but could they have something to do with the call? It was paranoid, of course it was, *Can't be,* she thought wildly, but she stared at the phone as if it were a wild animal loose in the house. There was no explaining it, no understanding it. But for some indescribable reason she was filled with the most hideous fear. For a moment the idea of letting the phone ring off the hook drifted through her mind as a hazy, half-formed thought, but that too was interrupted by the insistent wailing.

Ring... Ring... Ring...

She stood slowly. The world converged on the telephone, magnified as if by some great telescopic lens through which she was forced to peer. A sense of compulsion rushed through her as she stared at it. Was there ever any choice in answering? Certainly not, as certain as the sun sets and the moon rises—as certain as the rain still stubbornly drip-drip-dripped from the gutter into her garden.

Ring... Ring... Ring...

If anyone had asked later, she would not have remembered walking over. But suddenly she was there, picking up the receiver, the ringing stopping abruptly as she raised it hesitantly to her ear.

"Hel"—cough—"Hello?"

* * *

Tommy watched the great yellow bus grind to halt, jogged with a youthful effortlessness down the driveway and up the giant green steps into its cavernous interior. His backpack, almost as big as he was, lumbered awkwardly behind him in the rhythm of his footsteps. The driver, with her curls still in, a cigarette perched precariously on her lip and another burning in the ashtray, nodded matter-of-factly as he found a seat alone near the back, and with a lurch the bus sprang back to life. He looked around with interest as if to acknowledge the presence of all the other children and their own supersized backpacks, but none acknowledged him back, and so he turned to the window to watch with some bereavement as his mother disappeared behind a row of trees. Then he focused on his shoes.

His mother had bought him the shoes only a few weeks ago, and although they were soggy with rain, they still bore that ultra-bright, fresh-out-of-the-box look. Tommy loved new shoes; he couldn't have explained it if he wanted to, but there was something magical and invigorating about putting them on. In his childlike way he imagined they made him look more sophisticated, maybe more special, faster and cooler. He was just beginning to outgrow it, but he had always loved going to the store with his mother, to walk the aisles with her searching for the perfect pair, to try them on, to walk around feeling like the man of the hour, like the whole day was about him, to find these shoes that would take him on all manner of boyhood adventures. His mother would treat him to lunch while they were out, and they would sit and laugh like old pals, just the two of them...

...He and his mother—her smiling face had just disappeared behind the branches. He glanced up and out the window with a pang of grief. He knew she worried. He worried too. Even when he was a toddler he could sense it, intuit it—the horrid thing that kept her up at night, the one that left her with a turbulent undercurrent of misery and fear. His daddy didn't know...he didn't notice....but Tommy knew, knew that she carried it around with her everywhere, even when she didn't think of it consciously. He felt its awful weight following them but usually remaining at a safe distance, only emerging when they parted—a terrible cloud that grew in size and energy as the space between them also grew. What the secret was remained a mystery, but its presence was all too clear to Tommy, who feared he would one day discover the truth of it. After all, he had his own secret; one which came slithering out of the darkness when he tried to sleep, one which haunted him when he was alone, one which he hoped would never see the light of day—

—*mewling and mewling and breathing in great shuddering breaths, rattles, death rattles, rattles like the toy, oh how funny, just funny, ha ha yes that rattling, oh God oh God oh GOD, look at the BLOOD! I didn't do it Mommy, I didn't I didn't I didn't please believe me Mommy it was that thing in the trees, the thing that watches us—*

—because it was so frightening and he tried not to believe it. His thumb inched toward his mouth and he fought the urge to suck it. That was a baby habit. And Tommy was no baby. He was eight. He would be nine—a big kid, or almost anyway—in just a couple months. One year until double digits, and no self-respecting *ten*-year-old would ever suck his thumb. Plus Daddy hated it, said it would mess up his teeth—which confused Tommy because his teeth always fell out anyway. But still, it wouldn't do, not here, not in front of the other kids. He surveyed the rows of bench seats and willed himself to relax.

As a real youngster, only five, he had been terrified of the school bus, terrified and excited, but now it was old news. He suppressed his home-sickness with a swell of pride at how very grown-up he was, and imagined the bus driver and maybe even some of the other kids could tell too. He looked over at a huddle of kindergartners talking excitedly across the aisle and felt a quiet superiority for having conquered the few years between them. One day they would be as old and experienced as he was, but not yet—not for a lifetime. He was in *third grade*, a truly advanced age. While they learned how to spell their names, he studied arithmetic, wrote whole paragraphs. And who knew what he would learn in a year or two, it was almost breathtaking to consider. He imagined them stealing looks at him and his shiny white shoes with a mixture of respect and awe. It was the same way he had looked at third-graders when he was in kindergarten, and the same way he looked at middle-schoolers now.

It wasn't long before the bus squealed to a stop and the children jostled for position in the line forming to disembark. Tommy interjected himself cautiously, pushed his glasses up higher on his nose, gripped the straps of his backpack with purpose. One by one they clambered down the steps and onto the covered sidewalk, trotting off at once or waiting for their friends. Tommy went alone.

"Hey Four-eyes!"

It was Billy Baker. Tommy ignored him and pressed on.

"Sorry—Tommy! Hey Tommy, wait up!"

Billy was one of Tommy's regular tormenters. He would not have qual-ified as a bully, but he was mean and direct, handsome and popular, every-thing Tommy was not, and he relished the power he held in the eyes of his schoolmates. No one knew this (certainly not Billy), but sometimes he was mean just to see if he could get away with it. He always could. The other children, well, they practically loved him for it. *Oh me, pick me, yes, me with the snaggle tooth. Isn't it funny? I laugh at it myself sometimes...* The best that could be said was that Billy was equitable with his meanness, sparing no one—unless of course that someone was even more popular, but there were few enough of those. Someone who was a victim today could feel that dizzying rush of power by laughing alongside him the next, and they were only too eager to do so, thinking perhaps that Billy was their friend. He was not.

"Hi, Billy."

"Hi, Tommy. Dude, what's up with your glasses?"

Tommy reached up without thinking and wiped the fog from his lenses with his wrist, but they clouded over again almost instantly. He felt a stab of embarrassment and hurried on.

"It's the rain," he said, walking quickly.

"If I had to wear glasses I'd kill myself," Billy said cooly, admiring his reflection in the glass door as they passed inside. Billy had started school a year late and was half a head taller than everyone else, a fact some children might have found embarrassing but which only fed Billy's considerable ego.

"Uh-huh." Tommy secretly liked his glasses, thought they made him look smart *(like my Daddy)*, but he wasn't about to admit this in front of Billy. He quickened his stride, hoping to get away, but the rush of warm air fogged his lenses up even worse, so that now he was nearly blind. Billy continued:

"So listen, Fred and Al and me are all going to the pond at recess. Have you been? It's way more fun than that boring old playground, that's for sure. Anyway, Elise is coming too, and I know how you like her. And Jenny of course."

Tommy's stomach did a somersault. "I mean, I don't *like* her like her," he said, an incredible lie, one which turned the somersault into an ache. He grasped for a distraction and found one easily, straight from his ready supply of goody-two-shoe-isms. Tommy was an old pro at being a wet blanket, a comparison that was especially appropriate as he stood blinking through his still-dripping hair. "I thought we weren't allowed over there."

"Of course we aren't, dummy," Billy scoffed. He lowered his voice conspiratorially. "Look, Eddie Miller already backed out, but he's just a big baby. Have you seen the notes his mom leaves in his lunches?" He wrinkled his nose. "*Yech.* But we need one more for even teams or it's not gonna work. Look, it's not like Weirdo Will'll be there, it'll be cool."

Weirdo Will was a quiet boy who loved superheroes just a little too much and whom the other children teased mercilessly. He had come to symbolize un-cool-ness in its incarnate form, so much so that his reputation had preceded him to the third grade all the way from the sixth. Billy and Tommy did not know, and may not have cared, but Will was the child of a troubled home. His father, home from Vietnam, usually drunk—in fact always drunk, and a mean drunk, a real bastard of the first order—was a man who had few nice things to say, and that was when he was sober. It was not uncommon for Will to spend an evening locked in the bathroom with his mother while she screamed through the door and his father pounded his angry fists on the other side in a towering alcohol-and-grief-fueled rage. But the other children knew none of this, and Will wasn't about to share—not with kids three years his junior or anyone else. Tommy felt an overpowering desire to be cool, to be a part of the group. He didn't want to be like Weirdo Will.

"Oh—okay Billy."

"So you'll come?"

He had the odd sensation of stepping across some invisible threshold. "Yeah, I'll come." And here he was on the other side. "What are you playing?"

"What are *we* playing, you mean. Capture the Flag," Billy said, effortlessly cool. "Groovy! We'll be by the swings. Come right at the start of recess, don't be late."

"I won't," Tommy said.

"Later, Four-eyes!" They were at the classroom now, and Billy broke off to hang up his jacket. Tommy dropped his backpack off by his desk and went to do the same. His stomach started rolling again, over and over on itself; his head drifted up into the clouds and he saw himself, strong, fast, faster than Billy, faster than all of them in his shiny white shoes. They couldn't catch him, he went a mile a minute, flag in hand, outrunning them all in a desperate leap across the goal line. Elise cheered...his cheeks glowed... Everyone shouted, cheering and happy, and finally Tommy was accepted, had friends, had people to play with. He grinned without realizing it and slid into his little plastic chair.

* * *

Rob was having a hell of a time driving to work. He cursed his eyesight and blinked furiously in an attempt to see what was happening through the windshield, but it was as much an enigma as ever. Actually it was *worse*, the rain pelting the car in explosive little bombs and running down the glass in fat cold ribbons. He thumbed the switch for the wipers but they were already working overtime; he cursed again and squinted at the taillights in front of him. They were two red blurs in a sea of gray, but they were the only things keeping him on the road. Leaning forward, straining to see, his body ached from the stress. Kristin materialized in front of him, hands on her hips, one foot tapping like always. God what a nag she could be.

Again, Rob? You left your glasses at work again? You know you can't see without them.

He snorted in frustration. *It's not my eyesight—it's this goddamn rain!* The two red blurs suddenly ballooned in size and he slammed on the brakes, and cursed a third time.

It wasn't a long drive and he hated the look of the glasses. *There, happy?* Rob was something of a man's man, burly and strong and bedecked in flannel and these goddamn motherfuckin Poindexter glasses were just not *him.* At best he could pass for some kind of mad scientist with them, and that was at best. At worst...hell, why even think about it. His boy, Tom, could never dream of living without glasses, and that was a real shame. The poor kid—his eyes looked like saucers behind those things. During their days on the lake, Rob would have to tie a string around the back of Tom's head to keep them from falling off in the water, and he could tell the boy was self-conscious about it. He wished they didn't have to do that, but the glasses were so damn expensive, they couldn't afford to buy another set. *Like father, like son,* he thought, rubbing his eyes with one hand uselessly.

The power station sat in a bend of the Elmwood River, it's giant futuristic-looking cooling towers presenting an anachronistic picture against the backdrop of wooded mountains and the calm, quiet water. Vapor rose in stately columns from the hyperboloid peaks, joining the clouds, dark and pregnant with rain. Rob glanced at what he could see of them with a tired sigh as he followed the road along the riverbank, stopping and starting with the traffic as he wound his way slowly to the gate. In his younger days Rob had dreamed of working in nuclear power. "The energy of the future," he called it when explaining this dream to others. What a crock of horseshit. He was five years old when the Bomb dropped on Japan, too young to appreciate the magnitude of the death and devastation, only barely comprehending the enormity of the scientific achievement. Despite the imminent prospect of radioactive fiery doom, the Cold War fueled a boyhood fascination with atomic energy, a fascination that peaked at seventeen (and had been sliding downhill ever since) when the first commercial power plant in the US opened in Pennsylvania. Now thirty-seven, his hair just beginning to gray and his once flat stomach beginning to sag, he had lost most of that enthusiasm. When he finally arrived at the gate in the cold February rain, blinking like a madman let loose with a car, he just felt tired and drawn. An equally tired-looking guard examined his badge with disinterest, exchanged cursory pleasantries, and waved him on through.

Rob worked on the third floor, in a room with no windows, one door, and an array of panels that read out reactor plant parameters on clustered dials. The job was much more exciting in name *(Reactor Operator, hold the applause, yes ladies, I do sign autographs after work)* as the parameters hardly ever changed, were difficult to read—with or without glasses—and required constant attention. He dropped off his coat and umbrella in a locker room on the first floor and took the stairs to the third—that was his exercise for the day—and joined the throng of people from the oncoming shift pushing their way into the conference room. Here it was, the capital *M* Morning Meeting, in all its bloated glory. The Morning Meeting never let Rob down. Somehow despite every effort to ruin it, it remained the best part of the day. The rest would be spent in relative isolation in the control room, where Rob would spend ten hours listening to his brains slowly leaking out onto the vinyl-and-asbestos floor. Next to that, the Meeting was a bonafide social event, one that Rob treasured. On a given day it might be duller than usual, but rest assured, everything that followed would only be duller still. Yes, there was always satisfaction to be found in sipping that first cup of coffee and making what Rob considered to be humorous—hell, insightful—observations of the various managers, as they made their usual soulless pleas for professionalism, integrity, *blah blah blah... Oh look, that guy still has a terrible combover. The night shift supervisor is wearing socks and sandals. Oh—my God—Blake's mole has grown to gargantuan size.*

Working in the control room was not actually a solitary experience, but the great mantle of tradition had been bestowed courtesy of the Navy and their hero Hyman Rickover to make sure, *please,* that operators were as bored as possible. The prevailing idea was that reactors were better operated in formal silence—that was the best—and second best (for those unable to handle *first* best) was to keep the conversation to the professional mini-mum, and always on topic. Well, it didn't make much difference one way or the other; Rob and his coworkers had long since exhausted their supply of topics for conversation—bled the well dry, so-to-speak, and they had dug deep. Still, he moved to the control room with dutiful quickness after the Meeting, stopping only for a second cup of coffee.

When Rob opened the door the night shift Reactor Operator barely had his eyes open, leaning far back in his swiveling desk chair, his own cup of coffee dangling precariously from one hand and a clipboard full of logs in the other. A row of other operators at similar panels sat in various states of doze beside him, and those that were awake turned hopefully for their own reliefs. Rob shut the door—*click*—and the Reactor Operator jumped upright with a snap, furiously scribbling down notes. After a glance he relaxed and set the clipboard back down.

"Oh—mornin," the man said, heavy fog across his eyes. The other operators peered blearily over at the two of them with visible disappointment, grunted, and stared silently back at their panels.

"Mornin, Karl," Rob said as gregariously as he could muster. It wasn't much. "Afraid I was someone else?" Karl had returned to the supine position, tenderly cradling what remained of his coffee.

"Oh, that? Nah, I just forgot a log, you know how it goes..."

Rob smiled. "Sure, yeah, I know how it goes. Well I'm ready to relieve you. Anything going on?"

"Nothin new," Karl said through a tremendous stretch. He rose to his feet and sighed heavily. "Same as always. Loading's just starting to come up, the usual stuff. Sample at three."

"Got it," Rob said. He took the logs, holding them close to his nose, and scanned them for anything out of the ordinary. As always there was nothing. "Well, I have no questions. Get outta here." He jerked his head back and to the side in a gesture that reiterated the sentiment.

Karl nodded silently with his eyes still halfway closed and ambled drowsily from the room. Rob watched him go, something between jealousy and concern painted across his face, then sat down in the chair and set his attention on the panel.

Damn.

Myriad little dials and gauges and he couldn't see a goddamn one of them. Where had he set his glasses? And here was Kristin again, her voice floating in from the wrinkled gray edges of his cerebral cortex:

Again, Rob? Again? You know you can't see without your glasses. If you just wore them home you'd know right where they were...

Yeah, yeah, sure, alright. A fine argument to be sure, but he was in no mood for fine arguments. What a *nag*, Jeezum Crow, just let me live in *peace.* He waved her away, her specter vanishing like mist, her voice disintegrating like a bad record. It didn't matter what she thought, what mattered was finding those goddamn glasses. He opened desk drawers one by one, thumbing through old records and logs not touched by human hands since they were dropped into these file folders to die. Perhaps they had fallen in with the old papers—it wouldn't be the first time. Top drawer...*nothing*...middle drawer...*nothing*...bottom drawer...

Ring... Ring... Ring...

He stopped, looked up at the phone on the desk. What could they want? And who were *they* anyway? He imagined it was his supervisor—that sonuvabitch Clif was always thinking of new ideas. He and his colleagues ("friends" would be too strong of a word) called it The Good Idea Fairy, that stroke of inspiration which led folks (usually supervisors) to try new and enlightened (some would say "boneheaded") ways of doing things, where time and practice had shown there was already a best way of doing things. Clif was visited by The Good Idea Fairy often.

Ring... Ring... Ring...

The others in the control room began to look over with a mixture of annoyance and rising anxiety. A thought drifted through Rob's mind then as he turned, first to the blurry mess of lights that was the panel and then, as if by instinct, back to the telephone: if Clif started asking questions about plant conditions, he, Rob, might be forced to admit he couldn't see the damned panel... and then he would lose the shift. *It's not that we don't trust you, Rob, it's just...well...a blind operator is not a safe operator...* He could just hear the words coming out of Clif's quivering little mouth, see the nervous way he played with his shirt corners. And that would be it. Money down the drain. Not to mention the slap on the wrist and the strained schedule. He scrambled for the spectacles, checking all the familiar places—pulling out logs, looking under audit reports, inspecting the little coffee corner—*Aha!* In an old coffee-stained US NAVY mug full of pencils. He pushed the lenses onto his face with a triumphant finger and picked up the phone.

Ring—click—and a relieved, almost imperceptible sigh from the rest of the room.

"Control Room—Rob Wilford."

"Rob, it's Clif."

With affected cheer: "Clif! Good morning."

"Morning. Listen—you remember that sample coming up, right? At three?"

Rob smiled mirthlessly, a smile that stopped below the nose. Another one of these calls. "Yeah, I remember."

"Okay...good. Just wanted to make sure," the slightly anxious voice on the other end of the phone trailed off in a tone that clearly communicated: *I trust you, I really do, I just...don't trust you. You understand—right?* Rob imagined Clif fiddling nervously with a corner of his shirt, like a small child—like Tommy—would.

"No problem. Anything else?"

"Nope. Guess I'll see you at lunch."

"Seeya."

He hung up the phone, ready to settle in now, and eyed the panel again. Reluctantly, he acknowledged that it was nice having everything in focus; and, of course, made a mental note to never mention this to Kristin. Then he grabbed his third cup of coffee from the corner and leaned back in his chair, scribbling down the hour's logs into the tiny gridded tables on his clipboard.

Hours or minutes, they were all the same in here, watching those little dials change by such tiny fractions they may as well not have changed at all. Without glancing over at the wall clock, he may never have known how long he sat there, musing on Clif and The Good Idea Fairy and the otherwise cold, sterile reality of his boyhood dream, burning through—five? six?—uncounted cups of coffee. But he also thought about the lake house, and the summer they had spent there, he and his son and wife, and the joy they had shared, finally, after several dark years—his irritation at Kristin relaxed like a coil slowly unwinding, replaced by a stab of guilt—and this job made it all possible. Another hour passed, another set of logs. And another. And another—how many now? He sat, watching and thinking and sipping and logging, his brain going slowly numb, some small part of him starting to gnaw in that oh-so-familiar way that perhaps—and it was ridiculous, but somehow it seemed increasingly less ridiculous each hour—perhaps he had never *not* been sitting here, perhaps his life outside was just a dream and really he was born and would some day die just like this, in this little room, taking logs. But no—that was nuts. *Wacko*. The day passed in a hazy, undisturbed blur and the clock ticked sluggishly, brutally—*painfully*—slowly, toward the end of his shift—until the phone rang once more.

Startled, he swiped the receiver off its holster with a sort of nervous rush, and took a breath as he held it up to one ear. Now he felt anxious—why was he anxious? He took another breath, steadied his voice.

"Control Room—Rob Wilford."

"Rob, it's Clif again."

"Clif! Hey, I was just—"

"Rob, your wife is on the outside line, she says it's urgent."

Rob's pulse quickened. "Well did she say what happened?"

"No, she won't say, she wants to talk to you. We've got Jim coming in to relieve you, just hold tight a minute."

* * *

Tommy was almost giddy with excitement as he sat at his small desk, his legs swinging enthusiastically under his chair, his eyes focused on the clock above the chalkboard and his mind not even the slightest bit engaged with the lesson his teacher was explaining underneath it to the rest of the semi-conscious class. He was only vaguely aware of what the lesson was about; in his mind he was out by the pond, preparing for the upcoming game of Capture the Flag. Through the window he could see that the rain had mostly calmed, meaning there was no chance of recess being canceled. Now he only had to wait as the minute hand edged ever closer to twelve o'clock. He glanced stealthily at Billy with a quiet, building thrill, but Billy was scribbling down notes and sharing his own quiet glances with Jenny on the other side of the classroom. She giggled and passed him a little slip of paper, and they both cracked up silently. Tommy blinked at this display of camaraderie and turned to Elise—unsure what he was hoping for but hoping anyway, maybe for some glimmer of acknowledgement or validation—but she was one hundred percent absorbed in the lesson, her head resting on her hands and her feet crossed under her chair, leaning forward with her eyes pointing attentively at the chalkboard. Tommy's heart felt very full looking at her, and he turned back to the clock.

Eleven forty-seven.

It was true that Tommy was not especially popular; he did not have his own giggling friend to pass notes with or anything else of that sort, he did not normally get asked to play with the other kids at recess, and no one ever pushed through the crowd to walk to class with him, as Billy had that morning. He did not have sleepovers at his or any other house; no parents stomped down the stairs at three o'clock in the morning to tell him and his rowdy compatriots that they needed to be quiet and get some goddamned rest. In his heart Tommy hoped that this was all because he was new in town—after all, he had only started at the school that year. But deeper down, in places he didn't like to think about, he sensed that it was just him, Tommy; that he was somehow inadequate; that the other children didn't like him, new shoes or no new shoes, because in some small way that he couldn't figure out—

—his face, speckled with blood—

—or understand, he was just different. *Weird.* A Weirdo Will in his own right. That insidious little voice crept to his ear in a whisper, reminding him that he had always been unpopular, even at his old school, always, and he had been there for three years.

But—and he brightened at the thought—Billy had asked him to play with them today. That had to count for something, right? He could have picked any of the other kids in class, heck, even from another class, but he had picked Tommy. *Four-eyes.* Not Weirdo Will or anyone else. Tommy scanned the room, watching his classmates, comparing himself to them in ways both great and small. What did they have that he didn't? *Nothing, that's what!* His heart started pounding with excitement as he imagined himself not just as their equal, but their better, a true and undisputed Master of that venerable game, Capture the Flag. He looked back at the clock.

Eleven fifty-two.

Eight more minutes, he thought, after counting down from ten on his fingers. It felt like class would never end. He leaned forward on the desk and propped his head in one hand, drumming on his cheek impatiently, the same way his father did. He breathed in frustration, hot air from his nose pushing out through his fingertips. It was an eternity. Somewhere off in the distance his teacher said, "...the cursive *F* has a tail like *this*..." and drew meaningless squiggles on the chalkboard, but Tommy was far past knowing how they had arrived at the cursive *F*, let alone why it was supposed to have a tail, or even what was the great big deal about cursive in the first place. He just wanted to go play. Now. He looked at the clock again: Eleven fifty-four. Time was moving even *slower*. He huffed again.

By the time the bell rang at twelve o'clock sharp, Tommy was beside himself. He put his notebook hurriedly in his desk and pushed his chair back, hard. Janet Parker in the desk behind him shrieked as the chair launched towards her, bounced off her desk with a cartoonish buzz, and fell on its back. The other students hushed for a moment, and then—*oh God*—the giggling started. Tommy flushed, embarrassed, and picked up the chair, now in more of a hurry than ever. *Oh no...oh no oh no oh no.* Elise was laughing too... It was too much. He wanted to run, to rush out of the classroom, to get outside and disappear. But the teacher had to walk them out to recess, so instead he stood humiliated as the woman's ample jowls shook with the effort of suppressing her own laugh.

"Tommy! We don't do that."

Tommy nodded, looking at the floor. His shoes looked back at him, the reminder of his mother flooding his senses with homesickness, and his eyes began to sting. He fought back the tears, knowing his face was turning a blotchy red, and went to grab his jacket in an attempt to hide this fresh embarrassment from the many eyes which watched him. Tommy hated himself in that moment, hated how his lip trembled and his cheeks burned with the effort of holding in the outburst that he knew would only make the situation worse. He pulled the plastic hood over his head and moved silently into the line forming by the door.

Outside there were a number of children already playing on the swings, jungle gyms, and other equipment sprawled across the sloping yard, most of them wild and excited. Teachers stood on the asphalt just outside the door and watched from a distance. At the bottom of the gentle hill was a row of trees, and Tommy knew, though he had never dared to venture there before, that the little stream which ran along its far side led directly to a similarly little pond nestled back in a clearing some fifty or a hundred yards from the playground. The trees provided a perfect cover for youngsters—hoping to slip away for a quick kiss or a cigarette swiped from a parent's coat pocket—and the clearing had become a popular spot for games. Tommy eyed the trees from the asphalt as the line of children made its way out the door onto the wet lawn, and wondered if Billy would still let him join. He sniffled a little, but as soon as they were released Billy idled up to him with a look that suggested he had forgotten all about the chair and was ready to play.

"We can't go all at once or the teachers will notice," Billy said in a tone that would have been equally appropriate for two inmates attempting a prison break. "We hang out at the swings and go one by one. I'll go first." He added this last with a self-important swelling of his chest. Tommy nodded and walked with him over to the swings, which sat at the bottom of the hill in an oblong mulch patch that bordered the trees.

Jenny, Elise, Al, and Fred were already there—they had taken off at a run as soon as they were able. They all sat down in the swings, where Tommy alone paused out of respect for the pooled rainwater. But he wasn't about to embarrass himself again, and with a grimace he plopped down in the seat. A few seconds went by, a few aimless swings. Then, with a knowing smirk, Billy hopped up and dashed behind the trees. One by one the others followed, each in their turn, until Tommy was the only one left.

"Psst. *Psst!* Four-eyes!" It was Al. Tommy risked a glance over his shoulder and saw the group of them back in the shade, waving frantically at him. "*Quick!* Before the grown-ups see!"

Tommy was not normally one to break the rules, and now eight years of being a wet blanket rose up inside of him in silent protest. He was wet, he was cold...he was still ashamed because of the chair...and suddenly he felt unsure about the whole enterprise. He stole another look at the trees. There was Elise...motioning for him to *come on, come on!* That was it, that was all it took, and with a nervous look at the row of teachers he too booked into the dark branches.

The first thing he noticed was just how high the stream had gotten. Normally frozen at this time of year, it was instead swollen and brown with runoff, a rapid in miniature. It had flooded its banks and now ran ferociously along a new trajectory, sloshing and splashing and spitting over roots and upturned rocks as it went. Even where Tommy stood with the playground just feet away, the rushing water was practically up to his shoes, his new white shoes. He pushed up against the nearest trunk, careful to keep them out of the muddy current. Up ahead, the other children already marched along the water's edge in a triumphant but silent parade, not looking back. Tommy, stepping carefully, hurried to catch up. When they finally broke out of the trees into the clearing, Billy was already there with an old rag and two long sticks. The stream churned loudly behind him, emptying into the pond, also engorged with rain.

"The flag goes on the stick," he explained, demonstrating. "The sticks go on different sides of the field, like this"—he fiddled for a moment pushing the stick into the soil, until it stood upright—"so those are the flagpoles. Steal the enemy flag and run back to your flagpole to win a point. If you get tagged, you're out. Got it?"

"There's only the one flag, Billy," Fred said, breathing through his mouth.

"I know that, stupid," Billy said, looking at Fred and rolling his eyes. "My mom would only give me one. So we'll have to find something else. Any ideas?"

"A shirt, maybe."

Billy considered this. "I mean, maybe. One of you planning to give up your shirt?"

Fred and Al both looked at each other as if hoping the other would feel suddenly inspired. Neither did, and the moment passed in silence.

"Well *I'm* not giving up *my* shirt," Jenny said, crossing her arms with a pout.

"Of course not, you're a *girl*," Billy said. The slightest tremor of discomfort tipped the words into higher pitch. Elise said nothing, but looked relieved. "Well..." Billy trailed off until he noticed Tommy. He brightened. "How about it, Four-eyes?"

Tommy didn't say anything. No, he did not want to let them use his shirt. For one thing it was cold, brutally cold. And getting past that, he liked this shirt, and it would probably get muddy. That alone would be enough to anger his parents. But most of all, Tommy was in the early throes of self-consciousness about his body. It was pudgy and flabby and freckled and—

—fat—

—and no no no he did not feel comfortable stripping down here in the woods, in the rain, at school, with girls—with *Elise*—around. He looked down at his shoes.

"*Please,* Tommy? You'd really be helping us out," Billy pressed.

"Yeah, Tommy," Elise said, "you really would."

Tommy felt his cheeks grow warm and red. The rest of them joined in a chorus of saccharine pleas. And Tommy knew—in some nagging place he knew—they were not genuine. That was bad enough. But he could not bring himself to say no...not when Elise was doing the asking. A strange fuzzy happiness blossomed in his stomach; he was the center of attention, the man of the hour in a group that for the first time did not include his mother. In fact, there was an overwhelming, almost heroic ring to it, to saving the day, to forking it over. Just a shirt. That's all. No big deal. Just a crummy shirt.

"Well..." Tommy kicked at the ground with his toe. He pictured his shame from only a few minutes ago, pictured himself never being invited back here again. "Well...I guess so," he finally said.

"Great!" Billy said. "Well then." He extended an expectant hand.

Tommy swallowed the lump in his throat, looking at the group of them looking back at him. He nodded slowly, then took off his jacket, which he hung on a tree branch, and then his shirt, revealing his dumpy little body, rippling with goose pimples.

Fred wolf-whistled.

"Nice jacket, Four-eyes," Al scoffed, taking it before he could put it back on and turning the shiny blue fabric over in his hands. Tommy shivered in the cold and crossed his arms in a useless attempt to warm himself.

"Alright," Billy said, grimacing with delight at this turn of events. "So I'm Team Captain of course." No one disagreed. "And I think Al will be the other Captain. And for my first pick, I want Jenny."

Jenny smiled and giggled and went to stand next to Billy.

"Then I want Fred," Al said, surprising no one.

"Elise," Billy pointed.

Finally it was just Tommy left, and even though he knew this moment would come—and he did, he really knew it—somehow it still hurt more than he expected.

"Aw, man..." Al sighed. He looked at Tommy, disappointment twisting his small face, then appealed to Billy for mercy. "But he sucks!"

"He's the only one left, Al. You have to pick him."

"Fine," Al said, "Four-eyes—but keep your shirt off, I wanna at least have some fun." And then to make sure he got his wish, he tossed Tommy's jacket in the pond.

It was as if time stood still. Up until that moment, even with everything else, Tommy had stayed relatively content. He knew he would be picked last. Just knew it. It was a foregone conclusion, case closed, no mystery there, and he really, truly wanted to be a part of the group and play Capture the Flag. He stood for an interminable second with his arms wrapped tightly around his chest, watching his little blue jacket disappear with a gurgle in the swirling brown water. His jacket...his mother had bought him that jacket...

"Why would you *do* that?" he whined, and shoved Al with all his eight-year-old fury.

Al stumbled sideways, recovered. His mouth hung open in shock and it snapped shut as he spun around. He came back with a vengeance to return the push. *Whoosh!* Tommy danced out of the way, his pulse skyrocketing. He had never been in a fight, had no idea what to do, was terrified beyond belief—and it suddenly occurred to him, all of it, all in a fraction of a second, that he was going to get beat up, really beat up. His hands and feet vibrated as a monumental fear gripped him. His head was spinning. He needed to run. He tried to take off and felt Fred's strong arms push him back. The girls were shrieking, God, Elise was *laughing* at him again. His face screwed up, he was going to cry, he was going to *cry*.

Stop it, Tommy, stop it!

Al lunged again, grabbed at him, closed his fingers around Tommy's wrist.

"Let go, let *go!*" Tommy squealed, yanking his arm back, and Al was sent staggering toward the pond.

"Don't *push* me!" Al protested.

"You threw away my jacket!"

"Stupid *Four-eyes!*"

Al dove in for another attack, his teeth bared. Tommy turned to run but once again he met hands pushing him back—Jenny and Billy. Tears burned in his throat. He felt them start to fall and finally hot anger roared in his chest, and as Al whizzed past he gave him another colossal shove. This one really landed—Al flailed, tripped, hit the ground hard. His face turned up, his eyes watering...he was bleeding, bleeding from his chin. A horrible red line split it in two. He lay sprawled on the ground for a minute, blood dripping through his fingers and into myriad little puddles as he held a hand up to his astonished face. Slowly astonishment turned to anger.

"You're DEAD, Four-eyes!"

Tommy's anger snuffed out, evaporated in smoke, replaced by panic. He tried again to run, but before he had made it anywhere there was a sickening *crack* and his face exploded in pain. His glasses broke—the pieces dropped to the ground with tiny splashes. Fred hopped up and down, howling and clutching his hand. Tommy fell like a brick, the girls' laughter loud in his ears, flopping around blindly trying to find the lenses that would show him the way back to the teachers at the top of the hill. A searing pain bloomed hot and wet over his left eye where the glass had cut him. And a noise...a colossal buzzing noise was building in his ears, drowning out everything, a droning sound that began as a whine and grew until he feared his eardrums would burst. He blinked and shook his head but it would not stop, and now a foggy red cloud spread across his vision and the world turned to hazy crimson. Hot liquid poured into his mouth, tasting like pennies, filling his throat. He spat it out, but the blood kept coming.

"I'm *bleeding!* You piece of SHIT!" Al screamed, his voice coming to Tommy in a disembodied howl. Tommy tried to look up through the curtain of red but his eyes jammed shut as a kick landed in his stomach. "YOU—PIECE—OF—SHIT—YOU—PIECE—OF—SHIT—"

The pain was enormous, unbearable. He tried to shield his gut but now the kicks landed in his face. Great purple fireworks burst across his vision. He shut his eyes tightly against the attack, but it was useless. He was going to die—oh *God* he was going to die. Al was going to kick his face in, was going to splatter his brains across the wet grass like the—

—*great shuddering breaths, rattles, death rattles*—

—snotty blood dripping from his mouth and nose and eyes and *everywhere*. Like a strange dream he heard birds singing...insects buzzing... And the droning noise growing, growing, how could they not hear it, it was deafening, roaring, it was everything, the pain and the noise and the purple-red cloud and the—

—*cat*—

—hot blood in his throat, and he curled into a ball, writhing with the incredible pain and wishing it would stop...*stop*...

"Stop! *STOP! STOP IT! Al, STOP IT!*" Elise screamed. And it did stop.

Tommy opened his eyes. Everything was a blurry red mess. The laughter was gone and people cried—wailed, screamed. The birds sang, the insects bit, he felt their stings on his skin. Somewhere behind him Al gave a confused grunt and was silenced. Droplets spattered in a rain from the wet grass as someone bolted past. Their squelching footsteps stopped abruptly and suddenly there was a new cry, a choked little retch. He looked over: a squirming body hovered over him, lifted quickly, unnaturally from the ground, thrashed in the air in the grip of something like a tentacle, green and gray and slender. Whoever it was landed hard, stood up, tried to run, and the tentacle impaled them cleanly through the middle. More tentacles...and two more dark figures, impossible to distinguish. Spikes erupted from their bellies, bloody and unreal, and the two bodies twitched and screamed as the tentacle, multiple tentacles, some strange beast, pounded them back and forth, pounded them into the ground and against the trees and against each other until with each incredible *whack*, their writhing shapes grew more and more limp, more and more red. A fine warm mist rained down. Tommy felt it on his face, steaming in the cold.

One of the girls screamed—a long, shrill shriek of terror. The scream fell away, away, away... Then something grabbed Tommy; it gripped his arm, both arms, and pulled him back; he stumbled and flailed across the clearing in its grasp until the light dimmed. He was dying, must be dying, this thing had him too, and with a start he felt wetness on his hands. Blood, *blood*, it was blood, blood everywhere, but...it was cold. It was the stream in the shadow of the trees. And Weirdo Will was there, eyes bulging from his blurry face, holding Tommy's arm in one hand, and with the other, a finger to his lips. Someone still screamed out in the clearing, running, he could just see them running, but then there was a terrific *crunch*, a long rattling gurgle...and silence.

The teachers finally arrived. But all that was left were three bloody corpses. They lay beaten and deformed in the clearing where that lonely old rag still hung stupidly from the stick in the mud. Al and Fred and Jenny—all dead. Tommy cowered in the shade, his thumb in his mouth, his eyes glassy, his nose broken and his new white shoes splattered with scarlet. Weirdo Will crouched beside him, shaking and jumpy and silent as the grave. Both covered in blood. Elise turned up at home hours later, bathed in red, soaked in it, shivering and refusing to speak. Not a whisper remained of the creature, or of Billy Baker. He was never found. The rushing current carried what was left of him in dizzying, twisting dark red lines out to the pond, where it bubbled and frothed, and then to the river, and then the lake, where it disappeared to the bottom along with Tommy's blue jacket, and was never seen again.

2

THE LAKE

JUNE, 1978

M onths passed. The spot in the clearing became the place where *those kids* were murdered, but before long no one could quite remember who *those kids* were. A fence quickly went up around the playground to keep more children from venturing past the trees. The outcries of disbelief—*I can't believe it happened here!* and *In Elmwood! Of all places!*—faded with the onward march of time. And the details of the incident, the uncomfortable *strangeness* of it, the unanswered questions—passed into myth. Tom would not be around to remind anyone—his parents removed him from school and kept him cloistered at home, where he spent uncounted days in mostly silence, staring out at the world through his enormous glasses and speaking almost to no one. A missing persons report was filed for Billy Baker, but it went cold immediately. The only surviving witnesses were Silent Tommy Wilford and Weirdo Will Ross, neither of whom had much to say (certainly not much that made sense), and Elise Smithfield, who had nothing to say at all. Period. Will, whether out of wisdom or fear, decided to pretend nothing had happened, and was allowed to return to school after just a few weeks. The other families moved away one by one. Not a soul questioned why.

The fence which was built at the school was wood plank; it left nothing to be seen and everything to the imagination. When it was first hastily erected in the weeks following the tragedy, children would crowd the length of it, the braver ones angling for a view underneath at the crime scene still being actively investigated on the other side. Within a few months no one was watching anymore, but the fence never lost that strange, mysterious power to enthrall. No one stopped, no one questioned it, but there was still a sort of fear lingering along its base and over its high beams. Over time it aged and turned gray and grew thick ivy leaves and was slowly reclaimed by the earth, but its menace remained and it still kept guard effectively over the small pond lying innocently nestled in the trees. Those trees aged too, filling in the clearing and expanding into massive trunks with limbs that hung out over the vine-covered wall. It was as if some great natural wonder clawed at the fence, had been clawing at it for years, even after just a few months. Some children—those with the most active imaginations, the kind that saw clammy hands reaching for their ankles from under beds and eyes staring out at them from every dark window—would gaze at the fence, picturing slimy green fingers, cold and alien, reaching from under the rotting planks and feeling blindly for flaws. Knots aged and fell out, leaving small holes for the children to peer through, their hearts racing with fear as they imagined some unseen horror emerging suddenly to startle them, or watching them from the other side with cold, dead eyes.

But in the summer of 1978 the scars of that awful day were still fresh and the wood planks still golden, almost resplendent as they stood against the onslaught of nature. Tommy Wilford remained shut up in his bedroom at home, seeing few and speaking to fewer. Elise, after months of therapy, had regained the use of her voice. Still, she was prone to long bouts of silence and often awoke screaming in the night, coated in sweat, drenched with the stuff, drenched like she had once been drenched with blood, screaming and screaming until her parents came and shook her from the nightmare, which seemed to go on even after she opened her eyes.

And to Will—Weirdo Will, the one, the only, whose reputation for being strange had only grown by leaps and bounds in the wake of the murders—to him it seemed almost as though he was the only survivor after all. He was the only one back at school, the only one capable of returning to *normal* life, if there ever was such a thing. Maybe it was some innate quality in him, some ineffable, unknowable strength, or maybe it was the hardness that had come with growing up in the shadow of his father. Or maybe it was simply that universal acceptance of the unknown which children so often have and adults do not. Whatever the reason, he had not lost his grip on reality, not even after seeing—well, whatever it was he saw. Sure, he had nightmares—who wouldn't? But there were bigger fears to face, or at least more pressing ones. Like what would happen if he lost his father's cigarettes.

It was a Saturday, the last Saturday before summer vacation, and even though he was facing the prospect of an entire summer at home with the old man, Will still felt the excited, almost electric energy of that late spring morning as he hopped, skipped, ran, lolly-gagged along the sidewalk that would bring him to the corner drugstore. He had a handful of bills in the pocket of his corduroy shorts and a mandate to buy five packs of cigarettes—Marlboros, or Camels in a pinch. Elmwood was a small town, remote and rural. Trifling matters like tobacco laws had yet to penetrate. Yes, he had money for cigarettes, and even a little extra for himself, for bubblegum or chocolate. Will was ecstatic at the thought of perusing the shelves of glittering wrappers in search of the perfect candy bar. He was vaguely aware of the occasional stares, the stares of people who knew his role in the events of that winter—probably after hearing it from some gossipy neighbor, or watching it on the nightly *News*—but no matter. He was a kid who was by now almost deaf to the opinions of others.

He rounded the corner onto Priscilla Avenue (*Prissy Avenue!* the girls in class had shrieked once), his imagination running at full tilt with childhood fantasy, the path seeming to light up before his eyes, glowing, shimmering in the morning sun: a river of molten lava that he alone could navigate. *Captain Ross, Intergalactic Explorer,* that was his identity, a hero of his own creation, one with incredible powers, powers used only for good. Ahead of him lay the demonic Volcano tribe, an evil cult that had captured the fair Princess Cartego—also his own creation—who stood screaming from the upstairs window. He danced from one crack in the cement to the next, picturing each as a tiny foothold, the only place he could land without frying to a crisp. *Hop! Hop! Shit!*—he lost his balance and nearly tumbled to what would surely have been a terrible and fiery end—or at least would have left him with a scrape or two—but he recovered and continued hopping along. The familiar edifice of the drugstore loomed before him in the form of the secret tribal temple, from which the lava river poured in a glowing ribbon.

Hopping, hopping—once, twice, thrice—and he was at the door. It was propped open to let the breeze in. Only one more leap separated him from the sterile white interior and the beautiful princess, when a hand tapped him on the shoulder.

Immediately he was out of one fantasy and into another, the events of that February day racing back into his consciousness like water rushing to fill a void; he felt his heart jump into his throat and in his mind's eye he saw those—those *things*—reaching out to grab him. He recoiled, his muscles tight, his sinews taut, ready to run. He whirled around to face the threat, his lips drawn back in an unconscious snarl—

But it was only a police officer, a portly (that was an understatement) man with a meaty face and blonde hair that was matted against his head with sweat.

"Take it easy, kiddo," the man—to Will he seemed impossibly huge—said, not unkindly. "You always jump around when you have places to be?"

"I was..." Will trailed off, his heart rate slowing, feeling the words on his lips: *I was running from that Thing! The Thing that killed the others!* Followed by, even more ridiculously: *I was jumping over the lava.* He thought better of both. "I was just playing around." He grinned a big goofy kid's grin and hoped the cop would buy it. He noticed the man had an enormous utility belt, something Captain Ross might wear on his next adventure, except this one had a pistol on it, gleaming dully. Captain Ross would never carry a gun because it was against his sacred Oath of Peace.

"I s'pose that's what a kid your age should be doing this time-a-year," the cop said. "But watch yourself going into the store, there's other people trying to shop. You get me?" He leaned over when he said "You get me?" and now he seemed bigger than ever. Will thought his hairy arms looked about as big as hams, which was appropriate considering his girth and the way his little eyes looked piggily out from his pudgy face. A Honeybun peeked out from the sausage-like fingers of his left hand, still in its wrapper.

"Yes sir," Will said, resorting to the version of himself that came around whenever his father was drunk.

"Good," the cop said, and leaned back again. "Well son, you have a—"

"Hey there, Officer Tibbs!" The voice came from behind him, and the officer turned in time to reveal a wiry high-schooler with hair that reached down to his chest and a beard that did not. Will recognized him as Billy Baker's older brother Clark. He couldn't remember having seen any of the Bakers since the Memorial Assembly at school back in March. At the time the family had seemed fairly close, tight-knit even, despite a public, messy, bitterly contested divorce. A funny feeling stirred in Will's stomach as he remembered the father crying, crying inconsolably into his ex-wife's shoulder. These days it was town gossip that the father had disappeared, was gone, vanished without a trace. Just like his youngest son. *But...not* just *like him,* Will thought with a fresh pang of unease. Clark was flanked by his friend Toby—also with long hair and a terrible beard—leaning against the wall of the drugstore cooly and smoking a cigarette.

"Baker," Tibbs said curtly. "Your eyes are looking a little red, son. You been smoking?" There was no need to speak the entire question: You been smoking *pot?*

Clark threw his hands up in front of him in mock deference and gave a squawk of laughter. "I dunno, your eyes are lookin a little glazed, officer—have you been eating doughnuts?" Then he laughed some more, evidently pleased with the joke, and looked to Toby for reinforcement. Toby smiled sagely.

"Very funny," Officer Tibbs said, the tone of his voice implying exactly the opposite. "But you just stay away from that stuff." He leaned over again and Will could almost see the words forming in his brain before he spoke them: "You get me?"

"Yes *sir!*" Clark barked, snapping to attention and smacking his hand to his forehead in a phony salute.

Officer Tibbs looked like he wanted to say something more, but instead just glanced back and forth between Clark and Toby with an expression that willed them to understand the gravity of his charge. Then he sighed and lumbered over to his squad car, parked on the curb, tossed the Honeybun through the passenger window and walked around and sat heavily in the driver's seat. The car bobbed down and up under his weight. Clark shrieked with laughter.

"Watch out, it's the Fuzz!" Clark trilled. "You better get runnin—he'll catch you as soon as he finishes his snacks!"

Toby chuckled. Tibbs glared at them both from behind the windshield, but the look on his face wasn't anger—well, it was, partially—but it was also embarrassment. Will felt a sort of indecent shame for having witnessed it, as if kids weren't supposed to see adults be embarrassed, especially not authority figures. The squad car lurched away from the curb and Officer Tibbs disappeared down the street. Will watched him go, strangely transfixed. He had never seen a kid talk like that to a grown-up before.

But then the high-schoolers were so *old*, they were practically grown-ups themselves...

"Hey—hey, kid."

Will turned, his reverie broken. Clark and Toby towered over him, standing between him and the door.

"Whatcha buyin?" Clark said. Then to Toby: "You know this is the little snot that was with my brother when he—when it—you know, when it happened?"

Toby nodded, cool and wise. "Yeah man, I thought I recognized him. Whatcha here for, man?"

Will stared up at the two of them, their faces greasy with pubescence, feeling the fear seep into him. "I uh... I was... I'm just here for cigarettes." He stared down at the ground after saying it, feeling stupid. "You know, for my dad."

Clark gasped with false sweetness. "For his *dad*," he said in a cringe-worthy falsetto, elbowing Toby in the arm. "Don't let the coppers hear it—lucky for you we came when we did, eh? Well don't let us hold you up there, boy-o. We don't wanna get in the way of your dad's cigarettes. 'Sides, we're not goin in anyway. We don't have any fuckin money, do we Toby?"

"Not a cent, man," Toby said serenely. From this distance Will could see his eyes were in a semi-permanent state of being halfway closed.

"Not a cent," Clark repeated, nodding matter-of-factly, his eyes never leaving Will's. After a pause he stepped sideways and gestured grandiosely at the door. "Well—by all means—this way sir!"

Will looked at each of them, then stepped cautiously through the gap between them and into the harsh fluorescent light of the drugstore. Behind him Clark shouted, "Buy your mom somethin nice too—for me!" Then he laughed, another series of howling squawks. The laughter faded as he and Toby walked away up the street.

Will felt a little flushed now. He wasted no time in picking out a Three Musketeers (the lights reflected off its silvery wrapper exquisitely) and getting his five packs of Marlboros and taking them all to the register, all the while stealing nervous glances out the door to see if the two older boys had returned. The cashier, a new girl approximately the same age as Clark and Toby with her hair sprayed to within an inch of its life, peered knowingly over the counter at him as she rang up the purchase.

"These ain't for you, huh?" she said, after giving him the total. All the while she chewed a wad of gum at a volume that could only be intentional.

Will shook his head. "For my dad."

"Mhmm. You know the age for cigarettes is seventeen in Vermont?"

"Um—yeah."

"You seventeen?"

Will was silent for a moment. "Well—I mean no, but they're not for me."

"Sure, sure," she waved her hand. "I'm just teasing you. You think I care? Have em, enjoy em too."

"Oh—okay, thank you."

He cast another glance out the door. The cashier looked him over, her face softening.

"You scared of them big kids?"

"No! No, well...not really."

"Sure," she said. "Sure, course not." She wore an expression that suggested the culmination of some fine detective work and popped a bubble with her gum, still looking at Will. "They're in my class. Dumb as a box of rocks. But harmless, mostly. You wanna bag?"

Will nodded again and fished the money out of his pocket.

"That Clark Baker thinks he's *sooo* funny. My friend Trish says he's an idiot. She says people just go along with him on account of what happened to his brother. You know the one? From a few months ago?"

Will nodded a third time, but it seemed his response was irrelevant.

"He had a little brother. I guess maybe he was about your age. Yeah," she said, sizing him up. "Ten or eleven, something like that. Anyway, he was playing with some kids over by that pond behind the Elementary school—you know where they just put the fence up?"

This time Will didn't nod, only stared straight ahead, holding the bag with the cigarettes and chocolate with both hands and fidgeting nervously in the hope she would spare him the details. She didn't.

"There were like five of them, maybe six, I can't remember. But something happened—no one really knows for sure, but Trish says there was *blood*. A lot of it." She smiled as if this delightful story was one he could share at campfires all summer, and popped her gum again. "And the brother was gone. Poof."

By this point she had given Will his change and he shuffled toward the door in the smallest footsteps that he dared without giving away his intention to escape. Oh, he remembered the blood alright. Cascading down in sheets, soaking the already soaked ground, running in rivers into the little stream and hurrying off to the pond, dark and thick with it. And that Thing, he had no name for it, but the Thing that killed them—he shivered thinking about it—in his mind it was Fear itself.

"Pretty crazy, right? Trish says that Clark spends most of his time high now, to drown out the feelings or whatever. But I asked her, 'Where does he get the pot from then?' Cause, you know, it ain't cheap. And she says 'Toby's got a cousin who lives down close to Mexico or something.' Anyway, no need to take that Clark Baker too seriously. He was a stoner before it ever happened. You know?"

Will nodded one more time, still backing away, images of Billy Baker and the others replaying in his head like some horrible movie. "Well I should probably..."

"You know, you look kinda familiar actually."

"I come get my dad cigarettes a lot," Will submitted dumbly, trying to smile.

"Maybe—I just started here Monday." She looked across the counter at him thoughtfully, biting her lower lip, her brow furrowed in an expression of complete concentration. Then her eyes widened. "I know! You're the kid—"

But Will was already taking off at a run, out the door, down the little walk, and off toward home, lava be damned. His mind raced and so did his heart. He ran hard, pounding his feet into the pavement in a vain effort to escape the images of blood, of death, of—of whatever that *Thing* was. Somehow he thought if he could just put distance between himself and those memories...and he might have made it too, but he had only gone about fifty yards when a foot suddenly appeared from nowhere and he flew, actually flew, he had just a split second between panicked surprise and bracing for the fall to wonder if this was what Captain Ross felt like, and then he slid along on his hands and knees, the sidewalk removing layers of skin like the world's worst dermatologist, and he skidded to a stop. He felt the urge to cry rise in his throat, fought it back. Somewhere behind him was a bark of laughter. A shadow moved over him.

"Jeezum Crow, I told you to stop im, not kill im!" the laughing voice said, still howling. It was Clark Baker.

"Yeah, man. I didn't expect him to be running so fast, man." Toby said. He grabbed Will's wrist and hauled him up, looking at him carefully through those half-lidded eyes.

"What do you guys want?" Will asked, in a tone that he hoped sounded both mature and appropriately respectful of their advantage in age. He glanced down at his bleeding knees and wiped the dirt from his shorts with the backs of his hands. His palms were bright red and speckled with little rocks.

"Well, to be honest," Clark said, the laughter fading from his voice but not his face, "a pack of those Marlboros, if you please."

Will followed Clark's gaze to the ground where the bag of goodies had spilled open, boxes of cigarettes scattered like shrapnel, the one lone Three Musketeers glinting in the sun like a piece of treasure.

"Those are for my dad," he said, imagining the afternoon that would await him if he came home *sans* cigarettes. "He sent me to get them."

"Oh come on, I'm sure your dad won't miss just *one little box*," Clark crooned, moving in close. Too close. Will could observe every pimple, blackhead, blemish, and acne scar dotting his face. He had never really paid much attention to such things before, but now he found they were all he could look at. They did not make Clark any less threatening; if anything, he looked like some sort of B-movie monster with only half his makeup on.

"He said five packs," Will said, flutters of panic rising in his chest.

"Well I'm telling you he'll be happy with four," Clark said, the last traces of laughter gone now. He reached down to pick up one of the little cartons, and for one crazy moment Will imagined himself body slamming him, grabbing the scattered merchandise and making a run for it. Instead he just watched (Toby still had a hold of his arm—the excuse was quick to his mind and in his view absolved him of all guilt) as Clark stooped, came back up with one pack...looked at it thoughtfully for a moment...then picked up another. "You know, actually, I think he'll be happy with three."

Will felt his eyes starting to sting with tears and he willed them not to come. *Please oh please oh please don't cry, Will,* please *don't cry...*

And then Toby released him and the two of them chortled to each other over their ill-gotten gains.

"Thanks for the donation, *Weirdo*," Clark said. They turned—Toby stopped to pick up the candy bar as well—and meandered away just as cool as can be, leaving Will with his scuffed up knees and hands, the bag and its remaining contents still adorning the sidewalk, his eyes hot and wet with tears that he was holding back only by tremendous effort.

He briefly considered his options. He had a few cents remaining in his pocket, but that would not be enough to replace the lost cigarettes. For a moment he entertained the idea that the girl at the store might give him the two extra packs for free, or maybe in some buy-now-pay-later scheme. He had heard of this before—he had a vague notion of what a credit card was, even if his parents had none, and the idea he might somehow acquire one drifted sweetly through his mind—but no...that was only for grown-ups. He hung his head. There was always the option to—well—*steal* them. His heart thumped in his chest as he imagined slipping the packs off the shelf and hiding them in his waistband...but after some thought he realized this too was a dud. The girl already recognized him. No way he'd get out unnoticed.

Finally Will resigned himself to the inevitable. He gathered up the remaining items, tenderly pinching them between two fingers to avoid touching them with his raw, tingling palms, and headed for home, all the fantasy gone from him now, his head down, staring at the sidewalk.

* * *

Officer Tibbs, or Harold to his friends (such as they were), had not always been fat, but he had been for a good long time. As he drove away from the drugstore, the Honeybun slowly warming in the rays of sun glaring down on the passenger seat of his squad car, he reflected that there was a time, a time during and shortly after the Police Academy, where he was downright—well, might as well come right out and say it—attractive. Well-built. Lean (or at least as lean as he would ever be) and muscular. The muscle he had not lost, thank God. The leanness he had. Too many graveyard shifts fueled by innumerable cups of coffee—cream & sugar, please & thank you—and munching on fast food. But dammit, he had been fit once! Was it his fault that there was nothing open at three in the morning

except the fast food joints? A man's gotta eat, after all. The honey bun
looked morosely up from the passenger seat as if to say *What about me,
then?* but Tibbs dismissed it easily. Sometimes a guy needed a snack too.

And that Baker boy...oh what Harold wouldn't give to teach that kid a
thing or two. He grinned sourly. That kid was nothing but trouble. Even
before his brother disappeared or whatever the hell happened, Clark and
Harold had had their fair share of run-ins. For one thing there was the pot.
Harold never could seem to catch him with it on him, but the red eyes, the
skunk smell, the general vagueness of expression—it was no mystery the
guy was lighting up. Aided and abetted by that good-for-nothing friend
of his, no doubt—what was his name? Tony? Toby? Whatever. And then
there was the petty thievery (once again never caught in the act, but Harold
just *knew* he was up to no good), the rude interactions with his elders, the
general *shitbaggery*—

Tibbs stomped on the brakes as the truck in front of him ground to
a halt and his hand flew instinctively to the horn. *What the hell—?* And
then a girl, maybe twenty-one or twenty-two, emerged from in front of the
truck in a skin-tight jogging outfit, waving and apologizing through the
glass. The driver of the truck gestured furiously and took off as soon as
the girl was out of his way, but Tibbs did not: he paused for a moment to
admire her. *Oh, but there was a time,* he thought. Back in the day. He could
have—*did* have—a woman like that, once or twice. He let off the brakes
and the car idled forward, his eyes still plastered to the girl's firm behind
until a small part of him suggested it was no longer safe to do so. Then he
drove on.

What was I—? Oh, yes. The Baker kid. What a Class A piece of shit if
he had ever seen one, and he had seen a few. And the little brother wasn't
much better, when he was around. Oh sure, he had been charming enough,
he charmed the hell out of people. But Tibbs knew, he could sense in his
not unimpressive gut, that Billy was every bit the sleaze that his brother

was, probably worse because he was so well liked. Well liked people were one of the many kinds that Tibbs disliked, along with Communists, gays, politicians, and of course the criminals that he dealt with on a nightly basis.

He rolled past the Elementary school, still lost in thought, and then something truly impossible, something so outrageous he didn't even have time to acknowledge that it wasn't possible, caught his eye and he slammed on the brakes again. Off to his right, way off in the distance by the new fence, he thought he saw—no, but that was crazy. He blinked, rubbed a sweaty hand over his face. Nothing there now, nothing out of the ordinary. Just a lot of trees, a lot of overgrowth. Damned groundskeepers couldn't take care of the place worth shit. He probably just saw some branches out of the corner of his eye—that was probably it. Because if he saw what he thought he had seen for a second... And of course there was what the Wilford boy had said after the murders, something about *tentacles*. And he could have sworn he saw them—tentacles—flailing from the area past the fence.

Suddenly there was a loud honk and he realized he was still stopped in the middle of the road. He pulled off to one side, waving the cars behind him on, and then looked back at the leafy grove behind the school. Something was not right. Something was *fishy*.

Hating himself, Tibbs climbed out of the car. He briefly regarded the Honeybun, getting well past fresh as it sat in the dazzling sun rays, but he thought better of it and shut the door. He gripped his pistol in one hand absently, and in the other his nightstick. Both were comforting touches. He released them and wiped his sweaty palms on his pants, and then trotted off toward the fence line.

As he drew closer the unmistakable sound of the trickling stream met his ears, and the unmistakable scent of nature run amok met his nose. Either one might have been relaxing, but they were not. Instead he felt his chest tighten with fear. He had been here back in February, oh yes, he had seen the three bodies beaten and mutilated past all hope of recognition. The images flashed into his mind now despite his efforts to stop them. At the time he had wondered, *Who could have done this to a bunch of kids?* Now, even after four months of calm, even after the school was reopened and there were children playing on the other side of this fence every day of the week, he felt that old unease creeping back under his skin. He reached the corner of the fence, the stream meandering alongside it with a peaceful little burble that seemed to say, *Don't be such a baby,* and peered around. Nothing. Nothing but the continuation of the stream and a line of geriatric, vine-covered trees.

One word rose to his lips, lingered there: *Spooky.*

He shuffled around the corner until he was standing between the fence and the bank, barely able to maintain his balance as his considerable belly kept pushing him off from the vertical wood planks. He moved gingerly along its length, grabbing the occasional tree branch for support, careful to keep his feet out of the water. There was something about the water he didn't like. Back in February the stream had been swollen with rain; it was brown and turbulent and farther downstream it mixed with the blood of those poor kids in a gurgling, churning mess. Now it was running a foot below the bank, but even as he looked it seemed to take on a red hue, a bloody hue; and images of that day kept flashing before his eyes. Tibbs was not a superstitious man, but he had the strangest feeling that if he dipped his foot in that quiet current something terrible would happen. He wiped the sweat from his face and proceeded cautiously, all the while still hating himself for having gotten out of the car in the first place.

Finally he emerged into that too-familiar clearing where the pond sat stagnant and green, and a chill stole over him despite the heat. He caught his breath—if there was anything going on, if there really *had* been tentacles (and he felt extremely stupid for even entertaining the idea), this is where they would be. He put a hand on his holster without noticing it and walked slowly toward the pond. The ground was dry, but in his mind, with each footstep, he could hear the *squelch* of wet soil, just as he had on that day four months prior. Yes, something was fishy alright, but maybe it was just his own nerves. It had been a stressful night, maybe he was cracking up a bit. Maybe he should just go home and get some sleep. Maybe...

But instead he kept walking. Harold approached the water's edge as if it were a vat of poison and peered across into the trees on the far side, expecting to see something—anything—that might explain the strange vision he had seen from the road. Only dark tree trunks and tangled branches looked back at him, although he knew the Elmwood River was back there somewhere. The tall towers of the power plant loomed ominously off in the distance. A mosquito alit on his arm and he slapped it, the tiny spot of blood smearing into his pasty skin.

Boy, but it was creepy back here, he thought. And so *overgrown*. Tibbs may not have had much of a green thumb (his thumbs were in fact decidedly not green) but this—back here behind the school, past the fence—even a botanist, a damn good botanist, would have been hard pressed to come anywhere close to matching it. Since he had last been here in February, it was like a bomb of green life had descended on the place. Part of that was just the spring growth, but no—Tibbs shook his head in absent-minded disbelief—he had never seen spring growth look so...so...*predatory*. The trees had encroached so much on the pond that the trunks actually *leaned out* across its flat surface, branches outstretched in the most hideous, desperate, twisted shapes, almost as though they were reaching for something. And looking down—had he ever seen so many *bugs?* He floundered backward in sudden disgust. How had he not noticed them before?

And then, just as he was making up his mind to leave, the worst of all: there in the trees on the far side, embedded in a trunk just as if it had always been there, twisted by knots into an agonized scream and slowly vanishing into the dark black tree bark, was a child's skull.

As he watched, it distorted further.

A breath of wind, barely more than a whisper, carried across the pond to him then from somewhere...somewhere *beyond;* it sounded less like the airy rustle of wind through trees and more like the damp, decrepit exhalation of air from a crypt. Something about it was...wet.

Tibbs froze. He wanted to leave, wanted to run, but he felt paralyzed. He was surely seeing things; he could come back later, or better yet, one of the other guys could come back later. He did not like it back here, he hadn't liked it in February when there were three bloody corpses, and if it was possible he liked it even less now. He wanted to be back in the safety of his squad car, Honeybun in one hand, stale or otherwise, and steering wheel in the other, whistling as he drove the last few blocks to his house. Why *did* he get out of the damned car? *Enough is enough,* he thought, and felt pins and needles as motor function returned to his limbs—or was it the mosquitos? They were everywhere now, the little bloodsuckers. He swatted them away, and tried to turn but discovered that he was rooted to the spot. Not figuratively—small vines had sprung up from the ground and across his feet. For one second he considered the idea that he had somehow walked into them, yes, surely that was it... Then panic set in and he wheeled around but the roots were hooked over the toes of his shoes and he stumbled painfully to the ground. Pain flared in his ankle and he let out a cry, and that was when he saw it. A face, a terrible, hideous *face,* rising out of the calm green water of the pond, evil and cruel, round black eyes staring at him...into him...

His eyes widened with an absolute, visceral fear. He couldn't look away. Those empty eyes pulled him in, down and down and down, and the Earth fell away, fell into darkness, swallowed him up. All was black. All was misery. A bolt of adrenaline coursed through him and he was back in the clearing. The eyes stared, oh *God* those eyes, and he struggled, Jesus he struggled, but the little vines were over his arms, and the bugs—centipedes, spiders, he wondered again wildly how he had not noticed them as soon as he entered the clearing—the bugs crawled over him. He felt a million pokes from their spindly legs, from their hungry little mouths. Somehow that was worse even than the rest and he flailed desperately. One arm came free and started scraping the grotesque things off of him, leaving bloody trails behind; he prised his other arm loose and tried to push himself up, but his legs were now bound up to the knees and he flopped down with a grunt. He reached for his firearm but his own fat stomach smooshed it into the dirt. The vines held him down so forcefully that he couldn't get to it. The trees swayed...swayed... Now there were flies, millions of them, descending on him, diving into his eyes and his nose and his mouth. He mashed his eyes shut and the world plunged into darkness, and still he felt them wriggling down his throat, squirming and crawling, deeper and deeper. He heard the chattering sound of birds, of rustling, fluttering, and then something sharp tugged at his arm, tugged at his leg, at his gut and his scalp and his fingers. Blood gushed from the wounds, hundreds of them, gushed into the grass as he was pulled apart, torn to shreds.

Tibbs did scream, once. The Thing in the water never moved. And like Billy Baker, when it was all over, there was nothing left—nothing but that sad, lonely Honeybun still going stale in the warm glow of the sun.

* * *

Just a few blocks away, Will pushed the screen door open at home and stepped cautiously across the threshold. He didn't know for sure yet, but it was a pretty safe bet that his father was napping in the next room over, drunk as a skunk. That was Standard Operating Procedure around here on Saturday morning. His father had spent the previous night out at Pesci's with some of his "buddies," drinking to life, to fallen comrades, to wives and women, to—well, anything would do—and then stumbled in the door around one in the morning, smelling like the piss on a dog. The fridge was well stocked and supplied his party of one until he passed out on the couch around three. Then it was up at nine, a little hair of the aforementioned dog to get the morning going right...and a nap. And there he was, the old bastard himself, sacked out on the floor with a beer bottle held loosely in one hand and a few crumpled cans in a ring around him. A shrine to drunkenness.

Will tiptoed carefully past the living room, willing his father not to wake up. This was not a significant risk—the man was plastered and snoring loudly. But oh baby, if he *did* wake up... It had happened before, and Will was not in a hurry to see it happen again. If Harry Ross was bad when he was drunk, Heaven help you if you crossed him hung over.

The living room door safely behind him now, Will entered their cramped kitchen and laid the three packs of Marlboros on the table. He looked at them thoughtfully for a few seconds, considering ways to arrange them that would make them seem...well...a little fuller. But even at twelve he could see this was a lost cause. He abandoned the effort as pointless and crossed back by the living room to get to the creaky wooden stairs that would take him to his room. If he could just wait it out up there... His mother would be home in the afternoon, and sometimes she knew how to talk to her husband, how to calm him down. He might even be sobering up by then, and that was as close as he ever came to being—well, what the heck—*nice*. It was during those times, those brief periods between all-out assaults on his liver, that Harry became almost fatherly. But there was something else as well: when he was sober, instead of angry he seemed...sad. Not just sad—miserable. And nothing Will or anybody else could do, no amount of love or affection, no amount of appeasing, could remedy it. Only booze made the suffering tolerable. Harry was drunk whenever he wasn't at work; and even then, sometimes. He would hide a flask in the inside pocket of his jacket as he dragged his sorry ass out the door and down to the loading docks.

Will arrived on the landing after a couple of heart-stopping moments, moments where the stairs creaked and his father's snoring lulled for a few seconds...and resumed. Will's breath caught in these moments, his body frozen, an old familiar fear washing over him, but he made it to the top without incident and relaxed. His room was at the end of the hall. It was a modest little house, and it had been handsome once, not that long ago. His mother still did the best she could, but with Harry around it was almost impossible. Right now she was working a double shift at the hospital, making time-and-a-half, God willing, and it was during these periods that Harry really had his way with the place. More beer bottles and beer cans littered the landing, some still dripping out their piss-yellow contents onto the floorboards or the threadbare rug, which had long ago been given up as a bad job and which bore the many crinkly stains of benders past.

Will moved down the hall, careful not to disturb the detritus—booby traps—and slipped into his room and shut the door quietly.

An assortment of toys met him: tiny figurines of soldiers, of fantasy characters; off in the corner was a small, partially constructed tower and a model plane. The pièce de résistance was his collection of superhero action figures, as evidenced by the six or seven that adorned the shelf over his bed and the many more hiding under it. He took several of them down now, wincing when the plastic touched his sore palms, and reenacted a favorite scenario in which the good guys lived together in an intergalactic space station of JUSTICE, dispensing goodness and vengeance to the villains living in their tower of doom.

This really was a favorite, a repeat number, although today the villains had personalities which were oddly reminiscent of Clark Baker and Toby Christiansen. The decision was not a conscious one, nor was the way that the heroes—especially Captain Ross—seemed to model their childlike personalities and notions of right and wrong on Will himself. Under other circumstances a child psychologist might have found valuable insight in these games, but Will's father would never have allowed his red-blooded all-American corn-fed son to see a *shrink*—those were for *losers* and *pussies*. It was all just another Saturday morning to Will.

Playing alone. That came with the turf. No one was in a hurry to come over and face the wrath of Will's crazy drunkard father, and that aside, no one was particularly interested in Will himself. It didn't bother him; he set out his figurines and his action figures with enthusiasm and within twenty minutes had almost forgotten the events of the morning, minus the sharp pains from his hands and knees. There were more pressing issues. For one thing, there was a terrible plot to enslave the kind people of the figurine army, a plot that could be thwarted only through the ingenuity of the intergalactic team of—

"Will... *Willll*..."

He stopped mid-action, his mouth hanging open in a startled O. For a few seconds he dared to hope that his father would drift back off to sleep. There were times when Harry would wake, perhaps from some terrible, beer-addled dream; he would call out, call for Fletcher, whoever that was, and then drift away. Maybe this time...maybe...

"WILLLL!"

Nope—no question about it, the man was up. Will heard the clink of bottles as his father shuffled drunkenly around the living room. He raced to the door and cracked it open so that his face stuck out into the hall. "Yeah Dad?"

"Willie, you get your ass down here!" Harry moaned.

Will wasted no time in obliging; he pushed out onto the landing and was down the steps in seconds. His father stood in the living room, greasy hair sticking up as if electrified, one corner of his work shirt still tucked in, beer stains and some globular stuff that might have been vomit down his front, his feet bare, one hand scratching his crotch absently, and the other—Will winced—holding the three packs of cigarettes. Time had not been kind to Harry since his discharge from the army: his hair was thinning sporadically, his body ached from the hours he put in down at the docks, and an increasingly impressive beer gut pushed its way out from under anything he could find to cover it up—which this morning was only that one half of his shirt that remained tucked in. The other side had wrinkled up into a tight roll, stretched across his stomach.

"What is it Dad?" Will asked, innocently enough. He tried with all his might not to look at the three small boxes fanning out from his father's hand.

"You know damn well what," his father grumbled. The words were slurred together in a string, like the world's longest Spelling Bee word. "My goddamn fucking cigarettes, Willie. Willie..." He stumbled a little and caught himself. "Willie. What the fuck happened to my cigarettes?"

Will felt a mixture of pity and fear. It was a familiar feeling. He thought about lying, thought better of it. "It was on my way home. I fell and..." His lip trembled. "These big kids took them from me! They knocked me down and they took them!"

Harry waved his free hand in a drunken, dismissive gesture and nearly lost his balance.

"No sense lyin, son. You know I have to beat you when you lie." This was a generous turn of phrase. Harry beat him for much less than that.

"I'm not lying Dad!" He gestured at his bloody knees, trying to make him understand. "I'm not lying, I'm not! Look at—" The back of Harry's open hand smacked him across the face.

"DON'T you talk back to me in my own HOUSE!" his father shouted, with startling clarity. Then he shook his head. "Bust my ass all week...yer mom busts her ass... And what do we get?" He was mumbling again, grunting, talking mostly to himself. In his left hand the three packs of Marlboros seesawed back and forth, back and forth, as he fidgeted. "Risk my life in the fuckin Army, God knows, and now this... We raise a fuckin *liar?*" He glared at Will. "What do you have to say for yourself, son? 'Cause if yer not a liar then yer just a goddamn fuckin *pussy*, 's what it sounds like. Are you a pussy, Willie?"

Will shook his head no.

"I thought not, I didn't raise no goddamn fuckin pussy," Harry said, speaking to himself again. In his mind's ear, Will heard his mother saying, "You should have known him before the war, sweetie. I wish you could have." And then she stared off glassy-eyed, and Will thought she might be holding back tears, but he was too afraid to ask. He did have a few memories of his father before Vietnam. Happy memories. The kind that are so distant they have neither shape nor meaning, only that warm glow, fading more and more each day but still *there*...

"Are you listenin, squirt?"

"Yes sir."

"I said if you ain't a pussy, you must be a fuckin liar. And you said you ain't no pussy. Ain't that so?"

"Yes sir."

"Well then," and Harry held his arms wide as if that was all that needed to be said, shifting his weight precariously from one foot to the other, a muddled expression of victory on his face. "It don't pay to be a liar, son. Now I give you a few bucks, and I say go down to the drugstore and get me five packs of cigarettes. I expect—" and he threw the Marlboros on the ground with a surprisingly loud bang that made Will jump "—*five fucking packs* of cigarettes! It ain't hard, boy!"

Will stood silently. It was generally the best course of action.

"You think I'm made of money? 'S that it?" Harry's eyes were wild as he worked himself up, worked himself up for the beating. "Lemme guess, you get down there and you think, gee, lemme just get a few more of these fuckin candies? I bet the old man won't notice? You think I got all the money I want to throw at yer fuckin candy bars and yer fuckin dolls, and the rent, and the electric, and everything else? No! Fuck no, man! Fuck no!"

"I'm sorry, Dad," Will said, his voice thick, tears in his eyes. It caught his father off guard for a moment, but he found himself again.

"No you ain't. You ain't sorry yet, boy, not yet. But I'll teach you a thing or two about *lyin*, that's the God's-honest truth. Now run and fetch my belt."

"But Dad, it's the truth—" The hand flew, fast for a man who could barely see straight, and smacked him across the cheek again. He felt a tingly warmth rise to the surface of the skin there, quickly followed by wet tracks as the tears started rolling.

"I said, run and get my GODDAMN BELT, Willie!"

Will did, feeling all the while like a death row inmate who is forced to dig his own grave. He knew exactly where to get the belt from, had retrieved it many times. It hung solemnly from one of the posts of his parents' footboard. He lifted it with a sort of reverence and carried it back to the living room, holding it like a snake about to bite. He handed it to his father, the tears flowing in earnest now.

"Pants down, Willie, you know how this goes."

He knew how it went alright. He dropped his shorts and there he stood in his superhero underpants. Harry sat down heavily in his armchair—*fell* might be more accurate—and gestured for Will to lay across his lap. Perhaps because he was drunk, or perhaps because he had grown blind to them, Harry did not notice the purplish-yellow bruises decorating Will's backside from some other, recent beating. Then he raised his arm back—for one terrible moment Will anticipated the blow, and that was the worst of all—and the belt fell, and painful red welts rose up, his skin rebelling against each *crack* as the leather smacked his skin like a whip. Once, twice, three times, and then Will lost count. At first he cried harder, but then his skin grew numb and he stopped and only grit his teeth. The normal rules of time no longer applied, it went on for what simultaneously felt like an eternity and no time at all. And then his father released him.

"That'll teach ya to fuckin *lie,* boy," Harry grunted as he flung Will away. "Go on now, stop yer cryin and go clean yerself up before yer mother gets home. Jesus Christ."

Will did as he was told, hating his father with every painful step. He wouldn't be able to sit down comfortably for days, maybe even a week or more, but that was old news. What he really hated was the *injustice* of it, the terrible injustice. It burned in him, burned and burned, he could feel it down in his insides, way down deep. Yes, he loved his father, somehow he still did, but he also hated him, really truly hated him. And he did not know this, but as soon as he was gone, Harry, too, began to cry.

JULY, 1999

Mr. Wilford. "Mr. Wilford. *Mr. Wilford!* TOM!"

Tommy returned to the present with a jump of shock that suggested he was actually time traveling, and looked up at the balding man in the dark suit sitting across from him. The man leaned across the table, his tie flopping solemnly against the table edge, his eyes wide and earnest. Tommy returned his gaze with a penetrating stare of his own. "Yes, *Special Agent.*"

"I said, where does the Highwayman factor into all of this? If it's not Harry, I mean. What does this whole..." the man gestured vaguely with one hand, searching for the word, "...saga...have to do with it all?"

Tommy regarded him with a dull expression. "I told you, you have to wait," he said, his voice that of a parent who, if he has said it once, has said it a thousand times.

The man—the *Special Agent*—leaned back in his chair and pushed his wire-rimmed glasses up on his nose. "Yes, Mr. Wilford, I hear you. But I guess I'm just confused. One minute you're talking about a massacre in Vietnam, the next you're on to monsters in the trees. Bugs—uh—*eating* people? Do I have that right?" He consulted his notes briefly. "Tentacles killing children? Forgive me—I just want to make sure we're getting to the point."

Tommy noticed how the man fidgeted nervously. Small movements, but tells all the same. How he avoided eye contact, how he clicked his pen, how he straightened his tie when he was searching for the right words. How generally uncomfortable he seemed. He found the man, frankly, pathetic. "Yes, Agent Nolan, we are. Unless you keep interrupting, of course."

Agent Nolan sat up a little straighter at this, and Tommy thought perhaps he was offended. Good. He lifted his hands, the chain making that rattling sound (*Death rattle* went drifting through his mind) as he did, and he stopped to watch Agent Nolan's face. It was pinched with discomfort, and Tommy slid his hands up and down against the bar, up and down, hoping it would irritate the man further, this man who had come like so many before thinking he could stick Tommy under a microscope and figure him out. They were all the same: the social worker, the psychologist, the *other* psychologist (the one trying to make a name for himself at his bleeding heart Ivy League school), a handful of police detectives, countless doctors who thought they would be the one to "cure" him, even a few of the nurses who thought they could befriend him. They all came, one by one, sometimes weeks apart, sometimes years, but they always came. And they sat and they listened to the story in whole or in part, and one after another they gave Tommy up as a bad job and went on their way. And this man—his eyes looking tired already behind his glasses, his face the boring, bored face of the career bureaucrat, his hands drumming impatiently on the table as he checked his watch with increasing frequency to know when he would finally have an excuse to leave—this man was just the same as all the rest.

Yes, Tommy hoped the man was offended. Tommy himself was offended by the man's visit. But Jeezum Crow, there was no reason *not* to tell the story...unless of course the fricking square kept interrupting him. He had many secrets, many unspoken things dying to be spoken, did ol' Tommy. But he wanted to be heard. He wanted someone to *listen*. For once in his fucking horror of a life, he wanted someone to *believe* him.

"I'm sorry," Agent Nolan said, not sounding sorry at all. But he smoothed his tie and folded his hands in his lap. "Please continue."

"You promise you won't interrupt?" Tommy asked, not recognizing that this was the question of a child. The man made a note with his pen, and Tommy studied his face carefully. In a way it reminded him of his father—his true father, anyway, the one who raised him—the way the glasses cast his face in strange angles; the light, hurtling through time and space, encountering their strange prisms and bending in ways both mundane and spectacular. For a fleeting moment Tommy pictured it: this light, on its journey from infinity, subject only to the laws of gravity and these stupid plastic lenses, being captured by the lowest of all monuments to mediocrity and bending to its will, as helpless as Tommy himself was to the will of those running Green Elm Home. And he pictured Rob: even now that he was many years dead Tommy pictured him just as he was in that spring of '78, aging and tired, old even for his age (not much older than Tommy now), full of warmth and love and hurt. He was sitting in their boat on the lake and the light passed through his spectacles with that same fascinating slant—a victory for his mother in the long and storied battle to get Rob to wear his glasses.

"You *promise* you won't interrupt?" Tommy asked earnestly.

"Of course not!" Rob said, smiling that fatherly smile as he studied the bobber bouncing in the ripples of whatever inconceivable engine drove the surface of the water in its eternal dance.

"Okay... Well, the thing is... Sometimes I *see* things."

"See what?"

"You said you wouldn't interrupt!"

"You're right, you're right, son. I won't."

Tommy chose his next words carefully. He had thought about this a lot, but he had never dared to mention it before. Why he was saying it now was a mystery, perhaps as deep as the mystery of the light through a prism, or the waves in a pool. He spoke slowly. "Sometimes I see things that I can't explain. I don't know if it's my glasses... I don't *think* it's my glasses."

Rob, still smiling, took a little slack out of the line. He exuded the warm confidence of adulthood, of a man who thought he knew exactly what his son was getting at: anxiety about the enormous spectacles sitting on his nose, perhaps, or simple childhood curiosity about the world around him. Perhaps in a dark corner of his mind Rob suspected it had something to do with the events of that February—in fact Tommy was sure of it.

"It's like... I dunno Dad... Sometimes I feel like there's something *watching* me. Well, not *watching* exactly. It's like I've done something wrong... Like...like I'm in trouble." He looked at his father, eyes shining with absolute trust.

Rob took his eyes off the bobber now and looked over at Tommy's magnified ones. They weren't full of curiosity. They were full of fear, real fear. He slowly, unconsciously, lowered the fishing pole until it was almost in the water.

"Tommy, what do you see? Is it a person?"

Tommy shook his head.

"Who's watching you?" Rob's face was a little drawn, a little nervous.

"I don't know," Tommy said, his lip trembling slightly. "Just sometimes when I'm outside...or by the window... Something in the trees..."

Rob looked around quickly as if expecting this something to make itself known at that moment, but nothing did. The lush green of virgin nature was all there was to be seen, the gentle burble of water from some nearby tributary all there was to be heard.

"Tommy—"

Suddenly the bobber took off on a furious dive and the line from Rob's reel spun out with a terrific noise that startled them both. And across the years it startled Tommy again, startled him back into the present, and he heard someone far, far away, saying:

"Mr. Wilford, can you hear me? Mr. Wilford?"

Tommy did wear glasses. Thick, enormous, huge glasses, and he supposed the light passed through them just like it had passed through Rob's glasses that day as they sat in the boat. He had liked his glasses back then, even loved them. And he had loved the man who raised him. But the man sitting across from him now, the one clicking his pen and jotting down notes and blinking away the sleep in his eyes, was not his father. As if to prove it, the man said:

"I said I'll try, Mr. Wilford, but I must ask you to please get to the point soon."

Tommy was silent for a long moment as he considered this. "Do you ever think about God?" he asked.

"I'm sorry?"

"Do you think there is a God who sees everything we do...who *judges* everything we do?"

"I suppose..." Agent Nolan said, not following. "Yes."

"That must be comforting for you," Tommy muttered.

The man peered over his glasses. "You don't?"

Tommy ignored him. "What about something you have no control over? Do you think He judges us for that?"

Agent Nolan watched Tommy very closely now, sensing the weight of whatever was coming next. "I'm not sure," he said. "What do you think?"

Tommy fixed him with that same x-ray gaze, the one that was becoming more familiar as their interview dragged on.

"Yes," he said. "I think He must."

JUNE, 1978

E lise was miserable. It was a feeling that had become all too familiar in the last four months. She barely ate or slept, and when she did sleep it was usually restless, punctuated by horrifying nightmares of the creature, that *Thing*, the one she saw in February. It came thundering into her drowsy mind like a runaway train, eyes black and lifeless and yet so very real, tentacles thrashing, mandibles dribbling with horrible hungry spittle. It charged at her with an alien swiftness and she turned, always turned, and a terrible hot liquid showered her back and she woke screaming. And now as she sat under the sterile glow of fluorescent white lights, tired, hungry, that indefinable (and somehow, extremely definable) fear washing over her again, she curled into a ball and glanced sideways up and down the length of the room.

It was an oblong room with a row of worn out chairs—mismatched colors, she noted—along one wall and posters of happy children along the other. Every time she glanced at these children laughing gaily at some secret joke she felt bitter resentment twist her stomach. It wasn't fair. It was cruel, a cheap trick. And worst of all, it didn't work. She snorted with derision—*derision;* it was a delicious word, one of those words her daddy called a "nine dollar word," but Elise was in no mood to appreciate big words today. Yes, she snorted with derision and averted her eyes from the fantasy children in their picture-perfect playground to gaze at one of the short ends of the room, where a door was set, with frosted glass into which the words *Connor Stephens, PsyD* had been etched in bland lettering which practically screamed: *You're broken! Ha ha ha!* Or at least that was how Elise felt. And at the other end of the room, so boring it was almost offensive: a Check-in Counter. A young lady, no older than twenty, sat there cheerily and smiled when Elise caught her eye; a sympathetic smile, a smile full of pity. Elise wrinkled her nose and looked back at the door.

"I was thinking maybe tomorrow we'd get some ice cream," her father, who was sitting to her left, said in a delicate voice.

Elise almost didn't notice. She turned her face slowly from the door and met her father's anxious gaze. Outside the sunlight was dazzling, but it looked like nothing more than a brilliant blue haze through the glass. Her father, on the other hand, looked like a nervous wreck. His brown threadbare suit jacket barely concealed an even more threadbare shirt, of which he had only three (not that Elise was privy to this information), and sat atop a pair of khaki slacks which had already seen better days when he found them at the local thrift store. His shave was patchy and rough and his eyes, behind square framed glasses, were a disturbed, stormy blue. His hair, once golden and thick, now sprouted in gray sleep-addled tufts which fell out if he ran a comb through them. A dingy badge hung forgotten from his breast pocket, spelling out his name, PAUL, in unenthusiastic typewritten characters. Elise, at nine, could have no idea that her parents were driving themselves to bankruptcy to get her this treatment (nor that they would have gladly done so ten times over), but even so, she had been so lifeless and devoid of emotion ever since that—that day—that they weren't sure she would have cared. She had some dim idea, maybe, but the old Elise was gone; the Elise who had giggled with delight when her mother made cookies and skipped home from the bus stop and relished playing word games with her daddy was either somewhere else entirely or buried so deeply that they feared she might never emerge again.

"Okay," she said quietly.

There was a pause then, a pause loaded with unspoken meaning, saturated with tangible worry about what to say next, and finally: "Do you and Doctor Stephens—uh—talk about anything interesting?" It was a nervous question, just small talk really, but Elise sensed it ran somewhere near the heart of things her father really wanted to know. She had a good intuition about these things—always had and presumably always would.

"Sometimes, I guess."

"Mm," her father nodded, feigning satisfaction, but she noticed that he did not say anything else, as if hoping the silence would encourage her to open up further. Part of her even wanted to, wanted to tell him more, to tell him what had really happened back in February, but a larger part was too busy looking for ways to bury it at all costs, and so she said nothing.

There was a time when she had not been miserable. Her father knew it, her mother knew it—in some vague way, Elise knew it—but it seemed so long ago that it was hard to remember when, or why. How was it possible that anything could ever have been so peaceful and happy and good when all she had known for four long months—a remarkable fraction of a young girl's life—had been fear? She considered the ice cream. Once upon a time that would have been a very special treat, a beautiful, treasured way to spend the afternoon with her father, who normally spent all day at work. Now as she turned it over in her mind, contemplating not just the taste, but the sweet smell of the creamery, the delightful *clink* as her daddy dropped the change in the tip jar, her fascination at the enormous jukebox in the corner, she found that what she felt was—nothing. No emotion either good or bad. Not one firing neuron to render the experience in any color other than black and white.

Perhaps it was the secret.

She gripped her legs harder and squeezed into the smallest ball she could manage. Yes, the secret, the awful secret, the one she had kept locked up inside for all this time, the one that burned with such terrible energy that

at times she felt she must burst into flame from the sheer effort of keeping
it hidden. That secret. It was too deep and too horrible to accept, too ugly
to recognize as the truth, too—

"Elise? Elise Smithfield?"

She looked up from the small dark space behind her legs and saw a lady
in a nurse's smock leaning through the door next to the Check-in Counter.

"Dr. Stephens will see you now."

Her father gave her an encouraging little push, nothing much, just a
friendly tap really, and she slid off the chair onto the floor. The happy
children were now extremely close; they seemed impossibly large as they
stood frozen in action with those big fake smiles plastered across their faces.

"I'll be right here, sweetie," her father said in that same delicate voice.
She nodded in a way that might have been just a small breath and floated—barely touching the floor, or so it felt—to the spot where the lady
stood, clipboard in one hand and doorknob in the other, smiling the same
sympathetic smile as the lady behind the counter. Elise glanced up at the
counter as she passed and saw the young woman there crinkle her eyes
knowingly, as if she herself were the keeper of all Elise's deepest secrets, as
if she were some great and all-knowing judge, passing silent judgement on
the poor girl walking beneath her elevated station and rendering a verdict
that was as secret as the charge itself. Elise looked away quickly and hurried
through the door, which shut behind her with a clinical sort of *thunk*,
a sound which suggested a strange and yet increasingly familiar sense of
finality.

She stood at the end of a short hall—no longer new to her, but still scary,
always scary; it seemed to contract before her like that room in the haunted
house at the carnival, shining with white light which only accentuated the
puke-like shade of brown that covered the walls. In a flash of adult understanding, Elise realized that she feared this place—dreaded this place—not
because of what it was, but because of what it represented; because this was

where she came to *remember*. When every hour, every tortured minute, she wanted nothing more than to forget, this man, Doctor Stephens, endowed from On High with gifts of insight only dreamt of by lesser men—he *made* her remember. She hated him for that, hated his wrinkled forehead and his self-important smirks and his fake sympathy; but most of all she hated the way that he could make her think things and say things that she did not even admit to herself. And somewhere deep down, somewhere in a dark, shadowy corner of her soul, where Connor Stephens, PsyD, seemed determined to reach, lay that *secret*...

Another door opened—had she really walked the entire length of the hall already?—and she arrived at the dreaded place, his actual office. The lady in the nurse's smock eased her through the door, pushed on her back with a firmness that was far greater than her father's, and shut it behind her; and now here was Doctor Stephens himself, sitting behind his desk and consulting the contents of a manila file folder, forehead wrinkles arched in an expression of concentration. They arched even further when the eyes beneath them looked up and saw Elise arriving.

"Ah! Elise—good to see you again, my dear."

She could not return the sentiment, and did not.

"Have you thought at all about the things we talked about in our last session?"

She considered how to respond and finally nodded silently, hoping it would appease the man behind the desk. It was better to appease him—he asked fewer questions that way.

"Good! Well, where shall we begin? Oh—have a seat, please, my dear, make yourself at home."

Make yourself at home. It was just a formality, a polite way to take the edge out of the request—no, not request, *demand*—but it stung all the same. How could he say that, did he have no idea, had all their sessions (two a week for the last few months) really impressed him that little, was he really so cold to her situation that he could suggest that here, of all places, *anywhere*, could be like a home to her, when her own "home" did not even feel that way?

But she took a seat.

"Good girl. Well, let's dive right in, goodness knows your parents aren't paying me for pleasantries." A self-satisfied laugh, *Ha ha ha!* "Now when we left off you were telling me about a creature, the one that attacked you and your friends? I thought that was very interesting. Could you tell me more about it? What did it look like?"

Elise stared into space, remembering; God she wished she wouldn't but she did anyway, and there it was again, the monster, the *Thing*, as large and as terrible as life, and she turned again, always turned, and that hot red blast of gore showered her back, sticky and clotted with hair and bits of flesh—

"I'm not really sure," she said, mostly honestly, tearing herself away from the memory with an involuntary shudder. "I turned before I could get a good look."

"Yes, I remember you saying that," Doctor Stephens said, jotting notes on whatever was contained in the manila folder. "Are you sure you don't remember anything? Anything at all?"

The flailing tentacles flashed across her consciousness like a bolt of lightning, the dripping jaws, the black eyes... She shook her head quickly.

"No? Nothing?" He consulted the folder again and made another note. "Well, not to worry my dear, we'll come back to it in due course. Now you were with several other children at the time, is that correct? Could you talk to me a little about them? What about this one—uh—Billy Baker? Was he a friend of yours?"

The memory rose to meet her at the mention of the name; yes, Billy Baker, he had been a friend—or had he? Even at the time she was never really sure; he had the kind of personality that made you want to be his friend, made you desperately crave his attention, no matter the way that he sometimes treated other people, because as long as you were on his side of things he was not treating *you* that way. In fact you felt empowered, you felt on top of the world, because here was this kid (and he was a good-looking boy) letting you in, into his circle, and you were part of that group, the *powerful* group, the ones that others wanted to be, and you were safe, safe from the bullies and the meanness, and things generally went your way. It was not a crush at all really—Elise did not suspect she had ever had a crush on anybody—but it was somewhere in that territory: a sort of admiration, a wordless awe, the kind that swept you up and brought you along without regard for how you might have felt about things or people beforehand.

She nodded uncertainly. "Yeah. He was my friend." It was simpler than the truth, and easier.

"What can you tell me about him?"

There it was. The open-ended question. She hated those most of all.

"He was tall," she said quietly.

"Was?" Doctor Stephens arched his eyebrows again, sending his fore-head wrinkles climbing into what had once been hair and was now just little wisps desperately clinging on for dear life. "Don't you think maybe he just ran away somewhere? Sometimes children do, perhaps you've thought about it yourself once or twice."

No, she had never thought about it herself; the idea was too awful to even consider. She loved her parents, both of them, desperately, and besides the fact that she was only nine and could never survive out in the world, she knew it would cut them to the bone. Even after it—it had happened—she had still found her way home. Even though it was cold and she was wet and miserable and scared, because where else would she go?

"Mm-mm," she said, shaking her head.

Doctor Stephens considered this answer and made another scribble with his pen.

"Well maybe you haven't. But children do, you know, many children. What makes you think Billy didn't? Maybe he saw what happened and was too scared to come back."

Elise could see it happening, she could see the thing he was driving at, and it came close, oh so close, horribly close, to the *secret*, he was practically stepping all over it, he would find it if he kept prodding and it had only been five minutes, she would be here an entire *hour*...

"He just wouldn't. Billy wouldn't," she said, dancing her toes an inch off the ground, staring at them intently.

Doctor Stephens let her sit in silence for a moment before continuing.

"Elise," he said in a quiet, serious voice, "was he taken by someone? I know you said it was a creature, but is it possible that it was a man? Is it possible a man took Billy?"

The ponderous weight of the question fell heavily on the room, and even though she knew there was no truth in it she paused out of respect for what it would mean. It was true that Billy had an estranged father who lived out in Essex. After his disappearance it was widely suspected that he had found his way out there, all that way, by whatever means, probably not good ones, and this theory was supported by his father's own mysterious disappearance. But no, Elise knew the truth, she knew but she couldn't say, it was just too awful.

She shook her head again, silently, still staring at her toes, although they had stopped dancing and were now very still.

Doctor Stephens looked like he wanted to say something more about this, but he didn't, only made more notes in the folder. "Okay," he said. "Well, what else can you tell me about Billy?"

Elise thought about what to say. What else was there? When she thought about her relationship (*"friendship"?*) with Billy she felt mostly embarrassed. When it came right down to it, he was not a nice boy, and when she was with him she was not a nice girl. She did not want to say this though; for some reason she did not want Doctor Stephens to know the truth of what she was beginning to suspect about her real, true self. And above all else, in some indescribable way, she felt that saying anything negative at all would be disrespectful to his memory—even thinking the things she had thought felt like some strange, disdainful act. *Don't speak ill of the dead.* She had heard that somewhere but she wasn't sure where. Even if it sounded weird and unnatural in her mind, she still understood its fundamental meaning.

"He was popular," she finally said. There. An answer that was both honest and gave away nothing.

"Can you elaborate on that?"

Elise made a funny face. "Ee-lab-o...?"

"Oh, I'm sorry, my dear," Doctor Stephens said condescendingly (she hated that as well, in addition to everything else), "you're so smart, sometimes I almost forget I'm talking to a child. Can you say more about how Billy was popular?"

So she had not quite escaped after all. "Well...people just really liked him, I guess," she said. Her toes started bouncing again; she was finding her footing, maybe she could climb out of this hole—

"Why do you think that was?"

"He was just..." The bouncing stopped for a second, she had to think, think fast. "He was really good at talking to people. Kids always wanted to play with him."

"And did you always want to play with him?"

She nodded, biting her lip. "Mm-hm."

"It must have been very hard for you when he disappeared," he said, leaning forward slightly.

"Yes," she said, her eyes glossing over. "It was."

"How exactly did it happen, Elise?"

His voice sounded far away. She knew how it happened, she had seen it, seen everything, but she could not let it out, would not let it out, because that would spoil everything. Her family, her whole life would be ruined, brought down by the *secret*, oh God the secret, he was so close to it again, why did he have to get so close—

"I don't know," she mumbled, her lip trembling, her eyes hot, "I didn't see. I don't *know*..."

Doctor Stephens sat back again for a moment...and then leaned in even closer.

"I think you do, Elise," he said gently. "Go on and tell me. It's okay—everything we talk about here is confidential. Do you know what 'confidential' means? It means that I can't talk about it with anyone else. So your secret—"

—oh God, the secret—

"—will be safe with me. I promise."

Elise looked up at him, blurry through the tears welling up in her eyes. Suddenly she wanted to tell him, wanted to tell him so badly because then it would be over, she would finally be free of it and no matter what happened she wouldn't be carrying around this terrible huge weight...

"No s-s-secret," she heard herself saying, stammering through the heavy sobs fighting their way up out of her chest. She couldn't explain it, she wanted to tell him, she did, she wanted it over with, but she just couldn't, no no no she could not, and the urge went sinking back down into those shadowy depths to stay, probably forever.

Doctor Stephens looked disappointed. Perhaps he knew just how close he had gotten. But he was a consummate professional and he sat up straight, scratched his slowly expanding belly and set the folder on the desk. "I'm going to level with you, Elise," he said, standing up. "Do you know what that means, to 'level' with someone? I'm going to tell you the truth. People are scared Elise. Your parents are scared. *I'm* scared." It was a masterful bit of acting, he pressed one hand into his chest to convey just how personal this was for him. "People are wondering if there's a killer around, a *child* killer, on the loose. Now if you know something—if you know *anything*—you should tell someone. It doesn't have to be me. But a grown-up, Elise. They can help you, and they can help other kids, like Billy. Do you want this kind of thing to happen again, to other kids?"

Elise shook her head no, of course she didn't, it would be crazy to want that.

"Then tell me, Elise, you have a chance right now, and remember what I said, I won't tell anyone." He put both hands flat on the desk as he said it and leaned forward until Elise felt so very, very small. "Don't you want to get it off your chest?"

She did, she really did, but she also didn't, and the moment had passed. Then a funny thought came to her.

"But if you can't tell anyone, how are you going to help the other kids?" she asked.

Doctor Stephens turned slightly gray. He blinked and backed off until he was merely bracing himself against the desk. "Well, you see," he said, eyes darting around the room, "I can tell the police what you know without telling them who said it. Now doesn't that sound good, my dear?"

Perhaps it did, perhaps it didn't; but something had crystallized inside her, something that she had long suspected but hadn't quite dared to believe, because this was a man that was trusted by her daddy or she wouldn't be here in the first place. Namely that she, herself, Elise, did *not* trust Connor Stephens, PsyD, and she especially did not trust him with her *secret*, the bad one, the one that scared her so much it hurt. He could never know, *no one* could ever know. And that was that. And anyway, there was no helping the other children or anyone else, because that monster, that *Thing*, was out there somewhere, and no one had believed her; not her parents or her pastor or the gray doctor standing across from her. It was no man; it was certainly not Billy Baker's father. And it was out there, she knew it, there was no stopping it, and she had no idea where it came from or where it was right now or where it was going; it was just *Out There*.

And no one could stop it. She was sure of that.

* * *

Will was sore. His backside ached with the memory of his recent beating, and although he could not see it himself, he was sure that his buttocks were a horrible, blotchy purple, maybe tinted with yellow. This was a familiar color scheme to Will, who had seen it at various times over every inch of his body. In the years since his father had returned from Vietnam it was a regular part of life. This beating, unpleasant though it may have been, was hardly the worst. What made it so terrible was the *unfairness* of it, the *injustice*; in the past Will could—and did—often rationalize to himself that he had indeed committed some offense, really *screwed things up*, to whatever degree. That his cuts and bruises were the natural comeuppance for whatever sin he had committed, large or small. There were exceptions of course, and this was one of them, but in his heart of hearts Will wanted only to please. Somewhere in his core, in some unconscious, unspoken place, he thought that maybe if he could please the man, his father would love him again, show him affection again, treat him the way he had before when Will was very small, so long ago it was almost beyond remembrance. Maybe his father would stop being so sad, that was the heart of it. But no, this...this was something else. This was wrong, it was *not right*. This stung all the more because it came after he had *already* suffered at the hands of Clark and Toby, the Dynamic Duo, when he could have used a friend or a father or even just some small word of encouragement. Instead he had paid—his bottom bore the proof—once again, for his failure.

Will stretched carefully and rolled over to take some weight off the bruises. His mother had gotten home just an hour or two after the beating, and then things had *really* blown up, you bet your bottom dollar they had. He still heard his parents' voices ringing in his head, shouting, screaming, saying things that at one time he never would have believed but were now so common they barely affected him anymore.

"You son of a bitch!" his mother had shouted. "You FUCKING *son* of a *bitch*, what did you do to our *son?*"

"Give it a rest, Jane," Harry had slurred dismissively, but he was just beginning to sober up and there was something a little guilty, a little defensive in it.

"NO! No, I will *not* give it a rest, LOOK AT HIM!" She had thrown a hand violently backward to where Will was curled into a ball in the corner. "He's scared of you Harry. He's *scared of his own father.*"

"GOOD!" Harry retorted. "Good, I'm *glad* he's afraid. The world ain't all sunshine and rainbows, Jane, the boy's gotta learn—"

"Oh *please,* don't give me that," his mother said, with an exhortation to the ceiling. "*Don't* give me that crock of *shit.*"

"YES! *Yes,* the boy's gotta learn, why, when—when I was in Vietnam—"

"Don't you say it, Harry, don't you give me some story—"

"—there were people blowing up into a thousand pieces, Janie, a *thousand fucking pieces*, and it could happen any time, you never knew—"

"—OH and here it comes, the same old bullshit. Harry, have you ever considered that I've *heard it all bef—*"

SMACK! and his mother staggered backwards until she sank onto the floor next to Will, clutching her face where a small rivulet of blood ran down from her nose.

"DON'T YOU CALL IT SHIT, JANIE! DON'T YOU CALL IT SHIT, THAT WAS MY FUCKING LIFE!" Harry roared, and Will sensed that a curtain of red was descending across his father's vision because it was times like these when he seemed to lose all sense of self or memory and the only thing in control was blind drunk rage. "RISK MY FUCKING LIFE, YOU DON'T EVEN KNOW WHAT SHIT IS, YOU DON'T KNOW WHAT KIND OF SHIT I'VE HAD TO DEAL WITH AND

YOU SURE AS SHIT DON'T KNOW WHAT SHIT I'VE DONE TO
OTHER PEOPLE JANIE, YOU HAVE NO GODDAMN FUCKING
IDEA AND I COULD DO IT AGAIN, I'LL DO IT, I SWEAR TO
GOD I COULD FUCKING DO IT—"

And they had retreated into the bathroom like so many times before,
Jane taking the few opportunities she had to pinch her nose with two
fingers but there was no stopping the blood, it kept running and running
and a little pool of it formed on the floor, and it would have been terrible if it
had not happened so many times already. It was almost a miracle Harry had
been so drunk because even now after several hours he could hardly keep up
as he stumbled and swaggered his way past the coffee table, the couch, the
lamp; he managed to find all of them and let out strangled cries as various
parts of his body erupted in pain. Jane was crying but calm, everything
calm except her hands, which shook violently, and she got Will into the
bathroom and slammed the door. She fumbled with the lock where a smear
of angry red remained behind and then she grabbed Will around the middle
and hauled him backwards until they were both on the edge of the tub.

BANG!

"JANE YOU OPEN THE DOOR! JANE!"

BANG BANG!

"JANIE WHEN I GET IN THERE YER GONNA FUCKING WISH
YOU HAD STAYED OUT HERE AND TALKED LIKE A GOD-
DAMN FUCKING ADULT! *JANE!*"

Will still heard the words as he lay in bed hours later, his father's snores
rumbling through the wall like some great slumbering beast; he could almost believe it really was some terrible beast lying on the other side and not
the flesh-and-blood man who had given him life. He heard them rattling
around in his skull like whispers: *Jane, Jane you open up, I swear to God, Jane
I'm sorry, okay, I'm sorry I didn't mean it, just come out, please come out, I'll
stop drinking, alright? Swear to God I will, just open the fucking door...* His

father had finally collapsed into a sobbing heap and then a sleeping one, and then Jane had carefully pushed the door open and she and Will had climbed out over the pathetic stinking hulk and she had gone to deal with the blood drying into a brown crust down the front of her nurse's uniform. Within hours Will might never have known it had happened at all if he (and his buttocks) had not been there to witness it. His mother showered and changed and did a decent job of cleaning up all the blood, and Harry eventually woke up mostly sober, and the three of them managed to sit down to a dinner in which the only thing harder than the biscuits was the silence. Not a word was spoken about it, then or later. As was tradition, the topic never emerged again. There was only the next explosion. And now Will finally sank into a troubled sleep in which the monster from the clearing chased him, blood dripping from what could only be a nose, like a skull's nose, showering him, going everywhere, and from its strange wet jaws came the voice of his father, screaming, *I'll do it, I swear to God I'll do it, you have no fucking idea Jane, I could fucking kill you and not blink an eye, I've killed children, CHILDREN Jane, I didn't want to but I did and I could do it again, I swear to God, Janieeeee...*

* * *

Tommy was bored. Not end-of-the-school-day, tired-of-math-class bored, but really, truly, Dear-God-help-me bored; the kind of boredom that starts somewhere in the toes and progresses to envelop the calves, thighs, crotch, midriff, neck, and finally the head in a numb, paralyzing fog. He was bored in the way that schoolchildren sometimes get bored at the end of summer, when their friends are on vacation, they've exhausted all the things they wanted to do and now wait in miserable anticipation for school to start. Except this was the last Sunday *before* summer vacation. Plus, Tommy, having only a child's frame of reference, could still recognize that that particular species of boredom existed on some lower plane and would have to have been multiplied by a thousand—maybe even a million, or a million-million—to come anywhere close to matching the boredom that he felt now.

He had not left his room since February. Oh sure; to use the bathroom, to eat lunch or dinner; but these tasks aside he had remained shut in for the better part of four months. This had begun as a measure of comfort insisted upon by his parents and grown into a punishment inflicted by himself. The fact of the matter was, Tommy was afraid. More than that: he felt a certain sense of guilt. Survivor's Guilt, perhaps. No—something more sinister, something that gnawed at him, ate him up from the inside, something about himself that he was just beginning to grasp. The fear was because a number of strange things had happened in the immediate aftermath of the killings back in February. And who could forget the nature of the killings themselves?

For one thing, there was the tree outside his bedroom. He would have noticed sooner, his parents said, if it hadn't taken so long to replace his broken glasses. Maybe so. But after two weeks—just two weeks—of near blindness, Tommy had awoken on the morning after picking up his new lenses to the sound of shattering glass. He had jumped upright and fumbled on the nightstand for the life-saving frames, images of tentacles and bodies dripping with blood springing like geysers out of the recesses of his traumatized brain, and finally slammed them onto his broken nose to discover that a branch of the tree had grown straight through his bedroom window. Not only that, but strangely the tree had grown into a noticeable lean, with several more branches outstretched toward the window as well, reaching for it, clawing at it, and the particular branch had not merely arrived at the window but somehow grown a full six inches past it and into the house. Rob had hauled out the old ladder and sawed off the last couple of feet and put particle board up to cover the opening, but within days there were more branches, first two, then three, then four, climbing across the length of the mutilated wood, penetrating it, curling around it, caressing it in an ecstasy of pain. Their anguished, twisted forms became in short order a hideous imitation of roots. Even the grass around the tree and throughout the yard on that side of the house had gone turbo; Rob found he had to mow it once a day just to keep it in check—and this was well before spring had arrived.

Yes, it was strange, alright. Rob would comment on it to Kristin in the dead of night when they were alone; he didn't dare mention it around Tommy. And it wasn't the only thing that was strange: as temperatures warmed and the ground began to thaw, it seemed that a colony of ants was not so much moving in as attempting to conquer the place. It began as a relatively normal spring infestation, but quickly grew into something much more curious. The pantry was the first thing to go, followed by the fridge, and before long the ants were marching one by one (hurrah, hurrah) along the walls, the ceiling, the floor, and hell if they weren't making their way with every six-legged step toward the same bedroom where the tree was quite literally growing into the now three-layer-thick boards covering the window. Soon after—drawn by the plentiful food, Rob suspected—there were other bugs as well, spiders chief among them, making the same bizarre pilgrimage, even gathering into circles around what remained of the glass and its steadily thickening cover.

The birds came in May. One might have been forgiven for thinking the Wilfords were attempting to start their own private wildlife sanctuary. They lined up like mysterious dark sentinels along every edge of the house: crows, vultures, owls, hawks, and some of the smaller ones as well. A splash of color here or there but generally grim and gray. They crowded onto the ledges and gutters and chattered at each other in their peculiar dialects...and Rob couldn't help but notice, even if he would never say it out loud, that they seemed to prefer the area above Tommy's bedroom.

Yes, it was all very strange. Rob felt grateful that their house by the lake was far enough away from neighbors to prevent too many questions. It served the additional purpose of allowing both Rob and Kristin to remain—somewhat willingly—oblivious to just how strange things really were. After all, it being their first spring in the area and with no neighbors around to compare, it was easy enough to convince themselves that this was all normal. At the very least, it was a great comfort to imagine that it was. After all, why not? Ants always come for food in the spring. Birds always fly north in the spring. Plants always grow in the spring. Yeah, you betcha. But Tommy knew; he knew in his gut that something was enormously wrong. These things were not a coincidence. For reasons he could not place, something—some terrible *power*—was after him. He felt it, he recognized it, he knew it from long ago, from the muddy depths of memory. He might have been a child, but even a child—especially a child—feels intuition. He was quite sure it was connected to whatever had killed his schoolmates back in February. Perhaps that *Thing*, whatever it was (*Fear*, Tommy thought with a lightning flash of terror; pure, absolute *Fear*), had unfinished business. Perhaps it wanted to finish the job...

So Tommy had stayed in his room and watched as the ants marched closer and the spiders scuttled nearer and the birds chattered louder and the branches grew into increasingly gnarled, incredible shapes. But oh, how he was bored. Bored and lonely. And with his father's encouragement, he finally left the sanctity of the house.

Sunday dawned bright and sunny, cool and inviting. The kind of June morning that grabs you by the balls with life affirming zeal. The kind that demands you take some time to enjoy the great outdoors. The late spring sun cast a dazzling ring around the edges of Tommy's window, backlighting the particle board with a warm glow. Outside it shone through the translucent green leaves of the deformed tree, rocking in the breeze, and made shifting, fluttering shadows across the lawn. Overhead a graceful assortment of clouds drifted from horizon to horizon in lazy trails, occasionally bringing shade and promptly taking it back. Even the birds in their endless watch sang peacefully at the coming of morning, the chorus of their chirps and chitters permeating the house. And Rob decided enough was enough.

At 8 a.m. there was a knock on Tommy's door.

"Tommy? Son, are you awake?"

Tommy was indeed awake, lying, as he often did, on top of the covers in his tractor trailer pajamas, watching as the ring-glow of the sun increasingly turned his room to orange. He had been awake for a couple of hours, as troubled as ever, but still possessed with that insatiable energy which is wasted on the very young, the energy which wakes children long before their parents and commands that their life force not be thrown away on such banal things as sleeping.

"Tommy?"

"Yeah Dad. I'm awake."

"Tommy, I thought maybe we'd go out on the lake today."

It was almost pleading, almost pathetic, but so infused with love and hope and genuine concern that Tommy couldn't help considering it. He scrunched up his nose—not that his father could see it—not wanting to say no, not wanting to say yes, and most of all not wanting to let his father down. But fear and something else, some terrible weight, had become good friends in the last few months, and he felt this weight press him back into the pillow. With a mind of its own, his thumb drifted toward his mouth. He lay silently, unsure of what to say.

"We could get the boat out of the garage," Rob's voice continued from the other side of the door. "We haven't done that all year. Maybe get a little fishing in. I've got a feeling about today, that Big Fish kinda feeling."

Still Tommy was silent. He *did* want to go fishing, really he did, and he wanted to spend time with his dad. He glanced over at the multitude of ant traps lining the floor by his window, where a cadre of the tiny insects marched in an orderly file, carrying the poison back to their hungry young. This was supposed to kill them, but they had been marching in these same lines for weeks with no sign that their numbers were dwindling, or even that their interest was waning. He looked at the small green tendrils pushing through the particle board, making their slow, unrelenting progress into the house, into his room—toward *him*, he was sure. His chest tightened and he pushed his glasses up onto his forehead, pushed his palms into his eyes. "I dunno, Dad."

"Son," Rob said, a little bit of an edge creeping into his voice, "you can't stay in your room forever. Now I know—I *know*—you've been going through a hard time this spring"—Tommy rolled his eyes in an almost teenagerish expression of misunderstood youth—"but getting out of the house will help you. I know it will."

Silence.

"Tommy? Tommy, I'm coming in." The door opened—another assortment of ant bait went skittering off to one side—and there stood Rob in his plaid pajama pants and a bathrobe, wielding a large cup of coffee in a mug which proclaimed *Never trust an atom, they make up everything*. Kristin stood behind him in her own pajamas, with an expression that said she had not meant to be caught listening to this conversation.

"Tommy, you have to leave your room," Rob said. It was gentle but forceful. "This isn't a debate. You have to leave your room."

"Good morning, sweetie," Kristin said nervously from behind him.

"G'morning, Mom."

"Your dad is right, sweetie. Why don't you want to go out on the lake? You love fishing."

Tommy stared at the floor, not because he was looking at the scattered ant traps—although he certainly watched them—but because he couldn't seem to meet his mother's gaze. Off in the corner sat a brand new pair of gleaming white sneakers, the end result of a previous attempt to get him out of the house, one which had ended in failure when his mother was forced to give up and buy the shoes alone. Tommy could not be motivated even by shoe shopping with his mother, something that quietly broke Kristin's heart. It broke Tommy's heart too; but even now as he glanced at the shoes, he imagined them spattered with blood—

—*screaming in the clearing as the water churned*—

—and felt his pulse accelerate. "Well—it's just..." He reached for the right words, but they didn't come. Finally he said, "I'm *scared.*"

"We're going fishing," his father said, a note of gruffness in his voice. "We're going fishing, and you'll see there's *nothing to be afraid of.* It's gotta happen sooner or later, son, and today's the day. You couldn't ask for a better day."

It was half true—the day was so beautiful, so perfect. But that left half wrong, just dead wrong, because there *was* something to fear, something terrifying and monstrous. Tommy had seen it back in February. But there was no more discussion. Within ten minutes Tommy was downstairs pretending to eat breakfast, where the radio crackled away happily that *"—a police cruiser was found abandoned last night by Elmwood Elementary School. The officer, Elmwood's own Harold Tibbs, was nowhere to be seen, but witnesses say they last saw him walking toward the site of spring's horrific child killings—"* at which Kristin, her eyes wide and apologetic, clumsily turned it off and declared that she didn't like listening to the news on Sundays anyway. Another thirty minutes after that, the echo of the broadcast still ringing in their ears, the three of them headed to the garage where Rob did his best to pretend he remembered how to hook up the trailer. The boat was not much more than a dinghy, a twelve foot flat bottom with an aluminum skin, but Tommy still felt an irrepressible twinge of excitement as he watched it reappear from under the canvas like an Old World relic. And finally, within two short hours, as the sun climbed higher in its arc across the sky and burned the last of the morning mist off the surface of the lake, father and son pushed off from shore and Tommy watched as his mother grew smaller where she stood on the bank, marking their progress with a forced smile. Once again he felt that nameless cloud of worry, that indefinable dread growing in size and weight as the space between them grew.

"Chin up, kid," Rob said with a cheeriness that was itself a concerted effort. Tommy turned to face him, the movement rocking the boat slightly in lazy bobs. "Feels good to be back out on the lake, huh?"

"I guess so," Tommy said. Truthfully it *did* feel good—the rumble of the motor hummed in his chest, an old familiar energy crept back into his limbs—but still the terrible uneasiness remained, cutting through the peaceful atmosphere like poison. He looked at his shoes but, still seeing the ghost of blood coating their white soles, quickly focused his gaze over the water.

"You'll feel better once we start fishing," Rob insisted, as much to himself as to Tommy. He gunned the throttle as they cleared the tiny cove behind their house and the boat reared back with its own infectious energy. A noisy silence descended while they motored out into deeper water, the morning breeze whipping Tommy's hair playfully, filling him with a sense of life. Real joy followed when they left the shallows behind and the boat skipped off a handful of waves. They raced out into the deeper water and angled left along the shoreline, leaving a wake that spun off on either side behind them and formed a foamy trail to mark their path. Tommy eased up to the bow of their little boat and felt his heart flutter—the faint echo of a smile began to cross his face—each time they skipped, and Rob, seeing this, steered around into their wake so that they could skip again—*pff! pff! pff!* Something miraculous happened then, something extraordinary that had not happened in four months: Tommy laughed. He felt embarrassed but he couldn't stop; he laughed and laughed and it felt good, and Rob started laughing as well, and the two of them spun in circles for several minutes, laughing like lunatics and crashing up and down, their problems suddenly seeming miles away. Rob pulled out of the turn and the boat snapped into a northerly course that took them farther away from the house, and Tommy felt for the first time that perhaps he was free, perhaps they could simply *outrun* those terrible things, perhaps he could leave them all behind and sail away with his father into the endless horizon. And then, just as quickly as this feeling came, it faded; Rob pulled back on the throttle and they settled into a gentle drift, the water swirling in microscopic whirlpools from the wash of the propeller and dancing in circles off and away.

"I think this is the spot," Rob said, his eyes still crinkled with mirth. "I've got a good feeling about this one."

Tommy could not have felt more differently; his own happiness evaporated at once as he looked out on the place his father had chosen. They had entered a sheltered area, where the menacing arms of what looked like a million trees stood in impenetrable lines on two sides, and extended in a dense copse halfway submerged in the high tide on a third. Perhaps it was a trick of the light, or just his imagination running wild after the strange events outside his room, but Tommy could almost believe the whole lot of them had leaned in toward their boat with an ancient sort of sigh as it pulled into their midst. A handful of logs and tangled branches poked out of the surf along the shore, the fallen comrades of this dense forest, and Tommy could not help but feel there was a bristling sort of anger at this sad fate, hanging in the air among the dark woods. Strange, yes, and probably it was his imagination. Probably. Tommy said nothing and slid his hands into his pockets. Rob, not noticing his son's trepidation or the unsettling energy of the place, immediately opened his tackle box and set about preparing the fishing poles. He tied off the hooks and cut the loose ends with a knife that Tommy had always admired but was too afraid to touch.

"D'you think you're ready to bait your own hook?" Rob asked, holding up the tiny barbed spike and looking at it with one eye shut. Tommy wanted more than anything to say yes, but one look at the worms wriggling in their bucket *(Dead*, Tommy thought without wanting to, *they're dead and they don't know it yet)* and he shook his head.

Rob nodded and grabbed a worm from the bucket. He pierced it once, straight down the middle, and Tommy winced—

—*splayed out in the grass, the blood dripping from its tail*—

—as the limbless little creature squirmed in apparent agony. Then Rob hung the dying thing out over the water where it swung side to side under the minuscule shadow cast by the bobber, and passed the line over to his son.

The reel felt heavy and adult-sized in Tommy's small hands, but even in the cruel shadow of the trees, misery coursing through his veins like some overcrowded freeway, he still wanted to impress his father. He swung the pole back over his shoulder and tried to cast the line to China. It sailed about ten feet through the air, and then worm, hook, line, and sinker disappeared into the ripples. *Plop.*

"Nice one!" his father said.

Tommy smiled in spite of himself and set his eyes on the bobber, hoping it would force the other feelings from his mind. In no time at all they were crowding right back in. He settled into a brooding silence. Rob cast his own line out, and they sat there for a while, now and then reeling in their soggy bait, sometimes freeing it from snags. Tommy still sensed that antediluvian wrath fixed on his back and remained mostly quiet. Rob watched him, casting and re-casting.

"What's bothering you, son? For a minute there I thought you were cheering up."

With effort, Tommy pulled his gaze away from the bobber and looked at his father. The sun was now high overhead and radiated heat. Magnificent rays reflected off the water and passed through his father's glasses—probably both of their glasses—in a spectacular assortment of colors that warmed the aluminum boat. *Strange*, Tommy thought, as he watched the edge of

Rob's face grow wider and narrower through the thick prisms. In the bright light his father looked tired. Wrinkles creased the edges of a pair of dark half-moon bags under his eyes, and for the first time Tommy noticed a line forming at the corner of his nose and curving around his mouth. In that moment he wanted to help, wanted his father to understand, wanted to share his secret. He wanted to feel the same connection that he used to feel. Last summer. Before the world went crazy.

"Well…" he said. "I mean, it's just…"

"What is it, Tommy?" The question was kind, not forceful.

"You won't interrupt?"

"I won't interrupt."

"You *promise* you won't interrupt?" Tommy asked again earnestly.

"Of course not!" Rob said, and he smiled in that fatherly way that always made Tommy feel better.

"Okay… Well, the thing is…" He took a deep breath. "Sometimes I *see* things."

"See what?"

"You said you wouldn't interrupt!"

"You're right, you're right, son. I won't."

Tommy stopped to consider how to say it. It was hard, but he wanted to say it—*needed* to say it. Somehow he knew that this was the moment. He spoke slowly. "Sometimes I see things that I can't explain. I don't know if it's my glasses… I don't *think* it's my glasses."

Rob took a little slack out of the line, still looking at the bobber, but Tommy knew that he had his father's full attention. This was what Rob had been waiting for. This was the conversation he wanted.

"It's like… I dunno Dad… Sometimes I feel like there's something *watching* me. Well, not *watching* exactly. It's like I've done something wrong… Like…like I'm in trouble." He looked at his father, eyes shining with absolute trust.

Rob took his eyes off the bobber now and fixed them on Tommy. They widened with unspoken understanding as he saw the fear on his son's face, and, unsettled, he dropped his fishing pole slowly until it was almost in the water.

"Tommy, what do you see? Is it a person?"

Tommy shook his head.

"Who's watching you?" Rob was scared now. It plunged daggers into Tommy's heart.

"I don't know," he said, his lip beginning to tremble. "Just sometimes when I'm outside...or by the window... Something in the trees..."

Rob looked around quickly as if this fearful something might be watching them at that very moment, as if the thing that had been plaguing his only son for months was standing on the shore right now in the darkness of the forest. He saw nothing and turned his head back to Tommy, but his eyes were still focused on a place in the distance.

"Tommy—"

Suddenly the bobber took off on a furious dive and the line from Rob's reel spun out with a terrific noise that startled them both. He grabbed the reel and pulled up, but the other end of the line turned and sped toward them, the translucent cord dropping in loose folds. It disappeared under the boat and pulled tight, so tight that Rob strained to hold it and the end of the pole snapped cleanly off and slid into the surf like a zipline. Rob stopped, transfixed, as the line spun all the way out and what remained of the pole was yanked out of his hands and disappeared with a messy splash. They were left in a deafening silence. For a moment, no one spoke.

"Reel in your line, Tom," Rob said.

Tommy did as he was told. Rob watched, stealing glances at the trees.

"I think we should go home." He revved the motor, but it guttered and failed. He tried again. Once, twice, and finally it started. Tommy looked back in the trees and saw them swaying in what could only have been a breeze, except that the air was still, deathly still. The rustling of the leaves was ominous, the creaking of the trunks threatening. If it was possible, they seemed to be leaning even closer than before. But no—Tommy tried to push it from his mind, because that was crazy. That was *unnatural*. He felt the overwhelming sense of it, the sense that something was *off*. A mosquito landed on his arm, then two, then three, and he swatted them absently, focused on the water's edge. Rob, at the tiller, looked calm but shaken. He threw the motor into gear and the water turned brown as they churned up silt in their wake, slowly gaining steerageway, picking up momentum.

A strange thing happened then: angry blotches of red appeared in the silt and bloomed fiercely, producing tiny solid things that looked unavoidably like some great bloody vomit.

"Dad, what—" Tommy began, but his father was already hitting the throttle and the boat reared back, as it had earlier in the morning but with none of that infectious joy, knocking Tommy on his butt. He grabbed the gunwale and peered over the side in time to see eviscerated bits of fish meat bob to the surface: tails, scaly hunks of flesh, fish heads. They brought with them a horrific stench, the smell of bloody death, of entrails ripped open and their contents spilled out. Tommy puked and then they left the red pool behind, speeding out and away from shore. A great churning wake followed them, but it was not the wake of the boat. It was gaining.

"Faster, Dad," Tommy said, watching this, his chest tightening.

"I'm *trying*," Rob said through his teeth.

"*Faster!*"

"I said, *I'm trying!*"

Whatever was following was now so close that Tommy could almost *see* its awful face through the swirling water. Lifeless eyes...that was what he saw. Deep, dark, soulless eyes, eyes that were watching him, unblinking, unwavering. And still gaining. A primordial fear gripped him and his fingernails sank into the aluminum side of the boat. His heart was in his throat. He felt like a mouse in a cage.

"FASTER, DAD! FASTER!" Tommy screamed. His father said nothing, but his eyes were full of fear. Tommy glanced forward and saw the worms in the bucket squirming ferociously until the boat hit a wave and the bucket overturned, sending a mass of wriggling brown slime cascading down the length of the boat. They washed around Tommy's feet and began climbing over his shoes in a sticky, gross mess.

"FASTER!!!" He pounded the side of the boat desperately, watching that bubbling, frothing shape in the water approaching with breathless speed.

"I'M TRYING, I'M TRYING!" Rob shouted, his voice high pitched, terrified. Suddenly the motor roared with effort, gave two great chugs, and died. There was a tremendous belch and black smoke billowed from the intake and hung on the still air, and the world became eerily silent.

"You sonuvabitch, NO!" Rob howled. "Dammit! God DAMMIT!" He tried to turn the engine over but the propellor was snarled in a bloom of seaweed and would not start. He tried again and again, but with no success. Tommy watched the churning wake disappear in a fizzle of bubbles.

"Dad..." he said, and then stopped as he looked up and saw the birds. They were circling directly overhead. He slapped another mosquito without looking at it, entranced by the strange avian dance playing out in the sky. All was quiet for a breathless moment, and then the entire boat lurched, sending worms careening into the water. Father and son cried out in shock.

"Get close to me, son!" Rob said, reaching out his hand. A great, scaly tentacle burst from the water then, slender, lined with spiny ridges on one side and suckers on the other. Before Rob could react it had wrapped itself around his wrist with merciless strength.

Tommy screamed. He scooted backwards into the bow of the boat until his back hit metal and then cowered as his father stood motionless, unable to comprehend the strange fate that had befallen him. That one second seemed to last an eternity, a moment frozen in time, and then Rob grabbed at the tentacle with his free hand, pulling on it with the kind of desperation known only to dying men.

"HELP ME! Tommy, HELP ME!" he shrieked. Tommy was paralyzed. He watched his father struggle but was too scared to move, too scared to help, too scared to do anything but watch. No...he couldn't watch. He threw a hand over his face, whimpering, crying. The other went straight to his mouth. A cloud of insects moved over him, gnawing, biting, feeding on any inch of him they could reach. His arms, his legs, his face, he felt their stings all over but was helpless to stop them.

"HELP ME!!!" Rob shouted again, and then the tentacle began thrashing back and forth. Rob was thrown like a rag doll from side to side and finally there was a horrible *crack!* as his arm broke and everything below the tentacle's cruel grasp bent backward a nauseating ninety degrees. He screamed then, but as he flailed past the tackle box he grabbed the knife with his other hand and buried it into the tentacle as deeply and as often as he could until it released him and disappeared back into the water. For a fraction of a second it seemed like it might be over and Rob dropped to his knees, cradling his wrist, covered in the thing's crimson blood, his glasses cracked and smeared, his breath coming in short, painful gasps; but then two more tentacles erupted from the frothy surface on either side of the boat, and the face, the awful face, rose out of the deep like some terrible ancient idol.

FEAR! The word flashed through Tommy's mind in huge red letters. *FEAR! FEAR! FEAR! FEAR! FEAR!*

It was a mottled dark green, like seaweed from the darkest depths, and gray, and those evil black eyes stared out from under a large wrinkled brow and over a set of grotesque dripping mandibles that scissored from side to side as though still working on their last meal—and perhaps still were, as scarlet bits of flesh dribbled down with the water and the spittle and made tiny splashes which only accentuated the remorseless gaze. Around these mandibles was a ring of small tentacles speckled with blood and gore. They slapped and slithered as the cloud of bugs abandoned Tommy and moved to attack the creature with an insane relish; a hideous, horrible sight. The rest of the enormous body was unseen, unknowable except for the slender tentacles which now flailed in the air above the boat, and the mystery of it, so deep and so terrible, went straight to Tommy's heart and froze it solid. Under the creature's dreadful gaze one tentacle wrapped itself around Rob's torso and squeezed, and when his arms flexed out involuntarily the other swung with spines down and severed the hand wielding the knife.

Rob stared at where the hand had been, stared almost as if he had not realized it had happened, and then he screamed again, screamed and screamed, screamed in a way that would burrow deep into Tommy's sub-conscious like an alien worm. It was worse than the cruel face, it was *much* worse, there was hardly anything worse in the whole world, how could there be, and the blood—it spurted from Rob's stump of a wrist in waves and showered the boat. The bugs—what a strange wonderland they had found—the bugs arrived in force to this irresistible meal, better even than the creature, and so did the birds, dancing out of reach of the slimy tentacles and making passes as they dared. They clawed at Rob with their talons, rending flesh from bone, and all the while they sang. The tentacle gripping Rob's stomach squeezed tightly and more blood spewed from his mouth. He convulsed and slumped over as it contracted again, and then with a pathetic sigh he was heaved over the side and the face, the awful *face*, disappeared with hardly a splash. Tommy finally regained his senses and flung his upper body over the gunwale, hands outstretched, reaching for his father, but he was far away, miles away, only Rob's head remained above the surface and he drifted farther and farther from the boat. In the murky water Tommy could just see the worms that had so recently made their getaway return to bask in Rob's bloody glory, and there, out there, almost beyond vision, the thing, the *Thing*—continued its brutal assault. Fantastic blossoms of crimson burst in a cloud below Rob's neck until all was concealed behind a brilliant haze. Flying insects alit on his forehead and marched in meaningless circles across it; they jumped when he struggled and then landed, jumped and landed, but he grew paler and weaker and his struggling grew less fierce until they covered him, coated his skin, devoured him. He screamed once more, a terrible, blood-curdling cry, and then all the fight went out of him. For a moment he was completely still and red ripples broke placidly against his ghostly face and the only movement was the black swarm as the mosquitos fed.

"*Tom*," he whispered, afraid, and then his face disappeared beneath the waves.

3

THE MONSTER

JUNE, 1978

HAWOOD

T ommy ran. He ran and ran. He didn't even notice the cuts and scratches as he scrambled over fallen logs, up the embankment, through the trees and underbrush; nor did he notice the blood, caked in grimy, glossy tracks over most of his body. It was better that he did not; if he were to stop, if he were to consider even for a moment that the horrific bath he had taken was in his own father's ichorous remains, it would have paralyzed him with such a profound despair that he may have met the same fate—if he did not drop dead on the spot from the sheer horror. So he ran. He ran without conscious thought of where he was going or what would happen next, only the primal, primordial knowledge that he must *escape*.

Escape, yes, he had done that. The bugs and the birds—he could still hear their singing off in the distance, their jealous whining—they had been distracted by his father's body, and the thing, the *Thing*—perhaps it was distracted too. He had flopped into the water with a splash that practically screamed to the world that he was there, that he was bait, like the worm, that wriggling worm; but nothing seized him, nothing gripped him in the vise of death, no squirming tentacle latched onto his foot and pulled him down into the yawning depths of oblivion; and he swam desperately, swam like he was drowning, and finally felt soft earth under his feet and climbed over the sharp sticks and logs and rocks and emerged in a shower of red water into the trees, towering over him with their own menace, and did not stop—don't stop, don't stop—and now ran, ran through the forest.

He ran until his chest hurt and his throat was dry and his lungs screamed for respite, ran until he could no longer run and there was no way that Thing could have followed him, and still he stumbled and pushed and clawed his way through the thorny vines and branches on all fours like a wild animal. He was in a panicky haze, desperate, feral, his heart pounding and his head screaming; aching, blind, his glasses smeared with blood and dirt—but mercifully not lost, thanks to the string his father had tied around the back of his head—

—*smiling as he tied the knot*—

—and the thought of it stopped him short. It burned him, seared into his mind like a tongue of flame and he finally collapsed from the pain into a stinking, sobbing wreck. A monumental sorrow welled up inside him, crushing him; he couldn't breath, he couldn't do anything. The image of his father's face returned to him, haunting, pale and ruined, bobbing in a ruby-red surf, that one word, *Tom*, echoing as if the inside of Tommy's head was a cathedral, clamorous and deafening. He clapped his hands over his ears and screamed for it to stop; begged, pleaded, but the noise continued. And underneath it, horrifying, building: that drone, the one he had heard in February, he felt it rising and he knew this time it would kill him, really kill him. He pressed his fingers into his ears until he was sure he would touch the eardrums but still the drone grew louder and louder, and he threw his head back and screamed to the heavens but only an indifferent sky looked down.

And then slowly...slowly...he felt the drone fading... Just as slowly, he pulled his fingers from his ears and listened breathlessly to the sounds of nature all around him. The whining of the birds had faded to nothing, but the air around him was still thick with the noise of chittering insects, of rustling leaves. A breeze drifted lazily from somewhere behind him, carrying the awful stench of blood and ruin, and he heard the forest sigh with it, breathe with it. And the trees—he looked up—they seemed to reach forever into the sky, up and up and up, and their tall dark shapes stared back, old and mournful. Gazing up at their swaying silhouettes, Tommy felt that suffocating fear grip his heart, the fear of inevitable, unavoidable death, and the urge to flee once again overtook him, but this time he was too weak to move. He lay there helpless, waiting for the end, for that beast to come lumbering through the underbrush behind him in a frenzy of bloodlust, but several moments passed and still there was nothing, no end, no terrifying monster. Finally the hammering in his chest subsided to a dull pounding and the adrenaline that had been electrifying his every nerve rushed out of him all at once, and was replaced with incredible, over-whelming exhaustion. It embraced him like a warm blanket, this weariness, this fatigue; it pressed him down into the dirt with the promise of relief from the storm of emotions churning in his aching head; it weighed down his eyelids and relaxed his clawing fingers and slowed his speeding heart. It called to him, sang to him, beckoning for sleep...sleep...

No...

No, he could not sleep. He knew he could not sleep. To sleep was to die, he was absolutely certain, but that warmth—that soothing, blissful darkness where the pain and the sorrow and the loss were nothing but a dream—wrapped itself about him and squeezed him tight until the only thing that remained was a swirling blue and green ocean as the sky and the trees swam before his eyes and finally they shut and the world was black.

***

The voice of Harry Chapin—*Cat's in the Cradle*—came warbling out of the jukebox in scratchy stops and starts and grew into stereophonic life as Elise sat with her head resting on her arms, watching from a table in the corner as her father paid for the ice cream. He turned while the girl behind the counter bent with the scoop—a moment Elise would have once watched with her face pressed to the glass—and he flashed a smile that begged Elise to be having fun. She returned it with an effort of her own, and it was an honest effort, but somehow the muscles around her eyes did not receive the memo and only her mouth curled in a joyless imitation. The laugh lines at the corners of her father's own eyes fell and the smile transformed into a pained look. He quickly turned back to the counter.

She watched him for a moment, the feeling of helplessness rising inside her. She felt bad for him, for both her parents; she wanted to be able to return the affection they were showing her, but somehow she just...couldn't. No matter how hard she tried, she could not seem to muster the energy even to fake it. That was a suggestion that came courtesy of Doctor Stephens: *You know, my dear, sometimes you have to fake it until you make it. Have you heard that expression? Fake it 'til you make it?* She could see him looking across the desk at her, that desk that might as well have been an endless gulf and his eyes two deep wells of condescension, and hatred boiled somewhere deep in her tummy. The appointment with Doctor Stephens was still fresh in her memory, still carried the taste of beautiful, horrible discovery. She pinched her lips together and wrinkled her nose as if there really were some awful taste lingering there on the tip of her tongue. The idea...the realization...that there were bad people out there, dishonest people, and Doctor Stephens might be one of them... Worse, that he might have tricked her daddy into thinking he *could* be trusted. It was beyond belief. The appointment had progressed in generally the same vein for the entire hour, with Elise increasingly determined to say nothing and Doctor Stephens increasingly determined to wrestle something out of her, until finally he was quite beside himself and the wisps of hair remaining on his head were standing straight up from the number of times he had run his hand through them. Now as Elise sat in the creamery listening to the jukebox hum and watching her father fumble for his wallet, she could not help but again picture the man leaning across the desk at her with his forehead wrinkles climbing ever higher into his scalp. *How exactly did it happen, Elise? How exactly did it happen?* And once again her skin crawled as the memory and the blood and the guilt raced through her mind.

Because she did know what happened to Billy Baker. She knew *exactly* what happened. She knew what happened when those kids, Billy and Jenny and Fred and Al (and she could hardly bear to admit she had been one of them too) had tricked strange little Tommy Wilford—quiet, bizarre, *weird* little Tommy Wilford—out to the clearing, to...(she paused, it was impossible to admit, surely *she* would never do such a thing...but yes)...to bully him. Her breath caught as her mind landed on the word *bully*; it was a dirty word, a *bad* word, a word for something so wicked, so vile...she squirmed with the shame of it, shrank in her seat. But that wasn't the worst. That wasn't the *secret.* It had all gotten out of hand so fast, she didn't even know how it happened, but Tommy was there on the ground screaming, and *she* was screaming, it looked like Al was going to kick his face in, the blood was gushing from his nose and mouth and eyes and—

"Hey kiddo, I got your favorite—chocolate with extra sprinkles!"

Elise looked up with a start and there was her father, her daddy, smiling, oblivious to her shame and carrying an ice cream cone that she suddenly felt she could not possibly deserve.

"Thanks, Daddy," she said in a small voice. His smile seemed to diminish again, but he held it firmly plastered across his face with an effort she would not truly appreciate until years later.

"Of course, sweetie." He handed her the cone and then sank into the seat across from her. The creamery was nestled along the main street of the little town, with a giant front-facing window that looked out onto rumbling cars, a handful of tiny shops, and the occasional passers-by. He looked out of this window now as if entranced by some magnificent vista, and stared hard. In his silence, the voice of Harry Chapin rose and fell.

Finally he spoke. "Doctor Stephens tells me you are not being very cooperative in your sessions."

Elise met his eye, surprised, and then looked quickly away, unsure of what to say.

"You know he's trying to help you—to help all of us, you and your mom and me..."

She stared at her lap. *He's tricking you!* she wanted to scream. *He's a stinking dirty liar!* But she did not know how to say this. She did not know how to make him understand.

"Yes, Daddy," she said in that same small voice. She continued staring down at her little summer dress, her father's face just a blurry shape in the corner of her eye. That shape now leaned backwards and shrank as he exhaled shakily. Then he leaned in again and put his face in one hand, and Elise realized with a jolt of shock that he was crying.

"Then what is it?" he said to the floor. "Why won't you let him help you? He says you're being difficult...you won't answer his questions... We can't afford—" and he suddenly stopped as though afraid of what he was about to say. "We just—we want you to be happy again. That's all we want, Elise. We want our little girl back."

Now more than ever she could not muster the courage to look back up at him. She could not stand the idea of her daddy crying. Somehow that was unimaginable. But the silence dragged on until the air was pregnant with it and finally she did look up, but only long enough to see the hand covering his face, and then she glanced quickly out the window. A young couple was there, walking by in the brilliant sunshine, holding hands, and they smiled when they saw her. The man tickled the woman behind the ear and she shoved him away playfully, laughing the whole time. Then he put an arm around her waist and they passed out of sight.

She blinked, staring at the sidewalk. The notion of being so cheerful and carefree reverberated like a cruel joke, an impossible dream hovering in the clear air beyond the window, just out of reach, like the stars on a cloudless night. Her stomach knotted, but she could not stop staring. And then that knot unravelled and inside was pure, sweet love for her parents, and this came boiling to the surface with overwhelming intensity that almost brought her to tears. The thought that she might tell her father the truth disintegrated into dust and all that she desired, all that she wanted, even if she might never feel joy again herself, was to at least make him happy. To make him stop crying. "I'll try, Daddy," she said, her eyes glistening and still glued to the window.

He looked up, his own eyes red and his cheeks flushed. "Thank you, Elise," he said, and his face broke into a joyless grin that was more sincere than any smile she thought she had ever seen. Then his eyes darted to her hand. "But look at your ice cream! You'll be wearing it if you don't eat up!"

He was right; the cone was soggy around its rim and great fat drops of sugary chocolate ran down its sides, over Elise's fingers, and dripped onto the table. She hadn't even noticed.

"I'll get you a napkin," he said quickly, and stood up from the table and hurried back to the counter. It was at that moment that the little bell over the door jingled and the pockmarked faces of Clark and Toby meandered into the creamery.

"—and an ass like a model," Clark was cooing, as Toby chuckled his agreement.

"Far out, man," Toby said cooly. "You sure know how to pick 'em, man."

"Can I get you boys anything?" the girl at the counter asked.

"Well hey there, sweet cheeks," Clark said. "You sure can, but I don't think it's on the menu."

Toby howled, but instead of his eyes squeezing shut with mirth they remained halfway open the entire time, lending him a stupid, vacant look.

"It's Trish," the girl fired back, unamused.

"Trish, right. Aren't you in my Spanish class?"

"Yes."

"Oh, *sí, sí!*" Clark shrieked, miming a woman in the throes of the most ecstatic passion. "*Sí! Sí! Sí! Sí! Sí, mi amor!*"

Clark and Toby both laughed at this display of wit, but Trish only scowled at them. Her voice was flat.

"What would you like from the bar?"

It took a moment for the two of them to calm down, but finally Clark caught his breath enough to say, "Well sweet cheeks, we don't really have any money. We were wondering what you have that's free." He put an elbow on top of the glass and leaned across the counter with what all present could only assume was his most charming expression.

Trish returned that expression with a look that clearly communicated she was waiting for the punchline, and said nothing.

Clark, recognizing this after several seconds, took his elbow off the counter and coughed. "We'll—uh—have a cone with cookies and cream, and uh—a float, right Tobes? Yeah, and a root beer float."

Trish rolled her eyes and started scooping the ice cream. By now the dulcet warblings of Harry Chapin had faded into silence and Toby slouched over to the jukebox to take a look. Elise's father, who had been watching the proceedings with a wary eye, returned to the table with a handful of napkins.

"It's all junk, man," Toby lamented with his face to the tiny window. "Fuckin trash, man, they don't even have the Stones. Fuckin whack, man."

"See if they have Led Zeppelin," Clark said distractedly, tugging on his beard and attempting to peek down Trish's shirt as she leaned over the tubs of ice cream. There was a moment's pause, then:

"Just *Stairway to Heaven*, man. I mean it's a good song, but fuck, they've got fuckin nothin—"

"Um, excuse me."

It was her father. Elise whirled to face him, her insides turning to ice, and made a face which conveyed that this was supremely embarrassing. Clark also turned, more slowly, as though the prospect of conflict with authority was an irresistible siren song to which he was helplessly drawn despite the opportunity to ogle a shapely girl.

"Can you please watch your language? There's a little girl here."

An uncomfortable silence hung in the air for several seconds while Clark studied his new adversary's face. Toby still leaned over the jukebox, his long hair and lanky figure presenting the image of an overgrown sloth, apparently oblivious.

Finally Clark laughed. "You hear that, Tobes? This guy here thinks you need to watch your fuckin language."

Toby lifted his head with a slightly astonished look on his face, greatly enhanced by the eternally half-lidded eyes.

"Well tell him to fuck off." And he returned to inspecting the jukebox.

Clark shrugged as if to say, *What can you do?* "You heard the man," he said.

Elise's father sat up straight, more than a little surprised to be met with such...*intransigence* (another nine dollar word) and made to stand up. Elise flashed him another meaningful look, one which begged him to shut up and leave the boys alone, but when that failed she hissed through her teeth, "Dad, *please.*" Her father raised a dismissive hand and gained his feet.

"Do we have a problem?" he asked Clark, and finally Toby pulled himself away from the little book of songs, evidently realizing that his backup might be required.

"I don't know, do we?" Clark said.

"You tell me, sport."

For half a second Clark looked slightly unnerved, but then his expression hardened. "I guess we might," he said, standing up straighter and puffing out his chest.

"I have your ice cream," Trish chimed in, perhaps hoping to defuse the situation. Her words fell on deaf ears.

"What's your fucking problem, man?" Toby asked in his usual monotone. "Why d'you gotta harsh the vibe, man?"

Elise watched her father's eyes widen with anger and increasing bewilderment. He was not quick to anger, her father, but he was not a man who liked being dismissed. He was also a man who appreciated the finer things in life, when he could get them—in particular, when it came to the English language.

"*Harsh* the *vibe?*" The words came out of his mouth with tangible disgust, like he was spitting out a rotten taste.

"Come on, Daddy, let's just *go*," Elise said, tugging on his shirt sleeve, but he would not budge. Clark saw this and his head cocked slightly to one side, his eyes widening minutely as he seemed to notice her presence for the first time.

"Elise Smithfield?" he said in an emotionless voice, all the antics temporarily gone.

"Yeah man, you're harshin the vibe, man," Toby said. "We just want our 'scream and some fuckin groovy tunes, man." Clark put one hand out to silence him.

"It must be my fucking week," Clark said quietly. The hand that he had used to silence Toby now wandered to his sleeve and produced a pack of Marlboro cigarettes that were rolled up there. He gave the box a couple of thoughtful tosses and then reached for the lighter in his pocket.

"You have a problem with my daughter, sport?"

Clark took his time lighting the cigarette and taking a long, deep drag. Toby watched all of this, looking perplexed. Finally Clark exhaled a great plume of smoke, stuck the cigarette back in his mouth and gripped it with his teeth.

"No sir, no problem," he said with his old bravado back. "Toby, get a load of this. Weirdo Will yesterday—now this bitch. She was with my brother too, can you believe that?"

Elise, with her hand still holding her daddy's sleeve, felt his muscles tense up on the word *bitch*.

"I knew it was gonna be a good day," Clark finished.

"Far out, man," Toby said for at least the second time that morning, nodding sagely, the corners of his mouth curling up in a ridiculous grin that was ill-suited to the occasion.

"Don't you—*ever*—call my daughter a bitch," her father said, and Elise sensed that deep, deep reservoir of anger bubbling up from wherever it normally hid.

"Come again?" Clark stuck his ear out cartoonishly. "Don't call her what?"

"You heard me," her father said, seething, his jaw working.

"You know, I think you're just a prude, man," Clark said, retrieving the cigarette and taking another puff. "What d'you think, Tobes?"

"Fuckin A right," Toby supplied.

"Fuckin A right. If you don't like my fuckin language," and Clark moved closer to them now, "why don't you just *fuckin leave*."

There was a long, tense silence. Elise was quite sure that if she wasn't holding her father's sleeve he would have already punched Clark Baker in the nose. The other hand still held the napkins, but it was only a matter of time before he realized that it, too, was available.

"Come on Daddy, let's go," Elise repeated, but he continued staring into Clark's greasy face.

"Don't you..." and he was trembling now, "*ever*...call her that. You get me, sport?"

Perhaps it was the way Clark was reminded of dearly departed Officer Tibbs, or perhaps it was just his nature, but he leaned into the approaching insult with visible relish contorting his face, twisting it into a hideous grin, leaned in until he was inches from Paul Smithfield's face and his eyebrows were hiked skyward in the most disrespectful expression he could muster. "Call her what? A fuckin *bi—*"

SPLAT!

Everyone froze. There was a moment of confusion as they all processed what had happened—all of them, but especially Clark, who wore most of Elise's half-melted ice cream on his face and clothes, sprinkles and milky brown goop dripping from his hair and out of his eyelashes; and Elise, still holding what was left of the cone, hardly believing it herself and staring at her hand. A tiny puff of black smoke popped from the end of Clark's cigarette as it was suddenly and unceremoniously extinguished, hanging on the silence like some comical punctuation mark.

"You're gonna regret that, bitch," Clark spat, wiping his eyes with his sleeve, but he had no time to deliver on that promise because he was suddenly leveled by her father's fist striking him squarely in the jaw. Trish screamed.

"I'm gonna call the cops! *I'm gonna call the cops!*"

"So call the goddamn cops!" Elise heard her father saying, shaking out his fingers, but then Clark rebounded from the floor, his mouth dripping red and pulled back in a snarl, and she pushed back violently from the table just before he crashed into it with his arms outstretched. Her chair tumbled backwards and deposited her painfully onto the floor, where she whipped around to face the threat and scurried backwards on her butt.

"Fucking *BITCH!*" Clark howled, spitting out blood as he wheeled around. "Toby, *help me!*"

Toby looked like he was completely unsure of what to do, his half-closed eyes darting from side to side with what may have been the greatest speed they had ever known. "Yeah man, sure..." he mumbled, still doing nothing.

Clark groped wildly, still wiping the ice cream out of his eyes with one hand. Elise's father reached to grab him but Clark flung his arm out and brushed him away, staggering to his feet and advancing on Elise.

"I'M GONNA CALL THE COPS! I'M GONNA CALL THE COPS!"
Trish continued screaming, motionless.

Paul Smithfield made another effort to latch onto Clark's wiry frame, but the boy was flushed with adrenaline and struggled savagely. Toby finally found his opening and grabbed Paul by the shoulders. They wrestled for a moment, knocking the table on its side, and then Elise's father ejected and slammed against the jukebox, where by a miracle of electronic malfunction the voice of Harry Chapin started in again.

Elise regained her feet and backed up into the wall, but once Clark was free of her father's grasp he rounded on her again.

"I know what you did to my brother, girl," he said, breathing heavily, a droplet of blood dancing precariously on his chin. "I FUCKING KNOW WHAT YOU CREEPS DID TO MY BROTHER!"

And somehow despite the immediate danger Elise plunged back into memory and the *secret* seared across her mind with burning intensity, a secret Clark Baker could only guess at, and she could see it, oh yes, every terrible detail: the beast rearing up before them with all it's fearsome horror; Fred and Al with those strange ridged tentacles erupting through their bellies, flailing like impaled insects; Jenny screaming and running, running, but not fast enough; Billy standing in front of her, paralyzed... Elise pushed him, pushed him toward the thing, shoved him desperately as she turned to run, nothing in control, no sane thought in her mind except for pure naked instinct, and that hot shower of gore exploded against her back and she knew that it was Billy, all Billy...

"Nooo," she moaned, and then reality rushed back to her and she jumped to the side as Clark slipped on the wet floor and smashed into the wall where she had been standing. For a breathless instant he stood dazed and blinking, but then the fog lifted and his eyes focused, shining with the steely glint of murder. She whirled to run but felt pain rip through her shoulder as Clark grabbed her small wrist viciously between his considerably larger

fingers and yanked her back, and for a terrifying second panic flooded her senses. Then...and it was hard to remember how...she sank her teeth into his arm until she drew blood and he released her with a small cry. Toby was battling her father by the jukebox and now there was nothing to stop Clark, nothing to hold him back, and he was no longer just a gangly troublemaker but a wounded animal, feral and dangerous. Elise flung herself at the door, skidding on the brown and red slick, the bell jingling innocently as she pushed it open a crack and slipped through, bruising her ribs on the push bar.

She was off at a run. Behind her the door banged open and she heard Clark's pained voice shouting: *"I KNOW WHAT YOU DID, YOU BITCH! I KNOW WHAT YOU FUCKERS DID!"*

His screams faded slightly as she dashed around the corner and down the narrow alleyway, the old painted brick walls rising like the uneven sides of a canyon on either side, and suddenly she felt them closing in, closing, closing, she would be crushed...and then she pushed through an open gate into a small backyard overgrown with weeds. She stopped for a moment and breathed in sharp, panicked breaths, clutching her ribcage where the ghost of a purple splotch was already forming beneath her dress. She looked around desperately for the next sign of danger, rapidly eyeing the flowerpots filled with dead soil, the small leafy vines climbing up the chainlink fence, the assortment of rusty tools leaning against the back wall, and at first there was nothing...but within seconds she heard Clark's voice echoing between the buildings like a great stoney channel, funneling his wrath toward her in rolling waves.

"...fuckers! YOU FUCKERS! Damn, my fucking LIP!..."

She whirled back to the fence, almost as tall as she was at four feet. It enclosed the tiny yard on all sides, all sides except for that little opening where the alley spilled out into it, and she knew she had only seconds. There was a large tank running beside the wall, a huge steel cylinder set on its side, and she ducked behind this just in time to hear Clark's footsteps emerge into the yard and slow down.

"Nowhere to run, girlie," Clark said, a hint of cool creeping back into his voice. She heard him padding around the other side of the tank, and knew with an instant sinking dread that of course he would find her, there were no other hiding spots, it was so obvious... Elise glanced left and right desperately and her eyes landed on a small rusty trowel in the grass. She picked this up silently and clutched it to her chest, trembling with fear. It did not seem possible that this moment could drag on any longer; Clark's careful footsteps were so close, so close, and getting closer, she could hear his ragged breathing, hear him wipe the blood from his mouth—

"GOTCHA!" Clark crowed as he came around the side of the tank and then screamed in agony as the trowel struck him in the face. His hands flew to his eyes and Elise was already running past him, dropping the trowel in the grass as she fled back down the alleyway and into the street.

Her daddy was here somewhere...her daddy... She looked back at the creamery window, saw the table turned on its side, saw the corner of the jukebox lit up with a carnival of colors, but no Paul, no Daddy—and then she let out an involuntary *Oof!* as she ran into something and the breath left her body.

It was Toby.

"Whoa, man," Toby said, and although his voice was as flat as ever his usually droopy eyes were slightly more alert, slightly more alive. His greasy hair was a tangled mess and along one side of his face from scalp to chin was a smear of chocolate ice cream and sprinkles that he must have acquired from the floor. There was a small cut across the bridge of his nose and the faintest hint of a shiner was beginning to form around one eye and along the upper ridge of his cheek bone. His shirt was slightly torn and one fingernail on his right hand was missing, leaving raw, bloody skin behind. All this she observed in one breathless second before he tried to grab her with his good hand, and she stumbled backward, nearly tripping over her heels.

"LEAVE ME ALONE!" she screamed.

"Chill out, man," Toby said, squeezing one eye shut with apparent pain and clutching his head where the shiner grew more purple by the minute. Then he opened the eye again, both eyes, revealing the hazy red whites for perhaps the first time in years, and gawked at something behind her. "DUDE! Look at your face, man!"

Elise spun around and there was Clark, a jagged red gash parting the skin in a slant from above his left eye down to his right cheek, standing in the alleyway with one hand bracing himself against the wall and the other holding his face. He pulled the hand away with a grimace and stared in shock at the blood covering his fingers. Then he looked back up at the two of them and his horror of a face screwed up with rage.

"GRAB HER! You fucking *idiot!*"

Toby looked as though someone had struck him over the head and his eyes narrowed back to their usual state. "Sure, man, I mean I fuckin tried..."

Elise did not wait for Toby to get over this slight; she sprinted past him, shoving him in the chest as she did, and Toby fell heavily onto his tailbone, gasping as the wind rushed out of him. Clark cursed and stumbled behind her, but his cries were left behind as she dashed across the street, past the post office, the library, the old church, and finally into the trees where the snaking arms of the forest pushed their way out to border the small-town hustle and bustle of Elmwood.

She crashed through the branches, thorns and twigs cutting her from head to foot and breaking off in her hair, but she knew she could not stop because Clark was still back there somewhere, knew he was angry, enraged. The memory of his accusation echoed in her head: *I know what you did, you bitch...I know what you fuckers did...* Hot guilt burned in her chest. What could he mean? There was no way he could really know...was there? Surely he just blamed the whole group of them—the ones who were still alive anyway. There was no way, no *way* he could know the truth. The muffled sound of his struggles carried up to her on the breeze, mixed with the nearby burbling of the lake, a cacophony of snapping branches and trickling water and muttered curse words, and even in her fear she felt a sudden pity, an overwhelming sorrow for the kid—really just a kid—who was no doubt grieving in the only way he knew how. Suddenly the pity was replaced with fresh terror as Clark's voice erupted out of the dense woods:

"YOU'RE DEAD, YOU HEAR ME? DEAD!"

She put on a fresh burst of speed, glancing behind her desperately for any sign of Clark's rabid face, and a magnificent pain exploded across her shin. She gasped and tumbled blindly forward, the right side of her body ricocheting off an enormous tree and sending her veering off to the left down a leafy embankment. She rolled violently down, down, until her head smacked into another tree at the bottom of the hill and the last thing she saw was the kaleidoscopic reflection of the branches as they danced and churned in the dark waters of the lake.

* * *

Will awoke with a start, awoke from the terrifying dream, the dream of the monster, the creature, the voice of his father gurgling from its unimaginable face, the grotesque syrupy liquid dripping from its sharp mandibles and from its hungry, wriggling tentacles. Immediately he regretted it, as the pain rolled across his backside and the rest of him in waves, and he grit his teeth for a moment until the shock subsided. God he was sore, even more sore than when he had fallen asleep. It felt as though his entire body had launched an impassioned protest against the angry red welts dotting his bottom and the bruises that had swollen up around them. For several minutes he lay still, breathing, feeling his young heart pound in his chest as the memory of the dream faded away, faded into foggy obscurity and finally vanished like so much mist.

He could hear his mother downstairs, making breakfast. The crackling of the skillet mixed with the enticing smell of eggs, of bacon, wafted up the stairs and through the gap under his door. Will was much too sweet to consider the possibility that his mother was anything less than an excellent cook, and when it came to breakfast he was mostly justified in this belief. Never mind the hard-as-rock biscuits and the shoe-leather beef and the lose-a-few-fillings fudge (when she made it), breakfast in the Ross household was a Sunday morning tradition, an unusually bright affair, an unconscious Hail Mary for normalcy that sometimes actually worked—for a few hours. Jane would rise early to fix the meal and make a stiff (sometimes very stiff) cup of coffee for Harry, who would come staggering semi-sober into the kitchen considerably later (how much later depended on the severity of the Saturday night explosion), and together the three of them would pretend the previous night had not happened at all until it was time for Jane and Will to go to church. Harry never went to church. Will knew better than to ask why.

The smell breathed life into Will's aching limbs and very slowly, very carefully, he sat up with the blankets bunched around his waist, looking toward the door. Each individual welt gave a spectacular cry of displeasure at this action and together they joined in a chorus of sharp pains that sent him leaping to his feet. The blood quickly rushed to his head and the dim room swam before his eyes, and Will stuck a hand out to grab the dresser, wincing as he was forcibly reminded of the raw, tingling skin on his palms.

God, he really was sore.

He slid into a pair of sweatpants and an oversized shirt—a gift from his grandmother, who never could seem to correctly guess his size despite innumerable efforts—and prodded the door open. Harry's snores were no longer rumbling from down the hall, and so Will supposed the man must already be awake and nursing his coffee. Will pushed the door open the rest of the way and slipped onto the landing, observing that while he slept his mother had cleared the myriad cans and bottles that only yesterday had littered the floor in abundance. This prompted a faint smile as he shuffled sleepily down the hall, feeling the familiar crinkly beer stains under his feet. At the top of the stairs was a shaft of light which beamed from a small square window onto the decrepit rug, and here he paused to let it warm his toes. Then he eased gingerly down the stairs.

"—fucking Carter, the man's a walking joke," Will heard his father saying as he reached the bottom step, and a small amount of levity drained from him like air leaving a balloon.

His mother, slightly short: "Language, Harry, it's Sunday."

"Sorry, Jane."

Will stepped into the kitchen. The sight was a familiar one: there stood his mother over the stove, the skillet handle in one hand and a spatula in the other, an assortment of butter, milk, cheese, salt, and other containers surrounding her in various stages of disassembly; and there sat his father, a weekend's worth of stubble adorning his gaunt face, coffee in one hand, and the other holding one side of a newspaper which lay propped against the table. As if in silent protest the paper kept refusing to stay upright, the top bending backwards solemnly like a depressed ballerina, and Harry kept snapping it straight. The headline read *CARTER GIVES STATEMENT ON SOVIET RELATIONS*. The other side said *Missing Town Cop Stokes Memories of Child Killings*. A bottle of Bailey's sat open next to the newspaper, and it did not take any imagination for Will to know that Harry was taking the edge off the morning.

"G'morning Mom. Morning Dad," Will said, sliding into a chair at the table.

"Morning, Willie," his mother said, turning her head from above the stove and smiling. Her voice was laced with sugar. She was mostly dressed for church and looked every bit the dutiful wife, but Will knew, could spot from years of experience, the thick layer of makeup barely concealing the swollen purple skin around her eye. His father grunted and returned to his newspaper.

There was a moment of quiet, and Harry flipped the paper over with a frustrated huff, revealing the article about the missing cop. He scanned the page for a few seconds and then lowered the paper slowly, looking across the top of it at Will with an expression that was something like tenderness, or at least as close as he had come to it in the last ten years.

"Willie, did you know this, uh—this Harold Tibbs?"

Will, just starting on a glass of orange juice, choked. He launched into a fit of coughing. Harry lowered his newspaper a little more, watching his son regain his breath.

"Sorry," Will finally said.

"We say, 'excuse me.'"

"Excuse me."

"'Excuse me, *sir*.'"

"Excuse me, sir."

"That's alright. Now did you know this man, Willie?" He held the paper up, held it with both hands to keep it flat, and turned it so Will could see the black-and-white portrait of a man in police uniform. The man in the portrait was trim and muscular and deadly serious, but his piggy little eyes and sweaty blonde hair were unmistakably those of Officer Tibbs, perhaps from a number of years ago. The somber, professional nature of the picture, complete with American flag resting in perfect majestic folds behind and to one side, suggested that this was a Police Academy graduation photo. Harry studied Will's face, watching for signs of recognition as Will in turn studied the face of the much younger Tibbs.

Jane frowned, glancing over from the stove. "Harry, don't show him that, there's no reason—"

"Not now, Jane," Harry said shortly. He turned the newspaper slightly so that he could look at the face again. "It says he disappeared right in the same spot where you and your friends got—uh—got into trouble."

Will nodded silently, still clutching his orange juice. The subtitle, in large, bold italics, read: *Experts Claim a Possible Connection.* For one surreal second Will was most curious about who these so-called *Experts* were, but then he imagined fat, dejected Officer Tibbs jerking away from the curb in his squad car, imagined him driving away, driving toward the Elementary School and leaving Will to face Clark and Toby alone...imagined the creature from the clearing, the creature from his dream...and he shook. Like a ponderous weight, the idea settled into his mind that he could very well have been the last person to see Officer Tibbs alive...and with it came the understanding that this was information best kept to himself.

"I think I remember him... I think from February," Will said, adopting an uncertain tone. Ten years at the mercy of his father had taught Will to be a good actor, when necessary. "After it happened... I think he talked to me and Tommy."

This was actually not a lie. In fact, it was one hundred percent true, and the truth of it made the uncertainty that much easier to invent. Tibbs had indeed interviewed them, or had at least fired off a few questions as the paramedics treated them and cleaned the blood from their faces. It was not a part of the day that begged to be remembered, not like the experience of seeing that *Thing*, of watching it bludgeon the other children like so many dolls. Will supposed the memory would have remained dormant forever if not for this sudden questioning, and with a jolt he realized he had not even remembered it when seeing Officer Tibbs the previous morning.

Harry nodded as though this was exactly what he had suspected and one side of his mouth hitched up in a lopsided smile, devoid of joy.

"Yeah, thought as much," he said, and took a bite of egg, staring into space. "Yeah, I knew the sonuvabitch too. Had a few encounters with ol' Tibbs myself, eh Janie?"

Jane did not turn around, but nodded stiffly.

"Not a fine man, Tibbs," Harry said, still staring forward thoughtfully. "Liked his women, I'd say a little too much. Fuckin hypocrite."

"Harry!"

"I said, not *now*, Jane!"

Will fixed his eyes on the empty plate his mother had set for him as an uncomfortable silence descended on the three of them. Harry broke it first.

"God woman, I ain't *said* nothin yet."

Jane remained silent, but her hand reached up to brush the hair from her eye. The purple one.

"Whaddaya want me to say, the fuckin prick arrested me? Jesus Christ."

Jane turned around, slightly red beneath the bruise and the heavy make-up. "No Harry, I want you to watch your language while your *son* is in the room."

"Oh hell, the boy's twelve, he hears worse every day. Ain't that right, Willie?"

Will continued staring down, wishing this was a rhetorical question, hoping his father would somehow forget he asked. But he knew an answer would be owed eventually. He could not quite find the breath to speak.

Harry leaned forward and lowered his voice to a dangerous whisper. "Answer me when I fuckin talk to you, boy."

Will finally glanced up from his plate and met his father's baleful gaze, looked into the jaundiced yellow eyes laced with angry red veins for just an instant, before turning his face back to the plate. "Yes sir," he said. As always, it was the only acceptable answer.

Harry leaned back again and took a sip of his coffee. "Sometimes I don't know where we went wrong with you," he said, shaking his head. Jane was silent. "Yeah, okay, the prick arrested me a few times, alright? But it was for nothin, always nothin, ain't that right Janie? You came to pick me up, you saw how he treated me, lower than the—than the shit on his boot. Fuckin prick. Prob'bly some kind of sexual deviant too, you shoulda seen the way he looked at girls, like he was fuckin em with his eyes. Fuckin pervert." He gave the newspaper another thoughtful glance and then tossed it on the table next to what was left of his eggs. "Got what he deserved, I reckon, and that's the God's-honest truth. But best you stay away from that clearing Willie, you hear me? I don't want you going over there, not that I reckon you would anyway, God knows, but you just stay away from there."

Will gave an obedient nod. "Yes sir," he said again, thinking that he would be crazy to ever set foot within a mile of that place. His mother now served him fresh eggs and bacon, and few more words were spoken. Harry occupied himself topping up his mug with more Bailey's and shooting bleary glances between the newspaper and his family. Jane slid the last of the eggs onto her own plate and then moved the skillet to the sink. The hot metal hissed and bubbled as the running water instantly vaporized and Will turned almost instinctively—catching his father's eye. He immediately stared back at the plate, feeling Harry's eyes drilling into his skull, and remained focused there until his mother announced:

"Alright Willie, it's about time to go. Run and put on something nice, and don't forget to brush your teeth."

Harry sighed tremendously, still looking at Will, a slightly hurt expression barely noticeable through the boozy pouches under his eyes. "I guess that about does it," he said, standing up with the groans and creaks of a man twenty years his senior, and heading for the door. "I'm off to Mike's."

Mike's referred to Mike's Gas, Hardware, & Sundries. Pesci's was Harry's usual haunt, a bar just around the corner from which he could walk home in a drunken stupor with a relatively high chance of making the journey safely. It was frequented by his "friends" from work and many of

Elmwood's other more colorful characters, but perhaps most important was that the barkeep knew Harry and allowed his tab to run long indeed, because he knew that Jane would be by at some point to pick up the bill. Pesci's only had one flaw, at least in Harry's mind, and that was that it was closed on Sundays. Mike's Gas, Hardware, & Sundries on the other hand was a twenty-four hour truck stop just off the highway, several miles away through the dense Vermont woods. Harry had no friends there, but it did not matter—the walk-in beer cooler was open twenty-four seven, and when Harry was of a mind (which was most Sundays) he could buy a pack or three and take them to the attached diner to knock them back. Incidentally, it was also on the return trip from Mike's that Harry was most likely to run into dear old Officer Tibbs, but of course this risk ran extremely low these days, and it was not lost on anyone why Harry would feel inspired to make the trip.

"Be careful, Harry," Jane said from the sink, where she was washing the dishes. Her food sat cold and getting colder on the table. Perhaps there was a time when she would have tried to convince Harry not to go, but that time was long past.

"Yeah, yeah," Harry said with a wave of his hand. The screen door bounced behind him and he was gone.

Jane stared after him for a long minute, and Will found himself struggling to dissect the emotions playing on her face. From the sink she could see straight down the hall to the door, and she watched as if in a dream as Harry's '63 F100 roared to life. The noise came through the mesh screen, sounding like the old pickup was growling right there in the living room. She kept staring as it sputtered slowly out of the driveway, the sound diminishing as it rolled away up the street, finally fading to nothing. Then she blinked, almost seeming to wake up, and turned to Will with her eyes blazing. "Go on, Willie, we'll be late!"

"Yes, Mom," he said, and hurried upstairs.

The hurrying was not easy on his tired, aching body, nor was it inspired by the prospect of church. Will did not especially enjoy church—he found it long and boring, and the old gray-haired congregants were nosey and touchy-feely—but he loved his mother, loved her tremendously, and he would never dream of disappointing her. Besides that, it was one of a few places where he could be with her without the grim presence of his father hovering over them. Sometimes when the fervor of prayerful singing heightened to such a pitch that for a moment Will felt truly religious, when the chords blaring out of the mournful old Wurlitzer organ hit just the right spot in Will's gut and elevated him into some spiritual stratosphere where he thought he might actually believe—during times like that even the fearful specter of his father would dissolve into nothingness, and instead he could listen to his mother sing. She would be hesitant at first, almost frightened of the dormant energy burning in her lungs, and then slowly gain in depth and volume until her real, beautiful voice joined the throng of worshippers and carried above them all. Will would stop mouthing the words and listen to his mother and feel that deep, deep love for her ache in his chest. Something about the singing reminded him of memories like those of his father before the war: just colors really, a warmth, a loving touch. He thought that perhaps this was her actual self, her true self, long buried, rising up for just moments before sinking back to its secret hiding place. It was during these moments that he found he enjoyed going to church after all.

But those moments were rare, and now as Will slid his slender frame into a button-down shirt and khaki slacks that he had outgrown a year ago, he wished that he could stay home and play with his action figures instead. This sentiment gained strength as the too-small slacks scraped over his skinned knees and bruised buttocks and clung there as if to ensure he could not forget. Even so, he hurried to get dressed and ran his toothbrush over his teeth and bounded—painfully—down the stairs to where his mother stood waiting by the door. She had donned a hat and a stylish purse, and put a gentle hand on his shoulder as she opened the screen door and the two of them stepped out into the sunlight.

It was a short walk to the church: left out of the house, then right onto Priscilla Avenue (*Prissy Avenue!* Will heard the ghosts of his classmates shrieking again) until they reached the corner where the drugstore sat, door propped open against the background of sterile white lights within—Will could just see the girl he had met yesterday sitting behind the counter blowing a bubble with her gum—and then right again onto Main Street. They walked up the street fairly quickly, but not too quickly because Jane was wearing heels. The buildings on Main Street were all smooshed together in tight rows. Here was the post office, an old building, one of the oldest places in town, with an impressive stone face and an engraved plaque over the door: *POST OFFICE AND COURTHOUSE*. It had not been a courthouse for many years, but the sign remained. And on the other side, not quite facing the post office, was the creamery. Will eyed it longingly. From here the glow of the jukebox turned the people sitting in the huge front window into dark silhouettes, but Will could tell there was an adult and a child. Then on past the library, which had been a bank many years ago and still had the huge vault door in the back, and finally they were at the church, its old New England colonial-style steeple rising severely into the clear blue sky. Just past the church was the edge of the forest, a place Will had fantasized about often, a place with tangled branches and deep shadows and, he was now certain, even deeper secrets. Will pushed the thoughts from his mind. The finger of woods that reached up and touched Main Street was short; the tight rows of businesses and municipal buildings continued on the other side as if the dense copse of trees was just an interruption in the onward march of progress. Somehow forgotten but one day doomed to the same fate.

And then they were inside where the calm, plodding notes of the Wurlitzer underscored everything in reverent tones as the crowd milled about exchanging pleasantries and finding their seats. Jane smiled and waved at a few of the other church-goers as they made their way to a pew in the back, but did not stop to speak to anyone. Within a few moments the general hubbub died down and the organist broke into a much louder Prelude, still solemn and stately, and the silver-haired, slightly rotund pastor made his entrance along with a meager choir of local volunteers, also silver-haired, all of them in white robs. They arrived at the altar and the choristers took their seats, while the pastor—Pastor Henry, as he always introduced himself after the first round of liturgy—waited patiently until the Prelude came to its joyous conclusion. He threw his hands wide.

"Welcome, welcome! God's blessings upon you and upon this house. We thank You, almighty God, for the opportunity to gather here today, to praise You and worship You. In the name of the Father, and of the Son, and of the Holy Spirit. *Amen.*" The congregation joined him on the word *Amen*, and Will dutifully crossed himself as he had observed his mother doing.

"Almighty Father," Pastor Henry continued in his shallow, quavering voice, arms still outstretched, "who knows all right and all wrong, who knows our hearts better than we even know them ourselves: purify our hearts and our minds. Lead us, O God, according to Your perfect will, strengthen us to know Your wisdom, and lead us always according to Your path. We pray in the name of Jesus Christ, our Lord."

"*Amen,*" the congregation intoned.

"The first letter of John says: If we walk in the light, as He is in the light, we have fellowship one with another, and the blood of Jesus his Son cleanseth us from all—"

"LEAVE ME ALONE!"

Pastor Henry stopped mid sentence and looked up at the still-open door, his mouth hanging open. A frigid silence swept through the congregants. It sounded like a little girl's voice, a little girl in distress. All throughout the church heads craned for a look at the owner of the voice, for the source of the interruption. Somewhere a baby hiccuped and started to cry. A slight rustle of whispers grew to replace the silence and moved through the congregation, from the back to the front. Pastor Henry blinked.

"Um—cleanseth us from—"

"GRAB HER! You fucking *idiot!*"

A male voice now, older, harsher. Now the whispers started in earnest, and Pastor Henry smiled apologetically as though someone had just suggested church was canceled. "Please, folks, please, let's just remain calm, remain calm," he said, waving his wrinkled hands in an attempt to illicit the reaction his words could not. "I'm sure it's nothing, let me just...well—" And he moved swiftly down the length of the small sanctuary until he was standing by the arched doorway, which opened onto the street.

"Willie!" Jane hissed, but Will was already sliding past her out of the pew. He recognized that second voice. He had heard it only yesterday...

Will arrived at the door next to the pastor, and sure as shit there was Clark Baker running past the church entrance into the trees. Except...except it looked like he had been mauled; there was a hideous red gash across his face and blood pouring from his lip, and his clothes were splattered with a mixture of red and brown. Toby Christiansen was hobbling along right behind him, his own face puffy and purple, a cut across the bridge of his nose, hunched over and sucking in ragged breaths.

"Jesus Christ!" Pastor Henry exclaimed and clapped a hand over his mouth. The people standing nearest to him gasped, but Pastor Henry was much too distracted to notice. Toby also glanced up at the church door in mild surprise as he passed, but put his head down and kept running.

"*Clark!*" Toby called out in a wheezy voice, with an expression that suggested he had been in a protracted struggle to get that one word out. "Fuck, man! CLARK!"

And then, heightening the confusion even further, a man Will did not recognize burst out of the creamery down the street, wincing at the enormous goose egg growing on his scalp and cradling his hand, from which blood seemed to be oozing in great fat drops. He stumbled onto the sidewalk, staggered into the road.

"STOP THOSE KIDS!" he shouted, his words slurred together and his eyes manic. "*STOP THOSE GODDAMN KIDS!*"

"Jesus *Christ!*" the pastor said again, but Will was already off at a run. Somewhere behind him he heard his mother's voice:

"*Willie! Willie, come back, where are you going?*"

He wasn't entirely sure himself, but he knew he would find it if he followed them into the dense woods, somewhere back there, somewhere in the trees. A strange warm courage was kindling in his chest, the same courage he had felt when he pulled Tommy Wilford from the jaws of that awful creature. He could hear Clark and Toby panting and breaking their way through the underbrush ahead of him, and then Clark's voice, murderous, terrifying:

"*YOU'RE DEAD, YOU HEAR ME? DEAD!*"

Will paused at the edge of the forest. Who was Clark shouting to? Who was the girl? The shouting and the crackling of broken twigs continued unabated, and finally Will gathered his courage again and pushed into the dark shadows after them. It was easier going, he imagined, for him than for the older, taller boys. He hurried along in their wake, gaining; their voices were growing louder all the time and now he could hear them clearly.

"Shit, man, shit! *Fuck!* What did you do?"

"Shut the hell up, I didn't do anything to her."

"She looks *dead*... Oh God, Clark, she looks dead!"

"I said *shut the hell up!* She's not fuckin dead—see, she's got a pulse. You want the whole fuckin town to hear?"

Will eased into a careful walk, trying with all his might to step onto soft broken pine needles and not the minefield of twigs. Ahead of him the ground dropped away in a steep hill, and the two teenagers were huddled at the bottom by the water's edge, crouching over a dark, limp shape. Will could just make out a small hand lying tangled in the underbrush. He sucked in a breath. Toby stood up suddenly and Will ducked behind a fallen log, but when he hesitantly raised his head Toby was just standing next to the body with a hand clasped to his forehead—and Will could recognize it now, could recognize the body, the long blonde ringlets, the unmistakeable slight form of Elise Smithfield.

"Her *head* though man... Clark, man, her fucking *head*. What are we gonna *do?*"

"How many times to I have to tell you to *shut the fuck up!*" Clark hissed. "I'm *thinking!*"

"Oh God, man... Oh *God!*"

"Can you be quiet for five seconds! Help me pick her up."

There was a pause then in which the only sounds were grunting and rustling and the quiet lapping of ripples against the shore.

"God, man, she's fucking *heavy.*"

"Just get her legs."

They struggled briefly and then traipsed off to the left, carrying the swinging body down the shore until they passed out of sight behind a rocky ledge. Will watched them warily, considering how best to follow, when a tremendous commotion exploded in the trees behind him and the man he had seen leaving the creamery erupted out of the woods, covered in leaves. Will said a silent prayer of thanks for the dense thorny vines that blocked him from direct view and slunk further out of sight, watching the man approach the edge of the embankment. From up close Will could see that the man had taken a beating; the goose egg on his forehead was a brilliant purple and oozed syrupy lines from a cut that angled jaggedly across it, matting his patchy hair with dark red clots. His clothes were ripped in a few places and covered with mysterious brown splotches that clung wetly to his skin. The knuckles on his right hand were cracked and caked with blood, which continued to drip through his fingers and splash noiselessly to the ground. And none of this he seemed to notice, as he stumbled to the top of the hill and peered down with eyes that were wild with rage.

"ELISE!" he called desperately, turning his head in all directions as fast as the huge bump on his head would allow. *"ELISE!"*

The man stood there for a moment, gripped with fear and anger, and then crashed back into the trees on his right. It suddenly occurred to Will that he should tell this man to stop, come back, you're going the wrong way... But he did not, and now the man's cries disappeared off into the distance. And the forest was silent.

* * *

You're dead, you hear me? Dead!

Tommy's eyes flew open and for a moment he looked straight up into a dizzying, spinning world of thick tree trunks stretching up into infinity against the cloudless sky, all of it obscured as though a pink film had been placed across his eyes. Then slowly the world stopped spinning and came into focus, and Tommy became aware that something soft was covering his limbs. The realization crept into his mind in an abstract haze, pushing through the dense fog of half-remembered emotions and some strange, blinding pain, but he was too exhausted for it to register as anything except the simple, matter-of-fact thing that it was: *there's something on my arms and legs.*

He tilted his head to one side and the world swam again, but once it stopped he saw through that pink tinge that his arm was buried under a thick net of ivy. The large, ear-like leaves covered his arm so completely that it was not even visible. Strange...definitely strange. He could not remember falling asleep in a bed of ivy. He rocked his head carefully to the other side and observed the same thing. And then down to his toes...

Suddenly he sat bolt upright, disrupting a cloud of mosquitoes and ripping up shallow ivy roots as he scrambled into a sitting position. Pain flashed through his legs and he clamped his teeth together hard, fighting the scream. The roots...the roots were growing *into* his legs. He looked back up at the sky, tears pooling in his eyes, and all at once he remembered everything, every horrifying detail. The boat, the *face*, his father's screaming...and the blood... He reached up with one sticky arm and tried to wipe the pink film from his glasses, but it was everywhere, it was everything, it covered his whole body, and the *pain*, oh God the pain.

He took several shallow breaths and gulped back the cries that were building in his throat. His father was gone...gone... That creature, that *Thing*, it had taken him—no, not taken...*murdered*... Tommy shivered uncontrollably as he pictured his father slumped over the spiny tentacle, blood dripping from his stump of a wrist and from his gut where the tentacle squeezed him, the birds ripping away his flesh in ribbons, the mosquitos sucking the life out of his face. A trigger went off in his gut and Tommy heaved violently, but there was nothing in his stomach but sour bile; it dripped down his front onto his already ruined clothes, stinking and yellow. He squeezed his eyes shut, willing the images to go away, but in the darkness they only grew monstrously, and when he opened his eyes again he was confronted with the hideous maze of tiny roots burrowing into his skin.

The buzzing sound started again...the droning sound... Very quietly, almost silent; he felt it more than he heard it, gradually growing out of nothing and filling every inch of his being. He fought it back. That sound was death.

He knew immediately that he had to move, to get out of there. The trees overhead swayed ominously and the sunlight filtering through their branches danced on his face, and Tommy could sense, could intuit, that there was danger here. But his *legs...* He grimaced as he grabbed a fistful of the leafy plants and felt microscopic daggers stab his legs in a thousand places—but the ivy could not stay, could not could not could not. He tried to pull and the pain crystallized into a fire of agony that swept down to his toes and up to his head and he nearly fainted again. The trees swayed more violently in the still air and for a moment Tommy almost thought that he could hear their anger pulsing through the forest, ancient, inhuman...

He gripped harder. The pain was unbearable, unimaginable, and the little specks of red showing through the green leaves nearly made him puke again, but he pulled hard and slowly the things started lifting off of him, showering him with tiny droplets of his own blood. He stopped to breathe and felt the air escape him in a long, low moan, and then hitched in a breath and pulled harder. Finally with a stifled cry the last of the ivy ripped out of his calves and Tommy hurried to his feet, panting, blood running down his legs in long sticky trails onto another ruined pair of shoes, and what little bile remained in his stomach upchucked onto the leafy bed. From far away the sound returned to him: the cackling of birds, the humming of insects. One hand reached up vacantly and wiped his mouth as he stared off into the distance, and then panic set in and he stumbled away up a gentle slope that he sensed must lead away from the lake.

Dead branches crunched under his feet; the sound was somehow both frightening and hypnotic. The swaying trees and the vicious calling of the birds faded away behind him and now Tommy settled into a strange kind of scrabbling march, one where he knew he must keep going—yes, keep going until he reached town, reached civilization...reached his mother. God, yes, his mother. His thumb popped between his teeth even as he walked. He could feel the huge weight of that terrible energy, that terrible cloud hovering between them and he suddenly wished to shrink that cloud down to nothing, to make it as small as possible, and he almost didn't care if he ever learned the secret so long as he could be near her again and maybe not feel this awful pain. But where was town? He shuffled forward with the blind hope that *away* from water meant *toward* safety, but churning inside him was the very real fear that he could be wandering farther and farther out into the Vermont wilderness, where he may never be seen again.

He reached the top of the slope and looked back the way he had come: the hill slipped away behind him, covered in pine needles and moldering leaves left over from the previous autumn, and disappeared into an indistinguishable mass of green and brown. No sign of danger, no sign that he was being followed. He turned ahead again and saw that the forest here was littered with fallen trees, and a vague memory that Vermont was logging country passed through his mind. He had learned something about it in school that year, but the specifics were hard to recall. Regardless, the carcasses were everywhere, scattered across the uneven ground among the living trunks like prehistoric monoliths, covered in moss and reeking with the sickly sweet smell of decay and sap. Tommy felt the air vibrate with that strange anger. Off to his left the ridge twisted away in a wide curve that vanished into the deep shadows of the forest.

There was a voice. He cowered and spun his head toward the sound, back to the left where the ridge curled around in its graceful arc. There were people there, two people, carrying something between them—something heavy. They had not noticed him, but staggered half-blindly up the hill, trying and failing to keep some piece of the thing from dragging in the dirt. Tommy squinted through his hazy glasses and could almost see it, could just...just make out...

His eyes widened until he could see blue sky around the pink lenses and the breath caught in his chest. It was a body. A girl's body.

His heart skipped a beat—two beats. He could hardly breathe. A child's lifetime of lessons about strangers and kidnappers rushed through his head in a fraction of a second and he knew immediately he needed a place to hide, fast. His eyes darted frantically and landed on the nearest fallen log, a massive old thing with enough leafy branches to keep him out of sight. He sprinted forward until he was level with it and ducked down as quietly as he could. The open wounds on his legs screamed in protest and he jammed a fist in his mouth to keep from crying. The people—he could only assume they were murderers, or worse—drew closer now, and he heard their ragged breathing over their shuffling footsteps.

"Could you walk any slower?"

"Sorry man, her fuckin legs keep trippin me."

Tommy recognized the voices...or at least one voice. Clark Baker—Billy's older brother. A chill stole over him as he remembered the day in the clearing...remembered Billy vanishing into oblivion. Like an awful replay he saw the blurry tentacles flailing in the air...saw the blood raining down... The scene of his father's own violent demise flashed before him and the enormity of it threatened to overwhelm him again. His fist was still pressed into his mouth and he bit down on it harder, tasting fresh blood as he attempted once again to drive away the droning noise that was building in his ears. He felt a sort of bizarre kinship with the gangly boy on the other side of the log, but it evaporated in seconds when he heard Clark's voice, so close, too close:

"Lay her down here."

And then the terrifying dry rustling of leaves just feet away—even without seeing it Tommy knew they had laid the body in the dirt just next to wear he sat leaning against the grimy trunk. His senses kicked into gear; he heard every shuffling step, every whisper, felt the tension rippling through the space between them, like electricity, saw the droplets of blood curling down his legs in glossy trails and pooling thickly in the wet soil, smelled the sour odor of sweat.

"What are we gonna *do*, Clark?" asked a voice Tommy did not recognize. It was flat and monotonous, and very scared.

Clark was silent for a long minute before answering, and in the stillness Tommy could clearly hear the clicking of a lighter—it seemed to take multiple tries, like the hand holding it was struggling with the simple act—and then a pause, a long exhale. "I don't fuckin know," he finally said, his voice small and shaking. "I just don't fucking know..."

"I thought you said you were thinking—"

"Yeah, Tobes! I am fuckin thinking. What the fuck do you want me to say?"

This time Tobes was silent, and when he did finally speak it began with a squeaky crack. "I—I mean, we could try to wake her up..."

"Go ahead, you can fuckin try."

"Or, you know man, take her to the hospital or somethin..."

"Jeezum Crow Tobes, are you out of your goddamn head? The whole fuckin town heard me sayin I was gonna kill her. How the fuck do you think this looks?"

Another pause.

"But you didn't really, you know...didn't... I mean, you didn't, right man? You didn't really—"

"Are you fuckin kidding me? No, I was just gonna...gonna mess her up a bit is all. I was just gonna mess her up, after...after... *Fuck,* Toby, have you seen my fuckin *face?*" There was a phlegmy spitting sound and some globular red stuff impacted the ground next to Tommy's ankle. "She must have tripped or something, I don't fuckin know."

"Yeah, man. What *did* happen to your face?"

"She *hit* me!" and Clark's voice cracked too, on the word *hit.* "She fuckin *hit* me, fuckin *bitch.*" There was a spasm of flapping clothes and a dull *thud,* and Tommy imagined Clark kicking the small body. "With a shovel. Right on my fuckin *nose.*"

"Far out, man," Toby said.

Clark let out another long breath and the smell of cigarette smoke drifted down in a dense cloud, filling the air. "But like I said, you can fuckin try to wake her up if you want."

All was quiet for a moment as Toby considered this. Then...hesitantly at first...there were slow, crackling footsteps, and Tommy pictured him walking carefully until he was level with the girl's head. What followed would have been humorous if it was not so deadly serious. There was a rhythmic rustling noise—quiet at first, growing louder and more hysterical the longer it went on. Tommy's curiosity finally got the better of him and he lifted himself carefully from the ground into a squat. His legs burned and polka-dots of fresh bright crimson bloomed across his thighs, but childhood curiosity overcame both pain and inhibition, and he turned, just as carefully, and raised his head so that he could watch through the thick branches of the dead tree. Slowly the scene on the other side came into focus through the veil of dried leaves, and he saw clearly the angry red slash across Clark's face where the girl had hit him. Dried blood was caked along the edges and the slightest hint of white bone shone brilliantly from between the flaps of skin across the bridge of his nose. Somewhere in the back of Tommy's mind a hidden door flopped open and out came...his mother's voice in a shrill scream, nothing like her real voice, shrieking like the steam from a kettle, terrified and angry all at the same time and threatening to crack his head wide open: Curiosity killed the cat! *Curiosity killed the cat! CURIOSITY KILLED THE CAT!*

He shivered. Curiosity killed the cat, he remembered, yes—

—*the cat*—

—but this was different, this was—

—*blood like you couldn't believe*—

—nothing like that, and he could not stop himself from leaning in closer, from pulling apart the branches for a better look...

Toby was hunched over the body, his long mangy hair falling in curtains around his face, his oversized clothes hanging off his slender frame, also in curtains, and his arms flailing wildly as he danced from foot to foot around the shoulders and head of the small figure in the dirt. Clark stood to one side, blocking Tommy's view of the girl's face, taking shaky drags on his cigarette and staring at nothing. For a moment Toby seemed to lose energy, but then he swooped down until he was practically nose-to-nose with the poor girl and a series of bizarre whooping sounds clawed their way out of his throat. These too grew in volume and pitch as he resumed his peculiar dance, until finally Clark chucked his cigarette at him and lunged with his palms out.

"Enough!" he snapped. "She's not fuckin wakin up, okay?"

He shoved Toby away from the body and Tommy had, for the first time, a view of the girl's face. He knew that face. The door in the back of Tommy's mind flung wider still and out poured perverse laugher, the laughter of two girls watching Al kick his eyeballs in, raucous and rotten and everywhere. His nose suddenly ached with the memory of being broken and the hairs on the back of his neck stood straight up. The droning noise swept over him once more and this time he was powerless to stop it, and it mixed with the laughter and the screaming in a cruel symphony of pain that swirled around and around him until it was all he knew, all he could sense, and the festering wound of his father's death, not even hours old, ripped apart and a stream of pitiful cries for mercy spilled out into the chaos.

...HELP ME! Tommy, HELP—

—CURIOSITY KILLED THE CAT! CURIOSITY KILLED THE—

—ME! HELP ME!!!—

—CAT! CURIOSITY KILLED THE CAT! CURIOSITY—

—Stop! STOP!—

—KILLED THE CAT! CURIOSITY KILLED—

—STOP IT! Al, STOP IT!—

—THE CAT! CURIOSITY KILLED THE CAT!—

—Tom...

His mouth dropped open and some kind of rattle came out, and the earth rushed up to meet him but then he blinked and he was still standing with his face pressed into the dead branches, staring at the world through his pink-tinged glasses. And through the branches, Clark and Toby stared back at him.

* * *

"Shit! Oh, *shit!*"

"Shut *up*, man, it's just a little kid."

"Yeah, but he saw... Clark, he *saw—*"

"He didn't see fuckin anything. Jeezum...is that Tom Wilford? It really is my fuckin week, just my fuckin *week!* Hey! Look at me... You didn't see anything...you didn't see *nothin*...ain't that right?"

Will crept up the ridge as quickly as he dared, taking care to maintain a safe distance between himself and the Dynamic Duo at the top of the hill. Even from here, Clark's voice—equal parts furious and frightened—carried easily to where he lay flat against the steep side of the ridge, only his eyes peeking over in an effort to see what was going on up ahead. This part of the forest was a massacre of felled trees, and between that and the spiny rock lining the edge of the ridge where it slipped away back into the denser woods below, there was little to absorb the sound but dirt and broken twigs. He gripped that spine with both hands and shuffled painstakingly along the side of the steep slope with his cheap brown dress shoes scrambling for purchase, determined to stay hidden. He eyed the commotion up ahead in between careful glances at where to place his hands and feet. His sore palms burned and his muscles ached, but he had the unexplainable sense that he was in too deep to turn back. If nothing else there would be hell to pay for the damage already inflicted to his church clothes, and he was in no hurry to face it. In for a penny, in for a pound—he pressed his body against the craggy hill and crept along. At the top, Tommy Wilford stammered out an incoherent reply, but the specifics were neither audible, nor impressing the two teenagers.

"Whoa whoa whoa, take it easy," Clark finally interrupted, in a tone that was anything but reassuring. "I still can't fuckin believe it. Get a load of this Tobes, this is *the kid*, I mean *the fucking kid.*"

Toby was silent and stood frozen in place, continuing to stare at Tommy through those heavy eyelids, his arms still spread slightly in the ghost of his wild dance. Even from a distance Will saw it as plainly as if he was standing right there, and his imagination supplied the usual dopey "Far out," even though Toby himself remained uncharacteristically silent.

"Well don't just stand there, kid. Come join us." There was a short beat, in which Tommy made a jerking motion like he was trying to bolt, then: *"Hey, what are*—I said—" and Will stopped breathlessly to watch as Clark threw his sweaty body across the log and hauled Tommy over in a tangle of arms and legs. Tommy's face screwed up with pain and he cried out pitifully as his shins scraped over the rough bark, and then he fell to the ground next to Elise, gripping his calves. "—*come join us!* What, you were so interested a minute ago, not anymore?"

Will continued shimmying along the rocky ledge, his heartbeat rising. His eyes were glued to the scene, hardly aware of where he was putting his hands anymore until he felt a pinch on his neck and slapped it. He looked down at the tiny red smear on his palm. A mosquito.

"I—I didn't—didn't mean to watch you," Tommy mumbled, his voice choked with emotion, his lip trembling dangerously.

"Oh yeah? That's not what it *fucking* looks like."

"Honest," Tommy said desperately.

"So you just normally hang around in the woods looking like—like—Jesus *Christ*, what's all over you, anyway?"

Tommy did not answer immediately, and instead his eyes squeezed shut and huge fat tears leaked out. Clark recoiled for a second, but his face was unmoved. Will slapped another mosquito.

"Answer the *fucking* question!"

"It's—it's..." Tommy stuttered and his lip trembled harder and finally he wailed, "It's my *daaaad*..."

Clark balked and his expression soured into a look of disgust, made horrible by the gory slash across his face. "What the fuck is that supposed to mean?"

Tommy opened his mouth but no sound came out; his breath came in short gasps and then he curled into a ball and cried harder.

"Dude, leave him be," Toby said, his flat voice rising slightly, a hint of color in his pockmarked cheeks. Clark rounded on him.

"Give me a fuckin break," he snarled. "Don't you know who he *is*?"

"Yeah man, but—"

"He was *there*, man! He was there too, the whole fuckin time, I mean, what are the—what are the *odds*? What are the *fuckin odds*, man?"

Toby looked confused, as if this was a serious calculation for which he was woefully unprepared.

"Impossible, right? Fuckin impossible, I mean really fuckin insane..."

Tommy was still crying, bawling, the tears running in trails down his face, clearing away the only places that were not colored a nauseating fleshy pink. His small hands were pressed into his ears and a long, silent scream was issuing from his mouth. Cackling, cawing noises drifted down from overhead, and Will looked up to see a trio of vultures circling above the place where Clark now paced madly, his eyes bulging out of their sockets, the spit popping from his lips.

"Give it a rest... *Give it a fuckin REST!*" Clark hissed. *"Agh!"* He slapped his own neck and pulled the hand away.

From his place over the hill, Will did the same.

"I'm sorry, I'm sorry," Tommy sobbed, squeezing his head between his palms and shaking it, his eyes still mashed shut. *"I'm sorry, I'm sorry, I'm sorry..."*

"YOU'RE *NOT* FUCKING SORRY!" Clark howled, "NONE of you! Not a fucking one of you, not fucking sorry at all, not... It's—it's not *your* brother that's fuckin d-d-*dead!*"

"I'm sorry, I'm sorry, I'm sorry..."

"SHUT—*UP!*" And Clark kicked Tommy, kicked him hard, and Tommy's hands flew from his head to his gut. For a moment neither of them spoke and the only sounds were Tommy's crying, Clark's labored breathing, the cawing of birds...the buzzing of insects...

* * *

"Clark, somethin's not right, man," Toby said, fear in his voice. It was the first sound Elise heard, and she cracked her eyes open slowly, her head pounding. Everything was dreamy and slow, so slow, she couldn't see straight, couldn't think straight. And oh *God* did her head hurt.

Floating far above her, moving thickly through the air as if it was made of honey, was Clark Baker. The world was spinning and so was Clark, round and round and round and somehow staying put all at the same time. Fear washed over her; she remembered something, remembered...oh, but it was impossible to recall, there was something about Clark... He looked hideous, his face was split down the middle and she had the vague idea that she was responsible for it. A hazy thought swam in and out of focus before her, the idea that she had been running, must keep running. The blood pulsed in her ears. She tried to lift her head but it felt extremely heavy and she gave up.

"Clark... Clark, man, something isn't *right.*"

"Would you be fuckin quiet! God, I can't hear myself think with you around!"

Elise blinked hard, tried to clear her head, but it was swimming in fog. It was so hard to remember anything, to remember where she was, or *why*, or... Still that fear kept racing through her. She felt something tickling her arms, something prickly, but...oh *God* her head, she couldn't lift it to see, and the only view was up, up up up, straight up, and way up there, way up in the sky, swimming through the honey-air high above Clark was a huge flock of birds. They made circles too, but unlike everything else those circles were not in her head. She squeezed her eyes shut and looked again, but they were still there, still circling, grim and black and deadly.

"So what is it, Four-eyes?" It was Clark again, his voice laced with poison, leaning over with his hands on his knees. Elise lolled her head slightly in his direction (and felt fireworks go off inside her skull), and now she saw a boy, a little boy, curled in a ball, his small chest heaving up and down, his fingers shoved into his ears, and he looked familiar, he looked like—

"What is w-w-what?" Tommy managed to say in between sobs.

"What brings—get your *fucking fingers* out of your ears! What brings you out here to the goddamn middle of nowhere?" Clark asked, hovering over him with his horrifying face twisted in rage.

"We w-w-were f-fishing," Tommy whispered, trembling all over. "W-we were f-f-f-f—" But then the tears started again uncontrollably and he was unable to speak.

Clark stood up straight, put his hands on his hips, and for one instant he looked quite grown up. Toby, meanwhile, began swatting at the air as if he had gone crazy.

"Fuckin—ah! Fuckin mosquitos!" Toby said, flailing and slapping his arms. Clark regarded him briefly and then turned back to Tommy.

"You're not making a goddamn bit of sense, boy-o," Clark said icily. The bugs were landing on his face, but he didn't seem to notice. "And—*hey!*—and you better start making sense real quick, you get me?"

Tommy's eyes were screwed shut, and Clark seized his collar and shook him violently.

"I said, *you fuckin get me?*"

Tommy nodded vigorously, his eyes wide now and glued to Clark's manic face through his smeared glasses. "Y-y-*yes!*"

"Doesn't fuckin seem like it," Clark said, and he pulled Tommy's face close to his own. "So I'm gonna ask again. What are you doin out here—what did you *see?*"

Tommy shook his head for several seconds before mustering the courage to speak. "N-n-nuh-nothing," he finally said. "I d-didn't see n-n-nothin, honest."

"You expect me to believe that when I saw you watching us through the fuckin tree?"

Tommy's eyes widened even more until it seemed impossible his head could actually contain them, his mouth working but nothing coming out. "Y-yeah," he finally said in a tiny voice, barely more than a squeak. "I j-just heard you w-w-wondering how to w-wuh-wake her u-up. I only came over because—because—because my dad was..."

His eyes jammed shut again and the air crackled as if energized by some great and terrible electric field, bristling with tension, vibrating with menace. Even Clark sensed it and loosened his grip, and Toby, off to one side, finally stopped slapping his arms and stared blankly at the sky with his mouth hanging open.

"Man, somethin's just *not right!*" Toby yelled. "I keep telling you, I'm telling you man, somethin is not right!"

"SHUT UP!" Clark screamed, his eyes still locked on Tommy, his grip tightening again. "Tell me what fuckin happened!"

* * *

Will was almost level with them now, and he felt the atmosphere ripple as the surge of energy swept past him. He stopped and turned to look over his shoulder, but all he saw there were the trees in the forest down below swaying in the breeze. They rocked back and forth like the trees he had seen in movies of hurricanes, except...his blood froze...the air was completely still. His heart beat faster—maybe in an effort to move the syrupy, cold blood—and he pulled himself fast against the side of the ridge. Another quick glance over his shoulder, and there again, behind him, the trees still swung from side to side, the air buzzing with some unknowable hatred. Immediately he imagined himself slipping down the ridge into those angry depths where God knew what fate awaited him, and he pressed his cheek into the rock.

"My d-dad was—was—he w-was..." Tommy's eyes were shut tight tight tight and now he clamped his hands down over his ears and screamed, screamed and screamed, screamed like he was experiencing the most exquisite torture, and there seemed to be no end to it, no gap, no breath, it went on for half a minute or more, maybe a full minute—hell, maybe an hour.

Clark released him, suddenly terrified, and scrambled backwards next to Toby. "OKAY MAN, OKAY!" he shouted above the scream. *"Okay, okay, okay..."*

And now the scream morphed, transformed, it formed into words, and the words were impossible to distinguish at first, all running together and then pulling apart like so much taffy.

"DEADDEADDEADDEADDEAD DEAD DEAD DEAD DEAD... DEAD... DEAD..."

A stone dropped into the pit of Will's stomach. From the look of it, Clark was experiencing the same. He staggered backwards from where Tommy sat in the dirt next to Elise's frail little—

—corpse—

—body, his mouth a perfect O of fright, his eyes stretched wide in terror, and suddenly he was covered in flies, yes, flies and mosquitos in an orgy of biting, of feeding. Tommy was covered too, and Elise, and Toby, and the two older boys flailed and cried with disgust as they swiped madly at their skin to remove the swirling black spots. Tommy sat completely still, that horrible, horrible scream still pouring from his mouth in clipped, broken verses of *"DEAD! DEAD! DEAD! DEAD! DEAD!"* Now two more sets of screams joined the first, as Clark and Toby jammed their fists into their eyes, trying to keep the flies out, but it was hideous, it was awful, it was useless, and the bugs swarmed in, into their eyes, into their mouths, into every opening they could reach, and still Tommy's piercing voice sang *"DEAD! DEAD! DEAD!"* even as the grotesque insects descended on him too, and on Elise.

That strange warm courage kindled in Will's chest and roared into flame, and in an instant he scrambled over the ledge and crawled across the short distance between them on all fours. There was nothing sane about it, nothing comprehensible or intelligible in his brain except for one thing, and that was CAPTAIN ROSS.

He reached Elise and grabbed her arm, swarming with spiders, with ants, and suddenly her eyes flew open, and in that short space before the flies descended her face was a mask of horror. Will pulled savagely, pulled as hard as he could. She was a dead weight, a *dead weight,* and the phrase bounced around inside his head alongside CAPTAIN ROSS in a cacophony of adrenaline and fear, but somehow she started to move, and then slowly she put a hand out, both hands, and now she was moving on her own, crawling and scrabbling her way sluggishly across the dirt floor next to him until they both reached the ridge and flopped over the side. Will stayed until Elise had slid to a gentle stop at the bottom, and he hesitated for a second, hesitated because some unspeakable feeling suggested that she was not safe down there in the trees. But that was crazy, and he flung himself back over the ledge to go get Tommy.

He did not get far. Within seconds there was a terrible *CRACK!* from deep beneath his feet, a soul-shattering rending of rock from rock that he felt more than heard, felt in his core, vibrating in his bones, and he stopped short. For one crazy moment the air was packed with a swarming mass of flies buzzing sickeningly as they leapt from the other boys in a frenzied cloud and descended once again to feast. Clark and Toby let out strangled gasping cries, but these were quickly stifled as the swarm moved in. Tommy abruptly stopped screaming, and his eyes, partially shielded behind those giant glasses, widened beyond all human possibility into an expression of pure terror.

The noise...it had not stopped, only elongated into a thunderous rumble that swelled from below. The earth shook and buckled and then parted in a wide gash that opened like a seam between Will and the others, and he dropped back onto his rear, gazing in shock. A mass of stones and dirt erupted out of the pit, and so too did one spiny leg, and then another, and another. The ground heaved and swelled, heaved and swelled as the strange creature breathed as if for the first time, in great, shuddering breaths, and then lifted itself in a tangle of legs and dead roots and suffocating dust up, up into the air, until it hovered over them, huge and horrible.

Will opened his mouth to scream but there was no sound, no breath. He scooted backwards on his bottom, his feet and hands throwing up small clouds of dirt until he reached the edge of the ridge. Behind him the world dropped away to the angry listless depths below.

It was a spider, or something much like one, enormous and brown and hairy and many-legged. Its body was sectioned in two just like a spider, and the nauseatingly fleshy abdomen, with a great black spot in its center, bobbed slowly, heavily, down and up in a rhythm that was terribly alive. Bulging, breathing, groaning under its own weight, the creature was at least ten feet tall, and its legs fell heavily in innumerable clattering steps as it situated itself above Clark and Toby and Tommy. The teenagers were on their knees now, clawing at their faces, tearing the skin clean off, and still the flies crawled in, more and more and more of them, and still more swarmed the creature. Its legs had the same spiny ridges that Will had seen four months ago on that *Thing*, the one in the clearing, and if that was not similarity enough there was the *face*...evil and cruel and cold...great black orbs staring from under a heavy wrinkled brow and over a set of sharp, dribbling mandibles. It turned this gaze on Clark.

Will wanted to scream—Clark couldn't see it, God he couldn't *see* it, he was flailing and clawing at his throat, at his eyes, and in one horrible motion the spider ripped Clark's head from his body, and a cloud of bugs flew wetly from the hole in his neck. Pulpy chunks of brain and skull rained down as the mandibles went to work, all the while his hands twitched madly in the air where his face had been, blood spurting in jets, spraying the trees. With an awful *thump* he hit the ground and kept twitching until the last of the blood had oozed into the dirt.

Toby stumbled to his feet, stood like he meant to run, like he sensed through the hundreds of spindly legs forcing their way into his every cavity that something far worse was here. But his body was a wreck, his face, his hands, all of him dripping with blood and pus, and after several agonizing steps he flopped back to the ground and carved fresh tracks out of his skin with his fingernails. The spider—the creature—moved over him, the legs scuttling, heavy and insectile, the great swollen abdomen lurching up and down, and with ferocious speed the face descended.

A hoarse, choked little cry gurgled from Toby's throat—just one pitiful, blood-curdling moan—and he was quiet.

The whole world, everything, *everything* started spinning, converging on Will as if he had just dropped into the middle of a giant magnifying glass. He wanted to move, wanted to hide, wanted to slide the last few inches until he was concealed behind the ridge, and he shoved back, hard. His eyes widened as he felt the ground disappear beneath him and then he tumbled, rolled, cascaded down the rocky slope until he landed with a *thump* in the grass next to Elise. His head swam and his vision dissolved in and out of focus, and he gasped painfully for air that would not come. His heart pounded, his chest spasmed. The sky and the trees and the crumbling hillside were still spinning...spinning...slowing...and finally settled. Elise lay next to him in a bed of ivy, white and still as the grave, almost invisible beneath the leaves. He waited to see one small, quivering breath, and rolled onto his back.

From high up on the ridge came a confusion of scurrying, scuttling footsteps, and the spider's spiny front legs preceded it over the ledge, so that it stood perched at the top with that hideous face staring down, brown hair matted with dark red. Those gleaming eyes, ancient, inscrutable, fixed directly onto Will and he felt a deep, nameless fear penetrate him, stab him straight in the heart, and suddenly he was sinking, falling through the Earth into a dark abyss where an evil older than time itself waited to devour him.

Down, down into the endless gulf, where all was darkness and ruin, a misery of wailing, of lost souls. And...there was Tommy, Silent Tommy Wilford...still curled in a ball and crying. And beyond him, another shape, cloaked in shadow, one that looked familiar, too familiar... It turned its head... Will drew in a sharp breath, but his chest was tight, still spasming... He reached out a hand...but the others vanished, disintegrated, and instead a pair of black eyes materialized in the gloom and that *face* followed, and the great dripping mandibles opened wide...

Wake up!

He was lost, he was lost in the dark...

WAKE UP! WAKE UP, WAKE UP!

"WAKE UP!"

Will's eyes flew open and Elise was crouched over him, shaking him violently, her pale skin covered in a maze of tiny red lines and—he was almost too dazed to notice—little sprigs of ivy. But she was alive, very much alive. Behind her the creature made its way torturously down the steep hill, down the crumbling rock face. Will's arm was still outstretched, reaching for something he couldn't see, couldn't remember.

"WAKE UP!" Elise said again, her voice scratchy and hurt, her words slurred and electrified with fear. Will sat up, his entire body feeling like one huge bruise, but adrenaline rushed through him in a wave and he bounded to his feet. He grabbed Elise's hand and together they retreated into the forest, into the dense trees. He glanced back as the creature stumbled to the bottom of the ridge, those cruel eyes never blinking, never looking away, and even as he turned ahead he could hear the thing's lumbering, clicking footsteps pick up speed as it followed them.

The trees...they still swayed, still rustled with that strange energy, and Will felt tiny pinches all over his arms and neck and face as more mosquitos bit him, but he was too terrified to care. They pushed deeper into the woods until the trees clustered together so tightly and the underbrush grew so densely that they could hardly move. The meager light filtering down was a sickly gray. Off to their right the sounds of the lake grew louder and louder. And the footsteps grew closer.

Through the vines, through the thorns, through the low-hanging branches and tangled roots, they pushed and clawed and scraped, their faces cut in what felt like a thousand places, every muscle screaming for respite. The scene of Clark's head tearing away, the stringy viscous stuff from inside pulling apart, the sticky wet flies pouring out, replayed again and again and again in Will's head, driving him forward. He was vaguely aware that they were going downhill, with no idea where they were headed, or what they would find there, but that was almost meaningless compared to the bone-deep visceral instinct that they must *run*.

Orange rays flickered across their faces, the trees thinned out, and suddenly they burst into sunlight. Rays beamed down from above and up from below, forcing Will to squint. They had reached the shore. Water lapped the rocks at his feet. His heart climbed up into his throat and beat so fast he thought it must burst. There was nowhere left to run, nowhere to go, and those chattering footfalls, unbound to shape or form, echoed through the forest—the unstoppable approach of death. He shut his eyes tightly, squeezed his fists into balls.

"Look!" Elise said, pointing.

He opened his eyes. Down the shore a ways, just past a copse of partially submerged trees, was a small aluminum boat—Rob's boat, not that either of them knew it.

...we w-w-were f-fishing...

It rocked gently in the surf, caught against a log.

"Come on," Will said, grabbing Elise's hand again, already taking off.

The creature was close behind, the sounds of it pushing heavily through the trees rising up to suffocate them; so close, oh so close, it was almost on them now. Through the dusky shadows its great hideous form emerged into violent life.

They reached the boat. It looked like the scene of a murder, and for one heart-stopping instant Will did not want to get into it. A handful of worms wriggled and flapped in the bottom, wallowing in great pools of what could only be blood. It coated everything, every surface. A small tackle box, open and waiting, and an overturned bucket bore witness that it had only recently been abandoned. But there was nothing else, no alternative, and Will scrambled over the side and splashed to the grimy deck. Elise, somewhat slower, did the same.

And now here it was, the beast, forcing its way between two old trunks that sighed gravely as their roots ripped up, and in a grotesque flurry of legs it was at the water's edge. Will wrestled desperately with the branches of the dead log, trying to push off, but it was no use, it was hopeless, and there was the *Thing,* the monster itself, black eyes staring evilly as the pincers sliced open and shut, hungry and wet. It's awful hairy body, bloated, disgusting, quivered and bounced as it splashed into the water, and with a pang of horror Will realized that it was over, that death had arrived, that in seconds there would be nothing left of them but strings of flesh and blood. Elise gripped him in a fierce hug and he returned it, looking away.

But it wasn't over. The boat heaved violently as the spider bore down, and with a metallic squeal it scraped across the tangle of branches and floated freely, bobbing and splashing as the ripples carried it out into deeper water. The spider thrashed in the surf, stamped its many legs and backed up onto the shore. Only the cold, cruel eyes stared after them, watching as they drifted toward the middle of the lake, where the current picked them up and carried them slowly away. And there it remained until they had passed out of sight and the only thing in the world was the terrible, terrible pain.

4

THE SECRET

JULY, 1999

D avid clicked his pen three or four times. "I see that you obviously survived this 'giant spider' attack," he said, unable to contain his frustration any longer. He watched the light diminish in Mr. Wilford's eyes.

"What?"

"I said, you obviously survived, since you're sitting here telling me about it." David shut his eyes and rubbed his temples. It had been several hours since the interview began, and in addition to being tired he suddenly wished he had accepted a doughnut from Mr. Cameron when he had the chance. The two large orderlies had not so much as knocked on the door since Doctor Alvarez stormed in about the coffee, and neither, for that matter, had anyone else.

"Yes, of course I did," Mr. Wilford said, his voice flat, a trace of indignation passing across his face like a ghost.

David returned his stare for as long as he dared. "So if all this is to be believed..." he waved his hand in the air in apparent reference to *all this,* "...why? What made you so special?"

"You're gonna see," Tommy replied in his usual childlike way. "But you have to wait. Good things come t—"

"To those who wait, yes, I know," David said, taking off his glasses and rubbing his eyes with his thumb and forefinger. Across the table the look of indignation returned, and it sank into Tommy's features so that he gazed reproachfully back at David, saying nothing. For a moment they stared silently at each other, until finally David bent over and retrieved his briefcase from the floor.

"I have an idea, and maybe this will help us cut to the chase a little bit," David said, rummaging in the briefcase and pulling out a manila folder. "It's true all the people you've mentioned are presumed victims of the Highwayman—Clark Baker, Toby Christiansen, Jennifer Collins...and some that were never found, your father included."

Mr. Wilford was silent, and only stared at David through those pale eyes.

"Now I can see how that checks with your—well, your version of the story," David continued. "Surprisingly well, really. Mr. Baker was even found decapitated." He produced a picture of Clark Baker's withered corpse, puffy and swollen from untold days in the forest, partly decomposed. "And there were signs of serious trauma inflicted by animals. Bite marks and the like. But you have to understand, Mr. Wilford, that the medical examiner determined those occurred *after* the time of death."

Mr. Wilford peered down his nose at the photograph, but there was no change in his expression.

"And the children killed in the clearing," he went on. "Stabbed, yes, beaten—hell, it was awful. But again, and this is from the medical examiner, nothing—*nothing*—about *tentacles*. So let's cut the crap. I have some pictures of the other victims, at least the ones we know about. And I want you to tell me what you know about them. Not wild stories—if you don't know, you don't know, and we move on. Fair enough?"

Tommy was completely still, completely quiet. That reproachful look had dissolved into a blank stare and now he only looked off into space, as he had when he was first brought in. David waited a few seconds and then flipped open the folder.

"Alright. Stacey Adams, age thirty-three. Died somewhere around the twentieth of July." He laid down a picture of a woman—or what had once been a woman, and was now just a bloody mess of arms and legs, with no discernible face and her gut ripped open. "Looked like she might have been trying to flag down some help after hitting a deer, there was considerable damage to her car and she was found on the side of the road."

Silence from across the table. Indifference.

"Nothing? Okay, what about this one?" And here was a picture of an elderly gentleman. From the neck up he was remarkably intact, but the same could not be said for the rest of him. "Edward Billings, sixty-eight, out camping with his two sons. Left for firewood and never came back." He glanced up at Mr. Wilford, but received no acknowledgement.

"No? Okay, let's see... Toby Christiansen you know. Jennifer Collins..." David thumbed through a couple of pictures without pulling them out. "You'll have to bear with me, these are alphabetized... Here's one: Ellen Gould." And another picture, this one of a teenager. "Age eighteen. Early September. Out partying with her friends to celebrate the start of her freshman year at UVM. Left for home and was found the next day by Highway Patrol. There's a reason the press nicknamed him the Highwayman..."

Nothing.

Picture after picture—no response, not even a nod. Mr. Wilford looked to have withdrawn back into himself; he was blank, unreadable. Catatonic. Staring forward as if in a stupor. David leaned back in his chair and considered for a moment that perhaps he really had stuck his foot in his mouth this time. *Well, hell, good job there Nolan, you really know how to work 'em.* The tape whirred loudly in the quiet room. How long since he had changed it? He had already swapped it out for a fresh tape several times, and this one had been going for a while. Shit, might as well take the damn thing out and call it a day. He caught himself staring at the recorder and looked back at his manila folder.

"Okay Tommy," he said, and noticed a hint of light flare in Mr. Wilford's eye on the mention of his first name. "Let's try one more. Should be familiar to you. This is Adrian O'Rourke." He set down a picture of a man with wispy black hair and scraggly sideburns...and no eyes. Instead two dark holes leered straight at the camera.

Mr. Wilford's head turned slowly, very slowly, until he could look at the picture without moving his pupils.

"Age forty-seven. Found by a truck stop, June fifth, nineteen seventy-eight. Long-haul trucker on his way to Montréal."

Click. The tape stopped.

Suddenly Mr. Wilford was out of his chair and climbing across the table. The chain at his wrists snapped taut and his eyes bulged out of their sockets, magnified into veiny spheres by his glasses. The muscles in his neck strained with effort and the skin of his face burned red.

"*Mother FUCKER!*" he bawled, snapping the chain tight again and again and again and breathing out through his nostrils like a horse. "*YOU MOTHER FUCKER, FUCKIN GODDAMN FAGGOT MOTHER FUCKER—*"

David reeled backwards and his chair tipped over, spilling him on the floor. Above him Mr. Wilford stilled strained at his handcuffs, trying to pull his large hands through, cutting slices out of his palms as he pulled with all his strength.

"*I'LL KILL YOU, YOU FUCKIN FAGGOT! GODDAMN FUCKIN FAGGOT, I'LL FUCKIN KILL YOU, I'LL KILL YOU, I'LL KILL—*"

The door burst open—*CLANK!*—and in rushed two guards. They tried to seize Mr. Wilford around the middle but he ripped out of their hands, still screaming.

"*—YOU, I'LL KILL YOU, YOU MOTHER FUCKER! I'LL KILL YOU, YOU FUCKIN GODDAMN IRISH FAGGOT MOTHER FUCKER, FUCKIN KILL YOU, I'LL—*"

They wrestled with him for a moment but he was bigger than them, stronger than them, and he squirmed from their grasp, knocking one to the floor. The other dove in and Mr. Wilford elbowed him in the nose, sending little droplets of blood flying in a spray. The guard's knees buckled and he hit the table face first, and now Tommy's large hands seized him by the throat and bashed him again and again into the hard metal. The man on the floor scrambled away on his hands and knees until he was against the wall and pulled himself up along the paisley wallpaper. He drew his nightstick, charged, and in a flash had sunk it deep into Tommy's stomach. Immediately the beating stopped and the tank of a man doubled over, the words still framed in his mouth and the guard still floundering in his strong grip. Down came the nightstick again, this time on his back, and now Tommy released the poor shaking bastard and collapsed to his knees on the floor, his face purple, wheezing and sucking in choked breaths.

In ran Doctor Alvarez, flanked by the two orderlies. He surveyed the scene: David on the floor; one guard bleeding heavily onto the tabletop; the other standing with his nightstick still raised above his head; and Mr. Wilford, blubbering softly, leaning against the table on his knees with his blood-speckled hands still caught on the metal loop. He swore.

"*What have you DONE?*" Doctor Alvarez hissed.

"Hector..." the guard with the nightstick said, panting, "he was...he was attacking—"

"Not *you!*" Alvarez spat, moving swiftly to Tommy's side. "Agent Nolan. My God, did you listen to anything I said? I told you not to get him excited! I told you he could get emotional!"

David was completely nonplussed. He clambered to his feet, his head still spinning from the outburst, so sudden, so unexpected. "Doc, I had no idea, I—I didn't mean—"

"No, no, of course you didn't! Of course you didn't!" Doctor Alvarez said, trying desperately to hold on to his genteel manner, failing. His voice rose hysterically. "No one ever means anything to go badly! And why am I surprised, why, when—when you gave him caffeine—when you gave him a goddamn *stimulant!* I should have been waiting outside the door, I should have been waiting outside the goddamn door..."

"I was just showing him pictures!" David finally managed to say, his temper rising. "It was nothing, it was crime scene photos, it was... I thought he might know something, something relevant, it's standard—"

"That's enough!" Doctor Alvarez said, and something in his voice shut David up. So much for THE LAW. He bent to examine the guard, still splayed across the tabled with his nose dripping red, and snapped his fingers at the two orderlies. The shorter one went immediately to a wall locker and pulled down a package of gauze and rubbing alcohol. "Enough. Mr. Wilford? Mr. Wilford, are you alright?"

Tommy said nothing, but snuffled softly against the table edge, his thumb tucked comfortingly between his lips.

"Mr. Wilford, it's okay now. Everything is okay. You don't have to talk to this man anymore."

David opened his mouth incredulously, but Doctor Alvarez flashed him a withering look and he shut it again.

"We'll get you cleaned up and back to your room," Doctor Alvarez continued, his calm demeanor returning. He gestured with his head to the two orderlies, who immediately came around to each of Mr. Wilford's arms and gripped them firmly. "Make sure you send a nurse for this man here. Mr. Kirk, I believe you have the key—"

"No," Tommy whispered.

All heads turned toward him, surprised. The guard whose face had been so aggressively acquainted with the table looked dumbstruck.

"Mr. Wilford, you've been hurt," Doctor Alvarez said carefully. "You need to rest."

"I want to finish...finish my story..." Mr. Wilford croaked, breathing heavily, his thumb still shining with spit. "I want to tell you about...about..." His eyes jammed shut and his face screwed up in pain. He shook his head slowly from side to side and his hands tried to move to his ears but were stopped as the chain snapped against the bar. A small moan came from his lips, and then he gulped down a huge breath and opened his eyes. *"O'Rourke."*

JUNE, 1978

The huge spider had trampled off into the underbrush and now all was silent.

Tommy sat alone in the pine needles—well, not *alone*... What was left of Toby's ghastly face grinned up at him. Lips pulled back in a scream, teeth bared, his insides stringing out from his belly and glistening in the moldering leaves, covered in a wriggling mass of ants. Clark's headless corpse lay at his side, flies still squirming out of the hole in his neck. Most of the insects had followed the creature down the hill, but some remained, flitting overhead in a cloud and feasting on the stinking, wretched remains. Tommy flapped his arms to shoo them away, but it hurt and he stopped quickly. Dark, thick blood oozed out of the dead boys in gelatinous streams, pooling in the dust. The birds, which had circled as the monster thrashed and spat, now alit on the tree branches in ungodly numbers, watching Tommy sideways out of their blank, emotionless eyes. A few fluttered down to the ground, cackling and crying, inching forward to the crumpled bodies and tearing away strips of flesh.

Tommy swooned and looked away. He was in a daze, somewhere between disbelief and utter despair. And in *pain,* yes, underneath the numbing shock was a monumental pain, both physical and emotional. His legs...his arms... He put his hands out in front of him, wincing as the skin around his elbows stretched. He was absolutely covered in bites, great pus-filled mounds. He reached up and touched his face, and felt them there too. And that web of red lines where he had pulled out the ivy roots still traced a painful maze across his legs. He felt the urge to cry, but he was too tired even for that, too numb.

The birds—they surrounded him. He gazed around, gritting his teeth slightly as his neck, too, burned from the many stings. All around, all sides, from high above, they sat like watchful gargoyles, observing his every move. He felt their stupid eyes piercing him, following him like a piece of meat. They twitched and cawed, and Tommy suddenly felt that numb pain darken with fresh fear. He was still not safe, he needed to get out of here.

Move, yes...but his legs were jelly... They trembled and ached, but with tremendous effort he raised himself to his feet, to the protests of several of the grim sentinels above. He swayed for a moment, his head cloudy, his thoughts jumbled, but he steadied himself against the dead log and shuffled forward into the graveyard of felled trees. Shadows from the thinned-out forest rippled over him with a sort of misplaced peacefulness, made terrifying by the way they swayed back and forth with the trees, swayed back and forth in the conspicuous absence of even a breath of wind. And the birds ruffled and hopped from branch to branch, trailing behind.

Away from the ridge, that was the idea, away from the spider, away from the horrible mutilated corpses. He pushed uphill, not even thinking about the huge expanse of wilderness that may lie ahead, barely thinking about anything at all. Minutes or hours, days even, he couldn't be sure, he walked as if in a trance, and slowly, so slowly, the fear and loneliness and desperate sadness slipped away, left in those fluttering shadows that grew steadily calmer as he put distance between himself and the nightmare that lay at his back. Finally he stumbled out of the trees—they barely moved anymore—onto a muddy twilit highway that stretched over a hill to his left and curved gently to his right down into a dark valley speckled with points of light.

Tommy stopped at the edge of the woods and gazed down. That consuming numbness stretched to his toes, to his fingertips, but even through it he could feel a slight glimmer of relief burn in his chest, and he set off toward the lights, following the road. The birds gathered in the last line of trees, crowing plaintively as he vanished into the growing darkness.

* * *

Will watched the spider disappear around a bend, watched its wet, gleaming eyes vanish behind the leafy green forest and disappear forever. A chill crept up his back and he shivered, still staring at the spot. He remembered...ugh, it was so hard to remember, but he remembered *something*, something about when he had locked eyes with the creature, something about falling into that great black abyss. He had seen something down there, he had reached for it... It *meant* something, that was the worst part, it really meant something, but no matter how hard he tried to concentrate, no matter how hard he stared at the place where he knew those eyes still watched him, evil and wicked and vile, he could not make the memory return. A little sniffle from beside him broke his reverie and he turned to face Elise.

She was sitting with her feet in the bloody pool *(And who's blood is it???)* at the bottom of the boat, and for the first time Will took stock of her injuries. Her arms and legs were crisscrossed with thin red lines, broken here and there (and his jaw almost dropped when he noticed) by actual living *roots,* tiny shoots of ivy, leaves and all, growing right out of her skin. That was the most shocking, but far from the worst. No, the worst was the enormous gash across the side of her head, bloody and speckled with dirt and bits of tree bark. It rose angrily in a painful lump, and as Will watched her eyes shifted in and out of focus. Her nose was running—she sniffled again—but her expression was mostly vacant now, as if the burst of energy that got her out of that bed of ivy and down to the boat had evaporated once the worst of the danger was over.

The bed of ivy...

WAKE UP, WAKE UP!

Yes, she had been the one to get him up, to pull him out of that place, that dream, if it was a dream, that vision of darkness, of death, of... God, what *was* it?

She sniffled again and he shook his head, and the hazy memories drifted further away.

"Hey, are you...are you alright?" he asked, unsure of what to say. He felt slightly uncomfortable, even more than usual. She was a *girl*, after all, and a few years younger, and it was bad enough when he talked to his own peers.

Elise did not respond at first. She raised her head slowly, shutting her eyes against one of what Will could only assume were many pains. *Geez, look...* She was covered in bites too, angry red spots rising into angrier red lumps, dotting her arms and legs among the strange webby lines.

"I think..." she whispered finally, "I think...I need to go...to the doctor..."

Now Will was quiet, letting this sink it. The Doctor, yes, of course, *Doctor* with a capital *D*. Doctors could fix anything, but he had no idea where to find one, or how to get her there.

"I think I hurt...hurt my head," she continued, letting her face droop back down to her toes. Her summer dress, once bright yellow, was cut to ribbons and brown with mud.

"I'll take you to the Doctor," Will said automatically, his voice firm, completely unsure of how he would do it. "I'll take you." He thought he saw her nod slightly, but it was almost impossible to tell. That fire of courage started to blaze again, and for one second he pictured himself carrying her across the threshold at the hospital, a hero in a cape; in fact maybe he had *flown* her there, Captain Ross in the flesh, huge golden *R* plastered across his chest, and all the nurses and Doctors would rush outside in fascination to take her from his muscular arms... But then Elise sniffled again and he was back in the smelly, bloody boat.

"Thanks," she said in a low voice.

Will nodded quickly, embarrassed. "Yeah, I mean...sure..."

He glanced around for something that would get them to shore. There was the motor, of course. He stepped awkwardly to the flat back end, the boat rocking from side to side, and kneeled down in the muck for a closer look. A pull string flapped from its holster, slightly loose, like on the lawn mower at home. He was used to operating the mower, and felt a surge of confidence that he could get this thing running. The mower had a priming button, and he searched for one...but there were only so many places to look, and none of them had that familiar soft cap. Wait... Under the deck plate was a little rubber bulb on a hose which ran into the bottom of the housing, and he squeezed this a few times hopefully. Then he took the plastic handle in his palm, breathed, and hauled it back with all the strength in his body. The engine wheezed pitifully. Again and again, but it would not turn over. He gave it up as a bad job and turned back to Elise.

"It won't start," he said, feeling the shame crawl up his neck.

"Under here," Elise breathed, reaching under the low metal rail. She stopped midway and put a hand to her head, wincing as sparks danced in her eyes. Will followed her gaze and found a large oar, mounted under the rail in rusty metal brackets. This would do. He pulled it out with effort, lowered it into the water alongside the rickety metal frame, and gave a good stroke from fore to aft. The boat inched forward and turned slightly, so he pulled the oar to the other side and did it again. *Left...right...left...right...* Now they drifted forward—a bit at a time, but still moving, still making progress. It was grueling work, and he felt his heart rate climb, felt his skin moisten with sweat. He glanced at the near shore—the shore where the spider had been standing, watching...waiting...and knew they could not go back. Could. Not. He gave several good strokes on the left (*port* side, his imagination supplied), and they slowly started bobbing across toward the far shore.

"What...what *was* that thing?" Elise asked, the fear cutting through her weakened voice like a knife. The weight of the question was huge, immense; her eyes suddenly darted to her feet as if afraid the unimaginable *hugeness* of it had just escaped and might now turn back on her. Neither of them had spoken of that *Thing* in the clearing since February, the visits to Doctor Stephens excepted, and no one had believed them back then. Maybe—as Doctor Stephens himself would be so happy to suggest—maybe it was all made up, some shared hallucination, some strange trick of the mind. An awfully violent, bloody trick, but a trick... But now here it was, the same (or similar), rearing up again, the same eyes, the same mouth, wriggling and alien and awful. Four long months that question had slept anxiously in her belly, unwilling to be voiced, but now, now that they had just escaped another...another *Thing*...undeniably similar...it passed from her lips without warning. That hugeness, that colossal weight, hung over them like a great dark storm cloud, waiting to burst.

Will stared at the trees they were leaving slowly behind, and for a moment forgot to paddle. "I don't know," he said. "I think... I *think*... " His eyes screwed shut and his nose wrinkled up in concentration.

"What?" Elise said breathlessly.

"It's so hard to remember," Will said, relaxing his face slightly and dipping the oar back in the water. It sat gliding in the current, motionless. "I think I...*saw* something...when it looked at me."

Elise watched him carefully, her now-and-then vacant eyes sharpening into focus.

"What did you see?" Her voice was tiny, barely present.

Will blinked and pushed the oar through the water, staring at the swirling whirlpools that followed the oar on its path. Anything could be down there in that dark water. Anything.

"I can't be sure," he said. "It was like I was falling into a big black hole. And something was inside. Something was...I mean some*one*...was in there with me."

"Who was it?"

"I'm not sure... I can't remember..."

Elise moved to pull her legs up to her chest, winced, and let them sink back to the deck.

"I wonder... I wonder if it was Billy," she said, eyes shining. Will looked at her, surprised.

"Billy?"

"Yeah...Billy B-Baker..."

"But why?"

"Because it...because it killed him! And I—" and she clamped her mouth shut, put one mottled hand across her lips to stop whatever was about to come out. "Because it got him and he never got found. He was just *gone.*"

Will thought about it, but wherever the vision lay buried in his subconscious, it smoldered in abstract denial. He shook his head, the vague memory of that deep darkness drifting across his mind like mist, obscuring every detail.

"It wasn't Billy," he said. "I know it wasn't Billy. Whoever it was, I feel like... I dunno, it sounds crazy to say it out loud. I feel like it was *them*. Ya know? They were *it.*"

Elise made a puzzled face.

"I'm not saying it right," Will said, flustered. "The people—"

—*oh yes, there were people down there, not one but two—*

"—the person, I mean—it was like that...*Thing*...was a part of them."

The fog was gone from Elise's eyes now; she looked alert, wound tight like a spring.

"Part of them how?"

Will breathed out through his nose, trying to collect his thoughts. It was hard to explain, especially when he didn't understand it fully himself, or remember much beyond that feeling, that pure naked instinct. The boat eased to a gentle stop as he sat holding the oar, the water calming to smoky glass, the current picking them up and carrying them in a lazy trail, lengthwise down the lake past the dark, watchful shadows of the forest. The spider, the creature, seemed closer than ever, its malevolent presence lurking behind every tree, its glistening eyes watching from every dusky hollow, its gruesome jaws working, dripping, waiting for them. And the monster from the clearing, that horrible beast—

—*I've killed children, CHILDREN Jane, I didn't want to but I did*—

—it had come from the water, from those invisible murky depths, all around them now, still and endless and God knows how deep... Will's pulse quickened with a stress that had nothing to do with physical exertion and suddenly his mouth felt very dry. The blood... Where *did* the blood come from? Fish in a barrel, fish in a barrel, *Easy, it's like shooting fish in a barrel* the TV had said. When? Don't ask, who knows, maybe in a dream... He licked his lips, tasting the salty-sour dryness caked all around.

"I think... I think whoever was in there..." He dropped his eyes, fiddled with the twining on the paddle. "It was like they were the source of it. Like they were creating it."

That great imaginary storm cloud hung heavy in the air over them, black and swollen and dangerous, electrified, broodingly silent, the stillness broken only by the lapping of water against the metal hull of the boat. The forest was completely quiet.

"That's crazy," Elise finally said, but she already knew she believed it.

"This whole thing is crazy," Will said.

"But how? *How?*"

Will scratched his head. "No idea..." he said. "When I was in there...in that place...it was like pain and fear and sadness all combined, everywhere.

It was like...like being in hell, but without the fire. It was..." He squeezed his eyelids shut, trying to remember. "It was like the people—"

—two people...

"—I mean the person, *they* were feeling all those things, and that—that *Thing*—was coming from them."

Elise looked at him for a long minute, some strange understanding settling into her face, gaunt and afraid. Then her eyes turned hazy again and her pupils contracted and she swayed in her seat. She shut her eyes and sighed. "I think..." she said, clutching her head and dropping her chin against her chest, "I think I need to...lie down..."

Will glanced at her, lowering herself across the flat bench, eyes closed. An alarm bell went off in his head, clearing away the mist.

"No! I mean—I don't think that's a good idea," he said.

"Why?"

"I don't know. It doesn't feel right."

"But I'm so...so tired..."

"Yeah, but..." He didn't know how to say it, wasn't sure if he should. Somewhere in the back of his skull he heard the faint echo of his father clocking himself on a doorjamb in a drunken fit... *Jane you fuckin bitch, fuckin BITCH, you come back here! Where you goin??? You come back with that boy, fuckin bitch, you come—mother FUCKER! God—DAMMIT! My head, my fuckin—oh God my head...* The Doctor told them not to let him sleep. "What if you...you know...don't wake up?"

Her eyes cracked open. "Why wouldn't I wake up?"

Will clenched his teeth, his lips tightening into a thin line as he recalled the finer details of his father screaming, flailing toward them in a rage, unable to stand up straight because he was so piss-drunk. The door was right where it had always been, sure, 'course it had, but try explaining that to a man who was so sloshed he had peed on the living room rug, and who, among other ailments, was now bleeding from his scalp. They should have let the man sleep, and good riddance, Will thought, and immediately regretted it as guilt flooded his senses. He went to put the oar back in the water but stopped, staring at his crude reflection shape-shifting across the rippled surface as the sun lowered on the horizon. Fear stirred in his chest, fear about what was behind those peaceful little waves. Fear about disturbing it. *Who's blood, Will?*

"I don't know. But one time my dad hit his head and the Doctor wouldn't let him sleep."

Elise shifted slightly on the bench. "You say that a lot," she said. "'I don't know.'"

The shame crawled the rest of the way up Will's neck and filled his cheeks with a warm burning glow. "Yeah, well..." he said, turning away from the water, "I still think you shouldn't sleep."

He stared resolutely at his feet, watching the red pool run in a wave from one side of the boat to the other, hearing Elise struggle back into a sitting position. In a strange way she seemed almost drunk, and the thought of it made a stabbing anger pass through him, but it disappeared at once when he turned his face up and saw her light frame shivering on the seat, her eyes wide.

"Okay," she said miserably.

Now the shame was back, purer this time. But he was right, he told himself he was right... He looked away again, out to the right towards shore. A small white house sat nestled in the trees there, quaint and perfect, like one of those photo calendar pictures his mother liked. Jesus, his mother! He had left her back at the church, and goodness knows where she was now, out looking for him probably, scared shitless that she couldn't find him, scared she'd have to tell Harry—

"Let's go...there." The voice came from beside him, and he turned back to Elise. She had one arm raised in a weak point, her finger trembling as she stretched it toward the little house. "We can...use the phone... Call 9-1-1..."

***

The cars whistled past him, sometimes minutes apart, sometimes seconds, barely slowing down, weaving into the middle of the road to avoid hitting him. Tommy watched their taillights disappear into the gloom, part of him wishing they would stop, part of him not wanting them to at all. Everything hurt, from his toes to his fingertips, and until now he had not devoted a moment's thought to how long he had been walking. The deep purple streaks stretching across the sky, spreading in ghostly plumes from where the sun blazed fiery red at the edge of the horizon, told him it must have been several hours. It would be nice to sit down. He suddenly yearned for his mother's coddling touch, for her sympathy and her warmth. That worrisome energy that he felt whenever they were apart had ballooned to astonishing size. But he felt something else as well...somewhere deep down...somewhere in his chest... A cold finger pressed to his heart, veins of ice curling out just like those ivy vines, and he felt cool indifference spreading through his body, spreading to his head, cruel and cold and emotionless. No, he didn't want to see anyone. He didn't *need* to see anyone.

A pair of headlights bloomed in the darkness behind him, casting his features in shadow and lighting the road in a hazy yellow glow that grew brighter as the vehicle approached. It was big, he could hear it, from the sound that came rumbling to him on the summer air. It shuddered and roared as it crested the hill, a giant tractor trailer, grayscale in the twilight, monstrous diesel engine coughing black clouds into the sunset, brakes squealing as it started down the slope. Tommy stepped as far into the grass as the guardrail would allow, but the colossal machine slowed to a stop behind him, air brake popping like gunfire in the still evening. The silhouette of a head leaned out of the driver side window, chewing on a cigarette.

"You lost fella?" The voice drifted down to Tommy in a cloud of smoke, coarse and gravelly. It sounded like the man had been gargling rocks.

Tommy stared up at him, unsure how to respond. A thousand different thoughts flooded his brain: fear of that voice, relief at being found, the knowledge that he shouldn't talk to strangers, the hope of seeing his mother soon, embarrassment at the way he must look. All erupted in his head at once, paralyzing him. And churning beneath those thoughts, monumental and overpowering and painted in stark contrast against the man's friendly words, was the sheer, utter horror of everything that had happened. The loss of his father, the monster, the *blood*, everything came rushing into full consciousness like a swirling storm. It was too much, too much to take, too much to even imagine, it rose up to crush him, swallowing him whole. He felt those icy tendrils break apart, shatter into a million pieces, dissolve in his chest. His eyes burned and his breath shallowed, and finally he collapsed to his knees in tears.

"Whoa, whoa!" the man said, alarmed, and he opened the door and hopped down to the pavement. "Whoa, fella! What's the matter? What's a kid like you doing way out here by yourself, anyway? What are—? Jesus Christ, you're a mess!"

Tommy choked and wiped his eyes and still said nothing.

"Come on, we'll get you where you're going," the man said. "Maybe get you home—you have a home around here?"

Tommy nodded, hiccuping into his clenched fist. "Yeah," he finally said.

"Do you know the address?"

He thought for a moment. Yes, he did, his father made him memorize it. His father...

—HELP ME! Tommy, HELP ME!—

...yes, he had wanted Tommy to know it. He had wanted him to remember it, just in case. Tommy squinted, thinking hard, and slowly the sequence of words and numbers came back to him, meaningless but so often repeated he could have recited them in his sleep.

"Yeah," he said again, barely more than whispered.

"Great! Well don't tell me now, God knows I'll forget. But I know a place where we can get a map and figure it out, maybe get you a bite, get you cleaned up a little bit. Does that sound alright?"

Tommy nodded that it did.

"Good—good, let's get you out of the road. Come around here—right this way, yessir—and climb up in the copilot seat. That's the one. You wanna be my copilot?"

The man had tree trunks for arms, and he lifted Tommy easily into the passenger seat of the truck as he spoke. It was huge and the cloth upholstered seats reeked of cigarette smoke. A hint of some tropical air freshener cut through the smell, vague and sickly sweet, but only enough to make it worse. Pictures of naked women adorned the dash. Tommy was dazed and still crying, but the man's friendliness and gentle manner were slowly putting him at ease. He said yes, he wanted to be copilot.

"Perfect, you'll do great," the man said in his scratchy voice, pulling an atlas from the floor and setting it in Tommy's lap. "The copilot is also the navigator. Think you can manage?"

"Yes."

"Well hang onto your seat."

He walked around the truck and climbed in on the driver's side and shut the door. It latched with a heavy *thunk*, and then he turned and flipped on the overhead light. Instantly the inside of the truck was bathed in a warm orange glow, illuminating the dark red cloth of the bench seat, the tired brown vinyl dashboard, the pink nipples of the ladies in the pictures (Tommy blushed furiously), a scattering of paper food bags, and an ashtray in the fold-down console, filled with butts. The man crushed his cigarette in the tray and glanced around in search of—aha!—the box, which he flipped open with practiced ease, drawing out the slim white cylinder. The last one.

"Don't smoke kid, it'll kill ya," he said, lighting up and taking a deep drag. "Name's Adrian, by the way." He reached out a hand.

Tommy accepted the hand, looking up into the man's weatherbeaten face. His skin looked like leather, tan and tough and wrinkled, his green eyes framed by bushy, scrappy sideburns on the sides and a Boston Red Sox ball cap on top. "Tom Wilford," he said.

"Tom, good American name," Adrian said, expelling a cloud of smoke and shutting off the light. "I suppose that's short for Thomas."

"Yeah, but my dad only says 'Thomas' when I'm in trouble."

Adrian grinned under his ball cap. "Well, we'll stick to 'Tom' then."

He fired up the engine and the truck vibrated like it had come to life.

"Ever ridden in a big truck like this before?"

Tommy shook his head, the tears drying as he distracted himself with the excitement of riding in a *real* tractor trailer.

"It's a little bumpy, but she's a good ol' girl. You just keep an eye on the mile markers and tell me when we're close to an exit, okay?"

"Okay," Tommy said.

"Here we *go!*"

The axles squealed as the tires gripped pavement and the big truck lumbered into a roll. Adrian eased onto the accelerator, shifting gears like he had been doing it all his life (which, Tommy thought, he probably had), and with a roar of the engine they climbed back to highway speed. From way up here it hardly looked like driving, it was much more like *flying*, and that overwhelming swell of emotions dwindled to a dull simmer.

"So Tom," Adrian said, blowing a puff of smoke out the still-open window and rolling it partway up, "I have to ask, buddy, now that we're not strangers. What brings you out here to the middle-a goddamn nowhere? If you'll pardon my French."

Tommy wrinkled his nose, trying to figure out which part of the question was French. Nothing that he could tell. Then his mind drifted to earlier that morning, watching his father pull the dusty old canvas off the boat and hook up the trailer, his heart racing with excitement, racing with anticipation even through the fear that had been keeping him holed up for four long months. Could it really have been just this morning? Regret welled in his throat, suffocating him with guilt. Oh God, why didn't he stay in *bed*?

"I was with my—with my dad," Tommy said, feeling the tears burning behind his eyes and swallowing hard. "We were f-fishing."

"Oh, fishing, gotta love it. I used to go with my old man out on Lake Iroquois. Good ice fishing out there."

Tommy nodded; his daddy had promised to take him ice fishing over the winter, but they had never gone. The idea of sitting out on the ice with the cold pressing in on all sides, the freezing water churning dark and unfathomable below, filled with creatures slimy and unseen and immune to the cold, was terrifying—but being there with his father, being there with his warmth and his guiding hand, just the two of them together in that great wilderness—that would have been thrilling. Thinking about it now made Tommy's stomach hurt, and he pushed it away.

"You ever been ice fishing, fella?"

"No," Tommy said, looking down at his ruined shoes.

Adrian watched him for a moment before turning back to the road. "Well, no shame in that, Tom, you're still young. So where's the old man now?"

Tommy was silent, his eyes glassy and still. Adrian glanced at him again and put a comforting hand on his leg.

"That's okay, sport. No need to answer."

Now Tommy looked at the hand. In the twilight it looked like wax. He felt chills flurrying out from where it sat on his thigh, and with them a sort of fluttering uncertainty rolling through his insides. He didn't like that. No, he didn't like that at all.

Adrian withdrew the hand and put it back on the wheel. Suddenly his lips spread in a broad smile.

"Say! Look at that, Tom, that didn't take long, did it?"

Tommy looked up and out the windshield as Adrian guided the old tractor in a steep turn off the highway. Resting there in growing darkness at the bottom of the gentle sloping curve was a dingy building, set back in a huge gravel parking lot. A handful of gas pumps stuck out of the pavement just off the exit ramp, side by side in a line that sat in brooding shadow beneath a huge flat roof. Panels were caving in along the top of this roof, sunken and rusted and dying. A few giant tractor trailers rested like slumbering beasts in the lot, windows dark and peaceful, and around front were two—no, three—cars, nearly invisible in the dwindling light. The store was lit from within in a cold fluorescent white, which spilled out the open door onto the nearest squares of cracked, weedy sidewalk. A huge sign, big enough to be seen from the highway, rose monolithically into the sky, neon lights beaming MIKE'S GAS, HARDWARE, & SUNDRIES & Stop-'n-Go Diner, now serving Ice Cold Beer.

They rumbled into the lot, air brake screaming and popping as they lurched to a stop beside the other trucks. Adrian cracked his door open and the cabin light gleamed in the darkness.

"Ol' Adrian is gonna grab a drink, if that's okay, sport. Won't be but a minute, and we'll find you that map. You got the address ready to go?" He tapped his head a few times with his finger. Tommy nodded. "Good. Alright, let's get on with it then."

He shuffled out the driver side and jumped to the pavement in one smooth motion, flicking his cigarette toward the woods. Tommy clambered down the opposite side and strained to reach the door to shut it. Then he hurried to catch up with the slouched, pudgy figure making his way across the parking lot. Adrian had what Tommy's father would have referred to as city miles on him—a reference which, like 'pardon my French,' Tommy did not fully understand—his breathing haggard, his steps shambling, his posture curved forward from untold hours behind the wheel. It was easy to keep pace, even with Tommy's shorter legs. They reached the door together and Adrian gestured for Tommy to enter first. The twangy sound of country music warbled despondently out into the night.

"O'Rourke, you Irish bastard!" came a drunken voice from the corner. "Where the hell you b—" *(belch)* "—been?"

"Same as you, pissing my life away," Adrian said, waving to a man seated alone in a flamboyantly orange vinyl booth. He was the only one in the whole place; to their right another door opened on a small convenience store where a handful of anonymous traveler types meandered the shelves of snacks and car accessories, each in his own world, safe and oblivious to the horror world Tommy inhabited. This man also had *city miles* on him, his bleary eyes glaring out from over massive swollen bags, his cheeks drooped and stubbly, his hair patchy and thinning, his white shirt stained and stretched across an impressive beer belly. A number of crumpled cans decorated the table, dripping and sticky beside a half-empty 24-pack of Coors Lite.

"Not much else to do, when the only beer around for a hundred fuckin miles is this piss water..."

"Oh, quit it. I see you in here every goddamn week drinking your life away, why don't you go on home to that pretty wife?"

The man waved his hand at them in a boozy dismissal. "Blehhh. She don't want nothin to do with me. Her or that pussy son-a-mine." His eyes stumbled over Tommy's rough appearance, still covered in the fleshy pink film, glasses caked and opaque, bug bites oozy and white. "Whatsa matter with im?"

"Harry, this is Tom—what was it? Wilford? Tom, Harry Ross. Picked im up on the side-a-the road, Harry, must have been walkin for a while, middle-a goddamn nowhere. Says he was out fishin with his ol' man, won't say where the guy is now. Figured he could use a bite and a shower."

Harry studied Tommy carefully, his eyes suddenly sharper, more focused, combing over Tommy's small frame from top to bottom. "Mmph," he grunted, looking back at the 24-pack and staring at it, a little too hard.

"Thought I'd leave the kid with you just a few minutes," Adrian went on, eyeing the convenience store.

"Sure," Harry said, still looking at the beer. "Have a seat, kid."

Tommy slid cautiously into the booth across from Harry, feeling extraordinarily out of place. Adrian nodded his thanks and ducked into the convenience store. Now they were alone. Uncomfortable silence rose up in a suffocating cloud.

"So, Tom," Harry finally slurred, fiddling with a corner of the box, his bloodshot eyes glued to the words *Coors Lite* as if they contained some perplexing mystery, "'s a small world, ain't it? You—you prob'bly don't remember, but I knew yer mom, long time ago."

"Oh," Tommy said, studying a ketchup stain on the table and not looking up.

"Anxious woman," Harry continued, more to himself than to anyone else, "real fuckin—oh, 'scuse me—real jumpy lady. And you here all alone. She's gotta be worried sick."

Tommy felt that terrible energy pulsing in the air and shut his eyes. "Yeah," he said.

"Well what the fu—Jesus—what the hell are you doin out here then?"

Tommy opened his eyes. Harry was looking right at him. His eyes were deep, two deep wells, black and starry. Tommy stared at him. "Fishing," he said, under his breath.

Harry took a sip of his drink. "Fishing," he said. "Eh."

"But something bad happened."

The words were out of Tommy's mouth so fast he clapped his jaw shut, wincing in surprise. Harry looked back up from his drink, brow furrowed. He squinted drunkenly.

"What happened?"

"Nothing."

"'S not nothin," Harry said, a gruff edge creeping into his voice. "What happened, boy? No sense lyin."

Tommy hesitated; he didn't mean to say it, didn't mean to say anything. It was too much, too awful, and somehow saying it out loud would make it real, would mean it had really happened... But...he had already said it...already said it to Clark—

—*the flies pouring from the hole in his neck, more and more and more and just like the—*

—*cat, white bone sticking out of that clotted red, sticky and dark and—*

—*I didn't do it Mommy! I didn't I didn't I didn't please believe me Mommy it—*

—already told them his father was...he was...

"*Dead,*" Tommy whispered.

Harry leaned closer, blinking through the mental fog. "What? Whadju say, boy?"

"My dad," Tommy said, still whispering, staring straight ahead. "My dad, he...he's *dead.*"

Harry leaned back again, dumbstruck. "Oh, I... Well, kid..." He took a nervous sip. "Well that's too bad," he finally said, burping softly. The fermented, hoppy smell drifted across the table in a wet haze.

"Yeah," Tommy said, almost inaudible. "Something...something *got* him. Something..." He screwed his eyes shut, he didn't know why he was saying it, why he was telling this man, of all people, but it was spilling out of him now. "It...it cut him...it *ripped* him... I...I swam away...through the...the...the b-b-blood." Suddenly he looked down at his arms as if seeing them for the first time, the horrible pink color coating his skin from head to toe. He had known what it was the whole time, oh yes, he had always known, but he hadn't thought about it... He was dizzy...so dizzy, and his breath was short, he couldn't breathe, he was choking—*oh my God...oh my God oh my God!*

"Calm down, boy, calm down," Harry said, looking in all directions for someone to step in and help him, but the only other souls in the place were on the other side of the wall. Heaven knows he had never had a soft touch, certainly not with Will, but the boy was having some kind of an attack, a real *freak out.* "Calm down now, 's okay." He gripped Tommy's arm in one large hand and Tommy slowly took in a deep breath. "I been there." His gaze was far away. "I been there, I get it."

Tommy shuddered and let out a sigh.

"Kid," Harry said, his jaw tense, and then stopped as the few remaining travelers passed through the empty diner on their way out into the night. He waited until they were gone, his gaunt face drawn and scared, still watching them through the door. "Kid," he said again, lowering his voice, "I gotta ask... This...this thing... The one that *got* im..."

Tommy stared into space, his eyes misting over as the horrible image of the monster, both monsters, breathed into vivid memory.

"Did it... I mean... Tom... Do you ever...*see* things?"

The country song scratched to a stop and now the diner was deathly quiet. Harry leaned closer.

"Things that...ya know...well they don't make sense. Strange shit... Things in the...in the trees."

Tommy turned his head.

"Do you...oh hell... D'you ever feel like...like yer bein..." He shut his eyes. *"Watched."*

A bead of sweat had formed on Harry's brow. Tommy focused on it, his heart racing. He nodded slowly.

"Yes," he whispered.

Harry opened his eyes, his expression dark.

"Listen, Tom." Harry fixed him with that stare again and Tommy's eyes were helplessly drawn to it, deep and dark like a bottomless pit. "There's somethin you should know—"

"Alright, Harry, I got it from here," Adrian hollered as he stepped back through the door, his own 24-pack under one arm, a few bags of chips in the opposite hand, and a new pack of cigarettes tucked in his shirt pocket. No map. "You don't like kids, I get it, I'm here to save you."

Harry froze, his face locked in an expression somewhere between bleary confusion at being interrupted and disbelief that he had somehow gotten as far as he did. "Sure, Adrian."

Adrian set the case and the chips down on a table and jerked his thumb toward the store. "Tom, there's a shower back there if you wanna get cleaned up. Wouldn't wanna deliver you lookin like you slept in the woods!"

"Adrian," Harry said, his face clearing. "I think we oughta call the p'lice."

Adrian looked taken aback for a moment. "Police? Harry, what're you—"

"The kid, man. The kid's in rough shape."

"Nothin a little shower and food can't fix, I'm—"

"O'Rourke," and Harry was deadly serious now, his voice coming in a low grumble through his grim hanging jowls. "The kid's dad is dead."

Adrian stopped with his mouth still open, shut it. "Oh, that's—that's awful, I'm sorry to... Well yes..." He sat down in the booth next to Tommy, looking slightly disappointed. "Well yes, I guess we should..."

"There's a phone in the store."

"Ayup," Adrian said. His expression went blank for a moment, and then he brightened. "Yes, could you—could you make the call, Harry? I was just gonna toss this stuff in the truck, won't take a minute. Tom, would you mind helping me?"

"I dunno if I should be the one... I'm a little buzzed," Harry mumbled with remarkable introspection, but Adrian was already standing up, already gathering his things.

"Tom?" Adrian said, pushing the chips toward him. "Can you carry these?"

Tommy stood dutifully, watching Harry frown at the two of them, and grabbed the chips off the table. "Okay," he said. He tried to look away but Harry was staring intently back at him, his eyes glittering and dark, and he continued frowning until they had disappeared around the edge of the door and were back outside in the warm night.

"I shoulda known better than to leave you with im," Adrian said as soon as they were clear of the building. "Just a sad, angry drunk. Better to leave im to his business, Tom."

Tommy looked up at him. Adrian was shuffling along in a bit of a hurry, his arthritic legs hardly bending, that enormous pack of beer hefted easily under one shoulder.

"He seemed okay," Tommy said, gripping the bags of chips a little nervously.

"He's in there every week. Every week I come through here on my run I see im. Mangy old bastard—not old, actually, younger'n me. Never once have I seen im sober. Not once."

Tommy considered this, recalling that *drunk* was *bad;* his father had said so, despite doing a fair amount of drinking himself, by the—Tommy gulped—by the end. There was a time when Rob never drank, or almost never, but in recent years a drink a week had turned into a drink a night, and then two, and then three...*but I'm not drunk, Tommy. Drunk is bad, you don't wanna be drunk, son...* Now he was dead, Tommy had said it out loud, it was real now, so real and it could never be taken back—

"Right," Adrian said, pulling open the huge door of the truck and folding the seat forward. Behind it was a cramped cabin with a handful of cabinets and a small bed nestled tightly in the back. "Hop on up there sport, I'm gonna pass you the box."

Tommy did as he was told, wondering how on Earth he was going to lift the box, but Adrian just set it on the floor and told him to push it into the corner. It was heavy and hard to push, but after several good shoves, each moving it forward a few inches, he got it back beside the bed. He smiled in spite of himself and turned around.

"I did it! I did—"

Adrian was already inside with him, shutting the door behind—*thunk*. Velvet darkness surrounded them for a few seconds and then he flipped on the cabin light. He gazed at Tommy for a moment through his green eyes, an odd expression spreading across his face. Then he undid his belt.

"It would have been better if you were clean," he said, pulling the belt through the loops in one smooth motion. "But you get what you can, ain't that right Tom?"

Tommy was confused, so he nodded and said, "Yes sir."

"Fuckin prick, I mean the nerve, am I right? We coulda got you somethin to eat, got you showered up. Hell, looks like it's just chips now."

Tommy looked at the chips. He had left them on the bed. "You don't like the police?"

Adrian looked up from where he was struggling to undo the buttons of his pants. "Huh? Oh, not especially, kid. We don't really see eye to eye, if you get me."

"My dad doesn't—I mean, he didn't...he didn't like them either," Tommy said, hanging his head. Adrian stopped fumbling for a moment and the funny expression was replaced with sympathy.

"I am sorry about your dad, sport," he said. "It's a tough life, all rotten to hell. My old man, well, he and I didn't really see eye to eye either, but it was still tough when he passed."

"What happened to your dad?" Tommy asked.

"Killed in a bar fight, can you believe that?" Adrian had his fly undone now and he dropped his pants down to his knees. "Makes a man wonder, but no sense dwellin on it. Tom, you like candy?"

Tommy looked squarely at Adrian's underwear, yellowed with age and sagging around his hairy legs. His confusion deepened.

"Yeah," he said uncertainly. "Last year for trick-or-treating I got two whole bags."

Adrian laughed, his scratchy voice rolling around the cabin in waves. "And twice the cavities, I'm sure! And you like ol' Adrian, don't ya sport? You'd help im out if you could?"

"Sure!" Tommy said, but he felt the heat rising in his neck.

"Well Tom, I don't want you to judge me now. The thing is, I normally pick up college kids up around Burlington. God knows they get drunk enough and even an old sonuvabitch like me looks decent. But I'm not gonna make it that far tonight. You think you could help me with somethin?"

Tommy blinked. "Help with what?"

"It would have to be a secret, Tom, just you and me. And we'll have to be quick before that old drunk brings the cops down on us."

"What is it?" Tommy asked desperately.

"Tom, it's been a while since ol' Adrian felt the touch of a woman—or anyone for that matter." He rolled his eyes. "Could you be a sport and just give me a touch. Nothin much, just—right here." He pointed at the bulge in his underwear. Tommy suddenly felt very flushed. "It'll be our little secret. I'll make it worth a candy bar."

Tommy took an unconscious step backward.

"I don't—I don't think—not that—" he said, the words falling out of his mouth in a nervous jumble. Adrian balked.

"Not even after I picked you up? Offered you a ride home? Come on sport, can't you just do this one little thing for me?"

Tommy's heart beat very fast, threatened to beat right out of his chest. "No, I—I can't," he said in a very small voice.

Suddenly those green eyes flashed with anger.

"Tom, we don't have time for this. You understand, right? We only have a few minutes."

Tommy took another step back and his foot hit the box of beer. His breathing shallowed.

"*No!*" he said, almost crying. Embarrassment at the outburst injected into the swirling storm of fear; he wanted to get out, to run away, but Adrian was blocking the door and in his panic he forgot all about the one on the passenger side.

"Ungrateful brat!" Adrian spat, all the pleasantness gone from his face, and he took off the Red Sox ball cap and threw it on the floor. Under his hat he was mostly bald, with a few wispy black hairs standing up in all directions. He pulled down his underwear and his manhood flopped in the dusky orange light. "You're gonna help me out, fella, I didn't waste half my night on you for you to say *no.*"

"*Leave me alone!*" Tommy wailed, really crying now, his hands brushing the faux-wood paneling behind him, feeling for an opening that did not exist. The droning noise started again, he felt it all the way down in his toes. "Don't touch me, *please!*"

"You're gonna give me what I want, goddammit," Adrian said, moving toward him. "Your hand or your mouth, Tom, up to you!"

"*No!*" Tommy whimpered, sliding down into a seat on the box. The noise was everywhere, was overwhelming, he could feel the awful life in it swelling into hideous form. Bugs pounded the windows, beat themselves to death against the glass. "NO! *LEAVE ME BE!*"

"*Give it up you little tease!*"

Adrian grabbed Tommy's head in both hands and pulled him closer, his arms flailing and pushing and useless against Adrian's strength. All was shadow and deafening noise and—

Suddenly there was a *thunk* and a shuffle of footsteps and Adrian flew backwards onto the floor.

"LEAVE HIM ALONE, YOU PIECE OF SHIT!"

Adrian's arms and legs flapped in the air like an overturned beetle. "Get off! *Get off!*" he yelped.

"I'll teach ya to go after a fuckin kid, goddammit!"

And now he was being dragged out the door on his back, kicking and screaming every step of the way. He hit the gravel head first and floundered to his knees, cowering in the dark.

"I wasn't doin nothin, I wasn't doin *nothin*, I swear!"

"Pull your fuckin pants up!"

Tommy scrambled to the door, feeling the droning sound dissipate slowly, watching the cloud of bugs thin out. In the hazy orange light spilling from the cabin he could just see Harry, disheveled and drunk, standing over Adrian's shadow with a tire iron in one hand.

"Come on Harry, we're friends, *friends,* you know I wouldn't—"

"I'm drunk you Irish fuck, not fuckin blind."

"Please, *please,* just let me go, don't hit me aga—*AGH!*"

"So you like little kids? *Do ya?*"

"Harry, please, *please*—"

"SAY IT! SAY IT YOU PIECE OF SHIT!"

"I DON'T, I D—*AGHHH JESUS!* JESUS CHRIST—"

"SAY YOU FUCKIN LIKE LITTLE KIDS, GO ON, SAY IT!"

"HARRY PLEASE, HARRY—*AGH PLEASE HARRY*—"

"FUCKIN SAY IT!"

"*AGH*—I DOOOOOO! OKAY, *OKAY I DO*, PLEASE, PLEASE LEAVE ME BE... Please let me go... Harry... Harry, please..."

Harry breathed heavily in the dim light, his eyes wild and dangerous. The tire iron hung from his right hand, blood dripping into the gravel. Adrian cried at his feet, cradling his arm, from which a pearly white shard of bone shone brilliantly in the rising moonlight. Tommy almost fainted—

—*THE CAT THE CAT THE CAT*—

—oh God, it was the cat all over again, and Clark, he could still see Clark's headless corpse slumping to the ground, blood rising in a fountain from the spongy neck—

—*I didn't do it Mommy! I didn't I didn't I didn't*—

"Please Harry... I'll do anything, I swear to God... I'll never do it again..."

Harry shook, seething, his breath coming in tortured gulps, staring down in wide-eyed fury at the man groveling in the dirt.

"That's *my* fuckin kid, you asshole," Harry said.

Adrian raised his head painfully, horror spreading across his bloodied face. "Harry, I—I didn't know, you gotta believe me, I had no idea—"

"*Shut the fuck up!* You think that makes it *okay?*"

"No, I... God no, I didn't mean—"

"I've heard just about enough out of you," Harry grumbled, raising the tire iron again.

"*NO! PLEASE, GOD NO PLEASE—*" and then he screamed. It was terrible, bone-chilling... Short. His broken body collapsed in the dirt, the back of his head caved in, blood running from the pulpy depression and filling in the gaps between the hundreds of tiny rocks.

Harry stood up straight, looking drunkenly at the bloody tire iron as if he wasn't entirely sure how it had ended up in his hand. Then his face twisted up with rage and he jammed the iron down lengthwise into Adrian's head. Once—twice. He stood up again, kicked the body as hard as he could for good measure. It twitched senselessly. He dropped the iron and looked up at Tommy, exhausted.

"Well," he said. "I guess you heard me say it."

* * *

She had been dreaming about the cat.

It was restless sleep, broken sleep, and she hadn't meant to sleep in the first place. Hours they had been gone. Hours. Fretting...pacing...cleaning everything... It was actually something of a miracle she had fallen asleep. And then the cat... Mewling...crying... She saw it walk in through the back door, face flattened into an oozy mess, tail gone, fur matted and brown... It cried at her, yowled and cried, cried because it was dead... She saw it on the thing's horrid face. Death. It looked just like it had when it was crushed into the lawn, but moving, walking, turning its dead face up at her, eyes clouded over with milky blue blindness, limping into the house on crumpled paws, leaving tracks of red slick behind.

Why did you let him kill me? the cat asked. The voice was like the wind through a door, all breath and no body, a whisper in a dark room.

I didn't. I didn't know.

The cat stared out of its blind eyes. Yesss. You knew what he wasss. You knew all along...

No! I didn't!

She turned away from it, folded her arms across her chest. Cats can't talk! No, this—this wasn't real. This was all a dream, a terrible, terrible dream. A touch like a feather ran up her back and she shivered. Something was behind her...something...

She twisted her neck...oh, but it was too frightening...she couldn't face it. But some strange compulsion, some deep need to see, uncoiled in her belly like a snake. She looked...

Vines.

Great leafy vines, ivy vines, ivy like you saw on old houses. The cat was gone and ivy flooded into the room, pushed in through the back door, covered the few feet of tile just inside the glass and then spilled out onto the carpet and kept growing, twisting, fighting its way toward her, and one lone vine was already next to her, wrapping itself around her body like some hideous green tentacle.

You knew what he wasss, the cat said. You knew it. You alwaysss knew.

I didn't know! she screamed, but it was just a disembodied voice, floating in the air, as weightless as smoke. The vine tightened around her neck. The ivy rose up to engulf her. The world grew dark.

It'sss all your fault. Your fault, Krissstin. Your fault...

Ring... Ring... Ring...

She had woken in a panic, her back damp with sweat and sticking to the couch. And there was the phone. It almost seemed unreal, the banality of it, the little black plastic box on the wall, ringing and ringing and ringing, and no ivy in the house, no cat, nothing, nothing at all but shadows. She shivered as she thought about the tiny grave Rob had dug for the creature, the little mound of dirt, the sticks tied in a makeshift cross...out in the woods...out in the dark... And it *was* dark, dark as pitch, deep and empty. She blinked. The phone was still ringing. A familiar fear paralyzed her as she looked at it, listened to it rattle—

—*death rattle...*

...thinking that Tommy and Rob had been gone for hours, hours, and now this. And it was her fault. All her fault, because of that thing, the thing she had done. She knew the one. And the phone was still ringing. She'd have to answer. Yes, she must. No choice. And finally she pushed off the couch and picked it up.

Even now as she drove through the all-consuming darkness, her hands bony and white on the steering wheel, shaking every time she had to reach for the gearshift, she could still hear that voice on the other end of the phone. It almost seemed to pass right in through the window like a ghost, hovering around her neck, whispering in her ear. Her feeling of isolation was absolute. The beam from the headlights was insignificant in that great darkness, that huge, overwhelming expanse of night. It pressed in from all directions as she wound her way through the pastures and forests and rocky hills, past fences and wilderness, beside trickling streams and fields of moonlit sunflowers bobbing sorrowfully in the summer breeze. The stars twinkled indifferently down from the vast beyond.

Mrs. Wilford, it's about your son, the voice had said, an anxious male voice, Sergeant Wilcox, Vermont State Police.

What—? What happened to him? What happened, is he okay?

He's fine, he's resting now.

What happened to my son?

We're...we're not entirely sure. He hasn't been making much sense.

Oh God... Oh God, what did he say?

He...um... Well, we'll go over it when you get here.

What did he say?

Please, ma'am, if you could just come to the hospital, we'll explain everything there.

She didn't even wait to get dressed, just threw on a robe over her nightgown and headed for the door. Thank God there was a box of cigarettes in the glove box. She had stopped to light one as soon as she reached the first stop sign, the flame from the match quivering delicately in her trembling fingers. So frail. So easy to snuff out. Snuff the life out and it would be dead forever, dead and turned to stoney darkness. The cigarette dangled from her lip now, already burned down to the filter and forgotten.

That swirling stormy ocean inside, that terrible sea, slammed against her consciousness in huge rolling waves, great foamy swells, black as the night. She knew what she had done. She knew it. She knew it would destroy them, knew one day it would come back. Pieces of it flashed in her mind like sea spray, harsh and chilling and gone. She tried to suppress it, tried to force it down like so many times before but she couldn't, she couldn't this time. It was like that day in February, that day when she had gotten a similar call, that same anxious voice, the same meaningless words, *It's about your son...*

She had thought that would be the end of her, the undoing, the ruin of her life and her marriage, but somehow she had survived. Against all odds and all reason she had managed to bury it again and keep it hidden, keep it a secret, forgotten almost even to her. But never entirely gone. No, never, and now it was back, fearsome and pounding in her skull, waves crashing, surf hissing as it sucked the base out from under that great seawall in her mind. That wall...it had been erected all the way back in 1968, and it had kept her safe. All this time it had kept her safe, and now it was crumbling, withering away, falling into the sea in a torrent of stone and spray.

This was a mistake. This was a mistake, you have to leave...

Her hands tightened on the wheel, trying to forget.

Go! You have to go, you can't be here.

Was she drunk? Back then, when it happened? Yes, she thought, yes or it never would have happened. Yes, she never would have done it if she wasn't drunk. But had *he* gotten her drunk? She frowned. No... No, that was her fault, all her fault...

She felt the wall cracking, felt the water coming through in mean little jets.

I said GO!

Kristin, I'm sorry, I... I didn't mean for this to happen, you know I didn't... Please, Harry—

And the wall burst. Exploded in a crack of thunder, and the memory rushed in, turbulent and cold, surrounding her, drowning her, pulling her down into its wretched depths.

She was twenty-one years old. So young, unbelievably young, Jesus, surely she could never have been that young. Nothing hurt, not her hips, not her wrists—not that swirling storm in her head, that was nowhere in sight. Instead there was a gentle rain. She remembered it, falling in soft sad sheets across her subconscious, that faint but ever present worry about her father's health. And not just in her head. Rain fell outside too, the sky a moody gray, distant thunder rumbling at the edge of the horizon.

It was July. She and Rob had tied the knot just three blissful months ago, and everything was just as perfect as perfect can be. He had graduated in May and started working at the local power plant a week later, got his foot in the door almost immediately. He still loved it, still raved about it. *The energy of the future,* he would say, his eyes lighting up with excitement whenever he had an excuse to bring it up. And now, already, just a short time later, he was off to Ballston Spa for some training courtesy of the Navy's nuclear power gurus at their site in upstate New York. He would be there a week.

And there was something else... Town rumblings... Because the local hero, Harry Ross, had come home from the war early. Come home in a sort of disgrace. Rumor was that he had suffered some kind of a breakdown, shot up a village or something, wouldn't pick up his gun anymore. And something darker... A superstitious sort of murmuring, the kind that has no basis in real fact any more than a ghost story. They said...they said terrible deaths had been following him ever since. They said six members of his company had been killed in unexplainable ways, unexplainable even by the standards of war. And now Harry had been dumped on the curb by an anonymous gray bus, he and his green Army bag, and he had stumbled home half drunk. Home to see his distraught wife and his disappointed father, shame and condescension painted across the father's face as he opened the door, and Kristin could almost hear him speak the words: *I knew this would happen, son.*

Kristin had known Harry from school. Before his enlistment he had been taking night classes, and she had seen him there, usually arriving when she was leaving. They had a flirty little rapport, although it had never gone anywhere. He was a little older, almost as old as Rob, and a little more worldly, and a little more handsome. Now he was all of those things, and dark and mysterious and quiet. He returned to school after a time, but he spoke to no one. Not even Kristin. And her heart broke for him, and not only that, it also...it also yearned for him, yearned in a way she had never acknowledged before he left for the war, yearned for his handsome face and his strong hands and his mysterious, deep eyes. Something about that quiet sadness, that deep, brooding sorrow...was intoxicating. And even though she was with Rob and she loved Rob, God did she love him, she could not help but try to speak to Harry, try to crack the shell, try to reignite whatever flame they had had (perhaps just a spark) and find out what was making him tick.

Explain it? No, she could never explain it, not even to herself. Nor would she admit it, not to Rob, definitely not to Harry. But she knew it, she felt it. And little by little she got him to talk, little by little she got him to open up about the fighting with his wife, the fighting with his father. Little by little she gained his trust, and before long he was calling *her* after a fight, calling *her* when he felt the depression swallowing him whole, calling *her* when he was piss drunk and couldn't drive home. She told herself it was all in the name of human kindness, told herself it was a good and righteous thing to help this man out, to help this man who seemed to have no friends, none even within his own family. Yes, she told herself she was right to do this.

One night he called, more upset than usual.

I tried, Kristin, I tried, he sobbed into the phone.

Tried what? she asked, a hand rising unconsciously to her lip. *Tried what, Harry?*

I tried...tried to end it... I tried to end it...

She froze, the blood curdling in her veins. She looked to see if Rob was in earshot and held her palm over the receiver.

Harry, what are you talking about?

I shoulda died, he said, the phone blowing up as his strangled breaths crackled into the line. *I ain't never shoulda come home.*

Don't say that, Kristin said at once. *Don't say that, she loves you Harry, Jane loves you, Will loves you—*

No, I... he paused. She could still hear his breathing but it was farther away, as if he was holding the phone out a few inches while he figured out the words. *I did somethin terrible, Kristin... Somethin...somethin unforgivable...*

Kristin mouthed wordlessly, searching for a response. *Well it... Whatever it is, Harry, I... I'm sure that's not true...*

It is true, he said. *It is. I shoulda died... I should let im kill me instead of...instead of what I did...*

Harry, Kristin said, curling the wire around her finger anxiously, not even noticing it. *Harry, stop it, you've been drinking. You've been—*

I ain't drunk, he said. *Not now. Not this time.*

You're not making sense! she said, grimacing at the shrillness of her own voice. *You're not... Harry, what are you saying?*

Harry sighed, a fearful little exhalation, choked with emotion. *Somethin came back with me, Kristin. Somethin... Jane doesn't know... I can't tell her...*

Harry, what are you talking about???

There was silence then, a silence so thick she could have cut it with a knife. Harry's labored breathing was the only sound and it was miles away. Finally his voice returned, flat and quiet.

You're right, Kristin. You're right, I have been drinking.

Harry, I—

I'm just drunk. Forget I said it.

And with a *click* the line was dead. Kristin stood completely still with the phone pressed to her face, her mouth hanging open in shock, her mind racing. Looking back on it now she knew she wouldn't see or hear from Harry again for weeks. She would fear the worst for all that time. And with the expedient grace of memory she suddenly jumped ahead all those weeks, jumped ahead to that day in July, the day everything changed, the day the first powerful waves of that internal sea first swelled into life.

Rob had gone on the trip.

Kristin was home alone, home in their little apartment—at this stage even the townhouse was little more than a dream. A small apartment was all they could afford, and things were stretching pretty thin. But the cat was there—

—You knew what he wasss. You knew it. You alwaysss knew—

—a small gray cat to keep her company. It was a gift from Rob after their first month of marriage. She loved it, oh she loved it. It was only a kitten in those days, precious and playful, chasing toy mice and pouncing on dust bunnies. She was watching it, sipping a cup of tea, dozing off and on. The rain...yes, the rain fell lightly against the window, sullen and peaceful. It was late—how late was hard to remember—but late enough that when the phone rang it woke her up.

'S me... 'S me, Kristin...

Harry. God, Harry!

He was drunk... He was in trouble... Jane had kicked him out of the house, he had nowhere to stay. It was raining... Would she mind...would it be too much trouble...could he come stay with her tonight?

Her heart hammered in her chest. *Yes, Harry, yes, of course you can. Don't go anywhere, I'll come pick you up.*

The entire ride home she felt icy fingers running down her back, felt a barely concealed thrill building in the pit of her stomach. Harry sat in silence. They finally arrived back at the apartment and Kristin opened a bottle of wine. Now Harry was talking. She didn't say much, only listened and nodded her sympathy. She opened a second bottle of wine. The feeling simmered...and intensified when Harry pulled off his rain soaked shirt to reveal the body the Army had created, not yet ruined by years of excess. She blushed and looked away...made an excuse to go to bed.

Please, Kristin, I... I don't want to be alone, he said. *Not tonight.*

You're not alone, she said.

I'm...I'm scared, he said, almost crying. *I'm afraid and I don't know what to do...*

Shh, she had soothed him. *Shh, it's okay.* She held him, held his strong body in her arms and felt her skin crawl with desire. *It's okay, you're here with me.*

He leaned back, looking at her hard from just a foot away, so close, close enough she could kiss him, even though she knew she shouldn't.

I'm sorry, he said, his eyes shining. *I'm sorry about before. I never...never shoulda...*

I know, Kristin said, squeezing his hand. *I know, it's okay.*

He looked down at the hand. *Thank you, Kristin,* he said, his face breaking out in a weak smile. *Thank you. Thank you for being there. Thank you...*

He leaned forward again...put his face against her shoulder. She didn't know what to do, didn't know how to react. Fear and pity and excitement coursed through her, electrified her; she felt alive, so very alive, more alive than she had felt in years, maybe ever, more alive even than when she had first slept with Rob. A small balloon of shame burst in her head but it was quickly overcome by the thrill, by the other feelings, the mounting desire. She kissed his hair...his cheek...

He looked up at her, locked eyes with her, and in that moment they were the only two people in the whole world.

Thank you, Kristin, he said again.

She stayed in that moment for a long time, perhaps a lifetime, and then leaned in and kissed him on the lips. He was surprised at first, and for that one horrifying second she thought she had crossed an invisible boundary that she could never uncross. But then he returned the kiss, returned it with a ferocity she had never expected, and they moved together, moved as one, and he unbuttoned her nightgown and took her hard nipple in his mouth. She closed her eyes and felt the pleasure burst from her nipple out to the rest of her body in electric pulses, and then she unbuttoned his pants and pulled them down and still they kissed, alone in the night. He slid her underwear down, slid it down to her knees and she kicked it off. It was all she was wearing beneath her nightgown. And then he was inside her, suddenly, passionately, just like that, and she gasped in pain and ecstasy. And then it was over.

She lay awake for a long time, Harry's head resting gently against her breast. That tiny burst of shame...it was growing now, growing into a monster, huge and terrifying, a hulking shadow that haunted her from beside the bed. She stared at the ceiling, feeling the awful weight of it, feeling it crush her, feeling it swell to unimaginable size, more and more and more with every second she lay there with Harry's warmth still pressed against her body. And the cat...

It was watching her. Watching through those yellow slitted eyes, only the eyes visible in the darkness, reflecting the moonlight into silver discs, unblinking. The cat... The cat knew what she had done. She could see it in those expressionless gleaming eyes. It knew. It knew everything. And it judged.

As soon as it was morning she kicked Harry out. Now the shame really sunk in. Deep. Bone deep. She swore to never see him again, to never speak to him again. To never mention this to anyone ever again.

But the horror only intensified a few weeks later when she realized she was pregnant. A flurry of panic rushed out to her extremities, made her feel tingly and lightheaded. This was it. This was the end of her picture perfect marriage, over almost before it even began. She had to do something. Had to hold her life together. And it was easy. So easy. She erected the great mental seawall. She told herself the baby was Rob's. She told herself so often that she came to really believe it. And it was possible, really possible. Once Tommy was born he looked so much like his mother, so much, it was impossible to tell... And with his glasses she was sure he was Rob's, just positive... Mostly positive...

Now she flicked on her turn indicator and pulled into the parking lot, mostly empty at this late hour. Outside the night had only deepened as the moon sank behind the mountains and disappeared into unknowable oblivion. And above her the hospital loomed, white lights from the windows peering down, silvery in the gloom and staring like eyes... Like the cat's eyes...

* * *

Tommy scrambled out of the truck, not wanting to be in there one second longer. He stepped carefully around Adrian and the puddle of blood, the empty sockets staring darkly up into the sky, and made his way toward Harry. He couldn't look at the body. Even after everything he had already seen he still couldn't stomach it. A gag jerked at his insides but there was nothing left to puke—he had lost it all hours ago. Harry stood over Adrian's crumpled form with his shoulders slumped, his hands shaking at his sides, his beer belly heaving. The tire iron lay at his feet, glistening in the dim light from the truck.

"Tom," Harry said, panting, "ya know what I'm sayin, don't ya boy?"

Tommy was silent, his glasses opaque in the darkness, the eyes behind them perfectly still and watching Harry as if he were an insect.

"You know what I—I mean...what I'm tryin to say... It ain't certain, Tom. It ain't a hundred percent certain, but it... Well it's better 'n even I'd say... What I mean is...what I'm sayin... I think...I think I'm your dad, Tom."

Harry immediately looked down at his feet, but seeing the corpse and the tire iron there, glanced up and away over the treetops. Tommy still said nothing and only stared.

"God, and to find out like this...to find out...I mean, Rob, he... God... I've wanted to tell you," Harry went on. His eyes were wet in the moonlight.

"God, I—I've wanted to talk to you boy, but yer mom, she...she uh...well, I stayed away..." He wiped his eyes with his sleeve. "Oh God... Jesus Christ... What have I done..."

He stepped backwards from the body and sank to the ground, his hands still shaking.

"We gotta...we gotta call the p'lice," he said, looking around as if hoping someone would hear him and take care of it, but the parking lot was like an alien landscape, deathly still, a gray postage stamp in a sea of black. No one had emerged from the other tractor trailers parked nearby. No one had come out of the store to ask about the screaming. No one had noticed—or they didn't want to notice. "Tom... We gotta call..."

Tommy looked down at Harry, looked down his nose at the man. He wanted to suck his thumb so bad it itched. His thoughts were going a million miles an hour, still trying to process what had happened with Adrian, nowhere close to accepting this new revelation. His father...his daddy...Rob had raised him, loved him, taken him out on the boat, taken him fishing, showed him how to bait the hook, taught him his manners, driven him to school, nursed him when he was sick, bought him his first baseball... This man crying in the gravel...*drunk*...

—*drunk is bad, you don't wanna be drunk, son*—

—this man who had just stabbed another man in the *eyes*... No. No no no. That wasn't possible. That wasn't real.

"No," Tommy said, hardly aware he was saying it. Harry choked and looked up at him.

"No? Tom, I just—I just *killed* someone..."

"You're not my dad," Tommy said. "You're *not.*"

Harry looked stricken. "Tom, I... I *am*. At least I think... B'lieve me, I know it must—"

"My dad wears glasses," Tommy said, reaching for the first thing he could think of. "He wears glasses and *I* wear glasses."

"A lot of people wear glasses," Harry said, struggling to his feet.

"And he's like me! He's just like me but bigger!"

Harry fixed him with a hard look. "Tom, he raised you. He raised you, boy, that's it."

Tommy was getting upset, was working himself up to real anger. This man was being impossible, was being really *dumb*—didn't he know how dumb he was being?

"You're wrong!" Tommy shouted, taking a step back. "You don't know what you're talking about!"

"Tom, listen—"

"No, you listen—"

"Shut the fuck up, boy!" Harry's bloodshot eyes bulged from his face, barely containing the rage that so usually accompanied his benders. For a moment he looked quite insane and his hands curled into claws, tense and furious, and then his muscles relaxed and he became sickly and pale. "Listen to me. Really listen. Please. There's a reason you feel like...like yer bein watched. There's a reason...there's a reason you see the things you see... It ain't a coincidence boy. It ain't just you..."

Tommy was silent again, his heart beating in his throat.

"I know what killed your dad... What killed your friends at school... Not what it looked like, only you an' the dead know that, but... I know what it was... I know why..."

Now Tommy sank to the gravel, the gory remains of Adrian O'Rourke—limbs contorted, blood pooling, mouth still frozen in his final scream—just feet away. He could hardly breathe. His lungs felt like they were full of water.

"How?" Tommy gasped. *"How do you know?"*

Harry's jaw tightened, the cords in his neck standing out, shining with sweat. He ran a hand through his hair, not meeting Tommy's eye.

"Tom, I... I did somethin once... Somethin I ain't proud of..."

He gazed off at something far away, something only he could see. His face twisted in anguish, twisted with some unseen hurt. His body seemed to diminish, seemed to shrink down to a shadow of itself.

"Somethin I... Somethin I can't ever take back..."

Harry lowered himself to the ground next to Tommy, looking like a ghost in the ruddy cabin light, his eyes never moving.

"Unforgivable," he whispered, his lip trembling. *"Unforgivable..."* He took a deep, shaking breath, squeezed his eyes shut. When he opened them it really was a ghost looking out, a husk, an empty shell. "And ever...ever since...somethin...somethin followed me, Tom... Somethin evil... Somethin that...*enjoyed* my pain... Somethin that helped me do pain to others. *Kill* people Tom, you understand?"

His eyes shut again and he shook violently.

Tommy heard, like an echo, that droning noise building in his ears, saw the face of the creature in the water, the face of the spider...saw the strange monster torturing the cat—

—*mewling and mewling and breathing in great shuddering breaths*—

—and ice-cold fear sucked the heat out of the summer air.

"What was it?" he whispered.

Harry only shook his head. "No name..." he said, his eyes still jammed shut. "No name... But it came when...when I thought...when I thought I would die..." He was still trembling, his whole body, from head to toe. "When I was afraid I would die... And it...it *killed* people... Anyone...anyone around me..."

Tommy could see it, could see the blurry tentacles impaling Fred and Al, could see their arms and legs flailing obscenely as it beat them to death...

"Or it *did*. It did until...until..." Harry lifted his face to the stars and gulped down a breath, dread and agony and regret etched into every line, every pouch, every crease. "...until you were born, Tom. Until you were born. Then it stopped."

The world started spinning. Slowly at first. The lights and the trucks and the big sign and the twinkling stars, faster and faster, spinning like a Merry-Go-Round with the brakes removed. Tommy felt a building ache in the pit of his stomach, a nauseating sense of understanding seeping in. He sensed where this was going, dimly at first, but more and more with all the welcome clarity of a bowling ball to the head.

"But why?" Tommy asked. His voice sounded like it was coming from a great distance, like he was listening to himself from the trees a hundred feet away. *"Why?"*

"I think it...passed...from me to you," Harry croaked, dripping with sweat. "I think it...I think it wants to stay alive somehow...I think that's why it kept me alive...and then you...you *were* me...a piece of me...a *purer* piece of me...a *newer* piece of me... My other boy...my Will... He was already born... It was like it was too late..."

"But I wasn't dying!" Tommy said suddenly, louder than he even meant, stronger. "I wasn't afraid of dying when we were...when we were fishing... When it...when it got my...my d—"

"I think..." Harry said, a shiver taking control of him for a moment, so strongly he was rendered mute, his mouth flapping open incoherently. "Once it's out there...once it's in the world...it seems to stay. Where it is and...and *how* it is...until...until the next time..."

Tommy's shoulders were up to his ears, his body collapsing into a ball, his thumb inching toward his mouth. "But—but why does it *look* the way it looks?" he asked, his voice pinching into a whisper.

Harry sighed.

"Who knows why a thing is the way it is," he said.

Tommy considered it, but he wasn't done.

"What about..." he was afraid to ask, afraid to even speak. "What about...the *bugs*? The *birds*?" He cast a nervous look at the dark edge of the forest, rippling in the breeze. "What about the *trees*?"

Harry swallowed hard, guilt and fear and some strange adult emotion passing over his face in shadows. He gave the trees his own nervous glance.

"Tom, what I did... It was evil...pure evil... It was...it was an affront to God...to nature... An abomination... And this...this *Thing*...I think it is too. It's like a disease on the world. I think nature wants to kill it, just...just goes crazy wherever it is and wherever it's been... I think all the natural world wants it dead, maybe even more than...than *it* wants to be alive..."

Tommy shuddered, stared at the trees again.

"But if...if it's alive...because *I'm* alive..."

Harry looked at him carefully, pity stretching across his face. Grown-up pity.

"I think that's enough questions, Tom," he said, pushing slowly to his feet. "We still need to call the p'lice. I...I think...I ain't gonna be around much after tonight. God, I could use a drink."

* * *

Will sat in the hospital waiting room, staring at the linoleum tile, crossing his feet and uncrossing them and crossing them again. It was the same sort of plain, glum, anonymous tile flooring he walked over every day at school, a thin coat of wax giving it the same vague, barely-there sheen under the light of the same dropped tile ceiling. One major difference stood out: the pervasive smell of rubbing alcohol, like the whole room had been swabbed with the stuff, hanging stalely in the air, tickling his nose, clinging to the chairs and the doors and the beige wallpaper with blank sterility. The chairs in the waiting room were alternating green and purple vinyl, with curved wooden armrests joining to the legs in solid, unbroken pieces. Every third or fourth seat sported some cut, scratch, hole, all-out laceration, the plastic cushions ripped crudely open along otherwise invisible seams, yellow-white innards puffing out or flattened into submission. The exposed padding reeked of alcohol even worse than everything else.

Will sighed sleepily. There were no other people in the waiting room. Just Will and the bleary-eyed male nurse behind the counter, who was doing more drowsing than talking. His bearded face nodded up and down to a rhythmless beat, slowly down...quickly up! And slowly down again... In one of those rare Emergency Room miracles Elise had been seen right away and it felt like she had been back there for*ever*. It occurred to Will in bits and pieces that he was not required to stay—and in fact Elise had her own family somewhere, her own worried parents who should be showing up any time. He was free to leave, free to go. Go home. His bruises itched—he was fully aware that every moment he was here instead of opening that screen door and walking inside was a moment he would regret later tonight. And Jeezum, his mother, she had to be worried sick, he had left her, just left her at the church by herself... But he could not bring himself to abandon Elise, not now. Not until at least *someone* showed up to claim her. And of course there remained the issue of *how* exactly he was going to get home.

His mind wandered to the boat. They had arrived at the little white house without any surprises, but that hadn't stopped Will from staring at the water with growing anxiety. The more he looked, the more he remembered those tentacles emerging from the murky depths of the pond, and the evil face with them, rising out of the water, curling and slicing and stabbing and *ripping*, blood everywhere...and then receding again, vanishing, disappearing back beneath the surface as if they had never existed at all. His imagination squirmed, picturing more of the wriggling things grabbing his hand where it stuck out over the side of the boat, grabbing it and tearing it straight off, or worse, pulling him down into that silent darkness. It took all his courage, all that fire blazing in his chest, just to put the oar back in the water and paddle the rest of the way to shore.

But he did. Somehow he did, and nothing stirred in the deep, no slimy tentacles rose up to destroy him, and finally the boat bumped peacefully against the bank with only the rolling puddles of scarlet—and Elise's various injuries—to remind him that anything at all was strange about their voyage. The owner of the house turned out to be an old lady with blue hair, who was horrified, just horrified, to see them stumble up her porch dripping blood. She called 9-1-1 herself and then fussed over Elise right up until the ambulance arrived. The paramedics let Will ride with Elise in the back, and despite the circumstances he could not help being fascinated by the sheer number of medical devices crammed along the walls, the thrill of hearing the siren blare from *inside,* the irresistible feeling of being a hero just like these bearded medics with their strong arms and cool uniforms. Will decided the whole thing was pretty *neat.*

And now he was here. One young doctor had asked him a few pointed questions about how he knew her, how she had gotten the injuries, did he have any contact information for her parents, and so on. Will said what he could without mentioning the spider chasing them into the boat, and of course beyond that he knew very little. The doctor had given up and returned to the area behind the big wooden door with the sign that said AUTHORIZED PERSONNEL ONLY. Will sat and waited and perused the magazines and—

Holy shit! The realization went off like a firecracker in Will's head. He *did* know something—the man! The man calling out for Elise, the one who had disappeared into the woods in the wrong direction. He could only have been her father; they had the same face, the same blonde hair. He had sounded drunk—another bolt of anger passed through Will and quickly subsided. There was something definitely off about his expression, his voice, the way he had staggered into the underbrush. Will was just standing up to make this revelation known to the sleepy nurse when the AUTHORIZED PERSONNEL ONLY door bounced open and a woman with a clipboard leaned out.

"Are you waiting for Elise Smithfield?" she asked.

Will had just reached his feet and he teetered on the edge of falling. "Yes," he said.

"Well come on back, you can see her now."

She held the door open and Will followed her outstretched arm beyond the door, feeling a small rush of excitement at this sudden access. In his mind's eye he was now a secret agent—for the CIA or MI6, dashing and handsome—strolling back with cool bravado to see what gadgets the whiz kids had dreamed up for him. In reality he hurried past the woman and turned to see the door shut with a wooden *clack*. But he wasn't in a CIA development lab—he was in a dreary hospital corridor with exam rooms opening off the main hallway on both sides, back and back and back until the hall turned sharply left and passed out of sight.

"She's just up here on the left," the woman said, and led him to a room where the door was mostly shut and only a few inches of light broke out into the corridor. She gave him a funny look before opening the door. "What was your relationship to her again?"

"Oh, I—I'm her friend," Will said, and paused as the strangeness of the *F* word rolled across his tongue. He had never said that about anyone before. And it wasn't exactly true—not really. Without counting their brief encounter in the clearing, his relationship to Elise, friendship or otherwise, was hardly more than a few hours old. With the ease of practice he dismissed the lie and moved on. "I brought her to the hospital."

The woman had thin lips and she pressed them together so that they were even thinner, nodding, looking at her clipboard. "Well you're a good friend to wait with her. We've been trying to reach her parents for the last hour."

Another firecracker went off in Will's head and he remembered he had been about to tell the nurse about the man in the forest. He wondered if Elise's mother was out right now looking for her father, the phone hanging on the wall at home, ringing off the hook. He saw it all clearly in his head, the plastic box vibrating with urgency, the empty house...

"I think I saw her dad in the woods," he said all at once.

The woman stopped with her hand on the door and her lips grew thinner still.

"I'm sorry?"

Will didn't want to admit that he had had a chance to stop Mr. Smithfield from running blindly off into the woods, and he hesitated, the story forming behind his lips.

"What I mean is... When I first saw her I also saw a man. He looked just like her and went running in a different direction. I don't know where he went after that."

Will looked up into the woman's eyes, willing her to believe that was all there was. She looked back at him sternly.

"I forgot until just a minute ago," he added.

Now she nodded again...stared as she slowly unpacked his words, examined them from every angle. She stood up straight. "Okay," she said finally. "Can you see yourself in? I'm going to let the staff know."

"Sure," Will said.

"And, uh, young man."

Will froze. "Yes?"

"Do your parents have a phone? You should call them if you haven't already, I'm sure they're worried sick."

"Oh, right," Will said, knowing inside that this was never going to happen. "Yeah, I'll do that right after I check on her."

The lady nodded a third time. "Good boy," she said. And she walked away to the end of the hall and rounded the corner.

Will breathed a small sigh of relief and turned to enter the exam room. Once again he was stopped, this time by a small commotion behind him, back through the AUTHORIZED PERSONNEL ONLY door. He looked at the blank wood—no sign on this side—watching, listening. He counted three voices, faint, barely audible, and he tiptoed carefully back and put his ear against the door.

"I'm telling ya, what a night."

"Ayup."

"What can I do for you officers?"

"Well, a few things really. We've got a guy and a kid. Guy looks like maybe he's got a concussion. Kid's got—well I dunno what he's got."

"Real fuckin weird."

"Yeah, really weird."

"So two patients?"

"Well, and the third guy down in the car."

"Oh, him. Yeah, he can fuckin wait, Ramirez is with him. Cold blooded killer, that guy."

"Fuckin A."

"So do you have the other two downstairs as well?"

"Yeah, someone's bringing 'em up."

Will cracked open the door so that he could peer through with one eye. Two uniformed policemen stood at the desk, talking to the male nurse, who looked considerably more awake now. The door to the stairwell pushed open behind them and the policemen turned.

"Jackson, good. I see you brought the kid first."

Will's knees buckled. There was Tommy, Tommy Wilford, shuffling into the room with a third police officer at his elbow. Tommy looked just as bad as when Will had left him in the forest, his entire body coated in pink, his glasses opaque, his arms and legs covered in bites and webby red lines, just like Elise. He could hardly believe it. He had been sure Tommy was dead. The kid was shivering, either from the cold hospital air or from a day of unending trauma, but the shivering stopped at his eyes. They were perfectly still, perfectly straight. He stared off into the distance, maybe not seeing anything at all.

"Is he talking?" the nurse asked.

"No, not much. Kid's been through a lot I think."

"We've got another one back there right now who looks about the same."

"Jesus Christ, another one? Hear that, Wilcox? I told you it was fuckin weird."

"Fuckin A."

"Where'd you find him?"

"That truck stop off exit twenty-four. You know Mike's?"

"I heard of it."

"Found a body too. Probably shouldn't say that, eh?"

"Then don't fuckin say it."

"Yeah, yeah. Fuckin mess though, real—

"*Ahem.*"

"—right, sorry. Well can you get him checked out?"

"Yeah, take him on back through that door, I'll meet you inside."

"Thanks."

They took Tommy by the shoulders and steered him toward the door. His head swung around and his eyes settled on the tiny crack where Will stood watching. Like two pale magnets they went straight to Will's face and suddenly Will plunged backward, into infinity, into a world beneath the world. The lights in the ceiling snuffed out and he passed through the floor into cavernous darkness. All around, on all sides, he felt despair and misery. The walls were shifting, *moving,* the haunted specters of a thousand trapped souls straining at invisible bonds and wailing into the inky blackness.

His breath caught in his throat. He was here again, *here again,* he had been here before, a lifetime ago, it was all so familiar, he remembered it, and he remembered—

Tommy. His small, chubby body half shrouded in mist and walking closer, closer, and behind him another form, bigger, stronger, sitting in a chair, mist and shadow distorting his face. Hands cuffed together and head drooped in shame, crying, crying into a stained undershirt. He was cast in a deep blue light, now deep red, now deep blue. The mist parted. His face was gaunt, unshaven...and familiar... It was Harry.

Will's arm shot out in front of him. God, he remembered, he remembered *everything*—

DAD! he shouted, but he had no voice. *DAD, I'M HERE! I'M HERE!*

Still no sound came out, but Harry looked up slowly, looked up as if he could really hear it, as if it was coming to him across a great distance, maybe from underwater or across a windy field.

DAD! DAD, I SEE YOU!

Harry turned his head, turned it slowly to face Will, and there was none of his usual anger, none of his bluster or rage or meanness, just a deep, deep sorrow...and a strange kind of peace.

"I see you, son," Harry said, and his voice was real, it was real. "I see you. I—I love you, Willie. Always ha—"

And then Will flew backward onto the floor, the lights and the tile and the beige walls materializing in an instant, his arm still stretching out in front of him. The door stood open and Tommy Wilford was there, looking down at him out of those bottomless pupils, staring in his own strange surprise. Behind him was one of the cops.

"Kid! What're you doin? Are you alright?"

It came to Will dimly that he had been knocked over by the door opening, and he pushed himself slowly to his feet. The shock was still fresh, still coursing through his body in bright electric bolts. He couldn't speak. His mouth flopped open.

"Kid? Kid, are you...?"

And finally he felt control return, felt the buzzing in his limbs subside to a dull tingle. His jaw muscles spasmed and pulled tight.

"I'm okay," he said breathlessly, dusting off his pants even though they were already ruined. "I'm okay, I was just—just walking by the door when—"

"I saw! I saw, I—Jesus, you've got a strong arm," the cop said to Tommy, nudging his shoulder teasingly. Tommy continued to stare. "Well, glad you're okay, kid. Can we scoot by?"

"Yeah—I mean—yes sir, of course," Will said, and he stepped off to the side. The male nurse came around from the desk and gave Will his own curious stare.

"What are you doing back here?" He had been sleeping, after all.

Nerves fluttered in Will's chest. "The other nurse—the lady—she let me back to—she was bringing me to see—"

"Chill out, man, chill out," the nurse said, rolling his eyes. "I'm just asking. Your friend must be in that room there." He pointed at the one where the door was mostly shut. "Try not to get lost."

"Yes sir," Will said, anxiety rolling up and down in his gut, and he hurried into Elise's room, sensing the eyes on his back.

"Will!" she said as soon as he shut the door, and immediately she clutched her head, wincing. She was wearing a hospital gown and sitting on the exam table. A large pad of gauze was taped across her temple, already turning brown. "You're still here."

"Yeah, I mean—yeah," he said, almost tripping over himself as he moved closer. She was the only one, the only one he could tell. "Listen, Elise—I know who it was I saw." He lowered his voice, dropped his gaze. The enormity of the discovery was causing his hands to shake. He stuck them in his pockets, listened for when Tommy and the cop were safely down the hall. "In the—in that place. The dark place."

Her eyes widened, and shifted out of focus and back again. She swayed on the table and recovered. "Hu—who?"

Will replayed it all in his head, watched it all happen over again, watched Tommy and—and his dad—appear out of the mist.

"Tommy Wilford," he said, not looking up. "Tommy and—well, yeah. Tommy." His neck burned with cowardice, with the shame of concealing part of the truth, but there was no way he could say it. It was like someone dumped a bucket of water on that flame in his chest. He would never admit it. Even his old man, as much as he hated him—he couldn't do it.

"So you—you think Tommy is the one...*making* them? *Making* the...the monsters?"

Will gulped. "Yeah. I just saw him in the hall, he—"

"Tommy's alive?"

"Yeah... I was surprised too... But when he looked at me, I saw...I saw the same thing as...as before. When the—the spider—looked at me." He shivered. "It's definitely Tommy. It's inside him. Whatever it is, it's...it's like it was looking out through his eyes."

Elise's mouth hung open in horror, and she shut it.

"Tommy... Oh my God... What do we *do?*"

"What *can* we do?" Will said bitterly, seeing his father's face again, hearing the words: *I love you, Willie...* He couldn't even remember the last time his father had said those words, and now...

"We have to do *something!*" Elise said, a little desperately. "If we know the truth, we have to—"

"We're kids, Elise. Kids. Twelve, and—and what're you, eight?"

"Nine," Elise said, almost whispering.

"What can *we* do? Nothing. We just have to...avoid it, that's all."

Suddenly there was a tremendous crash from outside the door and Will and Elise both froze, listening. An angry voice made its way down the hall outside, struggling, panting. They could hear clothes flapping and feet stomping and skidding along the tile floor.

"Let me *go! Let me go!* They're coming! Don't you understand, they're *coming!* I saw them—I saw them in the trees! They're in the *trees!*"

The door opened—Elise opened it, her fingers trembling, her face paper white.

"Elise!" Will hissed. "What are you—"

"That's my *dad,*" she breathed, her voice almost nonexistent. "My *dad.*" She flung the door wide.

Two cops and the nurse dragged Paul Smithfield down the hall, dragged him with his feet skidding and scuffing as he fought every step of the way. His eyes bugged out of his skull, his patchy hair standing straight up, his tired suit torn to pieces and covered in twigs and leaves. There was blood on his chest...on his hands...

"Daddy..." Elise said in a soft voice, and Mr. Smithfield stopped suddenly. His head turned like a corkscrew until he stared straight at her with an expression of pure, utter terror.

"Elise," he said, his mouth quivering, "Elise, I saw it. I *saw* it. Like a spider, but...but..." Tears started rolling down his cheeks. "And bodies...I saw bodies...in the trees. They're coming, Elise. Get out of here. You have to—" He flailed again and the three men latched onto him harder, started dragging him the rest of the way down the hall. "ELISE! YOU HAVE TO GET OUT OF HERE! GET OUT OF HERE, GO, GET OUT! THEY'RE COMING! *THEY'RE COMING!!!*"

He disappeared around the corner, his voice fading. Will grabbed Elise around the middle to keep her from chasing after him.

"Let me go!" she squealed. "*Let me go! DADDY!*"

"No!" Will grunted, struggling to hold her. "No, you're hurt, you're—"

And she was; she collapsed to the floor, her eyes shifting in and out of focus and spilling tears, her arms and legs shaking. The female nurse appeared at the end of the hall and came barreling toward them. In seconds she had scooped Elise into her arms and carried her back to the exam room.

"*Daddy...*" Elise still cried, "*Daddy, come back, come... Come back, Daddy...*"

The nurse stroked her hair. "Was that your Daddy?" she asked, laying her gently back onto the table.

"*Yes...*" Elise gasped, trembling all over.

The nurse threw Will a murderous look. "Stay with her, don't let her move. I'm bringing the doctor." And she bolted from the room.

Elise was shaking so much now that she couldn't sit up; she buried her face in her hands and sobbed into the paper sheet stretched across the tabletop. Will stood next to her, completely unsure of what to do or say. Fear squeezed his heart, but it wasn't fear of the monster.

"It's *Tommy,*" she whispered, the hurt in her voice curdling it into a snarl. "*Tommy Wilford...*"

Will nodded slowly, staring at her. "Yes," he said, from far away, miles away.

Elise raised her head to look at him, every muscle in her body tensing and relaxing and tensing again as the pain and anger and despair gripped her in a cruel fist.

"We have to kill him," she said. "That's how. That's how we end it. Tommy Wilford has to die."

5

THE END

OCTOBER, 1978

They sat in the window of the creamery, watching the wind dash playfully through the vibrant autumn leaves, watching it pick them up in dazzling handfuls and swirl them across the sky. Will turned to see Elise finish her ice cream, thinking that it was strange, definitely odd, having a friend at last after all this time but one that was three years younger and a girl. He had tried to make sense of it several times in the last few months but could not, and finally decided that that was alright. They had very little in common and sometimes found there was nothing at all to talk about. It didn't matter. They were the only two people, the only ones besides Tommy Wilford, who had shared that bizarre trauma in the woods and survived, and that was connection enough. Usually there was nothing that needed to be said, only the tacit comfort that came with understanding what no one else could. There was strength there, real strength, enough that Will spent all his time with her now. His action figures were left to collect dust on the shelf over his bed.

And it had been a good few months, a good summer, having someone to spend time with, to play with, and without the constant fear of his father breathing down his neck. His father...Harry, bastard that he was, never came home from that trip to Mike's. After the initial shock wore off, the shock that his own flesh and blood was accused of *murder* (the worst of all crimes, although he had suffered enough beatings not to doubt it), he felt a strange sort of protracted release. It was like his muscles had been carrying around this unknown tension for years, and now with his father safely behind bars they were slowly unwinding, untwisting, unknotting. When school started his grades were the best they had ever been.

And his mother, Jane—she looked better than she had in living memory. He wondered if she felt any sense of loss, any amount of sadness with Harry gone. She certainly played the part when confronted by sympathetic neighbors and family. But she no longer had to wear such heavy makeup, no longer spent her Sundays cleaning the blood and beer off the floor, no longer flinched when she heard her name, no longer looked gray and drawn. In fact she looked beautiful, Will thought. She glowed. She moved with an energy Will could not remember her ever having.

So he sat across the table from Elise, warm from the morning sun pouring in through the large front window of the creamery, and he felt, possibly for the first time in ten years, truly happy. At ease in his own skin. He watched her polish off the last of her chocolate cone and look up at him thoughtfully. It had been one of those silent days. She had barely said a word and now her lip wiggled as if she had something to say but couldn't quite find the words. He waited patiently.

"Will..." she finally said, nervousness passing across her face. She gripped her spent napkin hard in one hand. "We haven't talked about...you know...how..."

Will frowned. "How what?"

She lowered her voice, leaned in close, stress tightening her jaw. "How we're...how we're gonna...*how we're gonna kill Tommy Wilford.*" The words rushed out in a tense whisper and she clapped a hand over her mouth, looking around frantically as if terrified of what she had just said out loud.

Will's heart skipped a beat.

"We—we can't. I mean, we... I thought you were just saying that. You were just saying that, weren't you?"

Elise shook her head, slowly at first and then faster. "No. I mean it. I..." She glanced around again, glanced around the empty creamery, just the two of them and Trish at the bar. "I have to. *We* have to. It's the only way, remember?"

Will was silent, his mind racing. She hadn't mentioned this since the night in the hospital. Not one word. He had hoped she had forgotten.

"You haven't seen...my *daddy*..." she continued. Her face twisted up, made a funny expression. "You haven't seen what...what *happened* to him... What *Tommy* did to him..."

Will shook his head.

"Elise... Elise, no! We can't just..." He dropped to a hiss. *"We can't just kill someone.* Especially, I mean... Tommy's just a kid! I don't think he can control it!"

Elise leaned back in her chair, hurt, eyes glistening. "We're kids too! He r-r-ruined everything! My d-daddy... They w-w-won't let him c-come *home!* They give him m-m-medicine... He doesn't even recognize me anymore! He just sits there, he sits there, he... I thought you..."

Will was at a loss for words. He squeezed his fists under the table, trying to think what Captain Ross would do. He would have the right words at a time like this. Will could only sputter.

"I can't, Elise... We can't... I don't even know how we would..."

Elise shifted uncomfortably, reached in her pocket. She produced a small silver pocket knife, haft sparkling in the sun.

"We could use this," she said quietly, not looking up from it.

Will looked at the knife, looked at it hard, the whole world narrowing down until all he could see was that shiny metal handle. His mouth was very dry.

"Elise..." he said, licking his lips. "Elise... Where did you get that?"

Now she looked up. "It's just a pocket knife, Will," she said, a little defensively. Then she looked back down. "It was...my daddy's..."

Will was still staring at the knife, an otherwise innocent object now imbued with the power of death. He suddenly remembered Officer Tibbs and the dull gleam of the gun on his utility belt. Officer Tibbs, who had disappeared...evaporated...in the same swampy clearing where the monster had been.

"It's sharp," she whispered, the light from the handle reflecting in her eyes. "I checked. It's sharp."

Will drew breath and realized he had been holding it. He exhaled slowly.

"Elise, don't..." he said. God, his mouth felt like the Sahara. "Put it away. Put it..."

Elise blinked as if returning from some distant dream, some fantasy of revenge, and her eyes flicked up to meet Will. Her expression hardened and she stood up, pocketing the knife, her face furious.

"Fine. That's fine Will. If you're too chicken..."

"I'm not!" Will stood up too, shoved his chair back into the wall. "It's not that I'm chicken, think of what you're saying—"

"He's killing people, Will! Killing people! Still, even with him locked up. It's still happening!"

Trish looked at them now from behind the bar, watched them with her nose wrinkled in suspicion. Elise moved for the door, pushed through it angrily. Will followed on her heels, calling after her.

"Even if it was right—even if—how would we get to him? He's in the loony bi—"

Elise wheeled around, glared at him, and he stopped short.

"I'm sorry—I'm *sorry!* I didn't mean it, Elise, okay, I didn't—"

"Some friend you are," she said, turning again and walking away.

"Elise, I'm sorry!"

"Drop dead!"

He stopped, watching her leave. The friendship—maybe it had never been a real friendship—was breaking hardly before it had even begun.

He felt it, disintegrating in the wake of that one phrase. Snapping like cheap plastic. It was four months old and yet it stung like the loss of his father—his father, who was dead to him. He felt a stab of bitter guilt at his own weakness, at his cowardice for not admitting—perhaps not even fully to himself—that killing Tommy couldn't work, *wouldn't* work, because it wasn't just Tommy he had seen in those eyes... But he could never say that out loud. Never. Anger and bewilderment reared in his chest, breathed life into the flame that kindled there, but it was a different flame now. It was spite, smoldering these four long months, maybe even these ten long years, hidden away and now rising to the surface in foul, burning tongues of flame. He had done the right thing. He knew it, just *knew* it. She was being crazy, she was being a real *nut. Stupid,* that was the word, just plain *stupid!* He whirled to walk the other way, and that was when he saw a huge gray cloud, a column of black shapes swirling in the sky above town. Moving toward him. He felt a cold wind on his face, felt fear tug at his heart. That cloud...

* * *

Tommy awoke with his heart in his throat. It was beating fast, thumping so hard he could feel it in his head. He had been dreaming. Dreaming about the monster. About what Harry had said. About Rob and his mother and the cat and the spider, everything, all the bad that had happened. Billy Baker. The kids in the clearing. Clark's head tearing away, the spider's cruel mandibles ripping his head from his body, the stringy innards pulling apart, the bugs streaming from the hole in his neck, his mouth frozen open in blind anguish. Harry's voice behind it all in a thin whisper...

Somethin followed me, Tom... Somethin evil... Somethin that...enjoyed my pain...

He was covered in sweat. Tommy reached nervously into the darkness for his glasses and pressed them to his face. Details materialized out of the murky gray. The room was dark, still dark, ghostly in the dim pre-dawn.

Even after several months in this place he was still disoriented, staring wide-eyed at the paneled ceiling, grasping for a clue to where he was. It never became normal. Never. Slowly the visions faded and he remembered...he remembered the place... *Green Elm Home.* A place for *crazy people.* The idea was frightening, terrifying—the idea of losing his mind. It had been four months since the loss of his father, since the freakish incident in the boat and the spider in the woods; four months since Adrian O'Rourke had his eyes gouged out in the truck stop parking lot; four months since Harry Ross was arrested for murder and since Tommy had been admitted to the mental hospital, and still he couldn't wrap his mind around it. He wasn't crazy. That wasn't *possible.* They just didn't *understand,* none of them, not even his mother. His mother... So he had finally learned it—the secret, the source of the awful cloud, the root of that terrible energy. It didn't exist anymore. A hard lump formed in his stomach, all the pain and misery and betrayal pressed together into a mean little ball. He still loved her, but he also...he also hated her. It was a feeling he had never known, not the way he knew it now. She had cried, cried and cried and cried and hugged him so tightly it hurt, but he didn't feel anything. Not anymore. He turned his head carefully to one side and saw the papered walls of his little room, skeletal white in the darkness. A door set into the corner. His mother had walked out of that door the previous evening, told him good night and walked away. He had stared after her, stared hard at the blank wood. Now he looked again. A narrow beam of light shone from beneath, radiant and white from the brightly lit hallway on the other side. Despite his resentment, that sliver of light remained a source of comfort. It meant someone was awake and watching over him. Someone just feet away...just on the other side of that door...

He turned to the other side and followed the beam of light to its pale imprint on the opposite wall, beside the window. Sometimes when feet walked by outside the door he could see their shadows on the wall, gray blobs that flicked past and were gone. During the first few nights they had scared him, but not anymore. Now he found comfort in them too. Those feet. They meant someone—

His heart stopped. An icy dagger twisted his insides, twisted them up into a tight knot and stayed there, not letting him breathe. There on the other side of the window was a shape, a great, hulking, monstrous shape, pale like the walls, gleaming darkly in the light from the door. It had no features, no form. But it was there, just beyond the glass. He blinked. It was still there. Tingling fear washed up from his toes to his stomach...out to his fingers... He felt nauseous. A series of feet walked by the door, flash after flash after flash of shadow, passing like ripples across the strange shape.

Tommy stared in breathless silence, feeling the thing's presence like a heavy blanket. His hands were gripping the sheets so tightly that his fingernails pushed up into his palms. His eyes stayed glued to the window. And then, almost without being consciously aware of it, he pushed back the bedding and set his feet on the floor. Usually he had a child's fear of slimy hands reaching for his ankles from under the bed, but the thought didn't even cross his mind. Left foot. Right foot. He stood. There was no telling what compelled him to do so, but he did, and moved slowly to the window. His feet padded softly against the tile, muffled in the quiet room. Closer and closer. The thing, whatever it was, remained stock still. Tommy passed in front of the light and suddenly the window was a black rectangle, a blank stretch of night. He sucked in a breath, not even realizing he had been holding it, and stopped. He was afraid to step out of the glow from the door. What if...what if the thing was still there...watching him... What if it wasn't? That would mean he was *seeing things*. Worst of all, what if he stepped to the side and those dark, glittering, evil eyes appeared at the window, pushing into his own, pushing into his soul... He was still staring at the window, his eyes burning with the effort not to blink, his own horrifying shadow covering the wall and the glass, huge and spectral and strangely shaped. Seconds or hours. His heart beat fast again, beat so high up in his throat it was practically in his mouth, and an absurd thought came to him. He wondered if he opened his mouth, if his heart would fall right out and splatter on the floor. It was crazy—the kind of crazy thought that could get you sent to a place like Green Elm Home. But he couldn't shake it. The thought. What if. He very nervously cracked his mouth open, and when there was no beating heart pressing the backs of his lips he opened it the rest of the way.

Nothing.

He laughed, one of those short, relieved bursts that was really just the stress leaving his body. It was stupid, so stupid, all of it, just some weird effect from his dream. A sort of delirious relief swept over him and he stepped out of the light.

There were eyes. Two eyes, black and glistening in the pale glow, deep and full of hate. Tommy went as stiff as a board, felt his bladder let go. The warm, pungent smell of urine filled the room, reeking of shame, but he barely noticed. He stared into those eyes and suddenly he fell backward, fell through the floor, fell into infinity, and the eyes followed him down, forever and ever and ever and—

He hit the floor, the breath exploding from his lungs and leaving him gasping for air. His head jerked up to window but there was nothing beyond it, nothing but darkness and now...the first feeble shimmer of dawn. He scrambled to his feet, chest burning with the effort to breathe, choked little coughs punching from his mouth. No eyes. No monster. His nose pressed against the glass, cool to the touch, fogging sightly as he struggled to fill his lungs. Out in the gloom, in the first rays of morning, was a tree, an enormous elm, wide arms stretching toward him in agonized twists. He took a step backward, into a warm puddle, and remembered that he had wet himself. His pajama pants clung to his legs in sticky folds. The realization made him feel stupid again, but he knew what he had seen. He knew it, and it was no dream. The bodies in the clearing were no dream. Nor were the bloody remains of his father, nor the disemboweled corpse of Toby Christiansen, lying beside his headless friend in a wriggling mass of ants. Harry telling him the secret was no dream, and neither was the grisly *squelch* as Adrian's eyes collapsed into his skull. Tommy's thumb itched with the familiar urge to move to his mouth. He grasped it in his other hand and gazed back at the window, still hitching in painful breaths.

It was a Saturday in mid October. Brisk autumn air rolled up the hill, up the castle-like walls of the asylum, and turned them to frosty white. Beneath the frost, the leaves on the elm and many like it scattered across the hillside were a masterpiece of reds and yellows, invisible in the ghostly dawn. A dark line of trees crowded the bottom of the hill, the edge of a deep forest, the gateway to a wilderness which Tommy knew was home to an unspeakable horror. In daylight it was hard to believe that anything was out there, out in those dense trees, hiding beyond the leaves and the frost and the picturesque hills. Even though the lawn and the gardens of Green Elm Home had already begun their feral growth, it was still unreal—in daylight. But at night was different. At night the forest came alive. From the window in his room, Tommy could see the deep, velvety blackness of the forest, could hear the bugs chirping and the birds whistling and the trees rustling... And sometimes...even before he had seen those eyes at the window...sometimes when he looked too long...he had thought he could sense the spider looming in the darkness. Watching the asylum. Watching him.

But day was breaking now, the orb of the sun just beginning to crest the horizon, magnificent colors snaking across the sky. Suddenly the whole thing, just minutes old, was turning into a distant memory, fading like the darkness itself. And through the shame, through the wet, dripping embarrassment, Tommy remembered...it was time to go home.

Home, yes. That was a distant memory too, so distant it was unreal. He had not even set foot in the house since that day in June. The idea of walking its empty rooms without his father's—without Rob's—voice drifting from around each corner, without his smell and his embrace and his laughter and his knowing eyes, was almost alien. It didn't even sound like home anymore. It sounded like a tomb, a grave, dug to bury the memory of a past life, a life which he could never get back. He wasn't sure he even wanted to go... He glanced around at the small room, at the hospital-style bed and the visitor chairs and the window...but staying was no better. He shuffled over to the bed, his wet pants chafing. There was a button there for the nurse, and that was the only way he would get cleaned up.

By 7:45 Tommy was cleaned, dressed, and waiting for his mother. The strange thing at the window was already far from his mind, already collecting dust in the back of his head. He had seen so many things, so many *horrible* things... Strange shapes at the window were hardly the worst. He couldn't even place why he had wet himself. Despite what he had thought only a short while ago, the whole event was taking on the hazy color of a dream. He kicked his legs impatiently under the chair, wondering how long it would take for his feet to reach the floor. He hoped not very long. His tenth birthday was somewhere out there in the future, and once he was a big kid he wanted to at least be able to sit like one. On his feet were two shiny white shoes, spotless, like they had just come out of the box. Tommy didn't care.

"—and you said that was twice a day, with meals?"

His ears perked up. It was his mother's voice, on the other side of the door. Two pairs of feet stopped in front of the thin white line, but they were hard to see with it fully light in the room now.

"Yes, ma'am. Just one pill with breakfast and dinner, we've found he responds well to that."

"Thanks. I'm sure you've noticed he hates taking medicine." And the door to his room opened and there was Kristin, skirt and black stockings growing from the bottom of a handsome autumn jacket. Beside her was the doctor who had been treating Tommy all this time. *Doctor Drabczyk. Call me Doctor Chris or Doctor D,* he had said, smiling a warm smile. Tommy tried to do neither and just avoid talking to him, but that had proved impossible.

"Tommy!" his mother shrieked with excitement, her eyes lighting up. It was fake, all fake. She had been forcing herself to act happy around Tommy for a while now. He saw right through it. "Are you ready to go home?"

"Sure," Tommy said, his voice flat, his legs still swinging.

She moved to the bed and sat down next to him. Her perfume was comfortingly familiar. It smelled like home. The lump in his stomach clenched tight, reminding him that he hated her.

"I'll leave you two alone," Doctor Drabczyk said. "You're all set, Tommy! Just check out at the desk, okay?"

"Okay."

"Mrs. Wilford, you have my number if you have any questions."

"Yes, thank you doctor."

He smiled at them, that same warm smile. Tommy hated it. Doctor D left the room.

"You all ready to go, sweetie?" She brushed his hair, studying his face carefully.

"Yes, Mom."

"I thought we'd get some breakfast on the way. How does that sound?"

"Sounds good."

Kristin frowned at him, her eyebrows pushing together. "Aren't you excited, Tommy?"

"I guess."

Now she looked hurt. "You'll feel better with some food in you." She said it almost to herself. "We'll get your favorite, okay? Anything you want, today is all about you."

"Sure."

Kristin pressed her eyelids shut, took a deep breath. Tommy wondered if she was trying not to cry. He felt sorry, but not completely. No, laced all through it was a kind of vindictive pleasure. Now she could know how he felt. How he felt to learn that she had betrayed him, lied to him. How he felt when he discovered the secret.

Kristin opened her eyes. "Well, let's get going then." She rose to her feet and pushed gently on Tommy's back for him to do the same. He did, casting one last look back at the window. The ghost of the eyes was imprinted on his memory, staring at him, wicked and cruel. His stomach churned. Then he was led out the door and the window disappeared, and the memory with it.

Tommy felt like he was walking through fog. Down the hall, through the glass door that opened out of the pediatric ward, down another hall, into a dingy old elevator, and finally out into the lobby. His mother made pleasant conversation with the young lady at the desk, a lady with bobbed hair and large glasses who sat scribbling away furiously on notecards. Then out the large wooden door, down the long walk, the October chill nipping at his ears and neck, and finally to the small gravel parking lot. It still didn't feel real. None of it. They climbed into the old station wagon and eased out of the lot and twisted their way down the hill toward the forest. Tommy's heart pumped nervously in his chest as they approached the dark woods, but they hurtled into the fluttering shadows and nothing bad happened. He had shut his eyes as they passed the mangled arms of the outermost trees, but when he opened them again they were zipping along a peaceful road, the sun erupting through the branches in dazzling spots, the horrors of that day in June seeming miles away. It took about twenty minutes to get back to town, and by the time they rolled down into the valley where Elmwood sat quaintly nestled between the mountains and the lake—the large cooling towers of the power plant puffing vapor over the twisting river in the distance—Tommy felt his mood begin to lighten. Maybe it was leaving Green Elm Home far behind...but for the first time in months he felt like maybe...maybe...he could forgive his mother after all.

They reached the bottom of the hill and leveled out at the edge of town. The elementary school passed on their left. Tommy hadn't seen it since February.

"How does Nemo's sound?" Kristin asked, a hint of anxiety in her voice. She had been silent for most of the drive.

"Sure," Tommy said, a little more brightly than back at the asylum.

Kristin's face relaxed and her shoulders dropped from where she had been holding them tensely. "Chicken nuggets and a milkshake sound pretty good, huh?"

"Yeah!"

They both smiled, and for a moment all the misery was gone, forgotten. The lump in Tommy's stomach started to disintegrate. It was just like before. Just like the old days, when she would take him shoe shopping and they would buy lunch. He could feel the first tiny bubbles of hope forming out of the remains of that hard little ball, fizzling up to his chest and making him dare to think that maybe all the pain was behind them. Maybe they really could get back to normal life. Maybe they would—

The world exploded in chaos, in a squeal of tires and a shriek of bending metal. Tommy slammed against the dashboard, felt his nose crack as it impacted the faux-wood cover, felt his teeth bite through his upper lip. Everything spinning, flying. Glass everywhere. They hit something, slammed into it like a freight train and stopped suddenly and Tommy was thrown against the driver door. The first thing he became aware of was that it smelled like gasoline. The next was that he was in pain, awful, unbearable pain. Blood gushed down his front, soaked into his shirt. He reached up with one dazed hand and felt his mouth. There was a jagged hole in his lip and part of a tooth was missing.

"TOM WILFORD!"

It was a voice from outside the car, a man's voice.

"TOM WILFORD, COME OUT AND FACE ME! COME OUT AND LOOK ME IN THE EYE!"

That voice... He didn't recognize it. Oh *God*, he was in pain. He pushed himself up to a sitting position, tried to take in his surroundings. His head was pounding. Everything seemed to be underwater, moving slowly, echoing, rolling around. Where was his mother? There was glass on the seat. Glass. Where did the glass come from? The driver side window was gone, just gone, and the door was crumpled and bent around a light post. The passenger side had a huge web of cracks. And the windshield... He blinked, trying to clear his head. But the windshield...it was red. Why was it red? And there was a hole in it, a great, gaping hole, the glass broken in a sawtooth ring and chips tinkling out.

"I'M WAITING TOM! I'M WAITING FOR YOU!"

Tommy eased gingerly over to the passenger door and pushed it open. It swung wide and he saw what looked like the whole width of the street, trees lining the opposite side in a blurry line, a jumble of colors, and the school in the distance. None of it made *sense*. He couldn't piece it together. He was still swimming, swimming, the world dancing before his eyes. And deep down...way down inside...he felt a dull buzzing...

"DON'T MAKE ME COME GET YOU TOM! DON'T MAKE ME PULL YOU OUT!"

He flopped out onto the street, the gasoline smell filling his nose, the blood filling his mouth. He spat out a phlegmy glob of it and then puked onto his hands. The buzzing was growing, swelling, taking over. He lifted his face from the pavement and looked around for the source of the voice.

There was another car, an old Challenger with its fender pushed in and its hood bent in half, sitting to one side with smoke pouring from the engine. One door hung open. It slowly came to him that they must have been hit, must have been struck by the Challenger. And beside it, favoring one leg and blood oozing from his scalp, was a man. He looked vaguely familiar, but Tommy was sure he had never seen him before. And lying on the pavement...maybe twenty feet away... Was that—

"Finally... Finally..." the man said. His eyes were wild, manic, sunken into deep, purple sockets. He looked terrible. One leg of his jeans had turned a dark, wet red, and his knuckles were skinned to the bone—

—like the cat the cat the cat—

—and dripping onto the asphalt. And hanging from his fingers, loosely, like he had forgotten it was there, was a pistol. The sun reflected off the barrel in a blinding flash. Tommy blinked in the light.

"I don't...don't know you..." Tommy slurred, his head still spinning. It was all too much, too much to comprehend. His brain felt fuzzy. The buzzing noise overpowered him, threatened to leave him writhing in his own sick. A mosquito landed on his arm.

"No, you don't," the man said, shaking. "But you knew my boys. You knew Billy. You knew Clark."

Tommy shivered as cold understanding wash over him.

"I don't... I didn't..."

"DON'T DENY IT!" The man's face twisted in anguish, his stubbly cheeks quivering and drawn. "Don't pretend like you don't know! You were there! You were with them!"

The noise... God, the noise... It was everywhere...everything... He knew what it meant, Jeezum Crow, he knew what the noise meant. And the thing on the ground... There in front of him... The car had been empty...empty...and the red hole in the glass... Fear welled up inside him and pushed out of his mouth.

"*Where's my MOM?!*" Tommy screamed.

"I wanted to see you. I wanted to look you in the eye before...before I..." The man swallowed hard, brandishing the pistol as his hands wrung at the air. "I wanted to see... I just...I needed to know..." Tears ran down his cheeks. "You saw them both. You were there when they...when they both..."

Tommy shuffled backward on his hands and knees, watching the blood from his mouth and nose follow him in a trail.

"I just need to know what...what happened to my boys... You were there, you..." He gulped again, choking on the words. "You know what happened... You do, I know you do... You know what happened..." He hitched in several agonizing breaths. "Tell me, Tom. Look me in the eye and tell me."

"I don't know," Tommy mumbled, his whole body shaking. There were more mosquitos now, landing on his arms and on Mr. Baker's trembling face. "I don't know, I—"

"YES YOU DO!" Mr. Baker bawled, and then all that anger seemed to turn inward and his face collapsed. "You do, you *have* to... You were *there*... You..." His eyes landed on the dark shape lying between the smoking cars and he went deathly quiet.

"It—it was an accident," Tommy whispered. "Just an accident. I didn't... I didn't mean..."

Terrible pain contorted the man's face, twisted it into an ugly scowl. "*Th-that's not possible,*" he finally said, the words tumbling from his mouth. "Not possible, not... That can't be..." He turned away from the shape, turned to stare desperately into the trees and then back at Tommy. "I lost everything." He staggered closer. "You understand? *Everything.*"

Tommy shuffled farther back, looking everywhere, looking for someone to show up, for someone to help him. There was no one. There were no houses or shops out here. Just the trees...starting to sway...

"Look at me, Tom. Look me in the eye."

"Please, my mom..."

"Look me in the eye. *Look at me, boy!*"

"I can't! *I can't!*"

"LOOK AT ME!"

And Tommy did. He looked up and into those deep-set eyes and immediately Mr. Baker froze in place. His mouth hung open stupidly, his tongue flapping like he was being choked. Flies and mosquitos were swarming now, were everywhere, and the droning sound was so loud that the earth itself shook. Mr. Baker swayed forward and back as if he were a marionette hanging loosely from its strings, his eyes widening with horror. And then in that same loose motion, he raised the pistol to his jaw and unloaded his brains into the sky.

CRACK!

Tommy watched in slow motion as bits of blood and gore shot from the back of Mr. Baker's head in a red cloud and drifted sideways with the breeze. He watched them fall, transfixed, watched Mr. Baker fall too, watched his head kick back and his body heave over and land with a lifeless thud. The flies followed him down. And the droning sound... It didn't stop. It grew and grew and grew. He pressed his fingers into his ears and now the tension in his chest unraveled all at once and he screamed, screamed until his voice was spent but it was no use. He hobbled forward on all fours, feeling the fear strangle him, feeling the dread crush him from all sides. He couldn't breathe. There were birds now, birds circling and landing in the street, vultures and crows and God knows what else. Landing on Mr. Baker... Landing on that dark shape...the shape... He drew level with it, turned his face up from it. He couldn't look down... Couldn't bear to see...

The black stockings. The autumn jacket. All in tatters, like the rest, torn to shreds, unrecognizable except for those strips of cloth and one open, staring eye, set into a face destroyed and pooling in a halo of red. Tommy reached out... It was like a disembodied hand stretched out in front of him, not real, not possible... He gave the bloody mass a tentative push, a little shake, as if somehow she might still wake up, might roll over and tell him she had one hell of a headache...but his hand only pushed heavy dead weight. He sucked in a breath. The world rushed up to meet him, closed in on him. He was trapped. Trapped in this awful dream, *Dear God please, please, let it be just a dream.* His eyes mashed shut and then opened and his mother's mangled body still lay in a broken, bloody heap. A pile of flesh and bones and flies and glass-eyed birds. Dead. *Dead. DEAD DEAD DEAD DEAD DEAD DEAD DEAD.* He dropped back onto his legs, slumped over on his side. The tears came, great fat drops. Spilling down from his eyes, spilling down onto the gaping hole in his lip, stinging, burning. He felt it burning but it was like watching someone else experience it. All that remained, all that existed from here to the dark edge of the universe, was that all-consuming sorrow, that mind-numbing despair. And the noise...

God, the noise. It was killing him, ripping him apart from the inside, tearing him to shreds in a swirling whirlpool of guilt and shame and fear and anger and crushing loss. Louder and louder. The ground...the sky...the whole world, heaven and earth and everything in between, vibrated with the insane pitch of it. Shaking...pulling apart. It was a feeling like Tommy had never experienced, never, not like this, not in the clearing, not on the lake, not in the woods, not at the truck stop. The power of it electrified his body, raised him to his feet. Hate. That was it. Pure, absolute, unbridled hate. Hatred for himself and for the Bakers, for Rob and for Harry, for everything, everyone. It swelled up inside him. Energized him. Pumped through his veins, vitalized his every nerve. He could feel the creature inside him, could feel it grinning with malice, could feel its strange perverse joy at the human suffering at his feet, and...he let go.

His head tilted back, his jaw dropped open. And out of his mouth, from deep within, from down his throat, came a rich, guttural purr. It clawed out of him, burst into the crisp fall air with all the grotesque *wrongness* of laughter at a funeral. His insides reverberated with it, quivered with its alien energy. For one heart stopping instant he was consumed with regret and then the *Thing* took over and he saw only red.

* * *

The trees dotting the sides of the road swayed in the wind, swayed like there was a storm blowing in, the leaves rippling and breaking away, the branches heaving savagely. Will looked back up at the dark cloud, watched it swirl like a tornado...realized it was made of birds and some other things, smaller things. He followed them down to the ground and there at the bottom was a small shape, a person, walking toward him. Except...it was not walking like any person he had ever seen. It was hunched over, bent in the middle of the back as if suffering a painful deformity, hands contorted into claws and legs kicking in a bizarre gait—almost loping. The face turned up at him, teeth bared in a horrible grin, eyes completely black, empty, two bottomless pits. The flame in Will's chest snuffed out and he realized with sinking dread who it was.

Tommy Wilford.

Will stumbled backwards, back onto the sidewalk. He looked down the street for Elise, but she was gone, nowhere in sight. The street was empty, no cars, not a single soul. He pulled his jacket tight around him, feeling cold, feeling the heat from that flame wither and die in his chest. Bravery burned bright. Spite did not.

There was something evil in that face. It was not Tommy staring out at him, not Tommy shuffling toward him with inhuman speed. The eyes... They burrowed into Will and he felt himself falling again, felt himself plunging into the void, down and down and down. Screaming filled his ears, screaming from all sides, everywhere, the screams of a thousand tormented spirits pulling him down into their sorrow, carrying him to damnation. Hands reached out of the darkness, hooked their slimy fingers around his throat, dragged him into the deep, into despair, into ruin...

"LEAVE HIM ALONE!"

His eyes—had they been shut?—his eyes flew open and he was lying in the street. Elise stood over him, stood between him and the creature, small knife drawn, hand outstretched and trembling. A storm of birds and insects raged around them, biting and cackling and beating the air.

"DON'T TOUCH HIM! DON'T COME ANY CLOSER!"

Tommy leered at her, black eyes cruel and unblinking. One nostril hitched up in a snarl. He took a shambling step forward.

"DON'T! I SAID STAY AWAY!"

Tommy's hideous grin widened, split his face in two. His head pitched back and his mouth opened wide, and out came...tentacles. Small, slimy things that twitched and flailed in the air, wriggling sickeningly as a deep, throaty growl gurgled up out of his chest. His head snapped forward and again that evil grin cracked his face in half, and the tentacles withdrew into whatever dark abyss they had crawled from, leaving only a trickle of pus. One bloodstained foot lurched toward them.

Elise shook, her small wrist flapping up and down so violently that the shape of the knife was no longer distinguishable, but still she held it in front of her.

"GET AWAY! *GET AWAY!"* She swiped madly once, twice, and then some unknown strength, be it fear or courage, swept up her thin frame and suddenly she lunged forward, plunging the knife like a dagger. It happened so fast Will could barely make sense of it; she swung the knife down, moved it with deathly speed, and then she flew sideways. She hit the pavement and rolled, over and over until she slammed into the curb, and did not get up. The knife tinkled away to a stop, tiny and pathetic.

"ELISE!" The sound burst out of Will in a roar. He scrambled to his feet. The creature shuffled toward him, the last few steps, clawed hands reaching,

tentacled mouth slobbering, black eyes staring, blank, hungry, rolled back with insane pleasure. And in that instant Will knew, felt all the way down in the desperate fibers of his being, that this Thing wanted him. That it wanted his flesh. That it had determined his fate at the bottom of that rocky slope and was here to finish the job. That he was marked for death.

A shriek from beside them rent the chill air and the creature stopped.

It was Trish. She stood in the doorway of the creamery, frozen in fear, the sanity vanishing from her eyes like a wisp of smoke. Puny and gone.

The thing screamed, a wet, nauseating howl, spiny pincers flailing from the confines of Tommy's mutilated lips. And Will ran.

Somewhere floating detached and unimportant in his mind was the notion that he should save Trish, save Elise, but he did not. He bolted for the knife, scooped it off the pavement and kept going. Past the sidewalk, past the trees. Behind him he heard Trish's shrill cries echoing down the street, louder and louder and then cut short. Terror swelled in him, filled his lungs. The air was thick, dense, he ran through molasses. He couldn't breathe. The sounds of the monster gained behind him, ripping over the grass and through the trees, closer and closer. He crested a small hill and there at the bottom was the fence, the schoolyard, the stream running out of the trees and trickling along its length. He stumbled down the hill and splashed into the water, every hair on his neck standing straight up, feeling the strange transgression of the act. The current swirled around his feet and he set off along the fence, making his way toward the clearing where...where it all began.

More splashes... It was behind him, right behind him, closing the distance with every sloshing step. The storm of insects swirled around him now, circling him, descending in vicious waves. A crow scratched at his face and he beat it away, never losing stride. There was panting...gleeful panting on the breeze... He could almost feel the thing's ragged breathing on his back; he was a boy possessed, flushed with fear, the fear of looking over his shoulder and seeing those demented eyes grinning, those spiny pincers scissoring, ready for the killing stroke. He burst out of the trees and into the clearing and crashed to a stop. Vines had grown up around the pond, ferocious thorny snaking vines, covering the ground and making it impossible to pass. Nestled in the center with one gnarled branch growing from its mouth was a skull, a man's skull, empty sockets staring, tiny specks of meat and dirt still clinging to its grimy surface, and in a flash of horror Will knew that it was Officer Tibbs, risen from some hellish grave to make his despair absolute. The trees on all sides rocked dangerously in place. He turned to face the creature, held the pocketknife at arm's length.

"Stay away! I'm warning you!"

It closed the last few feet without slowing and dove into him, pincers gnashing at his face, tentacles gripping his hair and pulling him into those hungry jaws, strings of gore dangling in a vile dance from teeth that had once belonged to Silent Tommy Wilford. They crashed together into the barbs and nettles, struggling desperately, the chaos closing on all sides. Will stabbed the knife outward blindly, stabbed until he felt it strike home and then kept stabbing. The creature trilled in pain, a clicking, insectile noise that sent shivers cascading down Will's spine even as he pushed backward into the thorns. He kept stabbing, not sure what he was hitting, but hitting something, *anything*, driving the monster back. It retreated to the edge of the clearing, blood running in rivers from a dozen cuts, scarlet dripping thickly from its chin. Black eyes stared with hate, pure hate. All the glee was gone, replaced with malice. It watched him, stared at him through a gust of brown leaves, the vines still twisting, still growing.

And then...most horrible of all...the head leaned back again, so far Will thought the neck must break, and out of the mouth pushed a squirming mass of snakes, more tentacles, spiny legs, out and out until Tommy himself should have crumpled like a discarded skin, and still they kept coming until a creature of unimaginable dimensions lay pulsating and trembling on the ground, stamping and writhing and pushing into the corners of the clearing. One lingering tendril ran down into Tommy's throat, glistening and alive, and then the end of it pulled free like a cork and hit the ground—*splat*. For a few breathless seconds the whole awful mass of it lay glistening in the grass, sighing with the weight of its new life, breathing in sticky, glittering breaths. In form it resembled some great, tentacular centipede, horrible and slimy and bloated with venom. Tommy collapsed with a shudder. The creature's gaze, empty as night and furious beneath its heavy, wrinkled brow, turned on Will.

He floundered backward on his rear end, fumbled with his hands and feet to push further into the thorny branches but there was nowhere left to go. A tingling sensation washed over his fingers, moved up his arms. He glanced down—spiders, ants, millions of them crawled up his arms and legs, tiny bodies thrashing in a sea of glittering black. Higher, higher, up to his waist, up to his chest. The mosquitos landed on his face, flies clouding his eyes so he had to pinch them shut. It was over. Done. Through the nauseating buzz of wings he heard the creature's many coils twist with obscene delight, saw in his mind's eye the face moving in, saw its horrible mottled jaws open wide, nothing but darkness inside, nothing but putrid rotting death...

CRACK!

The insects dissipated in a swarm, sickening and vile as they had come. The air was thick with a tumultuous wind as the birds and flies beat their wings, flapped into the sky.

CRACK!

The monster reared back, pain rolling through its hideous segments in a wave, sharp fangs bared behind those clicking pincers.

CRACK!

"YOU LIKE THAT? YOU LIKE THAT, HUH?"

The creature screamed, bellowed, unearthly and horrifying, spittle spraying from its mouth, blood dribbling from its long belly. Its many legs and tentacles clattered and oozed as it swung around, swung its great bulging body to face Elise. She stood at the edge of the clearing, stood over Tommy's lifeless form, one side of her face scraped raw, her hair matted with red, her eyes wild and insane. She had a pistol in her hands, both hands, stretched out in front of her and shaking with fright and exhilaration.

"*Come on and take it,*" she hissed. The monster roared again, screamed and wailed and advanced with terrifying speed.

CRACK!

The bullet struck one dark, soulless eye and the spot exploded in a splatter of black goo. "*COME ON! COME ON!*"

There was a sound from beyond all human knowledge, from beyond recognition, a sound full of misery and rage and contempt. The face plunged upward, up into the sky, limbs tensing and flailing, dark gray body writhing in agony, perhaps an agony this creature had never known. It howled into the blue, into the cosmos, into an eternity beyond human understanding.

"*LEAVE US ALONE!!!*" Elise screamed, her voice shrill and desperate. The face turned back again, loathsome and furious and dripping with blood, pincers clacking and eye staring directly into her soul and—

CRACK!

—she fired a shot straight into its mouth.

It squealed, a terrible, bone-chilling noise, the sound of thousands, tens of thousands, crying out for death. The whole squirming length of it crashed to Earth, bent and contorted and stamped and pushed back into the trees, into shadow, the raging cloud of insects and vultures and crows disappearing with it, until the swaying trunks concealed it beyond all vision and the nightmare faded to nothing. And the clearing became silent.

* * *

Elise turned the gun on Tommy, pointed it straight at his head, hatred boiling in her stomach. She could end this. She could end this right now.

"Elise!" It was Will, pulling himself out of the vines, cut to ribbons. "Elise, don't!"

"You saw him, same as me! You saw it inside him!"

"It came out of him! I think it's out of him now!"

Tommy stirred feebly, blood pouring from his stomach, tears pooling in his eyes.

"It's *his* fault!" Elise said, still shaking hard, still feeling the adrenaline coursing through her body. "It's because of him! *He* caused this!"

"We can't just kill him! Not like this!"

"Exactly like this!" She breathed deeply, shutting her eyes against the hate, against the storm of emotions racing through her. "What do you care, it looks like you did enough already!" And it was true. Tommy was bleeding, dying, turning paler by the second. She clenched her teeth. *"It's not gone.* We can make it go for*ever!"*

"Please..." Tommy whispered, trying to move, unable to. Elise centered the pistol on his forehead, struggled to hold her hand steady.

Will hurried to her side, wide-eyed and afraid. "Elise, it won't go away. *It won't go away!"*

"What are you talking about? It's Tommy, all Tommy, you said so—"

"It's not—it's not just Tommy..."

Elise's eyes narrowed to slits. Cold betrayal flickered inside her. "What do you mean, *not just Tommy?"*

"It's—there's someone else."

"Who?"

"Someone different. Someone—"

"WHO?"

"MY DAD!" Will finally cried, dropping to his knees, wracked with guilt. "My dad... I saw my dad down there... I saw him too..."

Elise was stricken. Confusion swelled up inside her, bitter and terrible. "You're dad... No that's... That's not right, that's—"

"I did. *I did...*" Will sobbed, gripping handfuls of grass in white-knuckled fists. "He was down there, down in the dark, he was...he was with Tommy, behind him...down there..."

The world swayed around her, unbalanced, uneven. All this time...*all this time...* She had obsessed over killing Tommy Wilford, four long months, consumed with secret hate, eaten alive by it, let it grow inside her like a weed. Now she had a weapon, a real weapon, finally, felt its power heavy in her hands, felt its destruction in her fingertips. No... No, she had seen enough, seen with her own eyes. This boy was wrong, stupid and wrong. There was only one way. Her heart beat fast, incredibly fast, high in her chest, up into her neck, right up to her head, thumping and pounding in her temple, deafening, clamoring, screaming for her to do it, to do it now, get it over with, pull the trigger, end him, end it, send that hot lead burrowing into his rotten skull.

"Please..."

She squeezed the trigger.

Click.

There was nothing, no fire, no bullet, no concussion, no kickback. Just that little metallic noise. *Click. Click click.* Out of bullets.

The pistol, the gleaming six-shooter, dropped from her hand, dropped to the ground. Elise followed, sinking into the tall grass. She felt nothing. Nothing at all. Her mind was suddenly blank.

Will lunged forward, grabbed the gun. He studied it, holding it as if afraid it would bite.

"Where did you get this?"

It all felt so distant, so long ago, even though it could hardly have been ten minutes. She stared forward in a daze.

"From the road. There was an accident in front of the school. I saw it on my way here. Picked it up. From a—a dead person."

"There were no cops? Nobody?"

She shook her head. "No one." A weird feeling bubbled up inside her and she let out a harsh chuckle. "Just the bodies. Funny right? Really strange." And then she cried.

JULY, 1999

D avid let out a low whistle, leaned back in his chair. The man across from him, the man he had come to see, was sweating profusely and staring hard at the wall.

"The cops actually did show up not long after that," Mr. Wilford said, his eyes returning to the present. "Thank God, or I would have been dead."

David looked at him carefully, not believing a word, not wanting to cause another outburst. Doctor Alvarez sat in the corner now, observing everything, mouth pulled tight in an uncomfortable grimace. David shot him a glance and then looked back at Tommy.

"And you came back here," he said.

Mr. Wilford turned his gaze back on David, fixed those pale orbs on him. "Yes. For good this time."

"And the killings stopped after that."

"They did."

"What happened to Will Ross and Elise Smithfield?"

Tommy gave a joyless laugh, an odd little snicker. "You think I ever saw those two again?"

David smirked. "No, I guess not."

"Never. Never again. That was the last time."

"Do you ever wonder what would have happened if Mr. Baker hadn't hit you with his car?" Funny, David thought wryly, that he actually did believe at least a few words. Some of it was public record. The car accident for instance. The self-inflicted gunshot wound.

"Yes, of course. Every day."

David nodded, clicked his pen. He looked down at his notes, a handful of pages—meaningless nonsense. He glanced at the tape. A fresh cassette was in the machine now, spinning idly as it recorded Mr. Wilford's strange confession. They had been at it all day. The light outside the window had turned over to dusky orange.

"So the takeaway—if I may be so bold—the takeaway is that *you* killed all those people. *You* did. Only it wasn't you, it was this...*Thing*."

Tommy nodded somberly, his eyes never moving. He took a breath, as if bracing for the admission. "Yes," he said. "In a fashion."

"You're the Highwayman."

Tommy's expression was as blank as ever, but his jumpsuit was dark with sweat.

"Yes."

David nodded again, clicked his pen a few more times. "Mhmm."

"Agent Nolan, I think you've had quite enough time with my patient," Doctor Alvarez said crisply from the corner, standing up and gesturing at the door. "If you would be so kind."

"Of course," David said, welcoming the excuse to leave. "I think I have what I need." *Like hell.* "Thank you for your time, Mr. Wilford."

"I can't say it was my pleasure, but...I hope you enjoyed our time together, *Special Agent,*" Mr. Wilford said with his usual chill, and turned back to stare at the wall. Waiting for the orderlies to return and escort him out, David guessed.

"It was...definitely enlightening."

"I'm sure," Tommy said, not moving an inch.

David stood, flattened his tie. He started gathering his things, reached for the *Stop* button on the tape—hesitated.

"This is essentially the same testimony you gave in nineteen seventy-eight," he said.

"Yes." Tommy's voice was flat, his body perfectly still. "Does that surprise you?"

"No, it's just... This is the testimony that got you sent back here."

Now Tommy turned again, turned until his eyes were glowing in the sunset and burying deeply into David's own. Once again he had the unsettling feeling of being taking apart, piece by piece.

"I told you before, I know why I'm here."

The voice was steely, expressionless, but David sensed an overpowering bitterness in those words. He turned off the tape. "Okay, Tommy." He put the recorder in his briefcase along with the yellow pad and his pen. "Thanks again."

"Don't mention it."

"Any time now, Agent Nolan," Doctor Alvarez said stiffly.

David's heat rose. "Coming Doc." He grabbed the bag off the table and followed Doctor Alvarez through the heavy door, Tommy's magnified eyes burning holes into his back. As soon as they were past the two guards Alvarez turned to him.

"You understand none of this is admissible anyway," he said quietly, the lines at the edges of his eyes creasing as he scowled.

"What? You think any of *that* is going to hold up in court?"

"It doesn't matter what you think. The man was under the influence of a mind altering drug."

David balked. "You can't be serious, Doc. Coffee? Really?"

"In his condition," Doctor Alvarez sniffed, working his jaw, "and in combination with his medication—yes."

"Well it's not like we had any great breakthrough today anyway," David said, trying to shrug off his annoyance at the fussy little man. "Monsters in the trees? Kinda ridiculous, don't you think?"

Doctor Alvarez was silent for a moment, looking at Tommy through the door.

"Doc?"

"I'm sorry?"

"Don't you think the story is a little ridiculous?"

"Oh, right. Yes. Of course I do. Please come this way, Agent Nolan, I have to see a few more patients before I can go home."

He turned and walked off down the corridor in his quick, precise footsteps, and David broke into a trot to keep up. He gave one last look at the open door to the visitation room before it passed out of sight behind a corner and disappeared. They pushed through another heavy door and then a glass one and finally came to an elevator that David recognized as having brought him here from the lobby.

"You can find your way out from here, I trust," Doctor Alvarez said, most of his good nature gone and only his unconscious gentility remaining.

"Yes, I think so."

"Good." He extended his hand. "Come back any time."

They were empty words. David took the hand and shook it. "You bet."

They parted gladly and David stepped into the elevator. It was ancient and the old wood paneling smelled of rotting varnish. He rode it down to the first floor and collected his things from Marie, still click-clacking away behind her desk, hair still flopping prissily along the tops of her glasses.

"Thank you for your visit, Agent Nolan," she said, handing him a small bowl without looking up.

"My pleasure," David said, reminded irresistibly of his last conversation with Mr. Wilford. He grabbed his gun and badge from the bowl and hurried out the door.

Outside the sun was still blazing at the edge of the horizon, rippling in the heat rising off the disc of the world. He breathed in the warm air and admired the sunset for a moment before heading off down the walk. Dead spiders and centipedes crunched underfoot as he left the porch behind. There had been more this morning, he recalled. Damned groundskeepers, couldn't take care of the place worth shit. Then he remembered that the groundskeepers were patients, and felt a stab of guilt. Well...they still couldn't take care of the place worth shit.

Down the hill, past the overgrown lawn, past the eerie, reaching trees. He came to the parking lot and sat down gratefully in his Ford Taurus, and cast one last glance at Green Elm Home, bloated and overgrown, sitting atop the slope like an Old World castle. He blew out through his mouth with a dismissive buzz and looked down at the dashboard...and froze.

He thought he had seen... No, that wasn't possible. He was just bleary-eyed from a long day of work. From listening to the fantastic ravings of a certified lunatic. That was all it was. Still, he felt his heart beat faster in his chest, felt goosebumps erupt all over his arms. He was afraid to look up. Afraid to see if it was really there. He shut his eyes, willed himself not to be going crazy—was crazy catching? He took a deep breath. Bent his neck until he was peering through the windshield.

There at the top of the hill, in a window of the great stone building, obscure in the fading light, was a large, pale shape. Watching him. Two deep, black eyes stared out from the glass, peered straight at him, pierced him right through. He gasped, reeled back in his seat. Blinked. The thing was still there. Still watching.

He fumbled for his keys, turned on the car with an urgency that he couldn't shake, even though he felt stupid. It was stupid, totally stupid. It was probably Tommy Wilford. Just Tommy Wilford and his huge, ridiculous glasses, watching him pull away. He threw the car in reverse and backed quickly out of the spot, and then against all reason or desire he paused. Looked up.

The shape was gone.

His heart was still pounding, still thumping madly in his chest, his breathing still shallow. He put the car into drive and let the tires squeal as he peeled out of the parking lot. Out onto the twisting, winding road. Out into the rapidly falling night.

He reached the bottom of the hill and followed the road into the darkening trees.

CPSIA information can be obtained
at www.ICGtesting.com
Printed in the USA
JSHW030208050523
41291JS00005B/302